Santa Evita

Also by Tomás Eloy Martínez

The Perón Novel

Santa Evita

Tomás Eloy Martínez

Translated from the Spanish
by Helen Lane

Doubleday

LONDON · NEW YORK · TORONTO · SYDNEY · AUCKLAND

TRANSWORLD PUBLISHERS LTD
61–63 Uxbridge Road, London W5 5SA

TRANSWORLD PUBLISHERS (AUSTRALIA) PTY LTD
15–25 Helles Avenue, Moorebank, NSW 2170

TRANSWORLD PUBLISHERS (NZ) LTD
3 William Pickering Drive,
Albany, Auckland

DOUBLEDAY CANADA LTD
105 Bond Street, Toronto, Ontario M5B 1Y3

Published 1997 by Doubleday
a division of Transworld Publishers Ltd

Copyright © 1996 by Alfred A. Knopf, Inc

Reprinted 1997

Originally published in Argentina as *Santa Evita* by Editorial
Planeta, Buenos Aires, in 1995.
Copyright © 1995 by Tomás Eloy Martínez
Copyright © 1995 by Editorial Planeta Argentina SAIC
Copyright © 1995 by Grupo Editorial Planeta

The right of Tomás Eloy Martínez to be identified
as the author of this work has been asserted in accordance
with sections 77 and 78 of the Copyright Designs and
Patents Act 1988

A catalogue record for this book is available from the British
Library.

ISBN 0385 408757

Printed and bound in Great Britain by
Mackays of Chatham PLC, Chatham, Kent

FOR SUSANA ROTKER,
LIKE EVERYTHING ELSE

Dying
Is an art like everything else.
I do it exceptionally well.

SYLVIA PLATH
"Lady Lazarus," October 23–29, 1962

I want to take a look at the world
The way a person takes a look at a postcard collection.

EVITA DUARTE
Interview in *Antena,* July 13, 1944

Contents

Contents

Santa Evita

1

"My Life Belongs to You"

On coming out of a faint that lasted for more than three days, Evita was certain at last that she was going to die. The terrible pains in her abdomen had gone away, and her body was clean again, alone with itself, in a bliss without time or place. Only the idea of death still hurt her. The worst part about death was not that it occurred. The worst part about death was the whiteness, the emptiness, the loneliness of the other side: one's body racing off like a galloping steed.

Although the doctors kept telling her that her anemia was in remission and that in a month or less she would regain her health, she barely had the strength left to open her eyes. She was unable to get out of bed no matter how intently she focused her energies on her elbows and heels, and even the slight effort of turning over on one side or the other to relieve the pain left her breathless.

She did not seem to be the same person who had arrived in Buenos Aires in 1935 without a penny to her name, and who acted in hopeless theaters where her pay was a cup of coffee with milk. She was nothing or less than nothing then: a sparrow at an outdoor laundry sink, a caramel bitten into, so skinny it was pitiful. She began to make herself look pretty with passion, memory, and death.

She wove herself a chrysalis of beauty, little by little hatching a queen; who would ever have thought it?

"She had black hair when I knew her," one of the actresses who took her in said. "Her sad eyes looked as though they were saying goodbye; you couldn't see the color of them. Her nose was rather coarse, a bit on the heavy side, and she was more or less buck-toothed. Though she was flat-chested, she had quite a good figure. She wasn't one of those women men turn around in the street to look at: she was likable enough, but nobody lost sleep over her. To-day, when I realize how high she flew, I say to myself: Where did that frail little thing learn to handle power, how did she manage to come by such self-assurance and such a way with words, where did she get the force to touch people's hearts in the place where it hurt? What lamb's bleating can have so stirred her blood as to turn her overnight into what she was: a queen?"

"Maybe it was the effect of her illness," the makeup man on her last two films said. "Before, no matter how much foundation cream and rouge we put on her, you could tell from a mile away that she was common, there was no way you could teach her how to sit down gracefully or use a knife and fork properly or chew with her mouth closed. It couldn't have been more than four years later that I saw her again, and what can I say? A goddess. She had such beautiful features by then that they gave her an aristocratic aura, an air of refinement straight out of a fairy tale. I took a good hard look at her to see what miraculous war paint she was wearing. But it was nothing you could see: she still had the same rabbit teeth that kept her from closing her lips, eyes that were sort of round and not at all provocative, and to top it all off her nose looked bigger to me. Her hair, I grant you, was different: dyed blond, drawn back tight into a simple bun at the nape of her neck. Her beauty grew inside her without a by-your-leave."

Nobody realized that her illness not only made her thinner but also made her all hunched up. Since they let her wear her husband's pajamas till the end, Evita drifted about more and more aimlessly inside that vast expanse of cloth. "Don't you think I look like a Jíbaro, a pygmy?" she said to the ministers standing around her bed. They answered her with adulation: "Don't say that, señora. If you're a pygmy, what can we be: lice, microbes?" And they changed the subject. The nurses, however, turned her reality upside down: "See how well you've eaten today?" they kept saying as they took away the dishes she hadn't touched. "You look a little plumper, señora." They fooled her like a child, and the rage burning inside her, with no way out, was what made her gasp for breath: more than her illness, than her decline, than the senseless terror of waking up dead and not knowing what to do.

A week before—a week already?—she had stopped breathing for an instant (as happened to everybody who suffered from anemia, or at least that was what they told her). When she came to, she found herself inside a liquid, transparent cave, with pads over her eyes and wads of cotton in her ears. After one or two tries, she managed to pull out the tubes and catheters. To her astonishment, she noticed that in that room where things seldom changed place there was a cortege of nuns on their knees in front of the dressing table and dim lamps on top of the wardrobes. Two huge oxygen tanks loomed menacingly alongside the bed. Her jars of cream and bottles of perfume had disappeared from the shelves. Prayers could be heard on the stairs, beating their wings like bats.

"What's the meaning of all this ruckus?" she said, sitting up in bed.

They all stood there paralyzed with surprise. A bald-headed doctor she barely remembered came over and said in her ear:

"We've just performed a little operation on you, señora. We've removed the nerve that was causing you such pain in your head. You won't suffer anymore from now on."

"If you knew that that was what it was, I don't understand why you waited so long." And she raised her voice, in the imperious tone she thought she'd lost. "Come, give me a hand. I have to go to the bathroom."

She got out of the bed barefooted and, leaning on a nurse, walked over and sat down on the toilet seat. From there, she heard her brother, Juan, running up and down the corridors, excitedly shouting over and over again: "They've saved Evita! Praise be to God, they've saved Evita!" At that very moment she fell asleep again. She was so exhausted she woke up only now and again to drink sips of tea. She lost all track of time, of the hours of the day and even of the members of the family who took turns keeping watch over her. Once she asked: "What day is it today?" and they told her, "Tuesday, the twenty-second," but after a while, when she repeated the question, they answered, "Saturday, the nineteenth," so she chose to forget something of so little importance to everyone.

During one of her waking periods she had them summon her husband and asked him to stay with her for a while. She saw that he was fatter and had big fleshy pouches under his eyes. He looked disconcerted and seemed to be eager to leave. It was only natural: they hadn't been alone together for almost a year. Evita took his hands in hers and felt him shudder.

"Aren't they taking good care of you, Juan?" she said to him. "You've put on weight from worrying. Stop working so hard and come visit me in the afternoons."

"How can I, Chinita?" her husband said apologetically. "I spend all day answering the letters addressed to you. There are more than three thousand of them, and in every one of them they ask you for something: a scholarship for their children, trousseaus, bedroom suites, jobs as a night watchman, I don't know what all. You have to get back on your feet soon, before I come down sick too."

"Don't try to be funny. You know that tomorrow or the day after I'm going to die. If I ask you to come it's because I need to ask you to do certain things for me."

"Ask me whatever you like."

"Don't abandon the poor, my little greasers. All the people around here who keep licking your boots are going to turn away from you someday. But not the poor, Juan. They're the only ones who know how to be faithful." Her husband stroked her hair. She moved his hands away. "There's just one thing I won't forgive you for."

"Getting married again," he said, trying to make a joke.

6

"Get married as often as you like. All the better for me. That way you'll realize what you've lost. What I don't want is for people to forget me, Juan. Don't let them forget me."

"Don't worry. It's all taken care of. They won't forget you."

"Of course. It's all taken care of," Evita repeated.

The next morning she woke up feeling so energetic, so feather-light, that she was reconciled with her body. After everything they'd put her through, she didn't even feel it now. She didn't have a body, only breaths, desires, innocent pleasures, images of places to go to. There were still some pools of weakness in her chest and hands, nothing special, nothing to keep her from getting out of bed. She had to do it as quickly as she could, so as to take all of them by surprise. If the doctors tried to stop her, she would already be dressed to leave, and with a couple of screams she'd put them in their place. Come on, she said to herself, let's go now. But the minute she tried to take off, one of the terrible drills that bored holes in the nape of her neck made her acutely aware of her illness once again. It was a very brief torture, but intense enough to warn her that her body hadn't changed. So what? she said to herself. I'm going to die, right? Since I'm going to die, everything is permitted. Another bath of relief immediately washed over her. Up until then she hadn't realized that the best remedy for getting rid of something bothersome was to accept that it existed. That sudden revelation filled her with joy. She would never object to anything again: neither catheters nor intravenous feedings nor radiation treatments that burned her back to a crisp nor pain nor the sadness of dying.

They had told her once upon a time that it wasn't one's body that fell ill but one's entire being. If that being managed to recover (and nothing was as hard, because to cure it, it was necessary to see it), the rest was a question of time and willpower. But her being was healthy. It had never, perhaps, been better. It hurt her to move from one side of the bed to the other, but once she pushed the sheets aside, getting out was easy. She gave it a try and was on her feet immediately. The nurses, her mother, and one of the doctors were asleep in the armchairs around the room. How she would have liked

7

them to see her! But she didn't wake them, for fear that among all of them they would force her to get back in bed. She tiptoed over to the windows facing the garden that she had never had the chance to look through. She saw the molted ivy on the wall, the tops of the jacarandas and the magnolias on the garden slope, the vast empty balcony, the ashes of the lawn; she saw the sidewalk, the gentle curve of the avenue that was now called the avenida del Libertador, the strands of dampness in the semidarkness, as though they had just come out of a movie theater. And all of a sudden a boiling of voices reached her ears. Or weren't they voices? There was something in the air that rose and fell as though the light were skirting obstacles or the darkness were an endless fold, a toboggan run to nowhere. There was a moment when she seemed to hear the syllables of her name, but separated from each other by furtive silences: *Eee vii taa.* The light of day was rising in the east, from the depths of the river, as the rain stripped itself of its gray mists and came to life again with a diamond light. The sidewalk was strewn with umbrellas, mantillas, ponchos, glimmers of candles, processional crucifixes, and Argentine flags. What day is today? she said to herself, or may have said to herself. Why the flags? Today is Saturday, she saw by the calendar on the wall. A Saturday nowhere. It's the twenty-sixth, Saturday, July 1952. It's not National Anthem Day or Manuel Belgrano Day or the festival of the Virgin of Luján or any sacrosanct Peronist holiday. But there the little greasers are, pacing back and forth like souls in purgatory. The one on her knees praying is doña Elisa Tejedor, with the same mourning kerchief she was wearing when she asked me for the milk cart on Christmas morning; the one who's walking toward the police barricades, with his hat tilted to one side, is Vicente Tagliatti, for whom I got a job as an apprentice painter; the ones lighting candles are the sons of doña Dionisia Rebollini, who asked me for a house in Lugano and died before I could hand it over to her in Mataderos. Why is don Luis Lejía weeping? Why is everybody embracing, why are their arms raised heavenward, why are they cursing the rain, why are they grief-stricken? Are they saying what I'm hearing: Eee vii taa, don't go away? I'm not thinking of going away, my

8

dear *descamisados,* my little greasers, go get some rest, be patient. If you could see me you wouldn't worry. But I can't let you see me like this, looking this thin. You've gotten used to seeing me look more imposing when I appear before you, dressed to the nines, and how disillusioned you're going to be, now that I'm nothing but skin and bones, my happiness so wasted away, my spirits so low.

She could record a radio broadcast to them and tell them good-bye in her own way, entrusting them to her husband's care as she always did, but she still had all morning to set her voice to rights, to order the microphones set up and have a handkerchief within reach in case she was carried away by emotion the way she'd been the last time. All morning, but all afternoon as well, and the next day, and the horizon of all the days it would take her to die. Another gust of weakness sent her back to bed, her body turned out the light, and the bliss of her weightlessness made her very sleepy; she went from one sleep to another and yet another; she slept as though she had never slept before.

Could it have been 9:00 that night perhaps, 9:15? Colonel Carlos Eugenio de Moori Koenig was delivering his second lecture at the Army Intelligence School on the nature of secrecy and the use of rumor. "Rumor," he was saying, "is the precaution that facts take before becoming truth." He had cited William Stanton's studies on the structure of Chinese tongs and the teachings of the Bohemian philosopher Fritz Mauthner on the inadequacy of language for dealing with the complexity of the real world. But his attention was focused on rumor now. "Every rumor is innocent in principle, just as every truth is guilty, because the truth does not allow itself to be contaminated, it cannot be passed from mouth to mouth."

He looked through his notes in search of a quotation from Edmund Burke, but at that moment one of the duty officers interrupted him to inform him that the wife of the president of the Republic had just died. The Colonel picked up his folders, and as he was leaving the classroom, said in German: "Thank God it's all over."

9

In the last two years, the Colonel had spied on Evita by order of a general of the Intelligence Service who cited, in turn, orders from Perón. His outlandish duty consisted of submitting daily reports on the vaginal hemorrhages that were tormenting the first lady, concerning which the president was to be kept better informed than anyone else. But that was how it was in those days: everybody mistrusted everybody else. A frequent nightmare of the middle classes involved the horde of barbarians that would come down from the darkness to take their houses, jobs, and savings away from them, just as Julio Cortázar had imagined in his story "House Taken Over." Evita, however, saw reality upside down: she was distressed by the oligarchs and traitors who were out to crush the shirtless people beneath their boots (that was the way she talked: in her speeches she sounded all the high notes of emphasis) and asked the masses' help in "flushing traitors from their foul lairs." As an exorcism to ward off the stampedes of the poor, in the living rooms of the upper class the civilized maxims of Lin Yutang's *A Leaf in the Storm,* George Santayana's lectures on pleasure and morality, and the epigrams of Aldous Huxley's characters were read. Evita was no reader, of course. When she needed to get out of a tight spot, she cited Plutarch or Carlyle, on the advice of her husband. She preferred to trust in God-given wisdom. She was very busy. She received between fifteen and twenty labor union delegations in the morning; she visited a couple of hospitals and a factory or two in the afternoon; she inaugurated stretches of highway, bridges, and day-care centers; she toured the provinces two or three times a month; she delivered from five to six speeches a day, brief harangues, pet battle cries: she proclaimed her love for Perón up to six times in the same sentence, taking the themes farther and farther and then bringing them back to their point of departure as in a Bach fugue: "My only thoughts are for Perón and my people"; "I hoist my banner for the cause of Perón"; "I can never thank Perón enough for what I am and what I have"; "My life does not belong to me but to Perón and to my people, who are my fixed ideals." It was overwhelming and exhausting.

No spy job was beneath the Colonel, and to keep Evita under surveillance he served for a time in the court of her aides-de-camp. Power is nothing but a tissue of facts, he kept telling himself, and heaven only knows which of all the ones I gather will be of use to me for loftier ends. He wrote reports as minutely detailed as they were inappropriate for his rank: "The Señora is losing a great deal of blood but she refuses to allow the doctors to be called in . . . She locks herself in the bathroom of her office and discreetly changes her sanitary napkins . . . Blood keeps pouring out of her. Impossible to tell when it is from her illness and when it is her menstrual flow. She moans but never in public. Her female assistants hear her moaning in the bathroom and offer to help her, but she doesn't want them to . . . Calculation of the blood she lost today, 19 August 1951: 5.75 cc. . . . Calculation of the blood she lost today, 23 September 1951: 9.70 cc." Such precise figures gave away the fact that the Colonel questioned the nurses, snooped about in the trash cans, wrung out her used pads. As he himself used to say, he was doing honor to his original name, which was Moor Koenig: King of the Moor.

The longest of his reports dates from September 22. That afternoon, an official from the American Embassy passed confidential medical information on to him after having been given a complete list of the hemorrhages, thereby allowing the Colonel to draw up a document couched in more rigorous language. He wrote: "When an ulcerated lesion was discovered in the cervix of señora Perón, a biopsy was made and the cause diagnosed as an endophilic carcinoma; as a first step, therefore, the affected area will be destroyed through the use of intracavitary radium and shortly thereafter a surgical intervention will be performed. In other words, in lay terms, she obviously has cancer of the womb. Because of the extent of the damage it is assumed that when she is operated on her entire uterus must be removed. The specialists who are treating her give her six months to live, seven at most. They have called in one of the heads of the Memorial Cancer Hospital in New York for an emergency consultation to confirm what there is no longer any need to confirm."

Once Evita was placed in the care of the doctors, the Colonel was left with very little to do. He asked to be relieved of his assignment to the corps of aides-de-camp and be allowed to pass on to an elite of young officers his vast store of knowledge in the fields of counterespionage, infiltration, cryptography, and rumor theory. He led the life of a contented scholar while honorary titles and decorations were heaped upon Evita as she lay dying: Standard Bearer of the Humble, Lady of Hope, Chain of the Order of the Liberator General San Martín, Spiritual Head and Honorary Vice-President of the Nation, Martyr of Labor, Patroness of the province of La Pampa, of the city of La Plata, and of the towns of Quilmes, San Rafael, and Madre de Dios.

In the three years that followed, everything imaginable happened in the history of Argentina, but the Colonel kept his distance, absorbed in his teaching and his research. Evita died, and her body lay in state for twelve days beneath the towering giraffe dome of the Secretariat of Labor, where she had been drained of her life's blood answering the pleas of the multitude. Half a million people kissed the coffin. A number of the mourners had to be dragged away bodily because they attempted to commit suicide at the feet of the corpse by slitting their throats or swallowing capsules of poison. Eighteen thousand wreaths of flowers were placed around the bier: as many more were hung in the funeral chapels erected in provincial capitals and district townships, where the deceased was represented by photographs ten feet tall. The Colonel attended the wake with the twenty-two aides-de-camp who had served her, wearing the conventional black armband. He stood there for ten minutes, said a prayer, and withdrew with bowed head. The morning of the funeral he stayed in bed and followed the movements of the funeral procession as described over the radio. The coffin was placed on a gun carriage drawn by an escort of thirty-five labor union representatives in shirtsleeves. Seventeen thousand soldiers were posted in the streets to render her military honors. A million and a half yellow roses, stocks from the Andes, white carnations, orchids from the Amazon, sweet peas from Lake Nahuel Huapí, and chrysanthemums sent by the emperor of Japan in warplanes were thrown from balconies.

"Numbers," the Colonel said. "That woman's only anchor to reality now is numbers."

Months went by, and reality nonetheless continued to take care of her. In answer to her plea not to be forgotten, Perón ordered the body embalmed. The work was entrusted to Pedro Ara, a Spanish anatomist famous for having preserved the hands of Manuel de Falla as though they were still playing "El amor brujo." On the second floor of the General Labor Confederation, an isolation laboratory was set up, kept off bounds to the public by the most rigorous safety precautions.

Although no one could see the corpse, people imagined it lying there, in a private chapel, and came on Sundays to recite the rosary and offer flowers. Little by little Evita began to turn into a story that, before it ended, kindled another. She ceased to be what she said and what she did to become what people say she said and what people say she did.

As her memory became incarnate and people unfolded within that body the folds of their own memories, that of Perón—fatter and fatter, more and more disconcerted—was emptied of its history. Among the rumors that the Colonel compiled for the enlightenment of his disciples, one about a military coup that was supposed to take place between June and September 1955 began to make the rounds. There was no coup in June; in September, Perón fell on his own.

A fugitive, hiding out in a Paraguayan gunboat that was being repaired in the Buenos Aires shipyards, Perón, going without sleep for four nights in a row as he waited for his murderers to find him, spent those nights writing the story of his romance with Eva Duarte. It is the only text of his life that construes the past as a tissue of feelings and not as a political tool, although its effect (no doubt deliberate) is to wield Evita's martyrdom, like a mace, to club his adversaries in the face.

What is most striking about these pages is the fact that, even though they are a declaration of love, the word *love* never appears in them. Perón writes: "We thought as one, with the same brain, we felt as one and the same soul. It therefore was natural that such a communion of ideas and of feelings should give rise to that affection that led us to marriage." "That affection?" That is not the sort of expression that one imagines coming from Evita's lips. At the very least what she used to tell her *descamisados* was: "I love General Perón with all my soul and would go through fire for him a thousand and one times." If feelings had a unit of measurement and if that unit could be applied to the two statements, it would be easy to determine the precise emotional distance separating Evita from her husband.

In those days of the coup against Perón, the Colonel's interests lay in other breaths taken by reality. The most trivial of them was a semantic respiration: nobody now called the ex-president by his name or by his military rank, from which he was soon to be demoted. The phrases used to refer to him in official documents were "the runaway tyrant" and "the deposed dictator." Evita was called "that woman," but in private they reserved crueler epithets for her. She was the Mare or the Filly, which in the Buenos Aires slang of the time meant "hooker," "B-girl," "nut case." The *descamisados* did not give up using these names for her altogether, but they turned their meaning around so that they were no longer taken as insults. To them, Evita was the lead mare, the one that guided the herd.

After Perón's fall, the higher-ranking army officers were decimated by pitiless purges. The Colonel feared that his retirement, forced on him because he had served as aide-de-camp to the Señora, would be announced any day, but his friendship with several of the revolutionary ringleaders—whose instructor and confidant he had been in the Intelligence School—and his acknowledged expertise in bringing conspiracies to light kept him afloat for several weeks in the liaison offices of the Ministry of the Army. There he drew up a complicated plan to assassinate the "runaway dictator" and another, even more involved, aimed at surprising him in bed and cutting his tongue out. But Perón no longer worried the triumphant generals. The headache that kept them awake nights was the remains of "that woman."

The Colonel was in his office writing a memorandum on the use of spies according to Sun Tzu and listening to Bach's "Magnificat" at full volume when the provisional president of the Republic sent for him. It was eleven at night, and it had been raining for a solid week. The air was saturated with mosquitoes, caterwauling, and the smell of rot. The Colonel had no idea why they could possibly need him and wrote down a few notes about the two or three delicate missions that he was perhaps about to be assigned. Perhaps tailing the nationalist agitators who had been driven out of the government that very week? Finding out who was going to be entrusted by the military with the job of governing Brazil after the hasty resignation of President Café Filho? Or something more secret, more clandestine still, such as discovering the dens where the wolf packs on the run were licking their wounds? He washed his face, shaved his day-and-a-half beard, and entered the labyrinths of Government House. The meeting was in a large room with mirrored walls and allegorical busts of Justice, Reason, and Providence. The desktops were littered with dried-out sandwiches and cigarette ashes. The provisional president of the Republic seemed tense, about to lose his self-control. He was a pale man, with a round face, who punctuated his sentences with asthmatic silences. He had thin, almost white lips, darkened by a large nose. The vice-president's round shoulders and the contractions of his jaws put one in mind of ants. He also wore big sunglasses, which he did not take off even in the darkness of the room. In a hoarse voice, he ordered the Colonel to remain standing. Their meeting, he informed him, would be a short one.

"It's about that woman," he said. "We want to know if it's her."

It took the Colonel a moment to understand.

"A number of persons have seen the body at the CGT," a navy captain reported. "They say it's impressive. It's been three years now, and it appears to be still intact. We've had X rays of it taken. Here they are, have a look at them. It has all its vital organs. Maybe the body's a hoax, or some other woman's. There's still an Italian sculptor around who was asked to submit plans for a monument to her, with a sarcophagus and the whole bit. The Italian made a wax copy of the corpse. They say that it's a perfect copy, and that nobody can tell for sure which is which."

"They hired an embalmer," the vice-president added. "They paid him a hundred thousand dollars. The country's going broke and they've wasted money on shit like that."

All the Colonel managed to say was: "What are the orders? I'll see to it that they're carried out."

"There's going to be a riot in the factories any minute now," an obese general explained. "We know that the ringleaders want to get into the CGT and carry the woman away. They want to parade her through the cities. They're going to place her in the prow of a boat full of flowers and go down the Paraná with her in order to stir up an uprising among the people living along the river."

The Colonel imagined the endless procession and the drums beating along the shores. The baleful torches. The fleets of flowers. The vice-president sat up straighter.

"That woman is even more dangerous dead than she was alive. The tyrant knew it and that's why he left her here, so she'd make us all sick. In any and every hovel there are photographs of her. The ignorant worship her like a saint. They think she can come back to life any day now and turn Argentina into a dictatorship of beggars."

"How, if she's only a corpse?" the Colonel managed to ask.

The president appeared to have had enough of all the wild fantasies; he wanted to go to bed.

"Every time a corpse enters the picture in this country, history goes mad. Take care of that woman, Colonel."

"I don't quite understand, General. What do you mean, 'take care of' her? Under ordinary circumstances, I'd know what to do. But that woman is dead already."

The vice-president gave him an icy smile.

"Make her disappear," he said. "Finish her off. Turn her into a dead woman like any other."

The Colonel spent a sleepless night, weaving plots and unweaving them straightaway because they were useless. Getting hold of the woman was easy. The hard part was to find her a destiny. Though bodies leave their fate a long way behind them, this woman's was still incomplete. It needed an ultimate fate, but it would have to pass by way of heaven only knew how many other destinations in order to reach it.

He went over and over the reports on the work of preservation, which had been going on since the night of the death. The embalmer's account was glowing. He maintained that after the injections and the fixatives, Evita's skin had turned taut and young, like that of a twenty-year-old. Through her arteries there flowed a current of formaldehyde, paraffin, and zinc chloride. The whole body gave off a delicate aroma of almonds and lavender. The Colonel could not keep his eyes off the photographs that showed an ethereal, ivory-colored creature, possessed of a beauty that made a person forget all the other felicities of the universe. Her own mother, doña Juana Ibarguren, thinking that she heard her breathing, had fainted during one of her visits. The widower had kissed her on the lips twice to break a spell that was perhaps the same as Sleeping Beauty's. The transparencies of the body gave off a liquid light, immune to changes of humidity, storms, and the devastations of ice and heat. It was so well preserved that even the tracery of the blood vessels beneath the porcelain skin and an indelible pink tinging the aureole of the nipples were visible.

As he went on reading, the Colonel's throat grew dry. It would be better to burn her, he thought. With her tissues that saturated with chemicals, she'll blow up the minute I touch a match to her. She'll blaze like a sunset. But the president had given orders prohibiting her body from being burned. Every Christian body must be buried in Christian ground, he had said to him. Though that woman lived an impure life, she made a last confession and died in God's grace. The best thing, then, would be to encase her in fresh cement and throw her into the river in a secret place, as the vice-president wished. Who knows, the Colonel reflected. It's anybody's guess what occult powers those chemicals have. Maybe they'd effervesce on contact with water, and the woman would float to the surface, more vigorous than ever.

He was consumed with impatience. Before dawn he called the embalmer and asked to meet with him. "In a café or at my house?"

the doctor asked, still entangled in the fogs of sleep. "I need to examine the body," the Colonel told him. "I'm going to where you're
keeping her." "Impossible, sir. It's dangerous to see her. The sub-
stances in her body haven't settled yet. They're toxic, unbreathable."
The Colonel cut him short: "I'm heading there this minute."

The fear that some fanatic would take possession of Evita had always existed. The triumph of the military coup also emboldened
those who wished to see her cremated or profaned. At the CGT nobody slept in peace. Two sergeants who had survived the Peronist
purges in the army took turns standing guard on the second floor.
On occasion, the embalmer allowed civil servants from the foreign
diplomatic missions to enter the laboratory, hoping they would cry
out to high heaven if the military destroyed the corpse. But what he
got out of them was not promises of solidarity but incredulous stammers. The visitors, who arrived prepared to witness a scientific miracle, left convinced that what had really been shown them was a
magic act. Evita was in the middle of a vast room draped in black.
She lay on a glass slab, suspended from the ceiling by transparent
cords, so as to give the impression that she was levitating in a state
of perpetual ecstasy. Hanging on either side of the door were the
purple ribbons of the funeral wreaths, with their inscriptions still intact: COME BACK, EVITA MY LOVE. YOUR BROTHER JUAN; EVITA ETER-
NAL IN THE HEART OF THE PEOPLE. YOUR INCONSOLABLE MOTHER.
The visitors fell to their knees before the marvel of the body floating in the pure air, and rose to their feet with their minds reeling.

The image was so overwhelming, so unforgettable, that people's
common sense ended up somewhere else. No one knows what happened. The shape of their world changed. The embalmer, for example, now lived only for her. He turned up at the CGT laboratory
every morning at eight on the dot, dressed in one of his blue cash-
mere suits and wearing a stiff-brimmed hat edged with a wide black
band. On stepping out on the second floor, he removed his hat, baring a shiny bald pate and a few strands of gray hair plastered down
with pomade. He then put on his apron, and for ten to fifteen minutes he would examine the photographs and X rays that recorded

the slightest change in the cadaver from day to day. In one of his lab notes is the entry: "August 15, 1954. I lost all sense of time. I spent the afternoon watching over the Señora and speaking to her. It was like taking a look at a balcony that is now empty. And yet that cannot be. There's something there, something. I must discover the way to see it."

Is there perhaps someone who presumes that Dr. Ara was trying to see the suns of the absolute, the language of the earthly paradise, the milky galactic orgasm of the immaculate conception? Nonsense. All the references to him confirm his good sense, his lack of imagination, his piety. It was impossible to suspect him of occultist and parapsychological inclinations. Certain of the Colonel's notes—of which I have a copy—may hit the nail on the head: what interested the embalmer was finding out whether the cancer was still spreading through the body even after it had been purified. The boundaries of his curiosity were limited yet scientific. He studied the subtle movements of the joints, the changes in color of the cartilage and glands, the network of the nerves and the muscles in search of a stigma. There was not a trace of one left. What was withered had been erased. Only death breathed in the tissues.

Anyone who reads Dr. Pedro Ara's posthumous memoirs (*El caso Eva Perón*, CVS Ediciones, Madrid, 1974) will readily note that he had had a look at Evita long before she died. Time and again he complains of those who think that. But only a conventional historian takes his sources literally. See for example the first chapter. It is entitled "The Force of Destiny?" and its tone, as can be sensed from that rhetorical question, is one of humility and doubt. The idea of embalming Evita would never have entered his head, he writes; more than once he drove from his door those who came to ask him to do so, but in the face of Destiny, of God, what can a poor anatomist do? It is true, he hints, that perhaps there was no one as well prepared as he for such an undertaking. He was an academician of the first rank and a distinguished professor. His masterpiece—a nineteen-year-old girl from Córdoba who lay immobilized in a dance step—left the experts openmouthed. But embalming Evita was like blowing up the firmament. Have I been chosen? Because of what merits? he asks himself in the memoirs. He had already said no when they pleaded with him to examine Lenin's corpse in Moscow. Why would he say yes this time? Because of Destiny, with a capital *D*. "Who is so fatuous and so vain as to believe that he could be chosen?" he sighs in the first chapter. "Why, after so many centuries of decline, does the idea of Destiny continue to prosper?"

Ara met Evita in October of 1949, "not socially," as he puts his reader on notice, but in the shadow of her husband, at one of the rallies of the populace that thrilled her so. He had come to Government House as the emissary of the ambassador of Spain and was waiting in an anteroom for the end of the speeches and the ritual of greeting the people. A tide of admirers bore him to the balcony where Evita and Perón, with their arms upraised, were being swept to and fro by the wind of ecstasy that arose from the multitude. He stood at the Señora's back for a moment, so close that he was able to observe the dance of the blood vessels in her neck: the agitation and suffocation brought on by anemia.

In his memoirs he maintains that that was Evita's last day without worries about her health. A blood test showed that she had only three million red cells per milliliter. Her fatal illness had not yet taken its mortal swipe at her, but it was already there, Ara wrote. "If I had seen her for a little longer than that brief second that afternoon, I would have captured the dense fragrance of flowers of her breath, the fire of her cornea, the indomitable energy of her thirty years. And I would have been able to copy those details in their entirety in the dead body that was so badly deteriorated when it reached my hands. Given the circumstances, I was obliged to make use of nothing but photographs and presentiments. Even so, I turned her into a statue of supreme beauty, like the Pietà or the Victory of Samothrace. But I deserved better, is that not true? I deserved better."

In June of 1952, seven weeks before Evita died, Perón summoned him to the presidential palace.

"You may have already learned that there is no way of saving my wife's life," he said to him. "The legislature wants to build a monument to her one hundred fifty feet tall in the Plaza de Mayo, but such grandiose displays don't interest me. I would rather have the people continue to see her looking as alive as she is now. I have been told that you are the best taxidermist there is. If that is so, it is not going to be difficult for you to prove it with someone just a little over thirty-three years old."

"I am not a taxidermist," Ara corrected him. "I am a preserver of bodies. All the arts aspire to eternity, but mine is the only one that turns eternity into something visible. The eternal as a branch of the tree of the true."

The unctuousness of Ara's language disconcerted Perón and plunged him into an instantaneous mistrust.

"Tell me once and for all what you need and I will place it at your disposal. My wife's illness scarcely leaves me time to do everything I have to do."

"I need to see the body," the doctor answered. "I fear that all of you have called upon my services too late."

"Go in whenever you like," the president said, "but it's better if she knows nothing of your visit. I will give orders this minute for them to put her to sleep with sedatives."

Ten minutes later, he showed the embalmer into the bedroom of the dying woman. She was thin, angular, her back and her abdomen badly burned by the bungled radiation therapy. Her translucent skin was beginning to turn scaly all over. Indignant at the carelessness with which a woman who was so venerated in public was treated in private, Ara demanded that the torture of the radiation therapy be suspended and gave them a blend of aromatic oils with which her body was to be anointed three times a day. No one took his advice seriously.

On July 26, 1952, as darkness was falling, an emissary from the presidential palace came to get him in an official car. Nothing more could be done for Evita; she was now in mortal agony and was expected to die at any moment. In the grounds outside the palace, long lines of women were moving forward on their knees, begging heaven to postpone that death. When the embalmer stepped out of the car, one of the devout women clutched him by the arm and asked him, weeping: "Is it true, señor, that misfortune has befallen us?" To which Ara replied, in all seriousness: "God knows what He is doing, and I am here to save what can be saved. I swear to you that I shall do so."

He had no idea of the arduous work that lay ahead of him. They delivered the body to him at 9:00 that night, after a hasty prayer for the dead. Evita had died at 8:25. The corpse was still warm and pliant, but its feet were turning blue and its nose was drooping like an exhausted animal. Ara noted that if he did not act immediately death would get the better of him. It was advancing, dancing on eggs, and wherever it set its foot down it seeded a nest. Ara removed death from here, and it glinted there, moving so swiftly that his fingers were unable to contain it. The embalmer opened the femoral artery in the groin, underneath the Fallopian arch, and at the same time entered the navel in search of the volcanic slimes that were endangering the stomach. Without waiting for the blood to drain away completely, he injected a torrent of formaldehyde, as the scalpel made its way through the interstices between the muscles, heading for the viscera; when he reached them he trickled paraffin over them and plugged the incisions with plaster tampons. His attention flew from the eyes that were gradually sinking in and the jaws that were coming out of joint to the lips that were taking on an ashen tinge. Dawn surprised him in the midst of the stifling battle. In the notebook in which he kept a record of the chemical solutions and the peregrinations of the scalpel he wrote: "*Finis coronat opus.* Eva Perón's body is now absolutely and definitively incorruptible."

He took it as an affront to be asked, three years after such a feat, to account for what he had done. Account for what? For a masterpiece that preserved all the viscera? What stupidity, dear God, what a misprision of fate. He would hear what they had to say to him, and then he would catch the first boat to Spain, taking with him what belonged to him.

Colonel Koenig's good manners nonetheless took Ara by surprise.

He ordered a cup of coffee, nonchalantly tossed off a few verses of Góngora's on dawn, and when he finally spoke of the corpse, the embalmer's scruples had long since vanished. In his memoirs he describes the Colonel in glowing terms: "After searching for a twin soul for so many months, I have just found it in the man I believed to be my enemy."

"Absurd rumors about the corpse have reached the government," the Colonel said. He had brought out a pipe after drinking his coffee, but the doctor begged him not to smoke it. A slip of the flame, an absentminded spark, and Evita could turn to ashes. "Nobody believes that the corpse is still intact after three years. One of the ministers surmises that you hid it in a niche in the cemetery and put a wax statue in its place."

The doctor shook his head in dismay. "What would I gain by doing that?"

"Fame. You yourself explained at the Academy of Medicine that giving a dead corpse the sensation of life was like discovering the philosophers' stone. Exactitude is the quintessence of science, you said. And the rest, rubble, a mule without a face. I didn't understand that metaphor. An occultist allusion, I presume."

"I have been renowned for some time, Colonel. I have all the fame I need. On the list of embalmers there is no name other than mine. Perón called me in for that reason: he had no alternative."

The sun appeared amid the curvets of the river. A spot of light chanced to fall on the doctor's bald pate.

"No one is unaware of your merits, Doctor. What is odd is that an expert like yourself took three years to do a job that ought to have been finished in six months."

"Those are the risks of exactitude. Weren't you just speaking of that?"

"The president is being told other things. Forgive me for mentioning them, but the franker we are with each other the better we'll understand each other." He took two or three sealed documents out of his briefcase. He sighed as he leafed through them, as a sign of displeasure. "I would like to think that you would not take these accusations to be more important than they really are, Doctor. They are merely that: accusations, not proofs. It states here that you kept the Señora's corpse because you were not paid the hundred thousand dollars that had been agreed on."

"That is despicable. A day before Perón fled the country I was paid everything I was owed. I am a believer, a militant Catholic. I am not about to lose my soul by using a dead woman as a hostage."

"I concur. But it is the nature of the state to be mistrustful." The Colonel began toying with the pipe and tapping his teeth with the stem. "Listen to this report. It's shameful. 'The Galician is in love with the corpse,' it says. The Galician is no doubt yourself. 'He paws it, he fondles its tits. A soldier has caught him putting his hands up between its legs.' I imagine that isn't true." The embalmer closed his eyes. "Or is it? Tell me. What you say is strictly between us."

"I have no reason to deny it. For two years and a half, the body that I left fresh at night was faded on awakening in the morning. I noted that in order to restore its beauty its vital organs would have to be put to rights." He averted his eyes, tucked the waistband of his trousers underneath his ribs. "There's no need to go on manipulating it. I've discovered a fixative that keeps it nailed to its being, once and for all."

The Colonel sat up straight in his chair. "The most difficult problem to resolve," he said, putting the pipe away, "is what the president calls 'possession.' He believes that the corpse cannot remain in your hands, Doctor. You haven't the means to protect it."

"And they've asked you to take it away from me, Colonel?"

"That is correct. The president has ordered me to do so. He has just appointed me head of the Intelligence Service to that end. The appointment was announced in the papers this morning."

A disdainful smile appeared on the embalmer's lips. "It isn't time yet, Colonel. She's not ready. If you take her away now, you're not going to find her tomorrow. She will be lost in the air; she will turn to vapor, mercury, alcoholic spirits."

"I don't believe you understand me, Doctor. I'm an army officer. I don't listen to reason. I carry out orders."

"I am going to give you only a few arguments. After that, do as you please. The body still needs a bath of balm. It has a cannula that's draining. I must remove it. But above all I need time. What are two or three days for a journey that is going to last for all eternity? In the depths of the body are faucets to close, quarrels that are not settled. And what is more, Colonel, the mother doesn't want anyone to take it away from me. She has granted me legal custody. If they take it away there'll be a scandal. She will appeal to the Holy Father. As you see, Colonel, there are certain reasons that must be listened to before obeying."

He began to rock back and forth on his heels. He tucked his thumbs underneath the suspenders that he was doubtless wearing under his lab smock. He recovered his aloofness, his air of superiority, his slyness: everything that the Colonel's entrance onstage had, for a moment, caused to disappear.

"You know very well what's at stake," the Colonel said as he too rose to his feet. "It's not the corpse of that woman but the destiny of Argentina. Or both things, which to so many people seem to be one. Heaven only knows how the useless dead body of Eva Duarte came to be confused with the country. Not for people like you or me. To the poverty-stricken, to the ignorant, to those who are outside of history. They would let themselves be killed for the corpse. If it had rotted away, that would have been the end of that. But by embalming it, you made history change place. You left history inside. Whoever has the woman has the country in the palm of their hand, do you realize? The government cannot allow a corpse like that to drift about. Tell me your conditions."

"I'm not the one to dictate conditions," the doctor answered. "My sole responsibility is to fulfill the wishes of Evita's mother and sisters." He read a few notes he had on the desk. "They wish, they tell me, to have her buried in sacred ground and have people told where it is, so that they can visit her."

"Don't worry about the sacred ground part. But the other proviso is unacceptable. The president has given me orders to have everything done in the greatest secrecy."

"The mother is going to insist."

"I don't know what to tell you. If anyone were to find out where the body is, there would be no human force able to protect it. There are fanatics searching all over for it. They would steal it, Doctor. They would make it disappear from under our very noses."

"Then watch your step," the doctor said sarcastically. "Because when I lose sight of it, nobody will have any way of knowing if she's her. Didn't you tell me about a wax statue? It exists. Evita wanted a tomb like Napoleon Bonaparte's. When the mock-ups were being made, the sculptor was here, reproducing the body. I saw the copy he made. It was identical. Do you know what happened? He went back to the studio one night, and the copy was gone. They took it away from him. He thinks it was the army. But it wasn't the army, isn't that so?"

"No, it wasn't," the Colonel admitted.

"Well then, watch your step. I'm washing my hands of the whole thing."

"Don't wash them too fast, Doctor. Where's the body? I want to see for myself if it's that marvel your notes speak of. Let me see what they say." He took an index card out of his pocket and read: "'It is a liquid sun.' Doesn't that seem like an exaggeration to you? Imagine, a liquid sun."

2

"I Will Be Millions"

When Evita went outdoors for the last time she weighed eighty-two pounds. Searing pains flared up every two or three minutes, making her pant for breath. She could not, however, offer herself the luxury of suffering. At three in the afternoon that day her husband was going to take the oath of office as president of the Republic for his second consecutive term, and the *descamisados* had flocked to Buenos Aires to see her, not him. She was the big show. The rumor that she was dying had spread all over. In the huts of Santiago del Estero and Santiago del Chabut the grief-stricken people interrupted their daily tasks to beseech God to keep her alive. Every humble home had an altar where photographs of Evita, torn out of magazines, were alight with candles and decorated with wildflowers. At night, the photos were carried in a procession from place to place so as to give them a moon bath. No recourse was neglected if it promised to restore her health. The sick woman knew these things and did not want to let people down after they had spent the night in the inclement weather to see the presidential motorcade and greet her from afar.

She tried twice to get up out of bed, and the doctors would not allow her to. The third time, blinded by a pain that drilled into the nape of her neck, she collapsed on the bed. She then decided to go out anyway, because if she was going to die that day she wanted to do it in front of everybody. She summoned her mother, the nurses, her husband, and asked them to help her get dressed. "Inject me with sedatives so I can stand up," she said. "Help me, stay with me, don't leave me alone." They had never heard her plead for anything, and now they saw her on her knees on the bed, with her hands joined.

Her husband was disconcerted. From the door of the room he observed that fit of rebelliousness without knowing what the most sensible response would be. He was wearing a full-dress uniform and a dark winter cape. Beneath the presidential sash he had hung a collection of his medals and decorations. "Have you gone mad, Chinita?" he said to her, shaking his head. The inconsolable look in Eva's eyes tormented him. "You can't go out. The frost hasn't melted. You're going to fall flat on your face." She insisted. "Take away this pain in the nape of my neck and you'll see if I can or not. Put an anaesthetic on my heels. I can. If I stay here all by myself I'm going to die. I'd rather die from the pain than from sadness. Won't anybody take pity on me?" Her husband ordered them to get her dressed and left the room muttering: "It's always the same with you, Chinita. You always end up doing whatever you please."

They gave her two injections, one so she wouldn't suffer and another to keep her clearheaded. They covered up the dark circles under her eyes with light-colored foundation creams and brush strokes of face powder. And since, despite the bad weather, she was determined to be driven alongside the president in an open car as he proceeded on foot, a corset of plaster and wire to hold her upright was hurriedly made. The worst part was the torture of the lingerie and petticoats because the very touch of them made her skin burn. But after having had a rough time for half an hour because of it, she stoically put up with the scratchiness of the dress, the embroidered cloche hat they pulled down over her head to hide how emaciated she was, the high-heeled pumps, and the mink coat that two Evitas would have fit into. Although she was carried down the stairs in a wheelchair by soldiers, she reached the doors of the palace on her own two feet and smiled as she went out as though she were in the pink of health. She felt light-headed from weakness and the joy of being in the open air, which she had been kept out of for thirty-three days. Clinging to her husband's arm, she allowed herself to be nearly crushed by the people on the staircases of Congress and, except for a slight fainting spell that forced her to lie down and rest in the infirmary of the Chamber of Deputies, she graciously endured, as in her best days, the protocol of the presidential swearing-in ceremony and the hand kissing of the ministers. Then as the Cadillac of grand occasions led the motorcade down the avenues, she stood on tiptoe so people wouldn't notice that her body had shrunk like a little old woman's. She saw for the last time the pitted balconies of the pension where she had slept in her adolescence; she saw the ruins of the theater where she had played a role in which she spoke just three words, "Dinner is served"; she saw La Opera pastry shop, where she had begged for anything and everything: a coffee with milk, a blanket, a bit of room in a bed, her photograph in a magazine, a wretched bit of dialogue in the afternoon soap opera on the radio. She saw the big ramshackle house near the Obelisk where she had washed in ice-cold water in a filthy sink twice a month; she saw herself in a courtyard with wisteria vines on the calle Sarmiento, treating her chilblains with camphorated alcohol and her plague of lice with floods of kerosene; she saw drying in the sun the cotton skirt and the faded linen blouse that for a year had been the only outfit in her wardrobe; she saw the frayed panties, the garter belts with the elastic straps missing, the cotton stockings, and wondered how her face had risen above the humiliation and the dust so as to be parading down the avenue now on the throne of that Cadillac with her arms upraised, reading in people's eyes a veneration that no actress had ever known, Evita, Evita dear, my beloved little mother. She was going to die tomorrow, but what did it matter? A hundred deaths weren't enough to pay for a life like this.

The following morning she was again prostrated by pains more unbearable than Saint Joan's at the stake. She cursed Divine Providence for torturing her and the doctors for advising her to keep calm. She wanted to die, she wanted to live; she wanted them to give her back the being she had lost. She spent two nights like that, until the sedatives made her groggy, and her illness, worn out from its long siege, withdrew to the deep shadows of her body. Her mother and sisters took turns at her bedside looking after her, but on the evening that Evita regained consciousness only doña Juana was there with her. They drank a cup of tea and held their arms around each other for a long time, in silence, till it occurred to Evita to ask what day it was, as usual, and why she hadn't been brought the newspapers.

Her mother was wearing tight bandages around her calves and every so often she put her feet up on her daughter's bed. Warm sunshine filtered through the windows, and although it was winter, the commotion of doves could be heard outside.[1]

"It's now the sixth of June," her mother answered, "and the doctors don't know what to do with you, Cholita. They're tearing their hair—they don't understand why you refuse to get well."

"Don't pay any attention to them. My illness has them all confused. They blame me because they can't blame themselves for it. All they know how to do is cut out and sew up. What I have can't be cut out or patched up. It's something deeper inside." For a moment she stared into space. "So what did the newspapers have to say?"

"What do you think they said, Cholita? That you were gorgeous in Congress, that you don't look sick. They liked your mink coat and your emerald necklace. *Democracia* carried a photograph of a family that came all the way from the Chaco to see you, and since they couldn't find a place where they could watch the parade, they waited in front of the store windows of Casa América till you appeared on television. They were so moved they burst into tears, and

---

[1] "Those last days of Evita's life were as sad as the radio serials of the forties," doña Juana told me the one time I saw her. "The things we talked about that day were like the ones that Alicia, the little girl who was an invalid, talked over with her housekeeper in a series that, as I remember, was called *Dream of Love*." Evita Duarte portrayed Alicia in the serial *Promise of Love,* by Martinelli Massa, which was broadcast by Radio El Mundo in June 1942.

at that moment the photographer took the shot of them. The worst of it is that the photo made me cry too. I don't know what else was in the papers. Do you think it matters? Look at these clippings. In Egypt the military is still threatening to boot the king out. They certainly ought to, right? That disgusting tub of lard. He's a year younger than you are and he looks like an old man."

"They'll say things like that about me, because I'm so skinny."

"Are you out of your mind? Everybody thinks you're really pretty. A couple of pounds more wouldn't look bad on you, there's no denying it. But there's not one woman who's prettier than you are, just the way you are. Sometimes I look at myself in the mirror and ask myself: How did I ever come to have such a good-looking daughter? Just think if we'd stayed in Junín and you'd married Mario, the one who ran the gift shop. It would have been a waste."

"You know I don't like remembering those days, Mama. Those people made me suffer more than my illness does. My throat goes dry just remembering. They were shits, Mom. You can't imagine the things they say about you."

"I can imagine, but I don't care. They'd die to be in my shoes today. That's life for you, right? To think that when you got engaged to that magazine editor—what was his name?—you thought you were in seventh heaven. Poor Elisa was desperate and begged me to get us to persuade you to break your engagement because they were driving her husband crazy in the military district with their gossip: your sister-in-law's having her picture taken in a tight-fitting bathing suit, she's getting herself kissed in dressing rooms, they're treating her like dirt. I stood my ground, remember. I explained to them: Chola isn't like the rest of you. She's an artist. Elisa wouldn't drop the subject. Mama, she said, where's your head at? Chola's living with a married man who's a Jew to boot. She's in love, leave her alone, I told them."

"I wasn't in love, Mama. I never was, till I met Perón. I fell in love with Perón before I even saw him, because of the things he did. It's not every woman that happens to. Not all women realize they've met a man who's made for them, and there'll never be another one."

31

"I know Perón's different, but the love you gave him isn't like any other love either."

"Why are we talking about things like this, Mama? Your life wasn't like mine and we could end up not understanding each other. If you'd fallen in love with anyone except Papa you might not be the same person. Perón brought out the best in me, and if I'm Evita, that's the reason why. If I'd married Mario or that magazine editor I'd be Chola or Eva Duarte, but not Evita, see what I mean? Perón let me be everything I wanted to be. I kept pushing and I used to say to him: I want this, Juan, I want that, and he never refused me anything. I could take as much room for myself as I pleased. I didn't take more because I didn't have time. I got sick from taking on so much. What would other men have said? I ask you. Get in the kitchen, knit a sweater, Chola. You have no idea how many sweaters I knit in the outer offices of magazines. It wasn't like that with Perón. I fell head over heels in love with him, you know what I mean? And every time you've heard me say I love Perón with all my soul, Perón is more than my life, I was also saying I love myself, I love myself."

"You don't owe him anything, Chola. What you have inside is yours and nobody else's. You're better than he is and better than all of us."

"Do me a favor?" She unfastened a gold key from her necklace, a little one as light as a fingernail, with curved notches. "Open the right-hand drawer of the writing desk with this. On top, in plain sight, you'll find two letters. Bring them here. I want you to see something."

She lay quietly in the bed, smoothing the sheets. She'd been happy, but not the way other people are. Nobody knew what happiness was, exactly. People knew all there was to know about hatred, about misfortune, about losses, but not about happiness. She knew, though. At each moment in life she was aware of what might have been and of what was. With each step she took she told herself: This is mine, this is mine, I'm happy. Now the moment of sorrow had come: an eternity of sorrow to make up for six years of fulfillment.

Was this life, was this all there was? She thought she heard the music of an orchestra in the distance, as though it were in the main square of her town. Or could it be the radio, in the nurses' room?

"Two letters," her mother said. "Are these the ones?"

"Read them to me."

"Let me see . . . my glasses. 'My dear Chinita.'"

"No, the other one first."

"'Dear Juan.' This one? 'Dear Juan'? *I am very sad because I cannot live far away from you . . .*"

"I wrote it in Madrid, on the first day of my tour of Europe. Or maybe on the plane, on the way there. I don't remember now. Look at the handwriting. See how uneven it is, how shaky? I didn't know what to do; I wanted to go back. I hadn't even begun the tour and I already wanted to be back. Go ahead, read some more."

"*. . . I love you so much that what I feel for you is a sort of idolatry. I cannot express what I feel but I assure you that I have fought very hard in my life because of my ambition to be somebody and I have suffered a great deal, but then you came along and made me so happy that I thought I was dreaming, and since I had nothing to offer you but my heart and my soul I gave them wholly to you, but in these three years of happiness not for a single hour have I ever ceased to adore you or to thank heaven for God's goodness in granting me the recompense of your love . . .* I can't go on, Chola. You're crying and you're going to make me cry too."

"Just a little more, come on. I'm a softy."

"*I am so faithful to you, my love, that if God were to will not to keep me in this bliss and take me away, I would continue to be faithful to you in death and would adore you from heaven.* Why did you write that, Cholita? What was going through your mind?"

"I was scared, Mama. I thought that when I came back from so far away, he wouldn't be there anymore. That there wouldn't be anything. That I'd wake up in my room at the pension, like when I was a girl. I was deathly afraid. Everybody thought I was bold and had gotten farther ahead than any other woman. But I didn't know what to do, Mama. The only thing that mattered to me was coming back."

"Shall I read you the other letter?"

"No, finish this one. Read the last sentence."

". . . *Everything they've told you about me in Junín is monstrous, I swear to you. In the hour of my death you must know this. It's all a pack of lies. I left Junín when I was thirteen, and at that age, what horrible things can a poor girl do? You can be proud of your wife, Juan, because I was always mindful of your good name and I adored you . . .*[2]

"What stories did they pass on to him?"

"The ones about Magaldi. You know which ones. But I don't want to talk about that."

"You should have told me about it, Cholita, and I would have come here to set things straight. Nobody knows better than I do that you were an innocent girl when you left Junín. Why did you stoop so low as to talk like that? If a man is mistrustful, God himself isn't going to restore his trust. But did he ever—"

"Read the other letter. And don't say another word."

"*My dear Chinita.* Look, he typed it. Love letters written on a typewriter don't mean as much as ones in a person's own handwriting. Maybe he dictated it to a secretary, or maybe it's not from him."

"Don't say that. Read."

"*I too am very sad because you are far away and I can hardly wait for you to come back. But if I decided that you were to tour Europe it was because I could think of no one better suited than you to disseminate our ideas and give voice to our solidarity with all those peoples who have just experienced the scourge of war. You are accomplishing a great mission and all of us here think that no ambassador would have done as well. Don't be upset by all the talk behind your back. I have never paid the slightest attention to it and it has no effect on me. They tried to fill my head with stories about you before, when we were about to marry, but I allowed no one to utter a word against you. When I chose you it was for what you were and your past never mattered to me. I too have fought very hard and I understand you. I have fought to be what I am*

---

[2] The letter reads like a parody, but it is not. It was reproduced in *El último Perón* by Esteban Peicovich (Planeta, Barcelona, 1976), in *Eva Perón* by Nicholas Fraser and Marysa Navarro (W. W. Norton, New York, 1980), and in *Perón y su tiempo, I. La Argentina era una fiesta* by Félix Luna (Sudamérica, Buenos Aires, 1984).

and for you to be what you are. Put your mind entirely at ease, then, take good care of yourself and don't stay up till all hours. As for doña Juana, don't worry about her. Your mother is very tough and can hold her own with no help from anyone, but I promise you by all that is most sacred that I shall see to it that she lacks for nothing. Many kisses and best regards, Juan."

"Do you understand now why I love him so much, Mama?"

"It strikes me as a common ordinary letter."

"He sent it to me in Toledo, the day after he got mine. And if he answered me, it wasn't because there was any need to. Why would there have been, when we talked on the phone together every night? It was out of kindness, to make me feel good."

"You deserved it. No other woman would have written him what you did."

"He deserved it. You know now that I was happy, Mama. Everything I've been through has been worth it. Keep the letters if you like. You've seen me naked so many times by now that once more doesn't matter."

"No. I've never seen you as naked as you are now."

"You're the only one. You and Perón. It's not this nakedness of my soul that bothers me. I've bared my soul all my life, as far as that goes. What worries me is the other kind. When I lose consciousness again or something worse happens to me, I don't want anybody to wash me or undress me, you hear? Not doctors or nurses or anybody else. Just you. I'm embarrassed at the thought that they might see me, Mama. I'm so thin, I look so awful! Sometimes I dream that I'm dead and that they're carrying me to the Plaza de Mayo bare naked. They put me down on a bench and everybody lines up to touch me. No matter how loud or how long I scream, nobody comes to rescue me. Don't let that happen to me, Mama. Don't leave me."

Doña Juana hadn't slept well for several nights, but the night of September 20, 1955, was the worst: she didn't sleep a wink. She got out of bed several times to drink maté and hear the news over the radio. Perón, her son-in-law, had handed in his resignation, and no one had taken over to rule the country. Her varicose veins were troubling her again. Above her ankles, a bluish swelling appeared to be about to erupt like a volcano.

The only thing they talked about on the news was the movements of the rebel army. Anything can happen to Evita, her mother had told the embalmer. Anything. "They're going to take her away to destroy her, Doctor. What they weren't able to do to her when she was alive they're going to make up for now that she's dead. She was different, and in this country that's unforgivable. Ever since she was a little girl she wanted to be different. Now that she's defenseless they're going to make her pay for that."

"Don't worry, señora," the doctor had said to her. "Let your heart of a mother rest easily. In moments such as this, no one viciously attacks the dead." He was an unctuous, fawning man. The more he tried to calm her, the more she mistrusted him.

Who was there not to mistrust in Buenos Aires? Ever since doña Juana had moved there, everything frightened her. In the beginning, the comforts of life and the flattering attentions paid to power dazzled her. Evita was all-powerful, as was her mother. Every time she made a bet at the roulette table in the casino at Mar del Plata, the croupiers added a couple of thousand-peso chips to her winnings, and when she played blackjack with the ministers she always found herself holding, as if by a miracle, a pair of queens. She lived in a house fit for a princess in the Belgrano district, amid palm trees and oleanders. But in the end Buenos Aires had torn her family apart and given her asthma. They had bugged the rooms of her house. To communicate with her daughters, she wrote little notes in a schoolchild's composition book. After Eva's death she couldn't even bring herself to visit her son-in-law, nor did he invite her to come. Her one remaining tie to power was Juancito, her son, but a spiteful mistress had accused him of petty thievery, and Juancito, despondent and overcome with shame, finally committed suicide. In fewer than nine months the family had fallen apart in this accursed weather. The glands of Buenos Aires secreted death. Everything was pettiness and arrogance. Nobody knew how people could put on such airs. Poor

Eva. She had given her life's blood, and they were paying her back for it with a vengeance. Poor little thing. But her enemies would screw up. In life, she had always kept throwing dirt on her fire, so as not to put her husband in the shade. In death, she was about to turn into a conflagration.

She looked out the window. Amid the torpors of the river the first streaks of dawn appeared. She suddenly heard the rain, and at the same time she heard the rain of the hours that had gone by. On the radio they announced that the navy, staging an uprising against the government, had just destroyed the oil storage tanks at Mar del Plata and would bombard the South Dock at any moment. Admiral Rojas, the commander of the rebel forces, promised to raze the port unless Perón surrendered unconditionally. Rojas? doña Juana asked herself. Wasn't he that aide-de-camp who always anticipated Eva's caprices? The little black one, the runt with dark glasses? Had he turned his back on her too? If the South Dock was set ablaze, her daughter would be trapped by the flames. The CGT building was alongside the port, and the fire would reach it in an hour or two.

She tried to get up out of bed, but a cramp made her legs give way. It was her varicose veins. They had gotten worse in the last few weeks because she'd been foolish enough to take walks that ended up nowhere. She walked twice a day to the outer offices of the deputies to plead with them to increase her pension for services to the country. The same ingrates who had once smothered her in orchids and boxes of bonbons were now unwilling to see her and put her off. She went from one shop on Once to another in search of swaths of cloth and crepe for her daughter's funeral chamber. Every other afternoon she entered the labyrinths of the cemetery where Juan, the suicide, was buried, so he wouldn't lack for fresh flowers. She didn't dare get into taxis for fear she'd be kidnapped and her dead body thrown in some garbage dump. These miseries were her life now.

She took one of the sedatives she always kept on hand on her night table and then massaged her legs. Although the pain was torture, she tried to pull herself together. She had promised Evita to

37

wash her body and bury it, but they hadn't allowed her to. Now she had to rescue it from the flames. If she didn't, who would? The doctor who covered it with waxes and seminal paraffins every morning? The guards who thought only of saving their skin?

Suffocated by presentiments that boded no good, she summoned one of her daughters, who slept in the adjoining room, and asked her to bandage her ankles for her. Then she left the house without a word and walked to the streetcar stop on the avenida Luis María Campos. She was determined to make the embalmer give Evita's body back to her. She didn't give a damn about what might happen later. She would lay the body in her own bed and tirelessly watch over it until the disturbances in Argentina came to an end and times returned to normal. If they didn't, she could go into exile as a last resort. She would seek asylum. She would cross the ocean. Any torment would be preferable to another night of uncertainty.

She got into a Lacroze streetcar that took a long detour through the backstreets of Palermo before heading for the Bajo district. The ticket cost ten centavos. She carefully tucked it into the slit below the button of her kid glove. It was a nasty, humid, unkempt morning. She got out her compact and covered up the traces of sweat that showed on her forehead. She regretted having given in to Dr. Ara's arguments two days before. A woman shouldn't receive anyone when she's alone, she thought. She must cover her face with her own weakness, shut herself up, and wait till the storm passes. She had made all the mistakes of her life out of loneliness and lack of love, and this one, perhaps, was the worst of them all: Ara had appeared at her house as the first news reports of the military coup were broadcast. Just in time. Grief deafened her inside as the doorbell kept ringing outside. The streetcar turned south on Soler, and just there she saw him, thought she saw him. The little Spanish Napoleon crossed the entry hall of her house in two strides, with the waistband of his trousers pulled up above his ribs, his sparse hair leaving a wake of dandruff behind him, his stiff-brimmed felt hat between his buffed nails, trailing an aura of Grath and Chaves cologne. Good heavens, she thought, this embalmer has turned into a fairy on us. "I've come to ease your mind," Ara said. And he repeated the same sentence three or four times during his visit. The streetcar jolted along amid the plane trees lining the calle Paraguay, crossing the void of the endless sad city. I would take Evita far away from here if I could, I would take her to the country, but the loneliness of the countryside would kill her all over again.

"I presented myself at the presidential palace yesterday," the doctor told her, "to speak to your son-in-law. In all these years he's never called me, and such a long silence surprised me. I arrived at nightfall. They kept me waiting in corridors and reception rooms for a long time until finally a captain came and asked me: What is it you want? I handed him my calling card and answered: To see General Perón. In the present difficult circumstances, I need instructions as to what last resting place we are to choose for his wife's body. You must understand that the general is very busy, the captain said to me. I will see what I can do. I waited for hours. Soldiers came and went with suitcases and bundles of sheets. It looked as though they were clearing the place out. Finally the captain came back with a message: For the moment the general is unable to decide anything, he said. Leave us your telephone number and we'll call you. But as yet nobody has called me. And I have the feeling that they aren't going to. There are rumors that Perón is leaving, doña Juana. That he's asking for safe-conduct passes in order to go into exile. So you and I are the only ones left. You and I must decide what is to be done with the body."

She looked out the window at the wet garden, the creeper in bloom—what else could she do?—wiping her sweaty hands on her skirt every so often. "If it were up to me, I would bring her here, Dr. Ara, and put her in the living room," she said. She was ashamed now at having said that. What would Evita do in the living room? "But just look at my varicose veins. They're a wreck. Neither injections of salicylate nor elastic stockings relieve the pain."

It was at that point in the conversation that the doctor took ad-

39

vantage of the opportunity to ask her for a letter of authorization. "I think it best," he told her. "With written authorization from you, I can treat the body with all due reverence."

"A letter of authorization?" the mother said in alarm. "No, Doctor. Such authorizations have been my undoing. Every one that I have put in writing has been used against me. My son-in-law has taken what belonged to my daughter. He didn't even leave me any keepsakes." Her voice broke, and she was obliged to remain silent for a moment to give the pieces time to fit together again. "Ah, by the way," she asked, "what happened to the diamond brooch that we pinned to Evita's shroud? One of the stones, the reddish one, was appraised at half a million pesos. Since we're going to bury her, I don't want to leave a piece of jewelry like that on her body. It would be a temptation for thieves. What do you advise me to do to get it back?"

The streetcar slowly turned into the calle Corrientes, as though it were hesitating. The metal blinds of the shops were already being raised, and the merchants were washing down the sidewalks. On the shady side of the street there had once been the famous Jewish brothels, and her daughter had lived on that side in a pension with flowerpots on the balconies. "Didn't I do the right thing to leave Junín, Mama? Doesn't it seem to you that I'm different?" Evita thought that that was happiness. But before she died she had to admit it: it was only sorrow.

The streetcar entered a nebula of cafés and movie theaters. She hadn't seen any of the films advertised on the marquees: neither *Three Coins in the Fountain*, in which those who saw it thought that they were visiting the Eternal City because of the cinemascope effects, nor *Naked Angel*, in which for the first time an Argentine actress appeared with her bare breasts showing, although only the merest glimpse of them could be seen. A tide of perfumes made her drowsy, and on the shores of sleep the doctor appeared again: "The belongings of the Deceased are still where you saw them, señora: the wedding ring, the rosary that the Supreme Pontiff gave her, and the brooch as well. But I believe that you are altogether right. It is risky to leave them there. I am going to ask that they be returned to you this very evening."

She had to write it out for him. The letter of authorization: *Dr. Don Pedro Ara. In my capacity as the mother of María Eva Duarte de Perón, I request that if her widower leaves no instructions regarding the corpse of my daughter, you, Doctor, be the person who takes the necessary precautions so as to safeguard it from any untoward eventualities.* "Perfect," he approved. "Sign here, and add the date: September 18, 1955."

Neither that evening nor on the following days did doña Juana receive Evita's brooch. It was always the same old story: men ripped her off, conned her, she didn't know how but they soft-soaped her. But what did that matter now? The streetcar negotiated the intersection at the Obelisk nicely and hurtled down into the dark sea of Bajo, where the barricades of the troops loyal to her son-in-law were still smoking. She saw the marble statues of the Treasury building riddled with bullet holes, the palms frayed by machine-gun fire, the photo portraits of Evita flapping in the strong wind, the busts, their hair disheveled, their noses knocked off, in ruins. Remembrance of her daughter was split in two, and now only the memory of those who hated her shone brightly. She lowered the veil of her hat and covered her face. The past weighed heavily on her soul. Even the best past was a misfortune. Everything a person left behind hurt, but happiness hurt much worse.

Tasteless and vulgar on the outside, the CGT building inside was a succession of corridors that led to labyrinthine staircases. Doña Juana had made her way through it more than once when she brought flowers for Evita, but always by following exactly the same path: the lobby, the elevator, the funeral chamber. She knew that Dr. Ara's laboratory had windows facing west and that at that hour in the morning she would find him restoring the body.

She caught a vague glimpse of the embalmer's bald pate through the frosted panes and went in without knocking. She was prepared for anything save the horror of coming upon Evita in a steam vat, with her private parts exposed. The only human odor emanating from the entire body came from her hairdo with the chignon still intact, as though it were a tree full of thoughts; but from the neck down Evita was not the same: that part of her body looked as though it were preparing to take a long journey from which it did not intend to return.

Doña Juana's entrance caught the embalmer by surprise as he was smoothing the thighs of the corpse with a honey-colored paste. He saw her grab, quick as a flash, a surgeon's apron hanging from the coat rack and spread it out on top of the bare-naked body as she moaned: "I'm here now, Cholita, what have they done to you?"

He raised his bald head and managed to grasp her by the arm. It was necessary to recover forthwith his dignity as a member of the medical profession.

"Go along with you, doña Juana," he said, endeavoring to be persuasive. "Don't you smell the chemicals? They are terrible for the lungs."

He tried to give her a gentle push. She didn't budge. She couldn't. She was filled with indignation, and indignation weighed a great deal.

"Stop making up stories, Dr. Ara. I'm old, but I'm not an idiot. If your chemicals don't make a wreck of you, they won't make one of me either."

"Today is a bad day, señora," he said. Doña Juana was surprised to see that he was not wearing rubber gloves as other doctors do. "The military is going to turn up at any moment to take your daughter away. We still don't know what they intend to do with her."

"I gave you a letter of authorization so that you would protect her for me, Doctor. What have you done to her? Nothing you tell me is true. You promised to send me the brooch and I'm still waiting for it."

"I did everything that was within my power, señora. The brooch has been stolen. By whom? There is no way of knowing. The sergeants of the guard say that it was the civilian revolutionary commandos. And the commandos to whom I talked deny it. They say it was the sergeants. It is my opinion that your son-in-law made off with it. I'm all confused. This seems like a no-man's-land."

"You should have telephoned me."

"How could I? The phone lines were cut. I can't even talk to my family. Believe me, my one wish is to see this nightmare over and done with."

"Then I've arrived just in time." Doña Juana put her cane on a chair. The pain from her varicose veins had vanished. She had to rescue her daughter and get her away from the formol, from the resins, from all the other evils of eternity. She said: "I'm going to take her away with me. Bundle her up well in the shroud while I ask the funeral parlor to send an ambulance. I've gotten her out of worse fixes in her life. Evita has no reason to stay here even one more day."

The embalmer shook his head. He repeated, more or less, what he was to tell the Colonel two months later:

"She's not ready yet. She needs one last bath of balm. If you take her away like this, she is going to fall apart in your hands."

"It doesn't matter," the mother replied. "After all, death has already done that."

The doctor let his arms fall to his sides, as though beaten.

"You are forcing me to do something I do not wish to do," he said.

He locked the door of the laboratory, took off his apron, and, guiding doña Juana down a short corridor, dimly illuminated by a grayish light, made his way to the sanctuary with her. Although the darkness in the place was fathomless, the mother knew immediately where they were. More than once she had lingered there to pray, before the imposing glass prism where her daughter lay, and had kissed her full lips, which always appeared to be just about to come back to life. The deep shadows smelled of desolation and of anonymous blood.

"Why are you bringing me here?" she asked, in an orphan voice. "I want to go back to where Evita is."

The doctor took her by the arm and answered:

"Look at this."

Spotlights beamed down on the funeral prism, as neon lights in the moldings of the ceiling went on. Stunned by a glare that took her breath away, doña Juana couldn't believe the reality that gradually took shape before her eyes. The first thing she saw was a twin of her own daughter lying on the glass slab, so identical a one that not even she herself would have been capable of giving birth to it. Another perfect replica of Evita was stretched out on top of black velvet pillows, at the foot of an armchair in which a third Evita, clad in the same white tunic as the others, sat reading a postcard sent seven years before from the post office in Madrid. The mother had the impression that this latter Evita was breathing and reached her trembling fingertips toward her nostrils.

"Don't touch her," the doctor said. "She's more fragile than an autumn leaf."

"Which one is Evita?"

"I am happy that you are unable to tell the difference. Your daughter isn't here. You have just seen her in the vat in the laboratory." He slid his thumbs underneath his suspenders and swayed back and forth on tiptoe, filled with pride. "When your son-in-law's government began to topple, I asked them to make these copies for me, as a precaution. If Perón falls, I told myself, Evita will be the first trophy that the victors are going to look for. I worked day and night with a sculptor, ruling out one figure after another. Do you know what materials these are?" Doña Juana heard the embalmer's words but was unable to make any sense of them. She was horrified, overwhelmed: she needed another lifetime to absorb so much grief. "Wax and vinyl, plus indelible dye to show her veins. The Evita in the armchair is an improved version: she's done in fiberglass. She's a magnum opus. When the colonels come to take her away, your daughter will already be in a safe place and what I shall give them will be one of these copies. As you now realize, I have not betrayed you."

"What worries me," the mother said, "is that I'm not going to know which is which either."

"They must be x-rayed. The internal organs of the genuine one can be seen. The only thing that can be seen inside the others is emptiness. What do physicists do when they wish to interrupt the natural flow of things? Something very simple: they multiply them." In his excitement, the embalmer had raised the pitch of his voice one or two octaves. "Oblivion must be countered by many memories, a real story must be covered up by false stories. Alive, your daughter had no equal, but once dead, what difference does it make? Once dead, she can be infinite."

"A drink of water," the mother begged.

"Take one of the copies with you now," the doctor went on, paying no attention to her. "And give her a solemn burial in Recoleta cemetery. I will send another one to the Vatican and another to the widower, in Olivos or wherever he may be. You and I, all by ourselves, will bury the real one, and we won't say a word to anyone else."

It seemed to doña Juana that the world was receding, as naturally as a tide. There was no longer a world, and grief occupied all the empty spaces. Sobs came and went within her, bottomless, contourless. She would never be able to depend on Ara or Perón or anyone else except herself, and she was a mere nobody. She leaned against the walls of shadow and spat into the embalmer's face the phrase that had been going round and round in her head for some time:

"Go to hell."

In this novel peopled by real characters, the only ones I never met were Evita and the Colonel. I saw Evita only from a distance, in Tucumán, one morning on a national holiday; as for Colonel Moori Koenig, I found a couple of photos and a few traces of him. The newspapers of the period mention him openly and, often, disparagingly. It took me months to meet his widow, who lived in an austere apartment on the calle Arenales and who agreed to see me only after putting me off time and time again.

She received me dressed in black, amid furniture that appeared to be gravely ill. The lamps gave off such a feeble light that the windows disappeared, as though all they were good for was looking inside. That is how Buenos Aires lives, amid semidarkness and ashes. Stretching out on the banks of a broad, lonely river, the city has turned its back to the water and prefers to go on spilling out over the bewildered pampas, where the landscape copies itself, endlessly.

Somewhere in the house bits of sandalwood were burning. The widow and her eldest daughter, who was also dressed in black, gave off a strong scent of roses. I soon felt dizzied, intoxicated, on the cutting edge of an irreparable error. I told them that I was writing a novel about the Colonel and Evita and that I had been doing some research. I showed them the Colonel's service record, which I had copied from a military archive, and I asked if the facts were correct.

"The dates of his birth and his death are the right ones," the widow admitted. "As for the others, we can't say a thing. As you perhaps know, he was a fanatic about secrecy."

I spoke to them of a short story by Rodolfo Walsh, "That Woman," as the two of them nodded. The story has to do with a dead woman whose name is never mentioned, a man—Walsh—who is looking for her body, and a colonel who has hidden it. At a certain point this colonel's wife appears on the scene: haughty, with a neurotic sneer, in no way resembling the resigned matron who was listening to my questions without attempting to hide her mistrust. The characters in the story talk in a living room with big picture windows, from which dusk can be seen falling over the Río de la Plata. Among the pretentious furnishings are plates from Canton and an oil painting that may be by Figari. "Have the two of you ever seen a living room like that?" I asked them. A certain gleam appeared in the widow's eyes, but no sign that would indicate whether she would help me in my research.

"The colonel in 'That Woman,'" I commented, resembles the detective in 'Death and the Compass.' Both of them decipher an enigma that destroys them." The daughter had never heard of "Death and the Compass." "It's a story by Borges," I said. "All the ones Borges wrote during that period reflect the defenselessness of a blind man in the face of the barbarous threats of Peronism. Without

Perón's terror, Borges's labyrinths and mirrors would lose a substantial part of their meaning. Without Perón, Borges's writing would lack provocations, refined techniques of indirection, perverse metaphors. I am explaining all this to you," I said, "because Walsh's Colonel is also awaiting a punishment that he knows is inevitable, although he doesn't know where it will come from. He is tormented by telephoned curses. Anonymous voices announce to him that his daughter will catch polio, that he is going to be castrated. And all because he has taken possession of Evita."

"What Walsh wrote isn't fiction," the widow corrected me. "It really happened. I was listening to them as they spoke. My husband recorded the conversation on a Geloso and left me the tapes. It's the only thing he left me."

The eldest daughter opened a sideboard and showed me the tapes: there were two of them, inside transparent plastic envelopes.

Every so often a sudden, uncomfortable silence set in, which I didn't know how to break. I was afraid that the women would not be able to go on confronting the past that had done them so much harm and would make me leave. I saw that the daughter was crying. They were tears for no particular reason that brimmed over as if they were coming from another face or were part and parcel of the feelings of another person. When she realized that I was looking at her, she allowed this confidence to escape her:

"If only you knew what a failure in life I've been!"

I didn't know how to answer. It was evident that the more time that passed, the more self-pity she felt.

"I've never been able to do what I wanted to," she said. "I'm like Papa in that way. When I was a bit older, he'd come and sit on my bed and say to me: I'm a failure, my girl. I'm a failure. We weren't the ones who made him feel that way. It was Evita."

I told them again what they doubtless already knew: the colonel in the story says that he buried Evita in a garden. A garden where it rains every other day and everything rots: the rose beds, the wood of the coffin, the Franciscan cord they place around the waist of the dead woman. The body, it says in the story, was buried standing up, the way they buried Facundo Quiroga.

I stopped at that point. Nobody, I thought, buried Facundo standing up.

"That story is exactly the way it was," murmured the widow, who had the bad habit of inhaling fragments of words. "When we lived in Bonn, for more than a month the corpse was inside an ambulance that my husband had bought. He spent his nights keeping watch over it through the window. One day he tried to bring it inside the house. I objected, as you can imagine. I didn't mince words. Either you get that trash out of here, I said to him, or I'm taking off with my daughters. He shut himself up in his room to have a good cry. At the time, his sleepless nights and alcohol had made a weakling of him. That same night he went off somewhere in the ambulance. When he came back, he told me he'd buried the body. Where? I asked him. Who knows, he answered. In a wood, where it rains a lot. And he refused to say another word."

The daughter brought a photograph of the Colonel taken in 1955. His lips were a thin line drawn in pencil; his cheekbones were crisscrossed by little dark veins; baldness had played havoc with his vast, oily forehead, tilted backward at a sharp angle.

"Ten years after that photo he was a wreck," the widow said. "He let hours at a time go by without doing a thing, without talking, with his mind drifting. Sometimes he disappeared from sight for weeks, going from one bar to another till he passed out and fell down. He had fits of delirium. He sweat buckets. Sweat that was rank, unbearable. Shortly before he died he was seen on a bench in the plaza Rodríguez Peña, shouting for death to come."

"And what about the two of you?" I wanted to know. "Where were you?"

"We abandoned him," the daughter answered. "There was a moment when Mama couldn't stand any more of him and told him to go away."

"It was Evita's fault," the widow repeated. "Everybody who had anything to do with the corpse came to a bad end."

"I don't believe in such things," I heard myself say.

The widow stood up, and I sensed that it was time to leave.

"You don't?" Her tone of voice was no longer friendly. "May God help you, then. If you're going to tell that story, you should be careful. Once you begin to tell it, there'll be no salvation for you either."

3

"Telling
a Story"

*The canonization of Eva Perón by the Pope and that of Jean Genet by
Sartre (another Pope) are the mystic events of the summer.*
             JEAN COCTEAU, Journal: The Past Definite

After that encounter, I spent several weeks in newspaper archives. If
the curse that the Colonel's widow had spoken of was true, sooner
or later I was going to come across a fact that would confirm it. One
era was carrying me back upstream to another, and so I went up trib-
utaries that no one had noticed. Rodolfo Walsh had given away
certain clues, however, in "That Woman," on mentioning the misfortunes of two intelligence officers: "I heard," Walsh hints, "that Major
X killed his wife and Captain N's face was disfigured in an accident."
But the colonel of the story scoffs at those catastrophes, attributing
them to confusion and chance. "Tutankhamen's tomb," he intones,
"Lord Carnarvon. Bullshit."

    As I dug farther into the heaps of papers, I discovered more and
more indications that corpses can't abide being nomads. Evita's,
which accepted any cruel treatment with resignation, appeared to
rebel when it was moved from one place to another. In November

1974, her body was removed from its grave in Madrid and brought to Buenos Aires. As it was being taken to Barajas Airport in a van, two civil guards began having a row about a gambling debt. As the vehicle turned onto General Sanjurjo, opposite the City Reservoir, the two of them started shooting at each other, and the van, out of control, crashed into the fence around the Royal Automobile Club. The cab caught on fire and the guards died. Despite the havoc wreaked, Evita's coffin didn't suffer the slightest damage, not even a scratch.

Something similar happened in October of 1976, when the corpse was transported from the presidential residence in Olivos to Recoleta cemetery. Evita was being taken there in a blue ambulance of the Buenos Aires military hospital, between two soldiers carrying rifles with—heaven only knows why—fixed bayonets. The driver, a sergeant named Justo Fernández, went down the avenida del Libertador whistling, from one end to the other, "Happiness, What a Joke, Ha Ha Ha." Shortly before crossing the calle Tagle, he had such a sudden heart attack that the man with him, believing that "Fernández was gasping for breath after all that whistling," applied the hand brake and stopped the ambulance just as it was about to land in the courtyard of another automobile club, the Buenos Aires one. Evita was all in one piece, but the soldiers guarding the body had severed each other's jugular vein with their bayonets in the panic stop and were lying in a heap, one atop the other, in a pool of blood.

Souls have their own force of gravity: they dislike high speeds, open air, anxiety. When someone breaks the glass panes of their slowness, they become disoriented and develop a will to evil that they cannot control. Souls have habits, attachments, antipathies, moments of hunger and of satiation, desires to go off to bed, to be alone. They don't want their routine to be taken away from them, because that is what eternity is: routines, sentences that form an endless chain, anchors that moor them to familiar things. But just as they detest being moved from one place to another, souls also aspire to have someone record them in writing. They want to be narrated, tattooed in the rocks of eternity. If a soul has not been recorded, it is as though it had never existed. Against transience, the written word. Against death, the story.

Once I began trying to narrate Evita I noted that, if I approached her, she withdrew from me. I knew what she wanted to tell and what the structure of my narrative was going to be. But once I turned the page, Evita disappeared from my sight, and I was left clutching nothing but air. Or if I had her with me, within me, my thoughts went away and left me empty. At times I didn't know if she was alive or dead, if her beauty was sailing ahead or behind. My first impulse was to recount Evita by following the thread of the sentence Clifton Webb uses as an introduction to the enigmas of *Laura*, Otto Preminger's film: "I shall never forget the weekend on which Laura died." Nor have I forgotten the misty weekend on which Evita died. That was not the only coincidence. Laura had come back to life in her own way, by not dying; and Evita had done so too: by multiplying herself.

In a long, discarded version of this same novel I told the story of the men who had condemned Evita to endless wandering. I wrote several terrifying scenes, which I couldn't find my way out of. I saw the embalmer desperately scrutinizing the nooks and crannies of his own past in search of a moment that would coincide with Evita's past. I described him as being dressed in a dark suit, with a diamond stickpin and gloved hands, practicing alongside the learned professor Leonardo de la Peña the techniques for preserving corpses. I told of the spiderwebs of conspiracies that the Colonel and his students at the espionage school wove, on sand tables colored like chessboards. Nothing of all that made any sense, and almost nothing of it survived in the versions that followed. Certain sentences, on which I worked for weeks, evaporated beneath the sun of the first reading, ruthlessly cut out of a narrative that had no need of them.

It took me a long time to get over these failures. Evita, I kept saying, Evita, hoping that the name would bear a revelation within it: that "she," after all, was her right name. But names don't communicate anything: they are only a sounding, a lapping of language. I remembered the time when I went looking for the shades of her shadow, I too in search of her lost body (as is recounted in several chapters of *The Perón Novel*), and the summers I spent gathering documentation for a biography that I was planning to write and that was to be called, as was predictable, *The Lost Woman.* Led by that thirst, I spoke with her mother, the steward of the presidential residence, her hairdresser, her film director, her manicurist, two actresses from her theatrical company, the comic musician who got her work in Buenos Aires. I spoke with marginal figures, and not with the ministers or fawning admirers of her court, because they were not like her: they couldn't see the razor's edge or the narrow lines along which Evita had always walked. They narrated her in sentences that were too frilly. What attracted me, however, were Evita's margins, her obscurity, what there was in her that was inexpressible. I thought, following Walter Benjamin, that when a historic figure has been redeemed, all of his or her past can be evoked: both the apotheoses and the secrets. This may be why in *The Perón Novel* I managed only to tell of Perón's most private side, not his public exploits: when I attempted to deal with the whole of him, the text fell to pieces between my fingers. It was not like that with Evita. *Eva* is also *ave,* a bird: what is read from right to left has the same meaning as when read the other way around. What more did I want? All I needed to do was go ahead. But when I tried to do so, my jumbles of voices and notes went nowhere, turning to dust in the yellowing files that I kept taking along with me from one exile to another.

What occasioned this book was an even worse failure. In mid-1989 I was lying in a penitential bed in Buenos Aires, expiating the disaster of a novel of mine that had been stillborn, when the phone rang and someone talked to me about Evita. I had never heard that voice before and had no desire to go on hearing it. Had it not been for the lethargy that my state of depression had brought on, I might have hung up. But the insistent voice made me get up out of bed, and I embarked upon an adventure without which *Santa Evita* would not exist. The moment to tell that story has not yet arrived, but when I do tell it, the reader will understand why that is so.

Several nights went by and I dreamed of her. She was an enormous butterfly suspended in the eternity of a sky without a breath of wind. One wing, a black one, was billowing forward, above a desert of cathedrals and cemeteries; the other wing was yellow and was flying backward, dropping scales in which the landscapes of her life lighted up in reverse historical order as in Eliot's verses: *In my beginning is my end . . . / And do not call it fixity, / Where past and future are gathered. Neither movement from nor towards, / Neither ascent nor decline. / Except for the point, the still point . . .*

If this novel resembles a butterfly's wings—the story of death flowing forward, the story of life advancing backward, visible darkness, oxymoron of similarities—it must also bear a likeness to me, to the remains of myth that I kept hunting for along the way, to the *I* who was *she,* to the loves and hates of that *we,* to what my country was and to what it wanted to be but could not be. *Mito* in my native tongue is not only "myth" but also the name of a bird that no one can see, and *story* means "search," "inquiry": the text is a search for the invisible, or the stillness of what flies.

It took me years to arrive at these central folds where I am today. In order that no one would confuse *Santa Evita* with *The Perón Novel*, between the two of them I wrote a family story about a male singer with the voice of a coloratura at war with his mother and a tribe of cats. From that war I went on to others. I learned my métier, writing, all over again, with adolescent fervor. Was *Santa Evita* going to be a novel? I didn't know and I didn't care. Story lines, fixed points of view, the laws of space and times, slipped through my fingers. The characters sometimes spoke in their own voices and sometimes in other people's, merely to explain to me that what is history is not always historical, that the truth is never what it appears to be. It took me months and months to tame the chaos. Certain characters resisted. They came onstage for a few pages and then left the book forever: the same thing happened in the text as happens in life. But when they went off, Evita was no longer the same: the pollen of other people's wishes and memories had rained down on her. Transfigured into myth, Evita was millions.

Huge figures, millions, were always the aura that surrounded her name. In *My Mission in Life* the reader comes upon this mysterious phrase: "I think that many men together, rather than being thousands and thousands of separate souls, are instead a single soul." Mythologists caught the idea on the fly and transformed the thousands into millions. "I will come back and I will be millions," Evita's most celebrated phrase promises. But she never spoke that phrase, as is readily noted by anyone whose attention is attracted for an instant by her posthumous perfume: "I will come back"—from where?—"And I will be millions"—of what? Despite the fact that it was often proved to be apocryphal, the phrase still appears at the bottom of the posters commemorating each of her anniversaries. She never said it, but it is true.

Until her sanctity little by little, with time, became dogma. Between May 1952—two months before she died—and July 1954, the Vatican received nearly forty thousand letters from laymen and laywomen attributing various miracles to Evita and urging the pope to canonize her. The prefect of the Congregation of Rites answered all the petitions with the usual formulas: "Any Catholic knows that in order to be a saint the person must be dead." And later, as she was being embalmed: "The trials for sanctification take a long time, hundreds of years. Be patient." The letters gradually became more and more peremptory. They complained that María Goretti had waited only forty-four years to be a saint, and Theresa of Lisieux just a little over twenty-five. The case of Saint Clare of Assisi was even more striking, they said; the impatient Innocent IV wanted to canonize her on her deathbed. Evita deserved better: only the Virgin Mary surpassed her in virtues. The fact that the Supreme Pontiff should take so long to acknowledge such obvious sanctity was—I read in the papers—"an affront to the faith of the Peronist people."

During those same years, all the impoverished adolescents of Argentina wanted to look like Evita. Half the girls born in the provinces of the Northeast were named Eva or María Eva, and those who weren't named that copied the emblems of her beauty. They dyed their hair peroxide blond and wore it tightly swept back and caught up in one or two plaited chignons. They wore flared skirts, made of fabrics that could be starched, and shoes with ankle straps. Evita was the arbiter of fashion and the national model of behavior. That sort of skirt and shoes never came back in style after the end of the fifties, but hair dyed blond appealed to the upper classes and became, in time, a distinctive feature of women of the northern section of Buenos Aires.

In the first six months of 1951, Evita gave away twenty-five thousand houses and almost three million packages containing medicine, furniture, clothing, bicycles, and toys. The poor started lining up before dawn to see her, and it was not until dawn the next day that some of them finally managed to do so. She questioned them as to their family problems, their ailments, their work, and even their love affairs. In that same year, 1951, she was matron of honor at the wedding ceremony for one thousand six hundred eight couples, half of whom already had children. Illegitimate children moved Evita to tears, because her own illegitimacy had been a martyrdom to her.

In the remote town of Tucumán, I remember, many people believed that she was an emissary of God. I have heard that on the pampas too and in the villages along the Patagonian coast country people often saw the outlines of her face in the heavens. They were afraid she would die, because the world might end with her last breath. Simple folk often tried to attract Evita's attention so as to attain some manner of eternity thereby. "To be in the Señora's thoughts," said a woman stricken with polio, "is like touching God with a person's own hands. What more does anyone need?"

A girl of seventeen who went by the name of "pretty Evelina," and whose real name nobody ever found out, wrote Evita two thousand letters in 1951, at a rate of five or six a day. All the letters had the same wording, so that all that pretty Evelina had to do was copy it and deposit the envelopes in a mailbox in Mar del Plata, the city where she lived, once she'd come up with the money for the stamps. In those days, Evita was the victim of frequent epistolary effusions, but she did not ordinarily receive letters that were also little works of art:

"Telling a Story"

*My dere Evita, Im not going to aks you for anathing the way everbody
else around hear does, cause the ony thing i want is for you to rede this
leter and remember my name, I no that if you keep my name in yore mine
even if its just for one little minate nothing bad can hapen to me and Ill
be happy and not have any ailments or misries. Im 17 and I sleep on the
matress you left at my house for a present last Chrismas. I love you lots.
pretty Evelina.*

When the rumor spread that Evita might be the candidate for
vice-president of the Republic and that the generals, indignant at the
prospect of taking orders from a woman, would be opposed, pretty
Evelina sent one last letter to which she added three words: *Long liv
wommen.* She immediately put herself on exhibit in the show window of a furniture store, lying in a large chest, with the intention of
fasting until the generals changed their attitude. So many people
came to see her that the store windows broke and the owner put a
stop to the show. Pretty Evelina fasted for one night in the rough
weather out on the sidewalks, until the Socialist mayor of the city
agreed to lend her one of the tents on Bristol Beach that were no
longer in use because the season was over. At the entrance to the
tent, Evelina hung a sign with her motto, LONG LIV WOMMEN, and
began the second stage of her fast. Six notaries took turns as witnesses to the fact that the rules were being strictly observed. The
fasting girl was allowed to drink only one glass of water in the
morning and another at dusk, but after the first week Evelina accepted only the latter. The news came out in the papers, and people
said that Evita would pay a visit to Mar del Plata to have a look. She
was not able to come because she was suffering from pains in her
abdomen, and the doctors made her stay in bed. The candidacy for
the vice-presidency was stalled, and pretty Evelina, whom nobody
now called pretty, seemed doomed to a perpetual fast. The curiosity
of the first days was lessening. When the autumn rains started, visitors to the beach disappeared and the notaries began to drop out.
The only person to take pity on pretty Evelina was a girl cousin of

her own age, who regularly appeared every night to bring Evelina her glass of water and left the tent weeping.

The story had an unhappy ending. On the eve of Holy Week a violent storm came up that kept people at home and tore trees up by the roots. When it died down, not a single tent nor the slightest trace of pretty Evelina was left on Bristol Beach. When it announced this news, the daily *La Razón* commented sarcastically: "The Bristol Beach episode clearly proves that the climate of Mar del Plata is inhospitable to fasting."

Pretty Evelina's sacrifice was not in vain. Thousands of imitators soon appeared, trying to force their way into Evita's imagination, though at less deadly risk. Two workers in a factory that made tin-plate artwork, who also backed her candidacy for the vice-presidency, beat the world record for continuous work by turning out decorations for facades for ninety-eight hours in a row, but they had almost no chance to savor their feat because seven foremen from another factory beat them by assembling and polishing cylinders for one hundred nine hours without stopping. The daily *Democracia* published on its front page a photograph of the seven of them, overcome by sleep at the foot of a huge column of tubing.

Evita's life was meanwhile sinking deeper and deeper into misfortune. She was obliged to give up her candidacy before a million people who wept and paraded past the presidential box on their knees. A month later she was hospitalized with fulminating anemia, another symptom of her cancer of the uterus. Almost immediately thereafter she went through two terrible operations in which she was gutted and scraped till they thought she was free of malignant cells. She lost more than forty pounds, and an expression of sadness that nobody had ever seen there before, not even in her days of hunger and humiliation, was now engraved on her face.

Nor did all this earn her the pity of her enemies, who also numbered in the thousands. Argentines who thought of themselves as the depositaries of civilization saw in Evita an obscene resurrection of barbarism. Indians, blacks with no morals, bums, hoodlums, pimps straight out of Arlt, wild gauchos, consumptive whores smuggled into the country on Polish ships, party girls from the provinces: all of them had now been exterminated or confined to their dark cellars. When European philosophers came on a visit, they discovered a country so ethereal and spiritual that they thought it had evaporated. Eva Duarte's sudden entry onstage ruined the pastel portrait of cultivated Argentina. That vulgar chick, that bastard B-girl, that little shit—as she was called at cattle auctions—was the last fart of barbarism. As it wafted by, you had to hold your nose.

All of a sudden, the champions of civilization learned to their relief that the knife blades of cancer were slashing into the uterus of "that woman." In *Sur*, the review that was the refuge of the Argentine intelligentsia, the poet Silvina Ocampo foresaw, in emphatic rhymed couplets, the end of the nightmare:

> May the sun no longer rise, nor yet the moon
> if tyrants like these sow more misfortune,
> by conning the country. May these be the last days
> of that creeping species, that accursed race.

On the walls that lead to the Retiro railway station, not very far from the presidential residence where Evita lay dying, someone painted an ill-omened slogan, LONG LIVE CANCER, and signed it PRETTY EVELINA. When the radio announced that Evita's condition was extremely serious, the opposition politicians opened bottles of champagne. The essayist Ezequiel Martínez Estrada, covered from head to foot with a thick black crust that the doctors identified as neuromelanoderma, was miraculously cured and began to write a compendium of invective in which Evita was referred to in these terms: "She is a sublimation of what is morally vile, despicable, abject, monstrous, vengeful, ophidian, and the people see her as an incarnation of the infernal gods."

In those same days, confronted with the certainty that Evita would go to heaven at any moment, thousands of people made the most exorbitant sacrifices so that when it came time for her to account for herself to God, she would mention their names in the conversation. Every two or three hours, a believer would establish a world record for work without stopping, whether by assembling safety locks or cooking noodles. Leopoldo Carreras, the billiard champion, hit a thousand five hundred caroms in a row in the atrium of the basilica of Luján. A professional named Juan Carlos Papa danced tangos for one hundred twenty-seven hours with the same number of partners. The *Guinness Book of World Records* was not yet published in those days, and unfortunately all these records have fallen into oblivion.

The churches were full to overflowing with petitioners offering their lives in Evita's stead or else praying to the celestial courts to receive her with the honors due a queen. Records were made for glider flights, distances walked carrying sacks of maize slung over one shoulder, delivering bread, horseback rides, parachute jumps, walking across a bed of hot coals or barbed wire, outings in a sulky or on a bicycle. The taxi driver Pedro Caldas covered the distance between Buenos Aires and Rosario, almost two hundred miles, by running backward on an oil barrel; the seamstress Irma Ceballos embroidered an Our Father three-eighths of an inch square in thirty-three different colors of silk thread, and when she finished it she sent it to Pope Pius XII threatening to renounce her obedience to him as a Catholic if the Sacred Heart of Jesus did not immediately restore the health of "our beloved saint."

But the most famous of all the undertakings was that of the saddle maker Raimundo Masa, along with his wife, Dominga, and his three children, the youngest of which was still nursing. Masa had just delivered a couple of saddles in San Nicolás when he heard some mule drivers talking about Evita's serious condition. That same day he decided to go on a pilgrimage with all his family to the Christ the Redeemer in the Andes, six hundred miles to the west, promising to return on foot as well if the sick woman recovered. At the rate of twelve miles a day, the journey there was going to take almost two months, he calculated. He loaded a few tins of powdered milk, jerky, hardtack, filtered water, and a change of clothes into knapsacks and wrote a letter to Evita explaining his mission to her and announcing that he would visit her on his return. He asked her not to forget his name and, if possible, to mention him in a speech, if only in code: "Just say regards to Raimundo and I'll get the message."

He stopped on the endless plain with the whole family to recite the rosary, without taking his eyes off the trail and with an expression of inconsolable grief on his face. Dominga was carrying the nursing baby in a basket hung around her neck; the other two were tied with cords to Raimundo's waist so they wouldn't wander off and get lost. Every time they went through a town the parish priest, the pharmacist, and the ladies of the social club in their Sunday dresses just taken out of their nests of mothballs turned out to welcome them. They offered them cups of chocolate and hot showers, which Raimundo firmly refused so as not to lose time, paying no attention to the despair of his two older sons, who couldn't stand their diet of jerky any longer.

After forty days they went into the dreary desert between the cities of San Luis and La Dormida, where a hundred years before Juan Facundo Quiroga had escaped from the talons of a jaguar by climbing to the top of the one carob tree that grew in those desolate expanses. There seemed to be no end to the inhospitable landscape, the sun beat down mercilessly, and owing to his lack of experience, Raimundo had allowed his children to drink up all the water. He turned off the main road and took the shortcuts laid down at the beginning of the century to confuse army deserters. The older boys fainted, and the father had to leave his knapsacks with the provisions behind so as to carry the two children on his back. On the third day he lost heart and was afraid he was going to die. Sitting at the entrance of a dusty cave, he prayed that all his mortifications had not been in vain and God would restore to Evita the health she had lost. It troubled Dominga, who was suffering in silence, that at this crucial hour her husband seemed to be giving no thought to the fate of his family.

"We are who we are, nobodies," Raimundo pointed out to her. "If Evita dies, though, those left without hope will number in the thousands. There are people like us everywhere, but there is only one saint like Evita."

"Since she's such a saint, you could ask her to get us out of this terrible predicament," Dominga said.

"I can't, because saints don't work miracles while they're alive. People have to wait till they die and are enjoying the Lord's glory."

The light of day went out like a match. An hour later a raging wind began to blow. Amid the clouds of dust the honking of wild ducks could be heard. When the windstorm died down, the horizon was suddenly aglow with lights. Raimundo thought it was the phosphorescent skeletons of calves devoured by jaguars, and he was afraid that they were also following their trail.

"We'd better stay right here," he said, "and wait for dawn."

"Those are kerosene lanterns," she corrected him. "If we can hear ducks from here, water and houses can't be far off."

They went on, dragging themselves along beneath the wavering moon. Soon they made out a row of carob trees, fences, and a mud hut with a tile roof. There were lights in all the windows. Raimundo timidly announced himself by clapping his hands. Nobody answered, although monotonous voices and soft music from a radio came from inside. Beneath the overhang of the porch roof they found a pan of fresh water and a jug. Fresh-baked loaves of bread were laid out on tables. The boys dashed toward the tables, but Dominga held them back.

"God be praised," she said in thanks.

"May He be forever praised," came the response from inside. "Help yourselves to whatever you need and wait on the porch."

When night fell, Raimundo had felt cold, an indelible frigidity he was never to forget, but all of a sudden the air was warm and filled with the deafening chirring of summertime cicadas. The children dropped off to sleep. After a while, Dominga too stretched out on a wooden bench. They heard horses' hooves, snorts, the flutter of hens.

When they awoke, they were out in the open again. They could make out the towers of a town in the distance. At their feet they found the knapsacks that they had left behind in the desert days before.

"I didn't feel like sleeping," Dominga said.

"I didn't either," Raimundo answered. "But we did, and there's no getting around it."

They made their way along a stretch of fertile, unfamiliar countryside, amid fields of strawberries, poplars, and irrigation ditches. They were surprised when nobody came out to welcome them as they entered the town. The bells of the church were tolling and from the loudspeakers hanging from the lampposts came a sepulchral voice that repeated over and over: "Last night, at twenty twenty-five, señora Eva Perón entered immortality. May God have mercy on her soul and on the Argentine people. Last night, at twenty twenty-five."

Raimundo stopped short.

"It was at that moment that we found the bread and the water," he said. "At twenty twenty-five. Who knows if we'll be able to get back now."

I found a sober article about the departure of the Masa family in the daily *Democracia*, but the details of the whole journey, recounted in what was called "poetic language" in those days, are in the last October issue of *Mundo Peronista*. I spent some time tracking down Raimundo Masa's sons and was about to meet up with the eldest, whose name was also Raimundo. He had worked for a few weeks in the Norma tire-repair shop, located on the road from Ramallo to Conesa, and then, I found out, he had emigrated to the south. But the south in Argentina is everything: Raimundo's vast world, as one of Drummond de Andrade's poems explains. On the late afternoon when I talked with the boys in the Norma tire shop, dusk fell swiftly over the fields. The roosters mistook their nature and gave out with a crowing that never stopped. They told me that Raimundo had told them the same story that had been in the papers, but that on account of their twisting his arm to give them more details, he'd ended up not knowing whether it had been a miracle, a dream, or only a desire. In those days of big records, people were full of desires, and Evita saw to it that all of them were fulfilled. Evita was an enormous net that went out to catch desires as though reality were a field of butterflies.

I had no more news of the Masas till I shut myself away in a little town in New Jersey and went on writing this book. One midday in January, after finishing a page, I went out to get my mail. Amid the mountain of junk mail was a square envelope that looked out of place, sent to me from Dolavón, Chubut, where nobody I knew had my address. The sender introduced himself by his initials, RM, and enclosed a list of twenty Peronist records. I copy some of them herewith, to give my reader an idea of the unusual document:

February 22, 1951 / Héctor Yfray / World record for a nonstop bicycle ride: 118 hours, 29 minutes / "With the desire to reach Evita to express my admiration for her."

March 25, 1951 / "Pretty Evelina" / To beat the record for a fast established by Link Furk (22 days on water). The challenger disappeared in a storm / "With the hope that Evita will be vice-president and to combat usury and speculation."

August 21, 1951 / Carlos de Oro / Record for number of times run around the Obelisk of Buenos Aires: he began at 23:30; he stopped on August 30, because of a cardiac arrest. / "With the intention of going on running until Evita agrees to appear on the presidential ticket."

April 6, 1952 / Blanca Lidia and Luis Angel Carriza / Endurance test: number of hours going around the Plaza de Mayo on their knees. They began at 5:45 and stopped at 10:30 because señora Carriza's knee was worn down to the kneecap / "To ask for the salvation of Eva Perón."

I didn't know whom to thank for the gift and felt a certain anxiety for the remainder of the week as I went on writing. That Sunday, one of my brothers telephoned to tell me that our mother had died a few days before on the other side of the continent. "We've already buried her," he said. "There's no sense in your coming." I protested at the family's not having let me know sooner. "We lost your phone number," he answered. "Nobody could find it. We looked and looked. Everybody had lost it. It was as though you were cut off from us inside the circle of a curse."

I was trembling as I hung up, because that was exactly how I had been feeling for days, tormented by a treacherous, unknown curse. Perhaps because of the despair into which my mother's death had plunged me, I began to suffer from dizzy spells at night that the doctors were unable to cure. From midnight till dawn the planets went round and round in my head, and I flew from one to the next, weightless and with no feeling of belonging, as though I were a faceless nomad unable to find a bit of air to moor myself to. If I managed to get to sleep, I wrote blank pentagrams in my dreams, with just one sign, Evita's face, where the keys to them should have been; in the distance the whole sky echoed with a musical score, but I never managed to find out how it went, however finely I attuned my ear. The diagnosis of one of the doctors, after two weeks of tests, was that these symptoms pointed to a case of acute hypertension, which he tried to relieve with Procardia, Tenormin, and other pills whose names I've forgotten. The dizzy spells, however, stopped only when I gave up writing, at the end of that month.

Every time I tried to take a trip somewhere there were heavy snowstorms that forced the authorities to close the airports and the main highways. As my imprisonment went stubbornly on and on, I began to write again. The sun came out then, and the benediction of an early spring descended upon New Jersey. It was around that time that I received the second envelope from Dolavón, Chubut, with the full name of the sender, Raimundo Masa. This time it was a handwritten letter, signed in a child's clumsy scrawl: "If you were looking for me, don't look anymore. If you're going to tell the story, be careful. Once you begin to tell it, there will be no salvation for you." I had heard that warning before and had scornfully disregarded it. It was too late now to turn back.

In the envelope there was also a number of clippings, brittle with age, of articles by the Colonel, published as a "worldwide exclusive, all rights reserved" in the Mar del Plata daily paper, *El Trabajo*, between September 20 and 25, 1970, a week before his death. The first four articles, signed with a pseudonym, told the story of the hijacking of the corpse and provided a number of minor details concerning what the Colonel called Operation Concealment. In the final one the real name of the author—Carlos Eugenio de Moori Koenig—was revealed, as was the existence of three perfect replicas of the body, buried under false names in Rotterdam, Brussels, and Rome. The real Evita, according to the text, was in a field on the banks of the Altmühl River, between Eichstätt and Plunz, in southwestern Germany. Only one person—whose name was not given—knew the secret, and that person would take it to the grave. The statement was so categorical it seemed like a confession. It moved me to learn that the articles had been written in the hospital, as the author lay dying. I felt worse, however, when I read the pseudonym that the Colonel had chosen for the first four articles. He had signed them "Lord Carnarvon," the name of the British archaeologist who awoke Tutankhamen from his eternal rest and paid for this daring feat with his life.

I was not about to let superstitions scare me off. I was not going to recount Evita either as a curse or a myth. I was going to recount her just as I had dreamed her: as a butterfly who beat the wings of her death forward as those of her life flew backward. The butterfly was forever suspended in the same place in the air, and that was why I wasn't getting anywhere either. Until I discovered the trick. One shouldn't ask oneself how a person flies or why, but simply start flying.

4

"I Am Giving Up the Honor, Not the Fight"

The only duty we have toward history is to rewrite it.
OSCAR WILDE, The Critic as Artist

At some moment in 1948, Evita accepted the advice of Julio Alcaraz, the famous hairdresser of stars in the golden age of Argentine cinema, and began to bleach her hair, in search of a flattering blond shade that would set off her features. During the second or third session the bleach seared the ends, and since she had to rush off to inaugurate a hospital, she wanted them cut off. The hairdresser preferred to solve the problem by sweeping her hair back, with her forehead bared and a big chignon secured at the nape of her neck with hairpins. This medal-like image, which came into being through the work of chance and haste, lingers stubbornly on in people's memory, as though all other Evitas were false.

When I met Julio Alcaraz, more than thirty years ago, it never entered my head that Evita could be a heroine of novels. I didn't think of her as a heroine or a martyr of anything. She struck me—why lie?—as a violent, authoritarian woman, who used rough language, who in reality had already burned herself out. She belonged to the past and to the realm of politics, which was no concern of mine.

Allow me to go back to March 1958. It was the time in my life when I got together at night with Amelia Biagioni and Augusto Roa Bastos, or stood waiting for dawn on the hostile train platforms on Constitución, where the air smelled of disinfectants and fresh-baked bread. In those days I was thinking of writing big novels; I don't know why I thought they should be big and intense, with the entire country as a background, life-size novels. I also thought of the women who had rejected me, of the abysses between a sign and its object, between a being and the chance that engenders that being. I was thinking of any number of things, but not of Evita.

Alcaraz's name was on the list of makeup men and hairdressers that I was given an assignment to write about for an illustrated history of Argentine cinema. He was credited with the creation of the sausage-roll halo that made María Duval the Argentine copy of Judy Garland and the crests of curls of vamps like Tilda Thamar. From the chairs of his beauty salon, decorated with plaster angels and Hollywood film posters, you could see the display windows of Harrod's and the cafés where students from the Faculty of Letters pretended to be Sartre or Simone de Beauvoir.

The first time, Alcaraz agreed to meet me at the door of his salon at nine p.m. To prompt his memory, I brought him a collection of photographs that showed him fashioning a helmet of curlers on Zully Moreno's head, spraying Paulina Singerman's hair with lacquer, and flattening down the curls of the Legrand twins with a hair net. My stratagem was a failure. His reminiscences turned out to be so opaque that when I transcribed them they slid clumsily over the glass of the text. Did Mario Soffici direct actresses by asking them to project themselves into a situation, or did he explain the characters to them? How many times did he interrupt a take to have a curl tucked in place? Let me see, let me see, Alcaraz kept answering, and froze up during these memory blocks. The only photograph that roused him from his indifference was one in which he was pasting a toupee onto the bald forehead of Luis Sandrini, during the filming

68

of *The Unhappiest Man in Town.* He brought the photo closer to the light and pointed out to me the blurred figure of a young woman in the background, wearing a ridiculous feather hat.

"See?" he said. "That's Evita. Many journalists come to see me about her, because they know I was her confidant."

"And what have you told them?" I asked.

"Nothing," he said. "I never tell anything."

Over a year went by without my having any news of him. Every so often, the scandal sheets spoke of Evita's metamorphosis from a slovenly adolescence to an imperial autumn and published before-and-after photos of her hair and nails. Nobody mentioned Julio Alcaraz. He seemed to have gone off somewhere far from this world. The letter he sent me in April or May of 1959 took me by surprise. "First of all," he wrote, "I want to thank you for what you wrote about me in your illustrated history. We keep the clipping in a frame in my beauty salon. Nobody can help but see it because it's reflected in the big mirror. I've thought more than once about what we talked of that day. And I realize that, after having lived so many stories, it's stupid not to want to tell them. I haven't any children. The only thing I have to leave behind are my memories. Why don't you drop by the beauty shop so we can talk, on Tuesday or Wednesday, around nine, like the other time?"

I dropped by, just so as not to hurt his feelings. I had no intention of writing another line about him. Even today I don't know what happened. Alcaraz brought me coffee, began to tell stories, and after a while I found myself taking notes. I remember the semidarkness, the long frieze of mirrors where pedestrians outside were reflected as they came and went. I remember the pungent odor of hair dyes and lacquers. I remember a neon sign with a multicolored parrot that went on and off. The opaque hairdresser of a year before now gave off light. Is it possible for one and the same person to be so different when he speaks and when he says nothing? Not different in the same way as a landscape when seen by day and by night; different like two landscapes on opposite sides of the globe. Let's see, let's see, he said, but this time it was only to cross over from one story to another, to catch his breath before dredging the delta of his memory. He evoked the deep twilight of swamps and mosquitoes into which Francisco Petrone and Elisa Christian Galvé plunged during the filming of *Prisoners of the Earth;* he imitated with perverse delight the heights of hysteria reached by Mecha Ortiz in *Sappho* and *The Kreutzer Sonata.* I felt that we were stepping into the screens of a number of movie theaters at once and many pasts whose waters flowed along simultaneously. It was April or May, as I said, a damp February wind was blowing, and the sidewalks of Buenos Aires were blue with the flowers that the lapacho trees shed in November. We were sliding little by little down Evita's slope, and when we fell to the bottom of it we weren't able to climb back up.

Alcaraz had met her in 1940, near Mar del Plata, during the shooting of *The Charge of the Valiant.* It was dawn, it was summer, and cows were grazing in a violet light. Evita had a complicated hairdo, with her face framed in dark corkscrew curls that made her features look bigger and a tiara of croquignole curls on her forehead. She interrupted him as he was heating some curlers in the embers in the kitchen and, ignoring his scorn, showed him some stills from *Dark Victory.*

"Do my hair like that, Julito, like Bette Davis's," she begged him. "I'd look a little better with curlier hair, don't you think?"

The hairdresser studied her from head to foot with brazen curiosity. A few days before, he had identified Evita as the young woman with the sad face and the skinny bosom who was being used as a model in a book of pornographic postcards. The photograph on the cover, which could still be seen at the newsstands in the Retiro railway station, showed her in front of a mirror, with minimal panties and her arms back, intimating that she was about to take off her bra. The photographs were meant to be provocative, but the innocence of the model spoiled the effect; in one of them, she was thrusting her hips to the left and trying to emphasize the roundness of her buttock with such a look of fear in her eyes that the intended eroticism of the pose was nil; in another one she was cupping her breasts and running her tongue over her lips so awkwardly that just the tip of it showed at one corner of her mouth, as her big round eyes remained veiled by an expression that put the viewer in mind of a lamb. If Alcaraz hadn't seen the postcards, he might never have agreed to restyle Evita's hair, and their lives would have taken separate paths from that moment on. But the amateurishness of those poses made him feel sorry for her, and he decided to help her. He wasted an hour and a half of his precious morning turning her not into the Bette Davis of *Dark Victory* but, rather, into the Olivia de Havilland of *Gone with the Wind*.

"So I kept the character she played from being an object of ridicule," he said to me. "An 1860 hairdo was more logical for a film with 1876 costumes than that other modern cut with the ends curled that she showed me. When you come right down to it, Evita was my creation. I made her."

Ten years later, Perón was to say the same thing.

To prove he wasn't exaggerating, he took me to the back of the beauty shop. He turned on the lights of a little salon whose walls were covered with mirrors. Perhaps they were an omen that reality was going to repeat many times, one after the other. Perhaps a warning that Evita was not resigning herself to being just one Evita and beginning to come back in hordes, by the millions, but at the time I didn't see it that way. I saw, that first time, only one face of reality or, if you will, the first light of a fire that was to burn for a long time. Spread out in a semicircle, I saw ten glass heads set on plaster pedestals, reproducing the same number of different hairstyles of Evita's. The one with black hair parted in the middle that had appeared in a brief scene in *The Charge of the Valiant* forlornly contemplated the girl with blond braids behind her ears who danced sambas in *The Circus Parade;* I saw an Evita wearing a turban next to another one with chestnut-colored bangs and an enormous rose made of white cloth at the peak of her forehead; I saw the woman with the beehive hairdo and curls in the shape of a cocoon acclaimed by the people of Madrid in the Plaza de Oriente and greeted by a discomposed Pius XII in the Sistine Chapel; I saw, finally, the Evita with golden-blond hair drawn tightly back who had been reproduced to infinity by the photographs of the last period, the one I had believed to be unique. Hanging from all the heads was a transparent reliquary with strands of blond hair inside.

"They're the ones I cut off when I did her hair for the last time, after she'd died," the hairdresser said. "I always carry a lock of it like this one inside my watch case.

"I lightened her hair little by little. I used stronger and stronger dyes. I did her hair more and more simply because she was always in a hurry. I had a hard time convincing her, because she had worn it loose all her life. Before she knew it, Evita was already different. I made her," he repeated. "I made her. I made a goddess out of the poor chick I first met near Mar del Plata. She didn't even realize it."

We began to see each other every Wednesday night at nine. I fell into the habit of sitting on the manicurist's bench, with my notebook open and a pack of Commander cigarettes, as Alcaraz gave away his memories little by little. Sometimes we drank gin, for a pick-me-up. Sometimes we were oblivious of all thirst and desire. I believe that those moments marked, without my knowing it, the birth of this novel.

He had no other news of Eva Duarte till 1944, he told me. When he came across her during the shooting of *The Circus Parade*, she was already a different person. Heaven only knows what abysses of misery that poor girl must have looked into, he thought then. The look in her eyes was full of scars, and she spoke in an imperious tone of voice. She didn't let anybody ride roughshod over her. Safeguarded by her pull with important figures in politics, she arrived on the set late, with deep dark circles under her eyes that the makeup girls couldn't manage to hide. She was obviously torn between the desire to be a big hit in her role and the fear of not living up to the expectations of Colonel Perón, the minister of war, who was her lover and paid for her *garçonnière*. Perón dropped by the studios of Pampa Films two or three times a week, drank maté with the director and the actors, and then shut himself up with Evita in the dressing room, hoping she'd change clothes.

72

"It was at that period in her life," Alcaraz said, "that she made me her confidant."

Of what followed I have preserved a few words here and there, skeletons of a dead language that no longer means anything as my eye runs down the page. Phrases like "Luna Pk, festival for earthq took him away then and there said to him Colonel thanks for exist Ditched Imb that night," nothing of any use to historians, nothing of any use to me when I wrote *The Perón Novel.* Only now and again do the notes get clearer and allow me to catch a glimpse of the pattern, as though it were a puzzle from which, here and there, pieces have disappeared at random.

The hairdresser's reminiscences have never been published. I didn't write them up at the time, out of laziness or because my imagination was a long way away from Evita. Writing has to do with health, with chance, with happiness and suffering, but above all it has to do with desire. Stories are an insect that a person ought to kill on the spot, and to me those stories of Evita were never anything but a pointless flapping of wings in the darkness.

Toward the end of 1959, out of sheer intellectual inertia, I transcribed Alcaraz's monologues and took them to him to have him look them over. I had the impression that, by passing his voice through the filter of my voice, his halting tone and the spasmodic syntax of his phrases would be lost. That, I thought, is where written language falls short. It can bring back to life feelings, lost time, chance circumstances that link one fact to another, but it can't bring reality back to life. I didn't yet know—and it would take longer still for me to feel it—that reality doesn't come back to life: it is born in a different way, it is transfigured, it reinvents itself in novels. I didn't know that the syntax or the tones of voice of the characters return with a different air about them and that, as they pass through the sieves of written language, they become something else.

What follows, willy-nilly, is a reconstruction. Or, if anyone so prefers, an invention: a reality that comes back to life. How can this be recounted? Alacaraz speaks, I speak, someone listens, or we all speak at once, we all have a free shot at the game of reading by writing.

Alcaraz is speaking. I am writing:

Evita never ceased to respect me. She shouted at everyone, but she was careful how she behaved toward me. She once asked me to teach her good manners, because every so often Perón would show up at her place with important guests for dinner. I gradually housetrained her, as they say. "Hold the silverware just by the ends," I told her. "When you lift a glass, curl your little finger." But what refined her most was her instinct. They say she mispronounced words, but her problem wasn't that. In company, if she was uncertain of the exact meaning of a hard word, she combined it with one she knew. I once heard her say "I'm going to the dentologist" instead of "I'm going to the dentist" or "to the odontologist." And another time, "I can't get by on my moluments," for "I can't get by on my salary" or "my emoluments." She gradually learned how to keep from making a fool of herself because she kept looking out of the corner of her eye at what other people were doing and because when someone corrected a word she'd said, she wrote it down in a notebook.

When she finished The Circus Parade, *she couldn't make up her mind about her future for several months. She cried in front of her mirror, not knowing what to do with her life. She didn't know whether to stay in Perón's shadow like a mere kept woman, since thus far he hadn't said anything about getting married, or whether she should go on with her career as an actress, something she'd fought so hard for. It's not easy today to put yourself in her place. You forget that in those days virginity was sacred, and women who lived with a man without getting married let themselves in for the worst humiliations. Girls from good families unfortunate enough to get pregnant were not allowed to have an abortion. Abortion was the worst of crimes. They were sent to an unfamiliar city to have the baby, and as soon as it was born it was handed over to an orphanage. Evita could count on her mother's understanding, since she too had gone through all the rough times of living from hand to mouth and being held in contempt, but she knew that the high-ranking officers of the army weren't going to allow the minister of war to make a woman like her his legally wedded wife. Staying with Perón was a way of committing suicide, because sooner or later they would make him get rid of her. But Evita be-*

lieved in soap-opera miracles. She thought that if there had been one Cinderella, there could be two. Placing her faith in that, she leaped into the void.
By sheer luck it turned out all right. In her worst moments of doubt she sought
Perón's advice, to no avail; he was unwilling to express an opinion: he answered that she should let her feelings be her guide. That left her even more bewildered, because what she took to be a lack of interest on his part was perhaps
a sign of confidence in her good judgment.

   History kept tugging her one way and then the other, and before she knew
it, films and radio were no longer of any importance on her horizon. I think
that her last doubts were dispelled in October of 1945, when Perón was imprisoned and, abandoned by everyone, she shut herself up in her apartment,
waiting for them to come to arrest her. She identified herself more than ever
with Marie Antoinette, the heroine of her adolescence; she was Norma Shearer
hearing the drums of the guillotine from her prison cell in the Conciergerie.
When Perón was freed and lived his night of glory in the Plaza de Mayo, Eva
was scared to death, brushing her hair in front of her mirror in the bedroom.
Her lips were swollen and one of her shoulders was injured. That morning, as
she was going to her brother Juan's apartment in a taxi, a crowd of students
had recognized her, and shouting "Finish off the mare, kill Duarte!" they
broke the windows and beat her with sticks. She escaped by a miracle. When
she saw herself in the mirror, she looked ugly, disfigured, and wouldn't leave
the apartment till Perón took her off to a friend's country house in San
Nicolás. Evita lived through those days in the worst uncertainty. She didn't
know what was to become of her life. One night she phoned me. "Am I bothering you, Julio?" she asked me. "May I talk to you?" She had never asked permission to do anything. She never did again.

   You already know what happened next. Before the end of October, Perón
married her in the apartment on the calle Posadas where they lived, and two
months later they sanctified their marriage in a church in La Plata. For the religious ceremony, I did Evita's hair beautifully, swept high in two big waves
with clusters of orange blossoms peeking out. Although the presidential cam-
paign was in full swing and they didn't have time even to sleep, Evita always
set aside a few minutes to come to my shop on the corner of Paraguay and Es-
meralda, where I was gradually lightening her hair and trying out simpler and
simpler hairdos for her. Her new role as a married woman confused her. Un-

til a few months before she had been an actress cast in radio serials that nobody listened to, a nobody who went around begging to have her photograph in magazines. And then overnight she found herself a woman married to the ranking colonel of the Republic. The change would have been a dizzying one for anybody, especially in those days, when women amounted to less than nothing, invisible shadows at their husband's side. But not Evita. On sensing that she had power over people's fate, she grew. Have you seen the photo taken of her as she was leaving the cathedral on June 4, 1946, clinging to the arm of the wife of Vice-President Jazmín Hortensio Quijano? Just look at those lips tense with fear, that cold, mistrustful look, the awkward way she's holding her whole body. I gave her a very sober hairdo that day, leaving just a hint of a curl peeping out from under her hat with a Turkish look to it, but in those imposing naves where Perón was anointed president of the Republic, amid the solemnity of the Te Deum, Evita felt herself falter. For a moment she thought she'd never take another step. And yet just have a look at her only a month later in the Colón Theater, stretching her arms out toward the curiosity seekers waiting at the entrance. Already there was no one who could stand up to her and look her straight in the eye.

She knew that sooner or later her star might fade, and she wanted to have in one year all the experiences that take others a lifetime to come by. She gave up sleeping. She'd telephone her aides at three in the morning to give them an order, and at six she'd call them back to see if they'd carried it out. In less time than it takes to tell she'd set up a network of ministers, spies, and sycophants who kept her informed of everything that was going on in the government. In this respect she was cleverer than Perón; but if she wove her web of intrigue with great care it was not to put him in the shade, as people say, but because when you come right down to it he was ineffectual.

One morning in February I went to the presidential residence to give her hair a brushout and braid it. I found her feeling low. I tried to take her mind off her troubles by telling her about two cousins of mine who'd come to Buenos Aires from Lules, in the province of Tucumán, to look for husbands.

"And have they found them yet?" she asked me.

"They're never going to," I told her. "They're really ugly looking, with big warty noses. Even the more passable of the two has a great big goiter that can't be operated on."

"I Am Giving Up the Honor, Not the Fight"

She interrupted me, her mind elsewhere. I had long since gotten used to her changes of mood, which her enemies attributed to hysteria. With unexpected gentleness she reached for my hands and said:

"Wait for me outside for a minute, Julito. I have to go to the bathroom."

In about half an hour, she called me back in. She was dressed in street clothes and wearing high heels and wanted me to do her hair up in the double chignon she wore on elegant occasions. When I touched her head I could feel that she was burning up with fever. She was tense, panting for breath from one of those inner storms that would eventually kill her. I wanted to bring up the subject of my cousins again, but she cut me short.

"Hurry up and finish doing my hair, Julio. They're waiting for me outside. And don't worry about your cousins. I'm going to find both of them a fiancé. Birds of a feather flock together: there must be men as ugly as they are."

In the living room downstairs I saw the bosses of the CGT and the delegates of the women's section of the Peronist Party gathered together. Evita greeted them and listened to their long speeches with a frown on her face. They were offering to make her the candidate for the vice-presidency of the Republic, and even though holding this office was the greatest ambition of her life, she answered that everything depended on her husband's approval. Then as now, politics was a Chinese puzzle to me. So you can imagine my surprise, then, when I saw that the general, as though he'd sensed that they were calling upon him, had appeared at the residence at that unusual hour in the morning. Evita's fever had gone up. Every so often her head bent over. As I watched her from the floor above, I suffered with her. I didn't see her falter for a moment. With astonishing presence of mind she told her husband what was happening.

"I've told these comrades that I'm not going to move a finger without your permission."

"And did they believe you?" the general asked.

"I've never been more serious."

"How am I going to oppose the wishes of all these people? Even little old Quijano has asked me to have you nominated as vice-president!"

With that ambiguous pronouncement, Perón made it clear that if Evita was given the nomination, it was because that was what he wanted. From that day on, I saw her only when she was in a rush. She would call me at six in the morning as often as she did at eleven at night to touch up her dye job, to re-

77

arrange her hair a little. I made two fake chignons out of her own hair, and once I'd fastened them on securely with hairpins, her coiffure was impeccable. I've kept one of those chignons. You've already seen it, in my museum behind the shop.

The cousins stayed on with me for several months longer. They helped me in the beauty salon in the afternoons, arranging appointments or helping do manicures. They spent their mornings at the state pawn shop, where they bought utterly useless objects: from hats that dated from the Victorian era and tortoiseshell mirrors to silver coatracks and funeral candelabra. Since the tenants of several sugar plantations always sent them their rent on time, the two of them were never short of money. They suffered because their youth was fading and their hymens were hardening. They still had hopes of meeting Evita, but the chance never came, because the Señora was already keeping impossible hours.

She was living, but only the life of a ghost. I was losing sight of her. She's a saint, she's a hyena—in those weeks I heard Evita called everything imaginable. I read in a Uruguayan rag that to humiliate Perón, she made him wear wedding dresses in private. I read in a clandestine tract that, in the brothel in Junín where her mother was the madam, Evita had put an end to her virginity at the age of twelve at a cattle ranchers' party, purely and simply because of a natural inclination toward vice. In almost all the libelous attacks there was some insult concerning her past, but those that spoke of the present were vicious too. They called her Agrippina, Sempronia, Nefertete; comparisons like that didn't affect Evita, who didn't have the slightest idea who those women were. They accused her of encouraging worshipful admiration of her and censorship, of turning the labor unions into servants of her will, of presuming that Perón was God and declaring a holy war against infidels. Some of these accusations had some basis in reality, but reality didn't diminish in the slightest the blind love that people professed for her.

I don't know how Evita did it, but she soon began to be everywhere. I heard that she had thwarted a couple of conspiracies against her life and that the ringleaders were about to be castrated so as to calm one of her fits of rage. I knew that she had caused a rift between Perón and Colonel Domingo A. Mercante, who was also aiming at the vice-presidency. I read that she was in Salta one morning and in Córdoba or Catamarca the next, giving away houses, handing out money, or teaching the alphabet to rural schoolchildren out of books in which the same sentences were endlessly repeated: "Evita loves me. Evita is good. Evita is a fairy. I love Evita . . ." She traveled thousands of miles by train, alone, triumphant as a criminal queen.

Between April and May of 1951, Buenos Aires was papered over from top to bottom with her face, and enormous streamers hung even from the Obelisk, urging people to vote for PERÓN—EVA PERÓN / THE TICKET FOR THE COUNTRY. *I was surprised when Evita repeated in almost all her speeches, over and over again, "I want to be officially nominated," as though Perón's promise weren't enough and she needed the backing of the labor unions. She knew her husband well and was careful not to overshadow him. She began to exaggerate the syrup she poured over him in her speeches. Read, if you can, the ones from those months. "I'm in love with General Perón and his cause," she kept saying. "A hero like him deserves only martyrs and fanatics. I am prepared to face anything out of love for him: martyrdom, death."*

She fainted two or three times at public ceremonies and was whisked out of sight, but as soon as she came to, she insisted on going on. She was diagnosed as suffering from anemia or lack of sleep, although since that morning in February in the presidential residence I had had my suspicions that she had cancer. The famous Dr. Ivanissevich turned up one night with a blood transfusion team. Evita whacked him with his satchel and threw him out, and the poor man, a minister who'd been placed in office at the insistence of the Church, was forced to resign. "I want to be officially nominated," Evita kept saying over and over. "I need to be the official candidate because even the doctors are plotting to keep me apart from you, dear workers. The oligarchs, the reactionaries, the doctors, the unpatriotic, the mediocre, are all plotting." The bosses of the CGT finally took the hint and decided to announce her candidacy at an impressive ceremony.

The preparations began almost a month beforehand. On the eve of the ceremony, which was announced as a Justicialist Party Open Meeting, the whole country had come to a halt, the trains were packed with people from the provinces who descended into the jaws of the unfamiliar capital without a cent in their knapsacks, everything was free, even the nightclubs and the hotels, just imagine those obscure multitudes, who had never seen two buildings side by side, dazzled by the lighted skyscrapers. I can't tell you how excited my cousins

79

*were at seeing that endless procession of dauntless bachelors. They wanted me
to get them seats in the viewing stand, but it had been more than ten days since
I'd seen the Señora and I didn't have the nerve to bother her. I thought that
maybe she didn't even need my services. Everything was beyond belief, blown
up out of all proportion, night was morning, words and their meaning were
two different things; it seemed to me that we were sinking up to our necks in a
lie, but I didn't know what it was or what truths it could be set beside. In the
papers you'll see a clearer reflection of what was taking place. Read this clipping from* Clarín *for example:*

> Men in ponchos and boots, people bustling about with card-
> board suitcases and bundles, have constituted, since yester-
> day morning, Tuesday, August 21, 1951, the advance party of
> the vast contingents that have poured into the city via the
> railway stations and the bus and shuttle terminals. How
> many of them can there be? A million of them? They number
> many more, no doubt. They will be seen, late this afternoon,
> at the foot of the triumphal arch erected at the intersection
> of the avenida Nueve de Julio and Moreno. The aforemen-
> tioned arch, beneath which the official box is located, has two
> huge photographs hung from it: one of the head of state and
> another of his wife, along with the emblem of the labor con-
> federation, and many pennants and banners, while all
> around it some of the countless organizations supporting the
> party have hung slogans stretching for several blocks over-
> head. A week of revelry? No. A historic week, of deep civic
> fervor.

*In the papers, it was the CGT that had organized the event, but it was
Evita who put the machinery in motion. The free trains and buses were her
idea; she was the one who ordered an official holiday to give people enough
time off to come, the one who had shelters opened and people served all the
food they could eat. Perón was an admirer of the way the Fascists staged events,
and almost all crowd ceremonies copied the Duce's. But Evita, whose only culture came from the movies, wanted the announcement of her nomination to be
like a Hollywood premiere, with spotlights, trumpet flourishes, and hordes of
people.*

*My cousins set out for the ceremony around nine a.m., made up fit to kill
and decked out like Christmas trees. I stayed home alone, listening to the radio.
Every so often announcements were broadcast urging people to take advantage
of the sun on their holiday and to camp out under the trees along the avenue.*

"I Am Giving Up the Honor, Not the Fight"

I had a presentiment that the Señora might send for me at any moment. And would you believe it? Almost the next moment the phone rang, around three. They were summoning me to come just as quickly as I could to the Public Works building, behind the presidential box. "How can I get anywhere near it?" I asked. "The radio says that nobody's ever seen such a huge crowd." "Don't worry. We'll come by in fifteen minutes to get you."

I was given a ride in one of the official presidential cars, and it wasn't stopped at any of the barricades. So I caught a few glimpses of the city, not knowing whether to believe my eyes. At the foot of Manuel Belgrano's sarcophagus they'd set up an open-air movie theater that was showing propaganda films on old-people's homes, orphans' villages, and halfway houses that Evita had founded. A legion of patriots who took the Open Meeting business seriously lighted candles from the torch of the metropolitan cathedral where General José de San Martín is buried and demanded that his casket be carried in procession to the triumphal arch on the avenida Nueve de Julio. An ocean liner drifted forlornly from one dock to another, and though we all heard its sirens wailing desperately, nobody came on the run to lend a hand; I found out afterward that it had run aground on the mud along the river and the seamen aboard had gone over the side to join the celebration. In the very middle of that magnificent outpouring of joy, Evita was all alone. She contemplated the jacarandas from the windows of an imposing office in the Ministry of Public Works. She had put on a dark tailored suit, simply cut, a silk blouse, and diamond earrings that followed the contour of her earlobes. She was pale, thinner, with taut cheekbones. When she spied me, she smiled sadly. "Ah, it's you," she said. "It's lucky they found you."

I don't know why I remember that scene as being enveloped in silence, when in reality the air was saturated with sound. Outside the strains of "Peronist Young People" thundered away, loudspeakers in the distance were playing Nicola Paone's "The Coffeepot That Goes Glug-Glug" over and over, and on the avenue torrents of big bass drums were being unleashed, and fireworks that were scheduled to be set off at midnight were going off prematurely. But my memory has retained everything I talked about that afternoon with Evita with no sound except for our voices, as though they'd been cut out around the edges with a pair of scissors. I remember that, instead of my greeting her as usual, a lie welled up from my heart out of pity for her: "How pretty you look, señora!"

81

I remember too that she didn't believe me. She was wearing her hair down, held back with a barrette, and hadn't put her makeup on yet. I offered to shampoo her hair and give her a massage to relax her. "Do my hair," she said. "I want the chignon pinned on good and tight." She collapsed in one of the armchairs in the office and absentmindedly began humming Paone's song, "that goes glug-glug," just to keep from bursting into tears.

"How are things going for people out there?" she asked me. And before I could answer, she said: "Politics is shit, Julio. They never give you what's rightfully yours. If you're a woman, it's even worse. They trash you. And when you really want something you have to fight for it tooth and nail. They've left me all alone. With every day that goes by I'm more alone."

You didn't need to be very clever to guess that she was complaining about her husband. But she'd have been furious if I'd let on that I understood. I tried to console her.

"If you're all alone, how about the rest of us?" I said to her. "You have all of us, you have the general. There are a million people there outside who have come just to see you."

"Maybe they aren't going to see me, Julio. Maybe I'm not going out there," she said. At that moment I felt how tense she was. Her fists were clenched, her veins rigid, her jaws tightly clamped together. "Maybe I won't speak to them. Why should I, if I don't even know what I have to say?"

"I've seen you this way more than once, señora. It's nerves. When you appear in the presidential box you're going to forget about everything."

"What is there to forget, if nobody talks to me so I can understand? The only ones who say things I understand are the little greasers. With all the others you have to use a dictionary. The generals meet with Perón in secret to ask him not to let me be a candidate. Do you know what his answer is? He tells them to stick it up their ass, that I'm me and do as I please. But I don't do as I please. Too many people are getting involved in this whole affair, Julio. It's a nest of intrigue, dirty tricks. Even Perón's beginning to get fed up. The other day I grabbed him by the arm and said to him: Do you want me to give up? Okay, I give up. He looked at me absentmindedly and answered: Do whatever you like, Chinita. Whatever you like. I've gone a week without sleeping a wink. Yesterday I was about to get into a hot tub, I felt cold, I'd already taken three or four aspirin, and all of a sudden I started thinking: He's the president.

"I Am Giving Up the Honor, Not the Fight"

If he wants me to be vice-president, he has to tell the people. I grabbed the phone and called him at the Casa Rosada. Take advantage of the Open Meeting ceremony, I told him. Begin your speech by announcing to everybody that you're the one who wants me to be a candidate. Say to them, Ladies and gentlemen, I chose her. That'll put a stop to the rumors. It's obvious that I've chosen you, he answered me, but for me to say so is something else again. It's not, I insisted. You and I have been fighting over this for months. If we give in now, they're going to eat me alive. Not you, me. We have to watch our step with the party, he said to me. You're the party, I answered. Let me think it over, Chinita, he said. I'm busy now. It's the first time he hasn't known what to do. This morning we had another set-to. I refused to drop the subject. He realized I was about to explode and tried to calm me down. It leaves a bad impression if I propose you, he said. Family should be one thing and running the country another. We have to be careful to observe the formalities. You may be Evita all right, but you're my wife too: the party has to nominate you. I don't give a damn about formalities, I interrupted him. Either you name me as the candidate or I'm not appearing at the Open Meeting; you're going to have to show your face all alone. You don't understand, he said to me. Of course I understand, I answered. And I left the room, slamming the door behind me. In just a little while, the CGT bosses knew everything. They begged me to come. Señora, you can't do that to the descamisados, *they said to me. They've come from heaven knows where for you. I'm nobody, I told them. I'm just a humble woman. They're here on account of the general. No, they insisted. The general's candidacy is a sure thing. They've come on account of you. I can't attend that ceremony, I answered. If the people clamor for you, the only thing we can do is go get you, they said to me. You'll know where to look, I told them. I'm going to watch the ceremony from the Ministry of Public Works. The minute I said that, I was sorry I had. But then I thought: That Open Meeting belongs to me. I earned it. I deserve it. I'm not going to lose out on it. Let them come get me."*

Every story is, by definition, unfaithful. Reality, as I've said, can't be told or repeated. The only thing that can be done with reality is to invent it again.

In the beginning I thought: When I put together the bits and pieces of what I once transcribed, when the hairdresser's mono-logues come to life again, I'll have my story. I had it, but it was a dead letter. Then I wasted a lot of time searching about here and there for fossils of what had happened at the Open Meeting. I dug around in the back files of the daily papers, I saw the documentaries of the time, I listened to recordings of radio programs. The same scene kept repeating itself, repeating itself, repeating itself: Evita not knowing how to keep her distance from the crowd's blind love, drawing closer, moving away; Evita begging them not to allow her to say what she didn't want to say, begging them not to keep her from having her say. I learned nothing, I added nothing to my story. In that useless heap of documents, Evita was never Evita.

Between 1972 and 1973, after her body was rescued from an anonymous grave in Milan and returned to her widower, I wrote a film script that attempted to reconstruct the story of the candidacy that hadn't come off, using fragments of newsreels and whole series of photographs. I wanted the story to be a well-woven plot and, at the same time, an interweaving of symbols, but I wasn't able to judge how much truth there was in it. At that time, the flutter of the truth was essential to me. And no truth was possible if Evita wasn't there. Not her ghost, but the tears of her childhood, her soap-opera voice, her background music, her will to power, blood, madness, despair, what she had been at every moment of her life. In certain films I had sensed how people and things step forward once again from the im-mortal background of history. I knew that that sometimes works. I needed help. Someone to say to me: *That's how they were, just the way you've recounted them.* Or to teach me where to move them so that they coincided with an illusion of truth. I remembered Julio Alcaraz and phoned him. It took him a while to remember who I was. He agreed to meet me at ten p.m. in the Rex Café. He had aged a lot, and com-plained of buzzing sounds in his ears and cramps in his legs.

"I don't know if I'm going to be able to help you," he said to me.

"Don't force yourself," I reassured him. "Just listen to me and let yourself go. Imagine that you're at the Open Meeting again, and if something I say doesn't jibe with what you remember, interrupt me."

"I Am Giving Up the Honor, Not the Fight"

"Read me that script," he said. "It's going to be like sitting in a movie theater watching my life."

"It's better than life. You can get up from your seat here at any time and disappear. Life is harder. And now," I told him, "forget the hubbub. Imagine that the lights are going down. That a curtain is opening."

(Exterior. Late afternoon. The avenida Nueve de Julio, Buenos Aires.) Pan shot of the crowd. It is jam-packed from the official box to the Obelisk. Flags are fluttering. The aerial takes show that the crowd numbers a million and a half. Forests of placards in the middle of the street. The light is harsh, with sharp contrasts. Warm sunshine, as can be seen from people's clothing. Takes of the triumphal arch above the official box. In the foreground, huge photographs of Perón and Evita. Pan shot: seas of handkerchiefs waving. A clock: 5:20 p.m.

The clamor slowly grows louder. Huge bass drums roar. Here and there a few off-key geysers erupt: "The Peronist March."

A stir in the official box.

VOICE (off):
Comrades, comrades. Entering this historic Justicialist Open Meeting is the president of the Republic, General Juan Domingo Perón.

Perón walks forward, open armed, to the first row of the presidential box. A dangerous surge of the crowd as it attempts to get closer to its idol.

The crowd bursts into applause. (An unexpected word grows louder and louder. Perón / Perón? No. It is unbelievable. What the crowd is chanting in chorus is Evita's name.)
CHORUS:
Eee viii ta / Eee viii ta.

Close-up: The uncomfortable expression on the general's face. The whiplash of a tic raises his eyebrows. The secretary-general of the CGT, a rather grotesque potbellied figure, takes the microphone. His speech is full of mispronounced words.

SECRETARY GENERAL JOSE G. ESPEJO (referred to below as ESPEJO):
General . . .

Close-up of Perón, stern faced.

. . . The people of this country have gathered here to say to you, their sole leader, . . .

Close-up of the huge photo of Evita.

. . . as in every momentous hour, "Present, General!"

Shots of the crowd.

CHORUS (instantly):
Present! (The word gradually fades away naturally, dissolving into an insistent shout:) *Eee viii ta . . .*

"I Am Giving Up the Honor, Not the Fight"

Perón looks dwarfed. His face remains gray, his lips pressed tightly together. Would it be cruel to show his annoyance now, making it stand out against the excited crowd shown in the background? I leave it up to the director. The general is vexed to find himself playing a supporting role at the largest gathering in Peronist history. He decides to attract the attention of the *descamisados*. He raises his arms, brings his hands to his heart. The *descamisados* leap up and down, answer his greeting with delirious gestures. But they do not chant his name in chorus. They call out instead the name:

CHORUS:
Eee viii taa / Eee viii ta . . .

The afternoon light slowly dims. Perón's face again shows the same frown, the same sullenness, as at the beginning. Wiping the invisible dampness from his mustache, Espejo tries to gain control of the situation, but only makes it worse.

ESPEJO:
General . . . (Spoken in a pleading tone of voice. The word is drowned out by the chanting of the crowd.) *General . . . We note one person absent here, your wife, Eva Perón, without equal in this world . . .* (Ovation.)
CHORUS:
Bring us Evita! Where is Evita?

ESPEJO:
*Comrades . . . Perhaps her modesty, which is her
greatest merit, keeps her from . . .* (What follows can scarcely be heard.) *Allow us, General, to go get her, so that she may be present
here.*

Delirium once again. The camera follows Espejo
as he leaves. Then it sniffs about amid a forest of sharply creased gray trousers, until it
stops at a shoe impatiently jerking up and
down. It is Perón. The camera climbs up his
body, stops at his malevolent eyes, alights on
the skating rink of his hair slicked down with
pomade. [*Note: Such a shot exists. If the director wants to use it, he can look for it in
one of the two editions of the Spanish newsreel
NoDo, August 22, 1951.*] Darkness falls on the
general's head. It is six-thirty p.m.

(*Exterior, same place, Buenos Aires.*)
Evita is seen arriving, followed by Espejo and
a retinue of officials.

"They were the ones who went to get her at the Ministry of Public Works," the hairdresser said. "I was following behind them. I
braided her hair in a double chignon, I put just a touch of makeup
on her. She looked lovely."

Pan shot of the ecstatic crowd. Cut to women
falling on their knees on the sidewalk leading
to the Spanish Club. Cut to workers' families
weeping at the foot of the Obelisk. Cut to

Evita herself, throwing kisses from the presidential box. She too cannot keep from weeping. Close-up of tears [*there is a marvelous
shot in* NoDo]. Espejo makes his way to the
microphone.

ESPEJO:
*And I ask that we proclaim General Juan Perón
the candidate for the presidency of the Republic and señora Eva Perón for the vice-
presidency.*

Evita seeks refuge in her husband's arms. Then
she appears at the railing of the box, looking
ill assured. "I . . ." Her lips move. "I . . ."
Nothing comes out. Finally, she begins her long
speech. [*It is really long. There are complete
versions of it in* NoDo *and* Events in Argentina.
*I suggest that the director use only one para-
graph, the one next to last.*]

"What for?" the hairdresser broke in. "She didn't know what to
say, she was scared to death, she sensed Perón's disapproving gaze
and that made her even more inept. Compare this speech with the
ones she made months before. In those, Evita makes her voice do
whatever she pleases. It fills the whole stage. Not here. She was out
of her head. If you show her in that sorry state, you ruin the imposing effect of what follows."

"It's only a paragraph," I insisted. "The one next to last."

EVITA:
*I have done nothing. It is all Perón. Perón is
the fatherland, Perón is everything, and the*

*rest of us are an astronomical distance away
from the leader of the nation. General, with
the plenary spiritual powers granted me by the
descamisados of the fatherland, before the
people vote for you, I proclaim you president
of the Argentines.* (Ovation.)

Perón embraces her. Tumultuous shots of the box
[*good takes in* Events in Argentina]. An uniden-
tified labor union leader, seen from behind,
goes over to Evita [*the scene is in one of the
two editions of* NoDo].

UNION LEADER:
*You haven't told us yet whether you accept the
candidacy or not, señora . . .* (Turning toward
the microphone:) *Señora! The people are awaiting your answer . . . What will you tell them?*

Below the box, a horde of women wave white
handkerchiefs.

CHORUS:
Say yes / Evita . . . / Say yes / Evita . . .
ESPEJO (off):
*Comrades, let us hear the words of General
Perón.*

Shot of Perón, triumphant, approaching the microphone. Suddenly the image seems to have
frozen, but it hasn't. It is Perón who isn't
moving, standing dead still from shock. He has
just heard a defiant shout, and then the frenzied chorus of the crowd.

"I Am Giving Up the Honor, Not the Fight"

A VOICE (off):
Let Comrade Evita speak!
CHORUS (off):
Speak / Evita! / Accept / Evita!
PERON (trying to recover from the shock):
Comrades . . . (The roar of the crowd contin-
ues.) *Comrades . . . Only strong and virtuous
peoples are masters of their fate . . .*

As the camera slowly moves upward and takes in
the dense swell of the crowd, the fluttering of
the flags, and the oases of a few bonfires, the
general's voice gradually fades. Seen from
above, the images dissolve to the same scene,
at night now. The sweeps of a spotlight beam
stir the foam of the million heads. Rivers of
torches rise out of nowhere. Suddenly the
screen goes black, total darkness. The warm
lips of a microphone move toward the viewer.
[*Does the director remember the last image of*
The Magnificent Ambersons, *that masterpiece of
Orson Welles's overshadowed by his* Citizen
Kane? *Look for it, plagiarize it.*] From this
nothingness flows the voice that all are
awaiting.

EVITA (off):
My dear descamisados, *my darlings . . .*

As it moves back, the camera reveals Evita's
aquiline profile, and she stands there, frozen
to the spot. The camera is hypnotized by the
waving reeds of her arms and the trembling of
her lips.

91

EVITA (off):
I ask the women, the children, the workers
gathered together here, to give me, before mak-
ing such a momentous decision in the life of
this humble woman, at least four days to think
it over.
CHORUS (off, but very clear, rhythmic):
No, no! Evita! Today!

"You would have to show the expression of the others now," the hairdresser said. "Espejo was deathly pale; he didn't know what to do. He was beginning, too late, to realize that the Open Meeting was one of those historic misunderstandings that could cost him his head. Perón didn't like what was happening at all. He was obviously uncomfortable, impatient. What nobody understood was why things had gone as far as they had. A million people had journeyed across the vast expanses of Argentina, and all for nothing! Did you see Evita's face? When she arrived at the ceremony she was convinced that Perón himself was going to announce her candidacy. If not, why had he sent for her? It was all a big fuss over nothing. So as not to vex her husband, she would have to lie. But she didn't want to lie. She couldn't do that to the *descamisados*. She and the crowd were suddenly caught up in a fumbling dialogue, a death leap without a net. Evita wasn't prepared to say any of the words she says from this moment on. They came from her soul, from her instincts. Why don't you use the entire dialogue in your film? It's moving."

EVITA:
Comrades. You must understand me. I am not giv-
ing up my role in the fight. I am giving up the
honor.

"I Am Giving Up the Honor, Not the Fight"

The crowd lifts torches on high, waves handkerchiefs. Evita tries to calm it down with
desperate gestures.

CHORUS:
An-swer! / An-swer! / Say-yes! / Say-yes!
EVITA:
*Comrades . . . I had thought differently, but in
the end I will do as the people say.* (Ovation.)
*Do you think that if the office of vice-
president were a heavy burden and I had been a
solution, I would not have already answered
yes? Tomorrow, when . . .*
CHORUS:
Today! Today!

Eva turns toward Perón. She says something in
his ear.

"Do you know what the general said to her?" the hairdresser
remarked. "He said to her: Make them go away! Ask them to go
away."

EVITA:

Because of the affection that unites us . . . (A
sob clouds her voice. She raises her hands to
her throat. From her gestures, it is apparent
that she would like to get the sob out and
doesn't know how to. She sighs. She regains her
composure.) *I ask you please not to make me do*

*what I do not wish to do. I ask you as your
friend, your comrade, to disperse . . .*
CHORUS:
No! No! (The voices mingle, blend into one.)
We'll strike! A general strike!
EVITA:
The people are sovereign. I accept . . .

Images of the crowd leaping up and down, dancing, juggling with the torches, lighting volcanoes of fireworks. Confetti falls from the
balconies, the beam of the spotlight disappears behind a forest of flags. The words "I accept" come and go like a psalm.

CHORUS:
She said she accepts! She said she accepts!

From the box, Evita shakes her head, lowers her
arms.

EVITA:
*No, comrades! You're mistaken. What I meant was:
I accept, I agree, that is, to do what Comrade
Espejo tells me to do . . . Tomorrow, at noon . . .*
CHORUS:
(Boos. And then, immediately:) *Now, now! Right
now, now!*
EVITA:
I ask you only for a little time. If tomorrow . . .
CHORUS:
No, now!

Evita turns around once again toward Perón. Her
face is drawn; she is stupefied, panicked. In

```
one of the two editions of NoDo, her lips
clearly form the question: "What shall I do?"
```

"Perón told her not to give in," the hairdresser explained to me. "To postpone her answer. 'It's a question of holding out,' he told her. 'And you have the last word. They can't force you.'"

"He was right," I admitted. "They couldn't force her."

"They did though. They were determined not to budge from there."

```
EVITA:
Comrades . . . When has Evita ever deceived you?
When has Evita not done what you wanted her to
do? Don't you realize that for a woman, as for
any citizen, the decision you are asking me to
make is a truly momentous one? And all I ask of
you is a few hours' time. . . .


The crowd goes wild. A number of torches go
out.


Lava flows. "Now!" The uncontrollable now
spreads its wings of a bat, of a butterfly, of
a forget-me-not. The nows of cattle and waving
spears of grain buzz; nothing can put a stop to
their frenzy, their lance thrust, their fiery
echo. [The mad feast of that word lasted, ac-
cording to the figures reported in the daily
Democracia, more than eighteen minutes. But in
the editions of NoDo and of Events in Argentina
only ten seconds have been preserved for pos-
terity. I suggest that the director prolong the
same shot until the viewers collapse from ex-
```

haustion. I suggest an erotic or, rather, a
venereal montage. Maybe that way a certain reality effect can be attained.]
CHORUS:
Now! Now! Now! Now! [Et cetera.]

Evita bursts into tears. She is no longer
ashamed of herself for weeping.

EVITA:
And yet, nothing of this surprises me. I had
known for some time that my name was being insistently mentioned. And I didn't deny it. I
did it for the people and for Perón, because
there wasn't anyone else who could approach
him, not even from an astronomical distance.
And I did it for all of you, so that you could
know which men in the party had a vocation for
leadership. By using my name, the general could
protect himself from dissident factions within
the party . . .

"This is the sacramental moment of her speech," the hairdresser
said. "Evita strips herself naked. *I am not myself,* she says. *I am what my
husband wants me to be. I let him hatch his plots in my name. Since he gave me
his name, I am giving him mine.* It was horrible, and nobody realized."
"She didn't realize what she was saying either," I said.

EVITA:
But never in my heart as a humble Argentine
woman did I think that I could accept this
post. Comrades . . .

The moment has come. The camera too is a living being. It shudders, becomes confused. Where
to look now? The camera sniffs at the fears of
the crowd. It too is drenched with fear. It
comes, it goes: the sea of torches, Evita.

CHORUS:
No! no!
EVITA:
*Tonight . . . It's seven-fifteen p.m. I . . .
Please . . . At twenty-one thirty, on the radio,
I . . .*
CHORUS:
Now! Now!

In the final edition of *NoDo* there is a pan
shot, possibly accidental, that takes in the
tense atmosphere in the box. It shows Espejo as
he offers Perón embarrassed, inaudible explanations. Evita asks what to do. She is no
longer looking at her husband. She ought to
hurl reproaches at him. She contains them, says
nothing. Perón, with his back to the crowd,
points toward the camera with his index finger.

PERÓN:
End this ceremony this minute!

Amid the commotion in the box, it is not easy
to make out whose voice is whose. At intervals
a hysterical, very high pitched panting, which
can only be that of Evita in her desolation,
can be heard above the voices.

97

ESPEJO:
Comrades . . . The Señora . . . Comrade Evita asks
us only to wait for two hours. We are going to
stay here until she informs us of her decision.
We are not going to budge until she gives an
answer that satisfies the desires of the work-
ers of this country.

As in an endless filmstrip, the white handkerchiefs and the spiderweb of torches wave on
high again.

EVITA:
Comrades: as General Perón said, I will do as
the people say.

Final ovation. The *descamisados* fall to their
knees. The camera disappears overhead, moving
away from the divine Evita and her marvelous
music, from the altar where she has just been
sacrificed, from the torches lighted for her
night of mourning. [*Did she accept? All is not*
lost. But she did not accept.]

"I didn't know what to do with Evita's last sentence," I told the
hairdresser. "It's indecipherable. I confess I was tempted to leave it out.
Or cut it in two, which would change the meaning of it. I thought
of showing Evita saying, 'Comrades, as General Perón said.' And
then there would be a silence, ellipsis dots, maybe a shot of the crowd
urging her to say yes. There are thousands of yards of film in newsreels showing all sorts of emotions. Those emotions could be catego-
rized, and two or three of the most suitable ones could be inserted.
At the very end, I'd go back to a close-up of Evita with the second
part of the sentence: 'I will do as the people say.' There's no need to

explain to you that techniques like that are common currency in film editing. A jump cut or a fade-out suffices to invent another past. In films there is no history, there is no memory. It's all contemporary life, pure present. The only thing that's real is the viewer's awareness. And time has turned that last sentence of Evita's, the one that got the crowds at the Open Meeting so excited, into empty air. Without the emotion of the moment, it doesn't mean a thing. Just look at the syntax. It's very odd. Perón told me to do as the people say, but as the people tell me to do isn't what Perón told me."

"All Evita's speeches are alike," the hairdresser broke in. "All of them except this one. She was very skillful with emotions but clumsy with words. As soon as she stopped to think, it screwed her up. What you've written is fine, what else can I say? You did the best you could. It's the official history. The other one isn't on film. It's beyond film. And it couldn't even be invented, because the actress who played the lead has died."

Day was dawning. The tables at the Rex were beginning to fill up with telephone receptionists and bank cashiers eating breakfast. At intervals, the sun made its way between the embroideries traced by the cigarettes and the idle flirting of the mosquitoes buzzing about, immune to the passage of morning and night, of drought and flood. I got up to go to the toilet. The hairdresser followed me and began to urinate alongside me.

"The most important thing is missing in that film," he said to me. "Something that only I saw."

He intrigued me, but I was afraid to ask. I said to him:

"Shall we take a walk?" I wasn't at all sleepy anymore.

We went down the steep slope of the calle Corrientes, past lottery-ticket vendors and stamp sellers' stands. I saw a woman with swollen cheeks and only one stocking running in and out among the cars, I saw teenage triplets speaking one at a time and all at once. I don't know why I noticed these things. My sleepless night was filling my mind with presentiments that came and went for no reason. As we went by the Hotel Jousten, almost at the bottom of the slope, the hairdresser offered to stand me a cup of hot chocolate. Along the en-

trance to the dining room were empty chaise longues that Alfonsina
Storni and Leopoldo Lugones had stretched out in before making up
their minds to kill themselves. In order to be able to talk together,
the people at the tables had to peer at each other through delicately
curved vases filled with a forest of tall plastic carnations. I won't
drag anyone through the swamps of the conversation that followed,
in which everything I said is superfluous. I shall confine myself to
transcribing the information given me by the hairdresser, which
complements, in almost the same tone, the account he had given me
fifteen years before:

*When the Open Meeting was over, Evita asked me to accompany her to the
presidential residence. There wasn't a soul out on the streets. We made our way
through nightmarish silences. Evita was shivering with fever again. I went upstairs with her to the little drawing room outside the bedroom and bundled her
up in a down comforter.*

"I'm going to have them bring you a cup of tea," I said to her.

"And another one for you, Julio. Don't go yet."

*She took off her shoes and undid the chignon. I don't remember now what
we talked about. I think I recommended a new nail polish to her. Just then we
heard voices echoing downstairs. The army personnel on the household staff
began bustling about, a sure sign that the general was there. Perón was a man
of austere habits. He ate very little, his entertainment consisted of listening to
comedy shows on the radio, and he went to bed early. His strident tones at that
moment took me by surprise.*

*"Evita, China!" I heard him call, in what seemed to me to be an irritated
voice.*

I didn't want to be in the way. I stood up.

*"Don't budge," the Señora ordered. And she ran out of the little drawing
room barefooted.*

The general must have been only a few feet away. I heard him say:

"Eva, we must talk."

"Of course we must talk," she repeated.

They went into the bedroom, but left the heavy door leading to the draw-

ing room ajar. If things hadn't happened so suddenly and so quickly, I would have left. But my fear of making a noise kept me from it. Perched tensely on the edge of my chair, I overheard the entire conversation.

". . . not argue anymore and listen to me," the general was saying. "In a little while the party is going to nominate you as its candidate. You're going to have to turn the nomination down."

"I don't intend to," Evita answered. "Those bastards who talked you into that can't force me to give up my candidacy. Neither can the priests nor the oligarchs nor those pricks in the military. You didn't want to proclaim me the party's candidate, right? My little greasers proclaimed me. If you didn't want me to be the candidate, you shouldn't have sent for me. It's too late now. Either they put me on the ticket or they don't put anybody. They're not going to shit on me."

Her husband let her vent her wrath. Then he said emphatically:

"Being stubborn isn't going to do you any good. They proclaimed you their candidate. But things can't go any farther. The sooner you announce that you're not running the better."

I sensed that she was backing down. Or was she only pretending?

"I want to know why. Explain it to me and I'll let it go at that."

"What do you want me to explain? You know as well as I do how things are."

"I'm going to speak on the national network," she said. Her voice trembled. "Tomorrow morning. I'm speaking and that'll be the end of that."

"That's best. Don't improvise. Have them write out a few words for you to say. Give up, but don't give any explanations."

"You're a bastard," I heard her burst out. "You're the worst one of all. I didn't want to be a candidate. As far as I'm concerned, you can shove the nomination up your ass. But I went this far, and it was because it was what you wanted. You brought me to the ball, right? Well, now I'm dancing. I'm speaking on the radio the first thing in the morning and I'm accepting. Nobody's going to stop me."

For a moment, there was a silence. I could hear both of them breathing hard, and I was afraid they'd hear me breathing hard too. Then he spoke. He spaced out the syllables and let them fall, one by one:

"You have cancer," he said. "You're dying of cancer and it's incurable."

I'll never forget the sound of the volcanic tears that erupted in the darkness where I was hiding. They were tears of real flames, of panic, of loneliness, of lost love.

Evita shouted:

"Shit, shit!" I heard the maids come running and left the presidential residence, walking in my sleep.

The hairdresser turned his face away. When our eyes met I avoided his gaze. He was a man too full of memories and old feelings, and I didn't want any of them to stick to me.

"Let's go now," I said. I wanted to get away from that morning, from the hotel, from what I'd seen and heard.

"I got back home around two in the morning," the hairdresser went on.

I sensed that he was no longer talking to me.

"My cousins were in their nightgowns, waiting up for me. From a refuge on the calle Alsina they'd seen the general arrive at the Open Meeting, but since the surging crowd swept them this way and that, when Evita spoke they were close to the presidential box, some twenty or thirty steps away. 'We saw her porcelain skin,' the one with the goiter told me. 'We saw her long fingers like a concert pianist's, the bright halo around her hair . . .' I interrupted her: 'Evita doesn't have a halo,' I said. 'You can't make me swallow that.' 'Yes she does,' the one with the nose bigger than the other one's insisted. 'We all saw it. At the end, when she told everybody goodbye, we also saw her rise three feet in the air, four maybe, who knows how many, she slowly flew up higher and higher above the box and you could see her halo very clearly. You had to be blind not to see it.'"

5

"I Resigned Myself to Being a Victim"

Two reproductions adorned the Colonel's desk at the Intelligence Service. The larger one was Blanes's inevitable oil painting showing the liberator José de San Martín resigned to the vicissitudes of war. The subject of the other one was order. It was a reproduction of a sketch in pencil and tempera in which Immanuel Kant is seen walking along the streets of Königsberg as his neighbors check the accuracy of their watches. The philosopher has an abscessed molar and a handkerchief tied round his head, but he is walking along at a good, steady clip, conscious of the fact that each one of his footsteps reinforces the city's routine and wards off the calamities of chaos. As they appear on the balconies or at the doors of their shops, his neighbors repeat their daily ritual of adjusting their watches to the precise moment that Kant passed by. Underneath the sketch, the work of the illustrator Ferdinand Bellerman, a caption in German proclaims: "My homeland is order."

Exactitude was habitual with the Colonel. Each morning he wrote down in a notebook the tasks that he had already finished and the ones that he planned to undertake. Among those for that day was one that had come as a sudden shock: Evita. Alone with the embalmer in the sanctuary, the Colonel had at last seen the body in the glass prism. Seeing it had not been as great a surprise to him as had his difficulty in recovering from something so abnormal as surprise. Just as Dr. Ara's notes had proclaimed, Evita was a liquid sun, the arrested flame of a volcano. In these circumstances it's going to be hard to protect her, he thought. What is moving there inside her? Rivers of gas, of mercury, of dry ice? Perhaps the embalmer is right, and the body will turn to vapor during the transfer. It must be poisonous. And what if the corpse that I've seen isn't hers? This suspicion kept nagging at him, like a piece of furniture out of place.

He wrote in the notebook: *November 22. How many bodies are there? Perhaps the mother knows more of the details. Talk to her. Make an indelible mark on the Woman: brand her like a mare. Find out where the copies are. Decide on the secret place where she is to be kept until further orders. Draw up plans for the transfer operation. Set the date and the time: on the twenty-third at midnight?*

There was too much work to do. He must begin at once. He picked up the phone and called doña Juana. He waited a long time while they went to get her: he heard over the phone her halting footsteps as she came to answer, her asthmatic breathing, her cracked voice:

"What is it they want of me now?"

"This is Colonel Moori Koenig," he announced in a voice that came flowing out in capital letters. "The president of the Republic has ordered me to see to it that your daughter is given a decent burial. There is no closer relative than you left in the country. I need to see you about a few formalities. May I . . . ?"

"They haven't asked my permission for any of the things they've done. I don't see why they're now—"

"I'll be at your house before noon. Are you . . . ?"

"I've been asking for my family's passports for days now," the mother said. After every word or two, she cleared her throat. "The police won't give them to me. Perhaps you can do something. Bring them to me. I want to get out of here. My whole family is leaving. This country has become unlivable."

"Unlivable?" the Colonel repeated.

"Come on over. It's time to put an end to all this."

He looked through the daily papers piled up on his desk for a news item about the corpse. They hadn't carried one line about it for months now. Out of superstition, out of fear? Everything could come to light at any moment. Now that the body was about to pass from hand to hand, nobody was in control of keeping the operation a secret. He read: "BUILDING LOTS ON THE MOON FOR SALE IN U.S. *New York (AP)*. A dubious development corporation founded by the ex-president of the Hayden Planetarium has rounded up four thousand five hundred clients prepared to invest a dollar each." "NO INCREASE IN FUEL PRICES FOR NOW. This was officially announced by the minister of industry, Alvaro Carlos Alsogaray, who is collaborating in drawing up a plan for the economic recovery of the country, which has been ruined by the policies of the deposed dictator. In a radio speech broadcast yesterday, the provisional president of the Republic, General Pedro Eugenio Aramburu, emphasized the unwavering solidarity of all the cadres of the military in the face of the crisis brought on by the Liberation Revolution . . ." The Colonel read even the fillers carefully. Nothing. What a relief. Nothing.

He looked out of the big, dark bulletproof windows of his office and contemplated the jacarandas, stubbornly flowering still, along the avenida Callao. Bees were buzzing above the tops of them. The peace of their hives was on a different key than the racket raised by the buses and streetcars. Bees in Buenos Aires? It was spring, an excess of leaves and litter blocked the street drains, the bees were not disrupting the symmetrical order of life.

Once the sun was up, doña Juana's garden was also full of bees. The mother had come out to get a breath of early morning air and suddenly spied the zigzagging of the swarm overhead. She went back into the house to tell everyone about this most unusual sight and just then someone knocked discreetly at the front door. At that hour?

Through the peephole she recognized the bald pate of the butler at the presidential residence who had devotedly served Evita till the eve of her death. Atilio Renzi. He had two folders in his hand and wanted to leave them with her.

"What's this you've brought me, Renzi? What am I supposed to do with these?"

"They are things your daughter wrote. I got them out of the residence with great difficulty."

"You keep them, Renzi. I'm just about to leave Buenos Aires. Keep them for me till I come back."

"I brought them to you at the risk of my life, doña Juana," the man persisted. "I shouldn't like to think that what I did wasn't worth doing."

When Renzi himself told me the story, fourteen years later, there was scarcely anyone who still remembered him. I had to search through several archives before I found a few traces of his past life. From what I could see, it had been a full one. Atilio Renzi. A blurred photograph in *Democracia* shows him asking the women praying, in the rain, for the Señora's health at the entrance to the presidential residence to do so in silence. A short, stiff-backed man with sweaty palms: the faithful butler who followed Evita about like a shadow and disappeared from sight when she died. I read that he had been an infantry sergeant before Perón put him on his personal staff, first as a chauffeur and then as the butler at the presidential palace. But Renzi very soon became a convert to the worship of Evita and served Perón only by his deference. Whenever she received her humble followers, the butler felt sorry for himself as well and shed a few tears. The Señora felt ashamed for his sake and she would say to him, sotto voce: "Go into the bathroom, Renzi. I don't like to see you making a spectacle of yourself." In the bathroom, he would think to himself: "I mustn't cry, I mustn't cry. She's putting up a good front and here I am, making a laughingstock of myself." But the thought made him weep all the harder.

"I Resigned Myself to Being a Victim"

Renzi arrived at doña Juana's around eight. His bald pate was beaded with sweat, his hat was trembling in his hands, and he couldn't manage to hide his frayed shirt cuffs. Doña Juana cleared a path to allow him to make his way through the suitcases piled up all over the entry hall, but Renzi informed her that it was no use bothering.

"I must leave immediately," he said, though it wasn't true.

The one time I spoke with him, he told me that his courage had failed him. "I couldn't wait to leave, God knows!" he said to me. "To simply hand her the papers and get out of there."

He had been the butler at the presidential palace for three years when the rumor reached his ears that Evita was slowly dying of cancer. To see her so emaciated, nothing but skin and bones, awakened in Renzi a devotion more powerful than his imperturbable decorum: he wiped away her urine, rubbed her swollen feet with oil, dried her tears, and wiped her nose. To persuade her that the cancer had not made her frightfully thin, he removed all the full-length mirrors and adjusted the bathroom scales so that they always read one hundred two pounds. And as she lay dying, and processions of women came from the outskirts of Buenos Aires to the Plaza de la República, crying out for a miracle that would save her life, Renzi tampered with the radio set so that Evita wouldn't hear the terrible, prolonged weeping of the crowds.

When the Señora died, Perón began to disappear from the residence for weeks at a time, and the butler, left with nothing to do, silently wandered about the empty corridors with a feather duster in his hand, chasing after impossible motes of dust. In Renzi's memory (a coward's memory, as he put it, from which the happy moments had disappeared), the presidential palace was gradually going to ruin: patches of mildew suddenly appeared on the damask upholstery of the armchairs, the gold tassels on the curtains fell off, and during the night the termites could be heard gnawing frantically away in the banisters along the staircases. Perón hated the house, and the house hated him. There was no truce between them until he was deposed and decided to flee the country.

The morning he took off, Renzi accompanied him to his car, carrying his valises, and when the general turned around to give him a farewell embrace, the butler pretended not to notice and went back inside with his arms akimbo. He paid the servants their last wages and ordered them to leave, paid himself, and decided to wait the night out in the Señora's room, which had been kept closed since the eve of her funeral. Everything was still there, just as it had been, the Dior bras and panties that Evita had ordered in her last hours and the evening dresses that the couturier Jamandreu had had made for her, three days before the end, believing that he was keeping her hopes up. Renzi stroked those belongings left in the wake of the body that he had worshiped with such devotion; breathed in the last remaining traces of rouge, of Coty face powder, of Chanel No. 5; spread out on top of the bed the silk slips and satin pajamas kept stored in her dresser drawers beneath layers of transparent plastic; placed around his neck the ermine stole that the Politburo of the Soviet Union had sent the Señora as a gift early in 1952, with a note from Stalin himself; and burst into tears on top of the pillows where she had wept and cursed the motherfucking death that had given birth to her.

As darkness fell he was suddenly overcome with curiosity. He opened the writing desk in which Evita kept her letters and photographs and examined them with the intention of taking a few of them with him. He found a message with instructions for the manicurist, written before her illness, and several photos of her, taken on her last ventures out-of-doors, which she herself had taken a pair of scissors to and cut off the legs, perhaps because in her state of extreme emaciation they looked more like sticks.

He turned a few lights on to scare off prowlers. In those first hours following General Perón's escape, the country was still without a government, and according to what they said on the radio, there was to be a cease-fire for the duration of the deliberations of the generals and the admirals. It kept raining and people stayed indoors out of fear of sharpshooters. Since early that morning the guards had been withdrawn from the presidential residence, inasmuch as there was no longer anyone there to guard.

There was a secret door between the drawers of the writing desk, which could be opened by pressing a hidden spring; behind it Renzi discovered some fifty manuscript pages that appeared to be a draft of the book, entitled *My Message,* written by the Señora during her illness. The handwriting was erratic. Some sentences, penned in angular characters, gradually broke down into uneven, separate letters, as though the breathing of the words were little by little turning Evita into different persons. Other pages, where the writing was regular and careful, must have corresponded to times when she lacked the strength to get out of bed and preferred to dictate. A second folder contained a copy of the same text, typed this time, although with noticeable changes and omissions.

In the bottom of the hiding place was a pile of school composition books dated 1939 and 1940, when Evita was embarking on her career as a stage actress. The odd-numbered pages began with words underlined several times, *Nales, Hare, Legs, Makup, Nose, Esercises,* and *Hospittle Espenses,* all of them followed by a list of reminders with all the items left unfinished.

Renzi began to read them but stopped, surprised at his indiscretion. He had always been most respectful of the Señora's privacy while she was alive, and he thought that he ought to be even more discreet now that Evita was no longer there to protect herself. Those notebooks corresponded to the most wretched stage of her short life and therefore should not be allowed to fall beneath the gaze of an outsider. They were things only her mother should read, Renzi thought, and it was at that moment that he decided to take them to doña Juana. He left the typed pages of *My Message* in the secret compartment of the desk and hid the school composition books and the manuscript of the book among the clothes in his suitcase. At midnight he double-locked all the doors of the presidential residence and went out in the rain in search of a taxi.

Two months later, when he finally worked up the courage to seek out doña Juana, she was too nervous to appreciate the real value of those documents. She carelessly dumped them on top of the valises and thanked him for his gift with one of those gauche, thoughtless phrases that had given her the reputation of being heartless: "Just look at the state this house is in, and then on top of it you come bringing me more papers. Have you seen the bees outside? Just look. They terrify me. There are thousands of them." Renzi turned around and without saying goodbye left, forever, both that entry hall and this story.

In the bedroom, the mother underwent another attack of cramps in her legs. It was hot and the damp air was as heavy as mire. She clung to a brief interval without pain, and as she lay there without moving she had the sensation that her fingertips were touching the end of something. The end of the world? I'm not the one who's taking off, it's everything around me. This is the end of my country. The end without Eva, without Juancito. The end of my family. We've fallen to the other side of death without realizing it. When I try to see myself in the mirror, I won't see anything, there won't be anybody there. I can't even go away from here, because I've never come.

She now remembered as happiness everything that she had once experienced as unhappiness. She missed pedaling the sewing machine that she'd ruined her eyesight using, the games of cards with the lodgers of her pension in Junín, the honeysuckle on the unwhitewashed walls, the afternoons when she went out for a stroll along the railroad tracks, the fights with the neighbors and the Wednesday night movie, when she used to get a lump in her throat over Bette Davis's fits of hysteria and Norma Shearer's lovelorn life. That was only half of what she missed, because she no longer had the strength to miss all of it. She had allowed that other half to work itself loose from her weary flesh and knock at the doors of other bodies. She couldn't take any more, blessed Jesus; even her soul had had enough.

She stayed in bed till her muscles that had come unhinged from the cramps came to their senses again. She heard the door knocker and the Colonel's guttural voice, introducing himself. She sighed. She powdered her face, hid the wrinkled pouches of her jaws with a scarf, and covered her disheveled hair with a black turban. This done, she went to meet her visitor, as though her day had just begun.

The Colonel had been waiting for her for more than fifteen minutes. In the living room with dark parquet flooring, there stood, helter-skelter, as in a bazaar, a plastic sofa with arms veined to look like marble; a provincial, vaguely Breton, sideboard; a rectangular oak table with mahogany chairs at each end, and on the mantel a rustic altar, with a fruit bowl full of fresh flowers beneath a portrait in oil of Evita. In spite of the unwelcoming decor, sunlight filled the room, pouring though the skylight in the ceiling. A spiderweb of scrabbling noises was also coming from overhead. Bees? the Colonel wondered. Or perhaps birds. From above, two expressionless faces were peering at him. Both bore a distant resemblance to Evita. At irregular intervals, a hand rose above the face on the left. It had long fingernails, painted a color that changed from green to violet. Every so often the fingernails landed on the glass of the skylight and slid across it. The sound was so faint, so muffled, that only ears as sharp as the Colonel's could hear it. Where had he seen those bright heads of hair before? In the newspapers, he realized. They were Evita's sisters. Or perhaps two women imitating the sisters? From time to time they pointed to him and broke off what they were saying, giving him foolish smiles. The moment the mother came into the living room the faces disappeared from the glass.

The Colonel was surprised to note that her voice and her appearance didn't go together. Her voice was fluty and she had to push and shove to get it out, as though it were having a hard time getting past the censorship of her false teeth. Her bearing, on the other hand, was imposing.

"You are Moori Koenig, are you not? Have you brought me the

passports?" she asked, without inviting him to sit down. "My daughters and I wish to leave the country at once. We're smothering to death in this hotbed of intrigue."

"No," the Colonel answered. "A passport isn't a simple matter."

The mother collapsed on the plastic sofa.

"You want to talk to me about Evita," she said. "Go ahead and talk then. What are you going to do with her?"

"I've just seen the embalmer. The government has given him one or two days to finish up with the baths and the salves. Then we'll give your daughter a decent burial, with all her decorations, as you've asked."

The mother's lips tensed.

"Where are you going to take her?" she asked.

The Colonel didn't know.

"Various sites are being studied," he improvised. "Perhaps beneath the altar of a church, perhaps in Monte Grande cemetery. At first we won't mark her grave, no tombstone, no plaque, nothing that would identify her. Until people have calmed down, we must be very discreet."

"Deliver the passports to me, Colonel. It's best. The minute I have them, I'm taking her with me. There's no reason for Evita to go to a nameless grave, as though she didn't have any family left."

"That's not possible," the Colonel said. "That's not possible."

"Name a date. When can I leave?"

"Today, if you like. Tomorrow. It's up to you. All I need is your authorization for the burial. And the papers. That's right. The papers."

The mother stared at him in bewilderment. "What papers?"

"The ones Renzi brought you this morning. You must give them to me."

He heard the scrabbling at the glass again and thought he saw, overhead, the face of one of the sisters. She had her hair done up in curlers and her round eyes were open wide, like Betty Boop's.

"That's the last straw," the mother said. "It smells to high heaven. What kind of country is this anyway? The lot of you take our passports away from me, you watch to see who comes in and out of my house, you won't leave me alone. They say Perón was a tyrant, but you people are worse, Colonel. You're worse."

"Your son-in-law was corrupt, señora. There are only gentlemen in this government: men of honor."

"You're all one big pile of shit," the mother muttered. "Honor that stinks. Excuse the expression."

"Renzi's papers," the Colonel said insistently. "You must hand them over to me."

"They're not mine. They aren't anybody's. Renzi told me they were Evita's, but I didn't even have time to look at them. I don't intend to give them to you. Pretend they don't exist."

"I'm going to take them with me anyway," the Colonel said. "These are the ones, right?"

He tried to gather up the composition book and the manuscript piled atop the jumble of valises, but the mother got there ahead of him. She grabbed them and defiantly sat down on top of them.

"Get out of here, Colonel. You've driven me out of my mind."

The Colonel sighed, resignedly, as though he were speaking to a child.

"I'll make you a deal," he said. "Give me those papers, sign this official release, and I'll send you the passports tomorrow afternoon. I give you my word."

"All of you lie to me," the mother answered. "I've already given Dr. Ara a signed authorization. And now you're asking me for an official release. You're all liars."

"I'm an army officer, señora. I can't lie to you."

"You're a man. That's reason enough for me not to believe you." She smoothed her skirt and sat there for a time shaking her head. Then she said:

"What do I have to sign?"

The Colonel took out of his briefcase a typewritten document, bearing a letterhead with the seal of the Ecuadorian Embassy, and showed it to her. It said: *I, Juana Ibarguren de Duarte, hereby accede to the*

*transfer by the Superior Government of the Nation of the body of my daugh-
ter Evita from the place where it is now located to another that will ensure its
eternal safety. I express this wish of my own free will.* At the bottom, two
witnesses attested to the fact that the mother had signed in their
presence, on October 15, 1955. It was all false, as we now know: the
date, the letterhead, the witnesses.

"I'll send you the passports tomorrow," the Colonel repeated,
handing her a pen. "Tomorrow, without fail."

The mother moved aside and handed him the folders. They
would take them away from her sooner or later. The Colonel or
somebody else would take them away from her, sooner or later, as
they pleased.

"You'd better keep your promise," she said, stressing the syllables.
"I'm not all by myself, Colonel. I'm not defenseless."

"You needn't threaten me. I'll keep my word."

"Go now," the mother said, getting to her feet. "Take care of my
daughter. Don't bury a copy by mistake."

The skittering at the skylight became stubborn and monotonous.
A long spindle of bees spun out their routine above the glass.

"Don't worry. The body has an identification mark."

"What about the copies? Have they handed the three copies over
to you yet?"

"Don't exaggerate," the Colonel said patronizingly. "There's only
one."

"There are three. I've seen them. The one reading the letter impressed me most. She seemed to be alive. I even thought it was
Evita."

She began to weep. She tried to keep the tears back, but they kept
welling up all by themselves, from somewhere else, from all the pasts
she'd lived in.

"Listen to the bees," the Colonel said. "They're all over the city.
It's odd. And the radio, I don't know why . . . They don't say one
thing on the radio about these plagues."

Once outside in the pitiless yellow weather, the Colonel gave in,
for an instant, to the disorder of fury. Three copies of the body. He

absolutely must get his hands on them at once. He pondered what the mother had said to him. All her sentences dissolved into a single detested, lethal word, the word or the name that would buzz about in his thoughts but never on his lips. He turned on the car radio. Antonio Tormo, Feliciano Brunelli's folk group, a Bach partita: it all exasperated him. He counted to twenty, to no avail. He tried breathing exercises:

EVITA. Verb. Conjug.: 3rd pers. sing. of *evitar* (from Lat. *evitare, vitare*). To avoid. To evade. To elude. To keep something about to happen from happening.

He would avoid the word. He would avoid the unwholesome words close to it: *levity* [noun], frivolity, lightness; *levitate* [verb] (occult), to rise in the air without visible support; *vital* [adj.], pertaining to life. He would avoid all language contaminated by the aura of bad luck surrounding that woman. He would call her Mare, Colt, Bug, Cockroach, Friné, Estercita, Milonguita, Butterfly: he would use any of the names that were now going the rounds, but not the accursed one, the forbidden one, not the one that rained down misfortune on the lives that invoked it. *La morte è vita,* Evita, but *Evita è morte* as well. Watch it. *La morta Evita è morte.*[3]

---

[3] Helvio Botana, who told me of the Colonel's obsession with etymologies of the word *Evita,* insisted (interview, September 29, 1987) that I should cite the exact sources of the other names she was known by. *Mare* and *Bug* were common ways of referring to Evita among the army officers opposed to Perón, at least from the beginning of 1951 on. *Friné* and *Butterfly* were nicknames for her popularized by Ezequiel Martínez Estrada's columns in the weekly *Propósitos.* According to Botana, *bug* and *cockroach* were words that meant "vagina" in Buenos Aires prison slang. *Estercita* and *Milonguita* come from the tango "Milonguita," composed in 1919—the year that Evita was born—by Samuel Linnig and Enrique Delfino. Its most celebrated verse is:

> Estercita!
> Today they call you Milonguita,
> Party girl, dancing in a cabaret,
> Flower of night and never day.
> Milonguita!
> Men have done you wrong,
> And today you'd give your soul
> To dress in clothes bought for a song.

I am going to tell of the other facts of the day, avoiding the overemphasis they have had to carry. I am simply going to set them down, one after the other, like a beekeeper.

With an escort of six soldiers, the Colonel reappeared in the CGT building at lunchtime. On entering the lobby on the ground floor, he noticed that the debris of Evita's bust, destroyed the previous night by an armored tank, had not yet been removed. The small escort was armed with Mausers and Ballester Molina pistols, not bothering to obey the orders for secrecy and caution issued by the new ruling authorities of the Republic. The Colonel disarmed the guards posted on the second floor, ordered them to return to their garrisons, and replaced them with soldiers loyal to the new regime.

Dressed in a work apron, Dr. Pedro Ara appeared in the corridor and tried to reason with the Colonel. It was useless, because the Colonel now accepted no other reason but force. He pushed the embalmer toward the laboratory and stood there interrogating him, unable to avoid (accursed verb) an occasional temptation to use violence. At first Ara pretended to know nothing of the existence of other copies apart from the one which, that very morning, he had claimed had disappeared. Then when the Colonel cited the mother's revelations, he collapsed. The copies weren't his, he said. They belonged to the Italian sculptor who had been working on the prodigious monument to the Señora and had left behind him, when he fled the country, a wake of cameos, bas-reliefs, coats of arms, sculptures, terra-cotta virgins, caryatids, death masks, and images of the Señora, surprisingly real because they were life-size, and because the Señora was captured in them, the copies, as though in a photograph of paradise.

The Colonel wasn't interested in explanations. He was interested in the copies. "They're here, within reach of anyone," the embalmer informed him. "Upright, in crates, behind the curtains of the sanctuary." Laboratory tests would later reveal that the false Evitas had been made of a mixture of wax, vinyl, and very small additions of fiberglass. They could be distinguished from the real body because they looked more deeply tanned—a precaution that anticipated the inevitable change of color of embalmed tissues—and because they were all looking down.[4]

"You are no longer needed here, Doctor," the Colonel said. "Leave the corpse in the glass case and go. I have ordered this second floor closed. I have declared it a military area."

Stretched out on the glass, Evita's body refused to obey orders and behaved according to her own funereal logic. Her nostrils began to give off blue and orange gases. What's troubling her now? the Colonel wondered. She's perfect, she doesn't need anything. She isn't suffering from nightmares or from cold. She's immune to illnesses and bacteria. She has no reason to be sad now. He examined her from head to foot. The tip of her left earlobe and the last joint of the middle finger of her right hand were missing. The coroners called in by the government had cut them off in order to identify her. It was her, it was her: there was no doubt about it. Nonetheless, he needed to put his brand on her: a scar that only he would be able to recognize.

He brought tweezers, scalpels, grooved catheters, from the laboratory. He raised the arch of her lip and studied the rows of teeth, being careful not to lose his composure. He stopped at her armpits. He saw the downy underarm hair clipped short, the plateau of her adolescent nipples, the flat round breasts: little barren breasts, half formed. A body. What's a body? the Colonel was later to say. Can the dead woman be called a body? Could that body be called a body?

The buttocks. The odd oblong clitoris. No. What a temptation the clitoris was. No; he must contain his curiosity. He would read the notes he'd taken on the clitoris. The passageways and spirals of the

[4]I have never seen the copies, but I can imagine them. At the end of 1991 I discovered, in the Whitney Museum in New York, human figures, made with polyester resins and fiberglass, that I mistook for live people. The sculptor's name is Duane Hanson, and works by him can be seen, I believe, in the Fort Lauderdale airport and the museum of the University of Miami. All the figures are looking down because, according to one of the catalogs, "the expression of the eyes is the only thing that art cannot reproduce."

ear: that was better. He lifted up the earlobe that was still intact. In the shadow of the cartilage, a gentle curve: a toboggan slide. He chose the tip. In the volute where the muscle of the human anatomy with the longest name, the sternocleidomastoid, ended, there was a virgin space still untouched by the embalming oils. He picked up a pair of the tweezers. Now. A hard pinch: a tiny bit of flesh. The removal of it had left an almost invisible star-shaped mark, an eighth of an inch across. Instead of blood, a trickle of yellow resin oozed out of it, evaporating immediately.

He ordered the doors of the laboratory and the sanctuary sealed with strips of tape with the warning: MILITARY ZONE. DO NOT ENTER. And then went out to breathe in the murky afternoon air, the clouds of vapor rising from the river, the rain of pollen.

What did he know about Evita, after all? He knew that she was vulgar, almost illiterate, a climber, a farm girl totally out of her element. In his notebook he had written: "A housemaid with the airs of a queen. Pushy, not at all feminine. Dripping with jewels so as to get her own back for the humiliations she'd suffered. Filled with resentment. No scruples. Shameless." But this was just letting off steam. He knew worse stories about her. He knew that, when she died, the letters asking for bridal dresses, furniture, jobs, toys, the inexpressible, had to be addressed to her in person in order to get an answer. Letters to Evita. And he knew that she promptly signed the answers to them, even after she was dead. Someone imitated her signature below phrases such as "I send you a kiss from heaven"; "I am happy here with the angels"; "I talk to God every day"; and so on. She had planned it that way, as she lay on her deathbed. Shameless.

He arrived at the office with a stubborn headache, a reflection of disorder of some sort. Food, sex? Certainly not: his life flowed on, following the same routine as always. Like Kant, like the seasons. The seasons? Something in the structure of nature was shifting, this minute. Tongues of fire were rising: columns a hundred and two degrees high. The branches of the trees were seething with honeycombs. He contemplated once again the meticulous reproduction of Bellerman's drawing. Other times. Kant's long, imperturbable stroll.

The watches obediently keeping time to his footsteps. There was no sun or dark of night or sign of a breeze, only the opaque light of eternity.

No one was listening. Nothing was moving now amid the folds of such a deep silence. No one was expecting an answer.

Then he wrote:

What do I know of the Character: the Deceased?

The documents I have examined show that she was born in two different places and on three different dates. According to the entry in the register of the parish church of Los Toldos or General Viamonte, she was born on May 7, 1919, on the farm and in the locality of La Unión, with a different name: Eva María Ibarguren. A ledger (for the year 1935) kept by the Comedia Theater shows altogether different data: "Evita Duarte, ingenue. Junín, November 21, 1917." The record of her marriage to Juan Perón gives her name as María Eva Duarte, born in Junín, May 7, 1922.

Forebears? Parents? Siblings?

An illegitimate child. Her father, Juan Duarte (1872–1926), was a descendant of Basque and Aragonese cattle farmers, vassals of other landholders. A man of average means, second-rate, a petty politician. Married, in Chivilcoy in 1901, Estela Grisolía, by whom he had three daughters. Arrived in Los Toldos in 1908 and rented several farms twelve miles from the railway station.

Juana Ibarguren (1894–),[5] her mother, worked as a servant on one of those farms. Also illegitimate, born of the chance relationship between Petronila Núñez, keeper of the post house in Bragado, and the Basque carter Joaquín Ibarguren, who was kind enough to give Juana his name before disappearing forever.

The mother began living with her employer in 1910, during the holidays celebrating the Centennial. At the beginning of the summer, shortly before the harvest, the Duartes and their legitimate chil-

[5] When he wrote these notes, the Colonel had no way of knowing that doña Juana's death date would be February 12, 1971.

119

dren came from Chivilcoy on a visit, and Juana had to hide in the farm huts. In March she had her first child, a daughter, Blanca. Duarte took up with her again in May, and from that time on, for nearly nine years, the couple repeated their monotonous cyclical routine of living together from April to November each year. Other children: Elisa, born in 1913; Juan Ramón, 1914; Erminda, 1917; Eva María, 1919. All except the latter were recognized by the father as his children. Four months after the birth of Eva María, Juan Duarte left Los Toldos forever. He visited his illegitimate offspring once or twice, but impatiently, distractedly, eager to escape from his past.

What happened after her father died in 1926?

(Report in code. Last line: oqlcjigntnwdabajwniofcioaohgefcjin-flfcjhgefcjinkfcjjiavigcvcjo)

When did the Deceased become an outstanding elocutionist? What were the first verses in her repertory?

In 1933, when she was in the sixth grade at School No. 1 in Junín, her teacher, Palmira Repetti, asked her to recite at the Ninth of July celebration. The Deceased chose for the occasion a brief poem entitled "How Nicely the Dead are Doing!" from Amado Nervo's famous collection *The Beloved Who Lies Motionless*. Urged on by señorita Repetti, that same day she appeared before the microphones of a housewares store, where she recited the poem of Nervo's she found most moving: "She's Dead!" from his collection *The Shadow of the Wing.*

When and why did she decide to leave Junín to try her luck as an artist in Buenos Aires?

(Report in code. Last two lines: ehngnfhczahdemekgaioqmen-qhcjigagqrgahckfnxfcznsafewcocadmqznafek8320xnfclkcbngga)

Did she take off from Junín with the singer Agustín Magaldi, age thirty-four, known as "the sentimental voice of Buenos Aires"?

(Report in code. Last two lines: kzcgaghgqnfecwgekfnxfczcjicfnx-clknnfmgaoocfhoahdemekgaxdcofcjhcigcocfzEIABCiejioddcinsafew)

The Deceased is known to have had difficulties making a reputation as an actress, remaining a minor figure until 1944. Who were the friends who furthered her career in the world of the theater and radio?

"I Resigned Myself to Being a Victim"

(List of names in code)

During the first seven months of 1943, the Deceased disappeared. She did not act either on the radio or in the theater, and the magazines covering the entertainment world scarcely mention her. What happened during this lapse of time? Was she ill, on a blacklist, back in Junín?

(Report in code. Last line: hdsioejadnfakhgeahgckeinnifcjhca-gezknwwenjcfcigafzochcwfck)

When the deposed dictator and the Deceased met each other in January of 1944, which of them seduced the other?

She introduced herself to him with a sentence that was a high-voltage come-on: "Thanks for existing, Colonel," and proposed that they sleep together that very night. She was always one to take the lead. She couldn't conceive of a woman's being passive in any domain, not even in bed, where it is nature's decree that she be passive. The colonel whose ambition it was to become dictator was, on the other hand, somewhat naive when it came to doing battle in bed: a sentimentalist, with unsophisticated tastes. It was she who seduced him. She knew very clearly what she wanted.

Is the Deceased known to have had a secret bank account in Zurich, Switzerland?

The Deceased owned 1,200 gold and silver brooches, 756 gold and silver objects, 650 pieces of jewelry, 144 ivory pieces, platinum necklaces and pins set with diamonds and precious stones valued at 19 million pesos, as well as real estate and stock in agricultural companies held jointly with her husband, the deposed dictator, valued for tax purposes at 16,410,000 pesos. This jewelry and these holdings were seized by the tax authorities in 1955. Both the diplomatic inquiries discreetly pursued by the government of the Liberation Revolution and the many investigations carried out by this Intelligence Service and others have revealed no secret bank accounts in the name of Juan D. Perón, María Eva Duarte de Perón, relatives of either spouse, or possible fronts.

On the death of the Deceased, the assets of the Foundation bearing her name were estimated to be more than 700 million pesos. Did she divert any portion of them for her own personal benefit?

She handled even larger sums exactly as she pleased, without accounting to anyone. She gave away houses, cash, and household equipment to faithful supporters with few means and to other nameless admirers. But despite scrupulous audits, there is no proof of any illegal misappropriations. The Deceased did not need to embezzle. She had everything she wanted and imagined that her power would be everlasting.

Is there any indication of marital infidelity on the part of the Deceased?

This matter has been thoroughly investigated. There is no such indication.

Is there any indication of marital infidelity on the part of the deposed dictator?

Strange as it seems, there is no indication of that either. Ex-ministers, ex-judges, ex–labor union bosses, and other accomplices of the tyrant's have been interrogated on the subject. The majority of them admit that he engaged in every sort of obscene and lecherous act imaginable, committed rape, sodomy, but only after the death of his wife.

Of what importance may this subject be to an Intelligence Service?

Of the utmost importance. The map of eroticism is the map of power. Instead of a wife's vulgar, nagging anxiety about keeping her husband, the Deceased pondered how to go about outdoing Perón. It was an absurd idea, but so were all her ideas. She turned it over and over in her mind, until she eventually arrived at a solution: she would outdo him by virtue of the weight of her love for him. The one who loves the most has the most power. There was no one more loyal, more loving, more reliable, more truthful than she. The vastness of her love included everything. It embraced her husband as well, it encompassed him. In other words, it devoured him.

According to the gynecological information available to us, the Deceased found herself unable to fulfill her intimate conjugal duties from the end of 1949 on, the period when she began to suffer from violent pains in her hips, bouts of fever and unexpected hemorrhages, and swelling in her ankles. In view of such a situation, how to explain the marital fidelity of the tyrant, who lacked erotic imagination but not desire?

Confidential sources explain it. Despite her dizzying round of activities, the Deceased never failed to satisfy her husband, until her strength gave out. She managed to make masturbation seem like penetration. Her tongue acted as a vagina. The dictator never had enjoyed such expert sex, nor did he ever find its equal after she died.

What was the last wish of the Deceased?

She told her mother what it was. The Deceased's last wish was that no man touch her naked, defenseless body, that no man speak of her body, that no one in the world witness her eternal emaciation and decline. The first to ignore that wish was the dictator, who had her embalmed and crassly showed her off to the masses for two weeks. I have no reason to respect anything. I would feel more at peace with myself if I could throw that last wish to the dogs.

When the Colonel raised his head, there was no longer a city round about him. There was semidarkness, a vague fog, the veiled light of the moon outside the windows. He must get to work, get a move on. At what pace? He still had to find the place where he would hide the real corpse, choose the contingent that would help him, set the time for the transfer. Then he would have to decide the fate of the copies, erase all the traces, take a shower, get some sleep. He leaned back and heard, far in the distance, the buzzing of bees.

6

"The Enemy Is Lying in Wait"

Shortly after midnight he went by his house. His wife was brushing her hair. Every time she wore it swept back, there was a hint of a re- semblance to the Deceased: the same round coffee-colored eyes be- neath eyebrows penciled in, the same white, more or less buck teeth. On other occasions, when they crossed paths, his wife would say to him: "I don't know you anymore. We've been married for fifteen years, and I know you less every day." This time that wasn't what she said to him. She said, rather:

"We must talk. It's lucky you came."

"Later," he answered.

"It's important," she insisted.

The Colonel went into the bathroom, and then, stretched out on the sofa in his study, he began to drop off to sleep. Hung on the walls were pencil sketches that he'd drawn for his own amusement: cities seen from above, rows of Gothic towers.

His wife knocked timidly at the door and poked her head in. The Colonel gave her an annoyed look.

"They keep phoning," she said. "When I answer, they hang up."

"Some maniac," the Colonel commented indifferently. "You can tell me about it later. I need to get some sleep."

"It's never the same person who calls," his wife said. "Sometimes it's someone who just stays on the line for a while, breathing. All you can hear is wheezing. At other times, somebody says: 'Tell your husband not to play with fire. To leave the señora where she is.' This morning they began with threats. I can't repeat them. They say my name, and then a bunch of obscenities. 'Who's the señora?' I asked. But they hung up."

"What are their voices like?" the Colonel said. "Voices of black Peronists or of military officers?"

"How should I know? Do you think I'd notice things like that?"

"Pay attention. Next time try to record their voices in your head."

"A while ago, around ten, they rang the doorbell downstairs. They told me they were bringing a letter from you. 'Leave it under the door,' I told them. 'We can't,' they answered. 'The Colonel has given orders to hand it to you personally.' They wanted me to come outside. I refused. After the phone calls, I was scared to death. 'It's something serious,' they told me. 'Very serious.' I thought something had happened to you. I put on a bathrobe and went down to the street. There was a car parked in front of the door, a green Studebaker. They pointed a pistol at me, and when I started screaming, they drove off. They didn't do anything: they just wanted to show me they could kill me whenever they liked."

"You were an idiot," the Colonel said. "Why did you go outside?"

"I went out so they wouldn't come up to the house. I went out of sheer terror. Who is that señora? What is it you're mixed up in?"

The Colonel was silent for a moment. He had always had a hard time understanding women. He could scarcely talk to them. Lace edgings, scarlet fever, hair curlers, braids, organdy, nail polish: none of the things that interested them were of any interest to him. To him women were like scales that had fallen from another world, afflictions like fever and body odor.

"Nothing's going on," he said. "Why should I explain something you wouldn't understand?"

Just then the phone rang again.

* * *

The sources on which this novel is based are not altogether reliable, but only in the sense that this is true of reality and language as well: lapses of memory and imperfect truths have found their way into them. One of Evita's most famous remarks reveals her idea of the way things were. On August 24, 1951, she said: "I am young and have a wonderful husband, respected, admired, and loved by his people. I find myself in the best of situations." Only one of these statements was not open to argument: the assertion that she was young. She was thirty-two years old. As for the rest, only Evita believed it. At that moment her husband was threatened by two simultaneous plots against him, and she herself, that very morning, had been informed by the doctors that she was suffering from pernicious anemia and should retire from public life. She was in the worst of situations. In eleven months she would be dead.

For historians and biographers, sources are always a headache. They are not self-sufficient. If a dubious source wants to enjoy the right to appear in print, it must be confirmed by another and that one in turn by a third. The chain is often endless and often useless, since all the sources taken together may add up to a lie. Take, for instance, Perón and Evita's marriage certificate, bearing the signature of a notary public of the city of Junín attesting that the facts recorded therein are true. The marriage is not false, but almost everything the document says is, from beginning to end. At the most solemn and historic moment of their lives, the contracting parties, as the phrase went in those days, decided to perpetrate an Olympian hoax on history. Perón lied about the place where the ceremony was performed and about his civil status; Evita lied about her age, her place of residence, the city she had been born in. Their statements were obviously false, but twenty years went by before anyone questioned them. In 1974, in his book *Perón, the Man of Destiny,* the biographer Enrique Pavón Pereyra nonetheless declared that they were true. Other historians settle for transcribing the document and fail to discuss whether the facts recorded are false. It has never occurred to anyone, however, to wonder why Perón and Evita lied. Did Evita add three years to her age so that the certificate wouldn't show that her bridegroom was twice as old as she was? Did Perón make himself out to be a bachelor because he didn't want to admit he was a widower? Did Evita make up the fact that she had been born in Junín because she was on record in Los Toldos as being illegitimate? These minor details didn't bother them. They lied because they could no longer tell what was true and what was false, and because, consummate actors both, they had begun to portray themselves in other roles. They lied because they had decided that, from that moment on, reality would be what they wanted it to be. They did the same thing novelists do.

Doubt had vanished from their lives.

Will anyone care to hear, nonetheless, how I came to know what I am recounting?

It is easy for me to list my sources: I know because of the interview I had with the Colonel's widow on June 15, 1991; I know because of my long conversations with Aldo Cifuentes in July 1985 and March 1988.

Cifuentes was the Colonel's last confidant and the person to whom he left his letters. He was a short man, a dwarf almost, loudmouthed, outrageous. He boasted of having read very few books in his life, but he had written sixteen of them: on the fathers of the Church, astrology, the Rosicrucian Enlightenment, the Sinn Fein movement in Ireland, the poorhouses of Monsignor De Andrea. His works were well documented, and therefore his professions of ignorance were, perhaps, just coyness. His father had founded a dozen periodicals in the twenties and had made a fortune from them by covering up for mafiosi and political bosses. Cifuentes used to tell how his father, before he died, had given him a notebook with the names of his nine hundred ninety-two mistresses. A number of them were ballerinas, spies, and famous actresses. "Forgive me," he had said to him. "I wasn't up to making it to a thousand."

Instead of mistresses, Cifuentes collected marriages. He was going on his sixth when Perón expropriated all the family's periodicals and left him bankrupt. Cifuentes strolled up and down the calle Florida to advertise his misfortune, dressed as a sandwich man with a board that read, in front and in back: LET US CULTIVATE A LOST REPUTATION. Within two blocks he was arrested for disorderly conduct. He took advantage of his two weeks or so in jail to write a libel against Evita entitled *The Kama Sutra of the Pampas*. The Colonel discovered him through this clandestine tract. He invited the author to lunch, expressed his admiration by citing the most obscene parts from memory, and, when he had finished, sealed an eternal pact of friendship with him, the first clause of which bound them to work together to overthrow the dictator.

Cifuentes was a virtuoso of gossip. He collected from all over the city stories about the Perón pair (that was what he called the two of them, emphasizing the alliteration) and then saw to it that they reached the Colonel's ears. The two men met once a week to scan the truths and lies of the stories and transfigure them into inside information that Cifuentes published in his tabloids and the Colonel used in his swaps of information with other Intelligence agents. Cifuentes' nickname in the army was Tom Thumb, not only because of his minimal size but also because, like the character in Perrault's story, wherever he went he left a trail of bread crumbs torn off an inexhaustible loaf of bread he carried about in his pocket.

When I met him, three or four years before his death, there was no way to satisfy his desperate urge to tell tales. I would toss out a name or a date, and he would catch it on the fly and transform it into a story from which many another flowed, like an endless delta. Nothing was harder than bringing him back to his starting point.

What is narrated in this chapter is based exclusively on my conversations with him (seven cassettes, each of them an hour long).

I listen to them again and note that Cifuentes stresses, so emphatically that it arouses my suspicion, how easy it was for him to go in and out of the Army Intelligence Service building in those last days of November 1955. A veteran Intelligence officer, insisting on anonymity, assures me that that was impossible. No civilian, he says, could get around the guards, the constantly changed passwords, the orders for the strictest secrecy that safeguarded the fate of the corpse. Neither Ara nor the mother could do so: it is even less likely that a man whom nobody knew would have been able to.

I don't know, though, which version I should keep. Why does history have to be a story told by sensible people and not the delirious raving of losers like the Colonel and Cifuentes? If history—as appears to be the case—is just another literary genre, why take away from it the imagination, the foolishness, the indiscretion, the exaggeration, and the defeat that are the raw material without which literature is inconceivable?

It is now dawn. The Colonel, in uniform, is crossing the avenue lined with bookstores and closed bars that separates his house from the fortress where his kingdom, the Intelligence Service, is located. He has scarcely slept.

A flash of lightning startles him; then he hears a peal of thunder. It is always like that in Buenos Aires: a swollen, ashen sky, clouds that scud about like madwomen, beams of light in a corner of the darkness where the plain may lie; and then nothing. The rain evaporates before it hits the ground.

The sentry at the Service opens the peephole in the gate halfway, recognizes him, and comes to attention. He is under orders not to open the gate until the entire ritual of the sign and countersign has been gone through. "Who goes there?" he asks. The Colonel looks at his watch. It is three minutes after five. "Tragedy," he says. If it had been one minute to five he would have had to say: "Grappling hook," and the reply would have been: "Gargle." Now, however, the sentry clicks his heels, answers "Trident," shuts off the alarms, and unbolts the gate. The countersigns change every eight hours, but once the Deceased is in his possession, the Colonel has decided that the intervals between will be reduced by half.

He goes upstairs to his office, on the fifth floor, and lights the kerosene lamp, now electrically wired. The room, remember, has large windows with panes of bulletproof glass in which the darkness is reflected, motionless, as in a painting. Two reproductions on the desktop proclaim the virtues of heroism and exactitude. Mention should also be made of the tall leather chairs, set around the oval table where the officers confer; the Venetian cabinet that contains the bookkeeping files and the military regulations concerning secrecy; the cedar Gründig hi-fi set, with two speakers, three and a half feet wide; the bookcase with the dictionary of the Royal Academy and several 78-r.p.m. records that the former head of Intelligence has left behind.

I now cite, almost verbatim, the story told me by Cifuentes, who repeated to me in turn the story that the Colonel had passed on to him twenty years before. I also cite some of the file cards that Cifuentes showed me and his notes recorded in a Rivadavia notebook:

"It must have been five minutes past five. At six, Colonel Moori Koenig was to meet with his general staff. Several details of the plan, as you know, had yet to be worked out. He told me that he had driven all through the city, several times. He told me that as he drove by the Waterworks, he remembered that in the southwest corner there were two empty, sealed rooms, originally built for the watchmen. You are familiar with the building. It is a ceramic absurdity that has nothing inside it except water pipes. Moori Koenig had seen the plans in the municipal archives and retained them in his memory out of professional habit. When he recalled this detail, he thought—he told me—of the Deceased. It was the perfect place to hide her.

"Moori Koenig, in those days, was a tiny, maniacal man. He had a perfect knowledge of the weak points of ministers, judges, division commanders. To talk with him was a bitter experience: you came away with a terrible opinion of your fellow humans. Imagine, then, how carefully he chose his assistants. He wasn't looking for men with spotless backgrounds. He preferred ones who had some sort of serious black mark against them, so as to be able to have a hold over them: a sister who was insane or deformed, a father with a criminal record.

"I have the file cards on which he summarized the history of the three officers from the Intelligence Service. It may be of interest to you to copy them:

My second in command is Eduardo Arancibia,[6] *an infantry major, married, age 34. Wife twelve years younger. (1) Amber eyes, eyebrows and hair black, no gray, 5'5" tall, small feet: wears size 8 shoes. Officer on the General Staff. His nickname in the War College: the Madman. Two of his uncles, his mother's brothers, are stutterers, mentally retarded. They are in El Carmen Home, in Mendoza. (2) Devout Catholic. (3) Infantile meningitis, with sequelae. Occasional attacks of asthma. (4) Worked for a year and a half in State Control under the tyrant, in the Ideological Repression division. Changed sides when Perón fell out with the Church. The president swears by him. (5) I include part of a letter that Arancibia sent his wife from Tartagal: "The only entertainment we have here is the shootings. We tie up six or seven dogs, place them against an adobe wall, and line up the platoon in formation. At the command 'Fire!' they must shoot them in the head. The soldiers are clumsy oafs. They always miss. Yesterday I began shooting. Out of seven dogs I hit six. The other one lay there bleeding for a long time. When I got tired of hearing it howl, I ordered them to finish it off." (6) Non-commissioned officer assigned him: Sergeant Major Juan Carlos Armani.*

Third in command, Milton Galarza, *former artillery captain, married, age 34, son 7 years old. (1) Wife with gallstones, latent nephritis, thyroid deficiency: a veritable catalog of ailments. Tall, nearly 6'7" (2) Plays the clarinet in secret (badly). This may be why they call him Benny Goodman. Has*

---

[6] On the Colonel's file cards, all the names of the officers and noncommissioned officers have been changed: Arancibia's name was not Arancibia; Galarza's was not Galarza. I am here being faithful to his wish for secrecy, as I am in chapter 11, where Arancibia's sister-in-law appears under a name not her own.

not finished his courses at the War College. Now too late for him to do so.
(3) An agnostic, perhaps an atheist. Hides the fact. (4) Was a support officer
in the failed attempt on the dictator's life in 1946. Worked as a double agent
in 1951. Was discovered. General L. saved his career, assigned him to a mili-
tary district in the jungle. (5) Confidential and secret paragraph from his ser-
vice record: "Report from the Clorinda garrison to commandant of the Second
Division, 04/13/54: Verified that in three routine truck runs from Misión
Tacaagle to Laguna Blanca, Captain M. G. fired at will on families of Toba
and Mocobí Indians. There is a written confession by the soldiers who drove
the trucks. M. G. used his regulation Mauser rifle and is short 34 pieces of
ammunition. M. G. was verbally reprimanded." (6) Noncommissioned officer
assigned him: Sergeant Major Livio Gandini.

    The last: Gustavo Adolfo Fesquet, *first lieutenant, age 29, sexual devi-*
ations highly likely. Bachelor. Called Plummy in the Military School. (1) Vase
of flowers on his desk, photograph of mama, blotter in a polished walnut
frame with tortoiseshell insets, bottle of Atkinsons perfume with an atomizer
in the second right-hand drawer, writer's handbook. (2) Catholic, regularly
takes Sunday communion. (3) Outstanding in cryptography. Uncertain evi-
dence against him in the archives of the Service: a voluntary declaration by
Private First Class Julio A. Merlini to the guard officer at R19 of Tucumán,
10/29/51. "Lieutenant Fesquet came and appeared in the enlisted men's bath-
room, where Private Acuña and I were urinating. He began urinating along-
side me. Private Acuña left. As I was shaking my penis to follow him out, the
lieutenant touched my member with the tip of one finger and asked me: Are you
happy? I said to him: Excuse me, sir, leaving immediately, with no further
consequences." Statement placed on record by order of the commandant of
R19. (4) Noncommissioned officer assigned him: First Sergeant Herminio
Piquard.

    "With those file cards, the Colonel thought that he had a clear
picture at last of the forces he could rely on, but this was not the
case. People, as you know, never stay the same: they get involved
with times, with spaces, with the moods of the day, and these hap-

penstances redesign them. People are what they are, and they are also what they are about to be.

"I know that at some moment early that morning he took the map of Greater Buenos Aires and spread out on top of it a sheet of tracing paper on which he had sketched Paracelsus's trident. Perhaps you've seen it. It has three tips in the form of isosceles triangles, joined together by a long base onto which the short, cylindrical handle fits. Paracelsus believed in the harmony of contraries. Thus the teeth of the trident symbolize inimical virtues, such as love, terror, and action.

"Buenos Aires is shaped like a pentagon and the trident consists of three triangles. Harmonizing those figures that call to mind so many symbols is a very delicate operation and, in inexpert hands, a very dangerous one. The trident is Satan, the eye of Shiva, the three heads of Cerberus, and also a replica of the Trinity. The pentagon is the Pythagorean sign of knowledge, though Nicholas of Cusa believed that pentagons attract or repel rains of fire. Moori Koenig studied the map as eagerly as an alchemist but also fearfully."

(Allow me to leave Cifuentes' recording for a moment to say that the fondness of the Argentine military for sects, cryptograms, and occult sciences has always surprised me. In the Colonel's cartographic operation, however, occultist influences were less evident than literary ones. I pointed out to Cifuentes that the Colonel's plan bore a certain family resemblance to the one that Borges describes in "Death and the Compass." He refused to concede the fact. Although I have read little of Borges, he said [or rather lied], I have some memory of that story. I know that it is influenced by the Kabbala and by Hasidic traditions. To the Colonel, the slightest allusion to anything Jewish would have been unacceptable. His plan was inspired by Paracelsus, who is Luther's counterpart, and at the same time the most Aryan of Germans. The other difference, he said to me, is more important. Detective Lönnrott's ingenious game in "Death and the Compass" is a deadly one, but it takes place only within a text. What the Colonel was plotting was to happen, however, outside of literature, in a real city through which an overwhelmingly real body was to be transported.

I now return to the recording. We have reached the point where side A of the first cassette ends. I listen to Cifuentes' voice.)

"When Moori Koenig placed the handle of the trident so that it exactly coincided with the South Dock, the ends of it went off the map and lay there pointing toward the milking yards and cattle ranges that can be seen in the distance beyond San Vicente, Cañuelas, and Moreno. These remote fields were of no use to him. He then moved the handle over the map until it was exactly at the corner of Buenos Aires, where he was standing underneath a lamppost. He looked at the time, he told me, because on the cutting edge of the reality he glimpsed, everything was a dizzying whirl. It was six minutes to six. His gaze was distracted for less than a second. This was enough time for the trident to contract and for the points of it to bury themselves, with incredible precision, in three specific places: the church in Olivos, alongside a railway station named Borges; the Celebrities Corner in La Chacarita cemetery; Ramón Francisco Flores's white mausoleum in Flores cemetery. That was the compass of chance that he had hope—"

End of the record(ing).

At the hour that the Colonel has set, they knock on the door. Arancibia, the Madman, sidles in; his regulation shoes have a humpbacked instep. Fesquet must have spent a terrible night. The ravages of it are etched into his face. Galarza, the clarinetist, leaves a wake of abdominal growls behind him as he enters. No one sits down. The Colonel rolls up the sheet of tracing paper with the trident and shows them the map, on which three red dots glisten.

It pleases him to overwhelm the officers with the revelations that he has been storing up since the previous morning. He tells them about the mother, about the embalmer. He explains to them that there is not just one body but four, and that this multiplication favors the Service's plans: the more traces the enemy must follow, the easier it will be to cover them.

"What's that you say?" Arancibia exclaims. "We haven't even begun and the enemy has already appeared?"

"There are several," the Colonel says curtly. He does not wish to alarm them by telling them that threats have filtered into his own house, over his private telephone.

Then he explains the overall outlines of the plan. Four identical coffins, modest ones, are needed: Galarza is to obtain them. The respective body assigned each of them will be buried between one and three a.m. the following day: Arancibia's at La Chacarita, Galarza's at Flores, Fesquet's at the church in Olivos. Each of them must see to it that there is no one around at the burial sites. The more secret their movements, the more difficulty their adversaries will have deciphering them.

"What reinforcements can we count on, sir?" Galarza wants to know.

"Just the four of us."

There was a long silence.

"Just the four of us," Arancibia repeats. "Too few for such a big secret."

"I'm the only authority on secrecy theory in this country," the Colonel goes on. "The one expert. I woke up thinking about it: infiltrations, counterintelligence, undercover activities, shortcuts, probability calculus, chance. I've planned every step of this operation down to the last detail. I've reduced the risks to two or three percent. The most vulnerable aspect of the plan is the support contingent. Each one of us needs four enlisted men and a truck. All of you have, moreover, a noncommissioned officer to assist you. They'll be waiting for us at midnight at commando headquarters. The men are coming from different regiments and battalions. They do not know each other. The trucks are closed ones and have no peepholes: just vents. None of the men must know where he's come from or where he's going. At zero-fifteen a.m. we meet in the garage of the CGT. The place looks like any other. And I don't care what the men think. All I care about is what they might say."

"Brilliant," Galarza says. "If the men don't meet each other again, they're never going to be able to reconstruct the story. And there is no possibility that they'll ever meet again."

"There's one possibility in a hundred fifty thousand," the Colonel points out. "They're draftees from the provinces. Day after tomorrow they'll be discharged."

"Impeccable," Galarza, the clarinetist, says emphatically, fighting back an avalanche of rumbling noises from his bowels. "Only one detail worries me, sir. In view of the need for complete secrecy, neither the enlisted men nor the NCOs ought to drive the trucks."

"Correct, Galarza. We're the ones who are going to drive."

Fesquet sighs and flops one of his limp hands in the air.

"I'm a very poor driver, sir. And I might not be up to it. The responsibility, the darkness, you know. I don't have the courage."

"You must drive, Fesquet," the Colonel orders in a cutting voice. "There are four of us. There must not be anyone else."

"There's something that puzzles me," Galarza comments. "That woman, the body: it's a mummy, right? She's been dead for three years. What do we want her for? We could throw her out of a plane into the middle of the river. We could put her inside a sackful of quicklime, in a common grave. Nobody's asking about her. And if anyone does ask, we don't have to answer."

"It's an order from above," the Colonel says. "The president wants her to have a decent burial."

"That Mare?" Galarza exclaims. "She fucked us all our lives."

"She fucked us all right," the Colonel says. "Other people believe she was their salvation. We have to cover ourselves."

"It might be too late," Arancibia, the Madman, says. "Two years ago it could have been done. If we'd killed the embalmer, the body would have decomposed all by itself. It's too big a body now, bigger than the country. It's too full of things. We've all kept putting something into it: shit, hatred, wanting to kill it again. And as the Colonel says, there are people who have put their tears into it too. That body is like loaded dice now. The president is right. The best thing to do is bury it, it seems to me. Under another name, in another place, till it disappears."

"Till it disappears," the Colonel repeats, still chain-smoking. He bends over the map of Buenos Aires. He points to one of the red dots, to the north, almost at the river's edge. "Fesquet," he says. "What's this?" The first lieutenant studies the area. He spies a train station, two railway tracks that cross, a yacht marina.

"The river," he guesses.

The Colonel looks at him, not saying a word.

"It's not the river, Fesquet," Galarza points out. "It's where you're going."

"Ah, yes: the church, in Olivos," the lieutenant says.

"This green square is a plaza," the Colonel says, as though he were speaking to a schoolchild in a classroom. "Here, on the corner, next to the church, there is a garden covered with crushed stone with an iron fence around it; it is thirty feet wide by about six feet deep. It has spurge, begonias, succulents, planted all over. Lay out a plot that looks like a flower bed over here, against the wall. Put flowerpots or something all around it. Have the enlisted men dig a deep grave. Hide it, so that nobody can see it from the street."

"It's a churchyard," Fesquet remembers. "What do I do if the parish priest won't let us do our work?"

The Colonel clutches his head. "Can't you solve the problem, Fesquet? Can't you? You have to. This isn't going to be easy."

"Don't worry, sir. I won't fall down on the job."

"If you do, say goodbye to the army. You must all get it through your heads that on this mission failure is unacceptable. I don't want anybody coming to me afterwards to tell me that something or other came up that he hadn't foreseen. Now is the time when you must anticipate every possible variable."

"I'll go to the church and ask for a permit," Fesquet stammers.

"Ask for it at the archbishop's," the Colonel says. He stretches, tosses back the toboggan slope of his forehead, and half closes his eyes. "Just one thing more. Let us synchronize our watches, and go over the sign and countersign again."

He is interrupted by a couple of timid knocks at the door. It is First Sergeant Piquard, his hair disheveled. One of the locks covering his bald spot has escaped from its prison of pomade and is drooping pathetically down toward his chin.

"Urgent message for Colonel Moori Koenig," he announces. "This envelope has been brought from the office of the president of the Republic, along with an order that it is to be delivered at once, to you personally."

The Colonel feels the envelope. Inside it, he notes, are two sheets: one of cardboard, the other of thin paper. He notes the wax seal on the back of the envelope. The embossed design is blurred: Is it the national emblem or a Masonic symbol?

"How did this message get here, Piquard?" he asks.

"Somebody high up, in uniform, brought it, sir," the first sergeant says, with his shoulders hunched, standing at attention. "He came in a black Ford with official license plates."

"Give me his name, the license number."

Piquard's eyes open wide in consternation. "Nobody asked him for his identification. The number wasn't noted down. We went through the routine procedure. We inspected the envelope thoroughly. The explosives expert didn't notice anything unusual and let it through."

"Very well, Piquard. You are dismissed. Have the men keep all five of their senses on the alert. Now then, anything we haven't taken care of?" the Colonel asks, turning to the officers. "Ah, the sign and countersign."

"And synchronizing our watches," Galarza puts in, pointing to the print of Kant.

"Do you remember the password we used when we overthrew Perón? 'God is just'? We're going to use it tonight, from midnight to four. Those announcing their presence must do so in a questioning tone: 'God'? The countersign is obvious. Now, our watches."

It is four minutes to seven. They all adjust the hands of their watches, wind them. The Colonel breaks the sealing wax on the envelope. He glances at the contents: a photograph and a leaflet. The photograph is rectangular, like a postcard.

"Gentlemen," he says, suddenly pale, "you are dismissed. Be careful."

The moment the officers have disappeared in the darkness of the hallways, the Colonel closes the door of his office and looks at the photograph again, unable to believe his eyes: it is her, the Deceased, lying on the slab in the sanctuary, amid little bouquets of flowers. She is shown in profile, her lips parted, her feet bare. To allow such photos is unwise. How many can there be? The odd thing, however, is the mimeographed leaflet: *Commando of Vengeance*, the Colonel reads. And underneath, in a clumsy hand: *Leave her where she is. Leave her in peace.*

7

*"The Night of
the Truce"*

The art of the embalmer resembles that of the biographer: both try to immobilize a body or a life in the pose in which eternity is to remember it. *The Eva Perón Case,* a story that Ara completed shortly before his death, links the two undertakings to form a single all-powerful movement: the biographer is at once the embalmer, and the biography is also an autobiography of his funerary art. This is evident in every line of the text: Ara reconstructs Evita's body only in order to be able to recount how he has done so.

Shortly before Perón's downfall Ara wrote: "I am trying to dissolve the grayling crystals in the femoral artery. I am listening to Liszt's *Funérailles* on the radio. The music is interrupted. The announcer's voice repeats, as it does every day: 'It is twenty twenty-five, the hour at which the Spiritual Head of the Nation passed on to immortality.' I look at the naked, submissive body, the patient body that for three years now has remained uncorrupted thanks to my care. Although Eva might not wish it, I am her Michelangelo, her creator, the one responsible for her eternal life. She is now—why not say it?—me. I feel the temptation to inscribe my name on her, above her heart: Pedro Ara. And the date on which I began my labors: July 26, 1952. I must think about it. My signature would mar her perfection. Or perhaps not: perhaps it would enhance it."

Embalmer or biographer, Ara puzzled me for several years. His diary devotes several pages to an account of the hijacking of the corpse. Although it offers abundant details, little of what it says coincides with what the Colonel told his wife and Cifuentes, the sources through whom I learned this part of the story.

Ara writes:

"By November 23, 1955, I had completed my work. I entered the CGT building before midnight. The emissaries sent by the government had not yet arrived. On the second floor, a number of soldiers were on guard duty, some of them in front of the funeral chapel, others next to the stairway doors.

"'It's the professor,' a police officer said. When they recognized me, the soldiers lowered their weapons.

"I opened the chapel door and left it ajar. As at other times, the soldiers timidly approached and peeked inside to see Evita. One of them crossed himself. They were moved, and asked me:

"'Are they taking her away tonight, Doctor?'

"'I don't know.'

"'What are they going to do with her?'

"'I don't know.'

"'Do you think they're going to burn her?'

"'I don't think so.'

"As the soldiers were returning to their posts, I inspected the laboratory. Everything was in order.

"I went down to the lobby to receive the military officers. Moori Koenig was the first to arrive and, immediately thereafter, a navy captain. Together we explored the complicated passageway leading to the garage. I heard a distant clock strike twelve. The new day was beginning.

"I returned to the chapel. The coffin was already there. I made a gesture. Two workers came over to help me put the revered body inside. One of them took Evita by the ankles; between the two of us, the other worker and I raised her up by the shoulders. We were very careful; we did not disarrange her hairdo or her dress. On her bosom lay the cross of the rosary offered her by Pius XII. We now had only to seal the metal lid of the coffin.

"'Where are the welders?' I asked.

"'It's late,' one of the army officers said. 'We're going to let that go for now.'

"I insisted, but no one sided with me.

"'Don't worry,' the Colonel said to me. 'Tomorrow we'll do everything that still has to be done.'

"That tomorrow never came. I tried to see the Colonel in his office on Viamonte and Callao, to make sure that the corpse was being respectfully protected. He refused to see me. Nor was I allowed to go up to the second floor of the CGT.

"Months after that twenty-fourth of November, I was awakened in the middle of the night by the insistent ringing of the telephone. A voice that was not altogether unfamiliar to me said:

"'Doctor, she has already been taken to another country. The information is reliable.'

"'Reliable?'

"'I saw it with my own eyes, Doctor. Goodbye.'"

Aldo Cifuentes, however, told me this version:

"In the beginning, that plan that Moori Koenig had drawn up went without a hitch. At midnight, his group left commando headquarters in four trucks. Each truck was carrying an empty coffin. Shortly thereafter, they all drove into the CGT garage. There was an incident in the lobby of the building because the embalmer, who had posted himself there that afternoon, refused to leave until he had talked to Moori Koenig. He wanted him to sign a statement that the corpse was in perfect condition. Imagine: as though it were a piece of merchandise. I think the Colonel went up to the lobby to tell him he could go to hell. In the guard room, where nobody was aware of what was going on in the garage, chaos reigned (as the newspaper reports were later to phrase it). The news was making the rounds that the Peronists from the suburbs were congregating at the warehouses at the port and were threatening to advance on the city. There was fear of another attack on the CGT, another October 17, 1945, another invasion of the city by workers and blackies to rescue Perón from prison and return him to power. In Argentina the masses have always wandered about restlessly, like animals in heat. Slowly, sizing up the situation, pretending to be humble folk. If you remember what's happened in the past, there's no one who can stop them. Moori Koenig knew that. He had the presence of mind to phone headquarters to report what was going on. He asked them to fire on the gathering to break it up. He said that if they didn't put down the rebellion before dawn, he'd do it himself. The embalmer roamed aimlessly about, looking downcast and very frightened. When the Colonel walked past him, he stopped him.

"'If you're going to take the Señora's body away soon, I would like to be present at the ceremony,' he said.

"Moori couldn't forgive him for having tried to trick him with the copies of the corpse.

"'There's nothing for you to do here,' he answered. 'This is a military operation.'

"'Don't leave me out, Colonel,' the doctor persisted. 'I took care of the body from the very first day.'

"'You shouldn't have. You're a foreigner. You shouldn't have gotten involved in the history of a country that wasn't your own.'

"Ara raised his hand to his hat and went outside in search of his car. He had the bewildered expression of someone who has lost himself and doesn't know where to start looking."

Cifuentes chose that moment in the story to slip in another of his self-portraits:

"I am, as you know, a buffoon of God. They call me Tom Thumb because I'm the size of God's thumb. Sometimes I'm gigantic, sometimes I'm too small to see. What has saved me from solemnity is my lost reputation. Thanks to that loss, I have always been free to do whatever I pleased. Don't judge me by what I am telling you. My style is less gloomy than the reality I am describing.

"I shall spare you some of the details. In the sanctuary, Moori Koenig removed the copies of the corpses from their crates, behind the curtains, dressed them in white tunics exactly like Evita's, and left them on the floor. They were flexible, and weighed almost nothing. He deposited the Deceased at the end of the sanctuary farthest from the door, after identifying her once again by the mark behind her earlobe. The real body could be distinguished from the copies because of its rigidity and because of its weight: it was twelve, perhaps fifteen, pounds heavier. But it was the same height: four feet eleven inches. Moori Koenig measured it several times, because he couldn't believe it. Seen from a distance, lying on the glass slab, the corpse looked huge. But the formol baths had shrunk the bones and the tissues. Only the head was still the same: pretty and perverse. He took one last look at it and covered it with a veil, as he had the others.

"The coffins were already lined up, lying open, along the second-floor corridor. There were no witnesses except for the three officers from the Service. Moori Koenig opened the doors of the sanctuary and, with the help of his men, placed the bodies inside the coffins. Each one had a tin plaque inscribed with a name and a date of birth and death. Evita's was a wink at historians—if ever one of them happened upon the inscription—because the name and the birth and death dates were those of her maternal grandmother, who had also died at the age of thirty-three: PETRONILA NÚÑEZ / 1877–1910.

"The lids of the coffins were screwed down. The enlisted men were ordered to take them down to the garage. The bodies were placed in the trucks: without flags, without rituals, in silence. Shortly before one a.m., their work was done. Moori Koenig lined the contingent up in formation in back of the vehicles. Arancibia, the Madman, was pale, from shock or overexertion. One of the NCOs, I believe it was Gandini, could hardly stand up.

"The Night of the Truce"

"'In a couple of hours, this mission will be over,' the Colonel said. 'The enlisted men will be taken back to commando headquarters. Tomorrow they will be discharged. I will be waiting for the rest of you at the Service, at three.'

"The air was humid, dank, unbreathable. When Moori Koenig went outside in the dark, he discovered on the horizon an enormous crescent moon with a black band across it, a sign of rain or bad luck."

Inventory of items found on the second floor of the CGT building on November 24, 1955:
- One triangular glass prism, with two broad sides that meet at the top, similar to the niches used in churches to display sacred images.
- One woman's nightdress or tunic, of white cloth, with noticeable stains and burns.
- Two hairpins.
- Three boxes made of ordinary wood, approximately five feet long. In one of the boxes a postcard was found, stamped Madrid, 1948. Both the text and the name of the person to whom the postcard was sent are indecipherable.
- Seventy-two black and purple ribbons with gold inscriptions in homage to the deceased wife of the tyrant who has fled the country.
- One flask of grayling crystals, unopened.
- Five liters of ten-percent formol.
- Nine liters of ninety-six-degree alcohol.
- A notebook with handwritten entries, apparently made by Dr. Pedro Ara. It is fourteen pages long. It has been possible to decipher only the following phrases: "we will make her an embroidered brocade shroud to replace the one she has that leaves her exposed" (page 2) / ". . . book not . . ." (page 9) / "revealing the calves to emphasize the contortion" (page 8) "of the subjects" (page 4) / "the trace or the penetration of the x-rays" (page 3) / "the lack of a lacework of nerves" (page 10) / "of dead skin" (page 6) / "to open her

145

up so that they penetrate" (page 11) / "the coughs of the poor" (page 13).[7]

• A fresh bouquet of sweet peas next to the prism.
• A tallow candle, lighted.

They began to cross the river at dusk. They gathered in groups of ten or twelve in the stations on Isla Maciel and waited for motor launches going to La Boca. Although it was hot and the humidity was close to a hundred, they had warm clothes in their knapsacks, as though they were prepared for a months-long siege. Once they were on board, they forced the ferrymen to enter the navigation channels of the south basin, amid the steamers returning from Montevideo, and disembarked at any clear space along the piers, after promptly paying for their passage. Other ferries took off from Quilmes and Ensenada, with little lighted lanterns on their masts, and tied up a bit farther north, near the warehouses. Some of the passengers were carrying half-finished painted placards, others huge drums. They silently found places for themselves at the foot of the tall grain silos and, immediately, like busy ants, found wooden planks to set up shelters so that the women could nurse their babies. They all smelled of leather-tanning chemicals, of burned wood, of bar soap. They were people of few words, although those spoken were high-pitched and shrill. The women were wearing flowered cotton housecoats or sleeveless dresses. The old ones, with aerostatic bellies, sported sets of shiny false teeth. New teeth and sewing machines were the gifts that Evita gave out most frequently. Every month she received, at the Foundation, hundreds of packages with plaster molds of gums and palates and sent off, by return mail, dentures with the following message: "Perón keeps his promises. Evita brings dignity. In Perón's Argentina, workers have a full set of teeth and

[7] In the original inventory, the phrases follow the order of the pages. Néstor Perlongher regrouped them around 1989 and included them in the second part of his poem "The Corpse of the Nation," dedicated to Evita.

they smile with none of the inferiority complexes of the down-trodden."

A number of families had ventured into the shipyards, skirting the army guard posts. Others found their way through the dense beds of reeds or followed the trail of the freight cars along the deserted tracks. By midnight there were more than six hundred of them. They grilled organ meats and spareribs on flexible metal supports from packing crates. They came over to the fire with a piece of bread, formed a line, and ate.

They were in imminent danger but didn't realize it or didn't care. For a week now, the leaders of the so-called Liberation Revolution had resolved to wipe out all memory of Peronism. It was forbidden to praise Perón and Evita in public, to display portraits of them, or even to remember that the two of them had existed. One of the edicts declared: "Any person who leaves images or statues of the deposed dictator and his consort in public view, uses words such as *Peronism* or *third position*, abbreviations such as *PP* (Peronist Party) or *PV* (Perón will return), or strikes up the Peronist march once again will be sentenced to a prison term of six months to three years."

Ignoring the edict, a couple of girls fifteen or sixteen years old, with mouths painted a furious red and wearing skin-tight dresses, stood alongside the barbecuers, singing, defiantly: *Eva Perón, / the one we adore, / your heart is with us / forevermore.* Behind the warehouses was an altar made of bricks with an enormous photo of Evita amid processional candles. People came to the foot of it to leave poinsettias, wisteria, and forget-me-nots woven into garlands as they chorused: *Our voices raised in song aren't faint / We proclaim our beloved Evita a saint.* The racket must have been heard a long way off. The chain-link fences around the port area were some five hundred yards away, and five hundred yards farther on, to the north, were the towers of the commando headquarters.

Why would there be any real repression? There was no reason to be afraid, they told each other. The government decrees must have to do with serious disturbances, with acts of vandalism in public buildings; it didn't mention private devotions. Everyone had a right to go on loving Evita. Hadn't the first declaration of the "liberators" spoken of an Argentina "with neither victors nor vanquished"? And on the day that Perón fell, when it was rumored that they were going to kill him, hadn't they allowed him to seek asylum on a Paraguayan gunboat and hadn't the chancellor of the Republic himself visited him on board, to make sure that he lacked for nothing? Rumors. Rumors never turned out to be true. The only thing people should believe was what they heard on the radio.

As the night went by, sick people, elderly people, joined the others. A woman with a vague goiter, who introduced herself as a relative of Evita's hairdresser, had just heard a news bulletin on the radio that said that the port area was filling up with undesirables. The army wanted to disperse them before daylight. "Can that mean us?" several old people who had come from the working-class district of Los Perales said. "Who knows who they're talking about. The port's a big place."

In the shelter of sheets of corrugated tin, they lit candles and waited. They had heard that Perón was going to return from exile that night in a black plane and would appear again on the balcony overlooking the Plaza de Mayo. Evita would be beside him, all lit up, in a glass coffin. The gossip going around was contradictory. People were also saying that the army was going to bury Evita's coffin next to San Martín's, in the cathedral. And that the navy was thinking of dumping it at the bottom of the ocean, encased in cement. The most widespread rumor, however, was the one that had brought them together there: Evita would be removed from her pantheon in the CGT and solemnly entrusted to the people for them to watch over and care for her, just as was written in her last will and testament. "I wish to live eternally with Perón and with my people," she had said before she died. Perón was no longer there. The people would receive her.

That tissue of different versions must have had some truth behind it, since from dawn on army troops kept going in and out of the CGT building. The body had been there three years now, on an altar that no one could visit. In the months following her death, the building had always been wreathed in flowers. Every night, at twenty twenty-five, the lights in the windows went on and off, intermittently. But the flowers had gradually disappeared, and even the crepe hanging from the windows on the second floor fell to the ground one day, ripped to shreds by storms. Something was about to happen now, but nobody knew what. Ever since Perón's fall nobody knew anything.

On the horizon of the river, the moon shone faintly, its light dimmed by bands of dark clouds across it. It was hot. The air was saturated with fine wheat dust. At one end of the warehouses, from atop cranes, some kids were taking turns as lookouts, watching the open ground between the city and the river: the deserted switchyards, the empty freight cars, the shipyards, the distant sentry boxes of the army guards.

Shortly after midnight, one of the lookouts spied a big black car with its headlights dimmed coming through the switchyards. He ran to warn the others, amid the sparks of a terrible din. Behind the warehouses hammers rang on wood. The carpenters were building shelters and altars. Finally, two of the men went out to meet the intruder. One of them was wearing glasses and walking on crutches.

The car braked to a stop under a street lamp, and the driver got out, straightening his hat. He was wearing a three-piece flannel suit. He was sweating. He took a few steps and looked around, trying to get his bearings. He was puzzled by the warehouses silhouetted in the bright glow coming from behind them: the candles, the bonfires. He could vaguely make out the vast river in the distance. There was so much noise coming from so many directions that a person couldn't think: the wailing of children mingled with the shouts of women and the defiant bets of card players. Before his senses cleared, the man on crutches barred his way, looking him over from head to foot.

"I'm Dr. Ara," the driver of the car explained. "Pedro Ara, the doctor who has cared for Evita all these years."

"He's the one who embalmed her," the second man put it, recognizing him. "What did you do to her?"

"She's in very good condition. She has all her insides. She's perfect, as though she were sleeping. She looks as if she were alive."

"What need was there to torture her like that?" the man on crutches muttered.

They were all ill at ease, disconcerted. The embalmer himself didn't know what to do. The entry for that day in his diary is confused: "I feel responsible for the corpse. I left the CGT for fear that the soldiers would ruin work that cost me years of research and many a sleepless night. I thought of going to the papers, but it would have been pointless. It is forbidden to publish a single line about the body. And the Spanish government doesn't want to get involved in the matter. The best thing to do, in my opinion, is to speak to the people who have gathered at the port."

When they spied the intruder, the old ones stopped playing cards. The man on crutches hoisted himself up on top of some planks and clapped his hands.

"This is Dr. Arce," he rasped. His lungs wheezed. "He's the one who embalmed Evita."

"Ara, not Arce. Dr. Ara," he tried to explain, but many other voices spoke up at once, drowning his out.

"Are they going to bring her here tonight? Or did they take her to the cathedral? Tell us, did they take her away?" people asked. "Or are they going to hand her over to the general? Poor thing, why are they moving her from one place to another? Why don't they leave her in peace?"

The embalmer hung his head.

"The soldiers took her away," he said. "I wasn't able to do a thing. They've put her in an army truck. Why don't you people do something?"

The phrase "you people" took everyone by surprise. They didn't know anybody who would have used that familiar form of address, except Evita in her earliest speeches. It seemed to them an old, lost form, from another language. "You people took her away," someone muttered. And the word gradually spread: "The soldiers took her away." A woman carrying two children on her back burst into tears and went off through the reeds.

"Do something? Like what?" one of the old ones asked.

"March to the Plaza de Mayo. Stage a revolt. Do what you did when the general was imprisoned, ten years ago."

"There could be a bloodbath now," the man on crutches said. "Haven't you heard that they're getting ready for a mass slaughter?"

"I haven't heard anything," the embalmer answered. "There are a whole lot of you. They won't dare kill all of you. You have to get them to give Evita back to me."

"They said they were going to bring her to the port. If they don't, Evita's going to come all by herself," an old woman full of warts said emphatically. Several small children were clinging to her skirt, like a system of planets. "We don't need to go looking for her. She's going to come looking for us."

"How can she? The soldiers took her away," the man on crutches repeated.

"But she knows us," another man explained. "She came to our neighborhood many a time."

The embalmer was dripping with sweat. He had a handkerchief with scent in his hand and every few minutes he wiped his bald pate with it.

"You don't understand," he said. "If there's no one looking after her body, my work could be ruined. It's a masterpiece. I've already told you that the general entrusted her to me."

"She could always look after herself," the old woman with the warts persisted.

"They're not going to bring her now," the man on crutches said. He stood up on the pile of planks and raised his voice: "They've taken Evita far away from here. We'd better leave."

The old woman with the warts shouted too:

"I'm leaving. It doesn't matter whether she's here or on the other side of the river."

She made her way among the heap of women who were beginning to grow tense, and took a seat in one of the boats, with her planets on her shoulders. A slow river of people followed her to the shore. Even the teenage girls with incandescent lips lined up on the pier, singing: *So it's good to say / your name this way / today and every day: / Eva Perón.*

"Why don't you people go get her?" Ara insisted.

But there was no way to keep them from hurriedly dispersing. The men who had been playing cards put out the bonfires and when the embalmer repeated, "Bring her to me, please, bring her to me," one of the men stopped in his tracks and clapped an iron hand on his shoulder.

"We're not going to go get her because they want to kill us all," he said. "But if you take the lead, Dr. Arce, maybe we'll follow you,"

"Ara," Dr. Ara corrected him. "I can't go with you. I'm not from here."

"If you're not from here, you're from there. If you're not with us, you're with them," the man exclaimed. "What's that you've got under your arm?"

The embalmer turned pale. He was carrying a starched white coat. He hugged it to his chest. He didn't know what to do with it.

In the distance, the growl of army trucks, the tramping of soldiers, the crackle of rifle fire, could be heard, as the first of the boats drew away, heading upstream.

"This was Evita's shroud," the embalmer murmured. He tripped over the words. He hesitated for a moment and unfolded the white coat. It was a plain, short-sleeved one, with a V neck. "Do you realize? This is Evita's shroud. If you march to the Plaza de Mayo and ask them to give the body back to me, you can take the shroud with you and do whatever you like with it."

The man on crutches took off his glasses and, drawing closer to the embalmer, said to him curtly:

"Give me that."

Overcome by feelings of desperation and helplessness, the doctor handed over the garment and went to pieces.

"Forgive me," he said. Nobody knew why he was asking anyone's forgiveness. "I'd like to leave."

"Quick, get in the boats," the man on crutches ordered. He let himself down into a sloop and cast off.

They tied the shroud alongside one of the sails and lifted the oars. Billowing in the breeze, the cloth flapped from one side to the other.

They heard the heavy breathing of the trucks, coming closer and closer.

The stragglers took down the shelters and piled the boards up onto the decks of the boats. It didn't take long. There were many of them, and they shared the work without getting in each other's way, as in a beehive. As they were leaving, someone sang: *Eva Perón, / the one we adore, / your heart is with us / forevermore.* The people who were disappearing amid the reeds and taking off in the other ferryboats sang too: *We promise our love is true / we swear to be faithful to you.* The voices faded away, but the embalmer stayed behind on the river-bank, peering into the darkness.

The story has been told many times, and never in just one way. In some versions, the embalmer is wearing the white coat when he arrives at the shelters at the port and takes it off as he gets out of the car; in others, the army trucks attack, and the man on crutches dies. Sometimes the shroud is yellow and has been rumpled by death; at other times it is not even a shroud but a trick of memory, the wake that Evita left on the smooth surface of that night. In the first of these versions, the gathering at the port is a wish, not a fact, and there were no announcements on the radio. Nothing is like anything else, nothing is ever just one story, but a net that each person weaves without knowing the overall pattern.

Can someone embalm a life? Isn't it punishment enough to put it out in the sun and begin to tell the story of it in that terrible light?

Since an intricate delta of stories is opening out, I am going to try to be concise. On one bank of the river is the story of the false bodies (or copies of the corpse); on the other, the story of the real body. Luckily, there is a moment at which the paths clear, and there is just one story left standing, which blinds or puts a quietus to the others.

During the run to Chacarita cemetery, Major Arancibia, the Madman, disobeyed the Colonel's instructions. He drove nervously, and at times he could hardly breathe. On reaching Centenary Park, he brought the truck to a stop at a bend in the road where there was no light and opened the door of the cab. He gave the enlisted men ten minutes' rest and ordered them to station themselves a short distance away.

He stayed behind with Armani, his sergeant major. The Madman trusted Armani: he had cured him of fever when he was posted to Tartagal, in the middle of nowhere; he had rid him of his obsession about dogs. Now he wanted Armani to share the secret of their mission. He needed to get it off his chest.

He ordered the sergeant to bring a couple of flashlights as he took the lid off the coffin.

"Prepare yourself, because this is Eva," he said in a low voice.

The sergeant didn't answer.

In the beam of the flashlights, the Madman undressed the figure and placed the shroud beneath her head, without disarranging its chignon. It had moles and dark, sparse hair on its pubis. It surprised him that the fuzz on the pubis was dark when the corpse had such fair hair.

"She was a dyed blond," he said. "She dyed her hair."

"She died three years ago," the sergeant said. "This isn't her. There's a strong resemblance, but it isn't her."

Arancibia ran his fingertips over the body: the thighs, the rather prominent navel, the arch of the upper lip. It was a soft body, too warm to be dead. Between the fingers was a rosary. They had cut off the tip of its left ear and part of the middle finger of the right hand.

"It may be a copy," Arancibia, the Madman, said. "What do you think?"

"I don't know what it is," Armani answered.

"Maybe it's her."

They closed the coffin again and called the men back. The truck crossed the avenida Warnes and then entered the calle Jorge Newbury, where the trees formed a long tunnel. Sergeant Armani rode in the cab this time, alongside the major. A watchman was waiting for them behind the grille at one of the entrances to La Chacarita. He was wearing sunglasses. In the dark, the sunglasses seemed more threatening than a weapon.

"God?" he asked.

"Is just," the Madman answered.

They drove straight down an avenue that duplicated the layout of the city. On either side were enormous mausoleums. Chapels and caskets could be seen behind the panes of glass. At the end of the avenue was a stretch of open ground. To the right a number of statues stood out, portraying a guitarist, a pensive man, and a woman making as if to throw herself from the top of a cliff. To the left was a jumble of tombstones, grave plots with plants, and a few crosses standing atilt.

"This is the place," the watchman pointed out.

The enlisted men unloaded the coffin and lowered it, with ropes, into a grave that was already dug. Then they filled it in with dirt and crushed stone. The watchman stuck a cross of cheap wood, with the tips in the shape of a trefoil, at one end of the grave. He took out a piece of chalk and asked:

"What was the name of the deceased?"

Arancibia consulted a notebook.

"María de Magaldi," he answered. "María M. de Magaldi."

"Talk about coincidences," the watchman said. "The man with the guitar you see over there, from the back, is Agustín Magaldi, the singer, the sentimental voice of Buenos Aires. He's been dead for almost twenty years now, but people still bring him flowers. They say he was Evita's first lover."

"Coincidences," the Madman echoed. "That's life."

The watchman wrote *María M. de Magaldi* on the traverse of the cross. The moon disappeared behind clouds. In the darkness, they heard the buzzing of bees.

Fesquet was certain he wasn't going to screw up. Before leaving for the commando headquarters he had had his fortune read by a neighbor woman: "Everything is going to turn out all right" the tarot cards said. "In your future are people pursuing you and the ghost of a dead woman. But for now the coast is clear." And it was. He drove the truck without clashing the gears, he didn't lose his way, and the avenues parallel to the river were free of traffic. Amid the neo-Gothic towers of the church in Olivos there appeared great stained-glass windows that gave off a grayish light. The muted sounds of a harmonium could be heard. When the men unloaded the coffin, the music stopped, and the parish priest suddenly emerged from the shadows, followed by a pair of altar boys.

"I must say the office," he announced. "This is the first person to be buried in the churchyard."

He murmured a couple of quick prayers. He hadn't a single hair on his head, and the yellow beams from the streetlights glanced off it as though all of them were in a ballroom. Fesquet was surprised to note that First Sergeant Piquard knelt and listened to the prayers with joined hands.

"Kyrie eleison. Christe eleison," the priest recited. "What was the name of the dead man?"

"Dead woman," Fesquet corrected. "María M. de Maestro."

"A charitable person?"

"Something like that. I don't know the details."

"Why was this time of day chosen?"

"Who knows?" Fesquet said. "I heard that it was a request in her last will and testament. She must have been an odd sort."

"She doubtless detested the pomp of this world. She must have wanted to be alone with God."

"Something like that," Fesquet repeated, eager to leave.

On the way back, he asked Piquard to drive. It was the only order of the Colonel's that he disobeyed. He thought it didn't matter.

A tire on Captain Galarza's truck blew out on the avenida Varela, and the sudden explosion wrenched the steering wheel out of his hands. The vehicle zigzagged, climbed up onto the sidewalk, and stood there with its front end bowed, as though asking for forgiveness. Galarza examined the damage and ordered the men to get out. They all thought they'd landed in the middle of a nightmare and looked at the city mistrustfully. Behind a long iron fence were the windows of the Piñero Hospital. Patients in pajamas appeared at them and exchanged comments. A woman with an enormous belly, arms akimbo, shouted:

"Let people sleep!"

Galarza took out his revolver, with an indifferent expression, and pointed it at her.

"If you don't close that window I'll shoot it shut."

He spoke without raising his voice, and his words were lost in the darkness. But the tone of them must have carried a long way. The woman hid her face and disappeared. The other patients turned out the lights.

It took them almost ten minutes to change the tire. At the entrance to Flores cemetery a watchman, with sleep in his eyes and one leg shorter than the other, was waiting for them. The gravestones modestly hugged the earth and formed mazes that blocked their path and obliged them to detour around them. The four enlisted men were carrying the coffin. One of them said:

"It hardly weighs anything. You'd think it was a child's coffin."

Galarza ordered him to shut up.

"Maybe it's just bones," the watchman said. "They bury bones here all the time."

They passed by the white mausoleum of the founder of the cemetery and turned to the left. The moon came out briefly from time to time and then hid in the clouds again. Behind a row of round vaults, in which lay victims of yellow fever, two big graves, lined with cement, lay open.

"This is the place," the watchman announced. He brought out a list and asked Galarza to sign it.

"I'm not signing anything," the captain said. "This is a dead serviceman."

"Nobody goes in or out of here without a signature. It's a rule. No signature, no burial."

"Perhaps there's more than one burial scheduled," the captain said. "Maybe there are two. Give me your name."

"Read it on my badge. I've been here at this cemetery for twenty years. Give me the name of the dead man."

"It's NN. In the army, that's the name we give bastards."

The watchman handed them the rope to lower the coffin with, and went off down the avenue of pines, cursing the darkness.

The Colonel pictured his mission in his mind's eye as a straight line. He left the CGT. He drove one mile along the avenida Córdoba. He entered the Waterworks building by way of one of the side doors. He ordered the men to unload the coffin. He hauled the body to its destination. "Two empty sealed rooms," Cifuentes had said, "in the southwest corner of the Waterworks building." The hard part was getting the men to transport the coffin, safe and sound, up the spiral staircase leading to the second floor. *Safe* and *sound* were adjectives that he had never used in connection with death. All words seemed unfamiliar to him now.

As he drove along, the Colonel drew up his plans for the second time. There was a new figure in the plot: Sergeant Major Livio Gandini. He had decided at the last minute to get rid of the clarinetist Galarza. Although none of the others knew it, he, Moori Koenig, was the one who was going to transport the real body. He needed more reinforcements, more certainties. Now, things were going to go like this:

The enlisted men would leave the coffin on the second floor of the Waterworks building. They would return to the truck, under Gandini's supervision. He, Moori Koenig, would light a kerosene lamp. He would haul the Deceased to the rooms on the south. He would cover the coffin with canvas. He would close the door and put a padlock on it. *Et finis coronat opus,* as the embalmer had said.

The Colonel had studied the place time and time again in the course of the afternoon. He went up and down the spiral staircase three times. The curves were tight, and the only way to get the coffin upstairs would be to carry it upright. He was ready for anything. He repeated the phrase, like an exorcism: *for anything.*

He drove the truck along the avenues in silence. He shuddered. History: Was this what history was like? Could a person quietly enter and leave it? He felt light, as though he were inside another body. Perhaps nothing of what was apparently happening was happening at all. Perhaps history was not made up of realities but of dreams. People dreamed facts, and then writing invented the past. There was no such thing as life, only stories.

After the next step in the operation, he too could die. Everything he had to do was already done. He had kept the promise he'd made doña Juana. He had recovered her family's passports and had sent them to her that very afternoon, by messenger. The mother sent him a brief note in reply, which was still in his pocket: "My daughters and I are leaving tomorrow for Chile. I trust your word. Take care of my Evita." The only thing left to do now was to hide the body. He could hear himself breathing. He was alive. His breathing was just another sound amid the folds of countless other sounds. Why die? What would be the sense of that?

In the distance he saw a column of smoke, and then the wisps of flames. He supposed there was a fire somewhere in the city. The flames then crouched down as if in shame and disappeared. All of a sudden, a couple of blocks farther on, they flared up again and reached toward the sky. Dogs were strolling by on the sidewalks, sniffing at the peculiarities of the night. The Colonel slowed down.

Other cars stopped. The street filled with curious onlookers and people wanting to help. Nuns ran alongside the truck with sheets in their hands.

"They're for those who have been burned, for the burn victims!" they cried out, in answer to the Colonel's rude look.

A woman was sitting underneath an advertising poster, cradling a sewing machine in her arms. She was weeping. Two teenagers waved their arms in front of the truck. The Colonel honked the horn. Nobody budged.

"You can't go any farther," one of the youngsters said to him. "Can't you see? Everything's on fire."

"What happened?" the Colonel asked.

"Some big bottles of kerosene exploded," answered a tall man who was holding his hat down as though he were fighting an illusory wind. He had spots of soot on his cheeks. "I've just come from the fire," he said. "One of the tenements is nothing but a pile of ashes now. It burned down in less than ten minutes."

"Was it far from here?" the Colonel inquired.

"A few blocks away. Opposite the Waterworks. If they hadn't connected several hoses to the water reservoirs, the flames would already have reached this far."

"There must be some mistake."

"No," the tall man said. "Didn't I already tell you that I've just come from the fire?"

It was chance, the Colonel would say years later, when he spoke to Cifuentes about that night. Reality is not a straight line but a system of forking paths. The world is a fabric woven of unknown threads. On the clear horizon of reality, plans can fall through with no forewarning or premonition. They are thwarted by nature, falling victim to a heart attack or the caprice of a bolt of lightning. Chance disconcerted me, the Colonel would say. In the light from the fire, I realized that the Deceased could not remain in the deserted rooms of the building, hidden among the cisterns. It was chance, but it could also have been a miscalculation with Paracelsus's trident. I misplaced its axes; I failed to calculate the position of the handle correctly.

He drove the truck up onto the sidewalk, waved the barrel of the Mauser through the window of the cab to clear the way, and slipped down a side street. On the other side of the empty city the river could be seen. And what if I left the body in a warehouse at the docks? he thought. What if I let it fall into the water? Buenos Aires was the only city on earth with just three cardinal points. People spoke of the north, the west, or the south, but the east was a void: nothingness, water. He remembered that by the compass the Deceased's astrological sign coincided with north-northeast. There must be some secret key in such knowledge. He stopped the truck. He read the index card he'd brought with him in the glove box. Eva Perón's sign of the zodiac. "Taurus: wetness triumphs over dryness, earth over fire. The axis of her body passes through her stomach. The musical note that corresponds to her eternal life is E. The finger with which her destiny points is the index finger." Toward the river, toward the east, he repeated.

He crossed the raised tracks of Retiro station. In the back of the truck, Gandini and the enlisted men were singing in the dark. A moment before, when the Colonel had slowed down, on reaching the anteroom of the fire, he had heard them knocking on the wall of the cab with the butts of their Mausers. Two or three knocks, and then that song with its grating disharmony.

The moon had just disappeared. To the left, he made out the main gates of a naval station. I'm not going any farther, he said to himself. This will be the place. This is where they hate her most.

He asked to see the captain in charge of the station. "He's asleep," the watch officer said. "He's just gone to bed. We've all had a hard day. I can't wake him up." "Tell him I'm here," the Colonel ordered. "I'm not going to budge till he comes."

He waited a long while. The sky was full of signs. There were several falling stars, and at times the only thing that could be seen overhead was the superstructures of ships. The sky was a weary mirror that reflected the misfortunes of the earth. "The captain's coming, he's coming!" the watch officer said. But it took him a long time, almost till dawn.

He knew the captain. His name was Rearte. They had taken several Intelligence courses together. He was an expert on secret lodges, on conspiracies. He kept a notebook with a list of every secret society: a whole collection of names and dates, of plans that had fallen through, of double agents. The Colonel used to say that, if Rearte wanted to, he could use his notes to write the unknown history of Argentina: the back side of the moon. Would he want to? He had always been an unsociable person, and also a suspicious one. Now that he thought about it, Raúl Rearte and Eva Duarte were almost anagrams.

He heard Gandini and the men singing again. He asked them, from outside the truck, if they were thirsty. Nobody answered: just the singing. The Colonel fell asleep leaning on the steering wheel. Finally he heard the creak of the wrought-iron gate opening and saw the navy captain come out, freshly bathed. His head was gooey with pomade. Though he had his beret and jacket on, he was still tucking the shirttails of his uniform inside his trousers. The Colonel signaled to him to ask to speak to him alone.

They walked over to the courtyard of the naval station. In the middle of it stood a solitary, scraggly tree.

"We carried out an important operation tonight, Rearte," the Colonel said. "We moved a body. But it wasn't all that easy. One of the steps didn't come off right."

The captain shook his head. "Those things happen."

"In this case, they shouldn't have happened. It was chance."

"And what can I do to help? The president doesn't want the navy to get mixed up in the army's affairs."

"I have one of the coffins in the truck," the Colonel said. "I need to leave it here. Just for a while. Till midnight."

The captain took off his beret and slicked down his hair still more.

"I can't," he said. "They'd cut my head off."

"It's a personal favor," the Colonel persisted. His throat felt parched with anxiety, but he tried to make his voice sound neutral, indifferent. "Just between you and me. Nobody need know."

"That's impossible, Colonel. I'd have to notify the top brass. You know very well how these things are."

"Take the coffin to a ship. If it's on a ship, nobody need know."

"On a ship? You surprise me, Moori. You don't know what you're saying."

The Colonel scratched the nape of his neck. He stared at Rearte.

"I can't go all over the place with this thing," he said. "If they take it away from me, everything's going to blow sky high."

"Maybe. But nobody's going to take it away from you."

"Oh no? They're all going to want to have it. It's impressive." He lowered his voice. "It's that woman, Eva. Come see."

"Don't kid me, Moori. You're not going to get me to bite."

"Take a look. You're a refined man. You'll never forget it as long as you live."

"That's the worst part of it. That I'm never going to forget. If that woman is here, take her away. She's bad luck."

The Colonel tried to smile and couldn't. "Have you swallowed that story too? We were the ones who invented it, in the Intelligence Service. How the devil could she bring bad luck? She's a mummy, a dead woman like any other. Come look. After all, what have you got to lose?"

He opened the doors of the truck and ordered the men to get out. The captain followed him in a daze. Dawn came up amid the fluttering of insects, the rustling of leaves, claps of thunder in the distance. After being shut up in the dark next to the coffin for so long, Sergeant Gandini stumbled as he got out of the back, like a blind bird.

"We heard that there was a fire, sir," he murmured, blinking.

"It was nothing. A false alarm."

"What shall I do with the men?"

"Get them out of here. Wait for me a hundred yards away."

"There's a peculiar smell inside, sir. I'm sure there are chemicals in that crate."

"Who knows what's inside. Explosives, alcohol. There's no way to tell."

"There's a plaque with a name, Petrona somebody," Gandini said, as he started to walk away. "And some dates. There's something old inside, from the last century."

The odor was a faint one, barely perceptible. The Colonel wondered why he hadn't thought of it before: the real body smelled and the copies didn't. It didn't matter. The different versions of Evita would never be together again.

"Rearte!" he called.

The captain answered with a little dry cough. He was already behind him, climbing into the back of the truck.

"You can't imagine what this is," the Colonel said as he clumsily unscrewed the lid. The screwdriver slipped out of his hands more than once, and three of the screws got lost. "There she is," he said finally.

He drew back the sheet covering the Deceased's face and turned a flashlight on. In the beam of light, Evita was a sharp profile, a flat image, split in two, like the moon.

"Who would have thought it." The captain slicked his hair down again, stunned. "Just look at that Mare who fucked up our lives. How tame she looks. The Mare. She looks just the same."

"The way you see her now is the way she's going to stay forever," the Colonel said in a hoarse, excited voice. "Nothing affects her: not water, quicklime, the years, earthquakes. Nothing. If a train ran over her, she'd still look just the same."

In the beam of the flashlight, Evita gave off phosphorescent reflections. Faint colored vapors rose from the casket.

"She brings bad luck, the bitch," the captain repeated. "Look at what she did to you. You aren't the same anymore."

"She didn't do anything to me," the Colonel said in self-defense. "How did you get that idea? She can't do anybody any harm."

The words escaped his lips without his thinking about them. He didn't want to say them, but the words were there. The captain looked away. He saw that two NCOs were amusing themselves playing darts in the sentry box.

"You'd best take her away, Moori Koenig," he said.

The Colonel turned the flashlight off.

"You're losing your chance," he answered. "You could be in history, and you're not going to be."

"What the hell do I care about history? History doesn't exist."

In the distance, Gandini imitated the cry of a seagull. Raising two fingers to his lips, the Colonel answered with a long, high-pitched whistle. The sounds echoed in the fog. The river was there, a few steps away.

The men returned to the truck, looking drowsy. Gandini was about to get in with them, but the Colonel ordered him to sit down beside him, in the cab of the truck.

"We're going to commando headquarters," he said. "We have to take the men back."

"And our load too," Gandini supposed.

"No," the Colonel answered, haughty, self-assured. "We're going to leave it inside the truck, day and night, parked next to the sidewalk outside Intelligence."

They drove through the dock area in silence. They left the men in the garage of commando headquarters and then drove round and round the empty city. They thought they saw shadows watching them on the corners; they were afraid that someone would fire at them from an entryway and grab the truck from them. They drove down the avenues, through the parks, through the open spaces, slowing down abruptly on the curves, Mausers at the ready, on the lookout for an enemy that must be somewhere, lying in wait. A wind came up. A torrent of low-lying, gray clouds shrouded the sky. They didn't want to admit it, but they were dead tired. They drove on toward the Service, by way of other roads that took them in a circle, other detours.

When they got there, the Colonel discovered another sign of bad luck. On the sidewalk next to the place where he was thinking of leaving the truck a row of long, thin tapers was burning. Someone had scattered daisies, wisteria, pansies about. He now knew that the enemy was not pursuing him. It was worse than that. The enemy had guessed what his next destination would be and was getting there ahead of him.

8

"A Woman Reaches
Her Eternity"

What are the elements that went into the making of the myth of Evita?

1. She rose like a meteor from the anonymity of minor roles in radio to a throne on which no woman had sat: that of Benefactress of the Humble and Spiritual Head of the Nation.

She managed to do so in less than four years. In September 1943, she was hired at Radio Belgrano to play roles of great women in history. Her new salary allowed her to move to a modest two-room apartment in the calle Posadas. On the first programs she murdered the language with such fury that the series was about to be canceled. Her Queen Elizabeth of England was heard to say: "I am dying of indination, Bycount Rolly," meaning perhaps Sir Walter Raleigh, who was not a viscount. And in an improbable exchange between the Empress Carlota and Benito Juárez, she exclaimed: "I cannot forgive you for having such a bad opinion of my beloved Masimilian." Perhaps they corrected her during the break for a commercial, because at her next entrance, she said, with noticeable effort: "Macksimilian is suffering, suffering, and I'm gonna go outa my mind!" To be the head of a company of actors gave a person no social standing.

To the upper class, which seldom listened to the radio, Evita was only a comedienne who entertained army colonels and navy captains. Nobody thought of her as a danger.

By July of 1947 it was a different story. Evita appeared on the cover of *Time* magazine. She had just returned from a tour of Europe that the newspaper correspondents baptized "going over the rainbow." She had no official mission, but she was received everywhere by heads of state, the pope, the masses. In Rio de Janeiro, the next-to-last stop on her trip, the foreign ministers of the Americas welcomed her and interrupted their conference to drink a toast to her. Those who had paid no attention to her as an actress detested her now as the icon of illiterate, barbarous, demagogic Peronism.

She was then twenty-eight. Judged by the cultural codes of the time, she acted like a male. She woke up and gave orders to the cabinet ministers at the most inconsiderate hours, broke up strikes, had journalists and actors fired as an act of revenge or a whim, and decided the next day that they should be hired back; she filled wayside hostels with thousands of blackies who were emigrating from the provinces; she inaugurated factories; she went by train to visit ten or fifteen towns a day, improvising speeches in which she mentioned the poor by name; she swore like a trooper; she stayed up all night. She always walked one step behind her husband, but he seemed to be her shadow, the reverse of the medal. In one of his memorable diatribes, Ezequiel Martínez Estrada described the couple in these terms: "Everything that Perón lacked or possessed only to a rudimentary degree in order to take over the country from top to bottom, she devoured or made him devour. In that sense too she was an ambitious, irresponsible person. In reality, he was the woman and she was the man."

2. She died young, like the other great Argentine myths of the century: she was thirty-three.

Gardel, who made the tango world famous, was forty-four when the plane he was traveling in with his musicians burst into flames in

Medellín; Che Guevara wasn't yet forty when a scouting party of the Bolivian army shot him to death at La Higuera.

But unlike Gardel and Che, Evita's death throes were followed step by step by the masses. Her death was a collective tragedy. Between May and July 1952, there were hundreds of masses and processions every day to implore God to restore to her a health that was past restoring. Many people believed they were witnessing the first tremors of the Apocalypse. Without the Lady of Hope, there could be no hope; without the Spiritual Head of the Nation, the nation was done for. From the time that the first medical reports on her illness were made public to the time that her catafalque was taken to the CGT by a cortege of forty-five workers, it took Evita and Argentina more than a hundred days to die. Funeral altars, on which photos of the Deceased smiled from frames edged in crepe, were erected all over the country.

As is the case with all those who die young, the mythology of Evita is nourished both by what she did and by what she might have done. "If Evita had lived she'd have joined the guerrilla movement," the freedom fighters of the seventies sang. Who knows? Evita was infinitely more fanatical and impassioned than Perón, but no less conservative. She would have done what he decided. Speculating about impossible stories is one of the favorite pastimes of sociologists, and in Evita's case the speculations fan out like a pattern of veins, because the world in which she lived soon turned into a different one. "If Evita had lived, Perón would have fought back against the revolutionary uprisings that finally drove him from power in 1955," almost all studies of the Peronist credo reiterate. That imaginary eventuality is based on the fact that in 1951, after an anemic, abortive coup, Evita ordered the commander in chief of the army to buy five thousand automatic pistols and one thousand five hundred machine guns to arm the workers in case of another uprising. Who knows? When Perón fell, the arms that should have been in the hands of the labor unions had ended up in the police arsenals, and the bewildered president did not speak on the radio to ask for help. Nor did the masses mobilize spontaneously to defend their leader, as they had done ten years before. Perón did not want to fight. He had changed. Was he different because old age was overtaking him or because Evita the indefatigable was no longer at his side? Neither history nor any individual can answer that question.

3. She was the Robin Hood of the forties.

It is not true that Evita resigned herself to being a victim, as her book *My Mission in Life* intimates. She could not bear the thought that such a thing as victims existed, because they reminded her that she had been one. She tried to redeem all the ones she saw.

When she met Perón, in 1944, she was supporting a tribe of mute albinos who had escaped from homes for the handicapped. She paid for their room and board, but her job on the radio did not permit her to take care of them personally. She once proudly tried to introduce them to Perón. It was a disaster. They found them naked from the waist down, paddling about in a sea of shit. Her horrified lover sent them off to an asylum in Tandil in an army truck. The drivers were careless and lost them forever amid trackless cornfields.

Nothing distressed Evita as much as seeing the foundlings turn out on Christmas Eve and the night before the national holiday. Their heads shaved to the skull so as not to attract lice, dressed in blue capes and gray aprons, the orphans posted themselves on the corners of the calle Florida with tubular metal containers, collecting alms for cloistered nuns and for vacation camps for sickly children. From their cars, the ladies of the Benevolent Association kept an eye on the behavior of their charges and acknowledged the flattering greetings of passersby. The finery worn by the distinguished ladies was made by the homeless young girls shut up in El Buen Pastor, where they were taught the art of cutting cloth and sewing, using scissors chained to the tables to keep them from being stolen. More than once, Evita swore that she would put an end to these humiliating annual ceremonies.

The opportunity presented itself in July 1946, a month after her husband was sworn in as head of state. As first lady, she would have been named honorary president of the Benevolent Association ex officio, but the estimable ladies were reluctant to mingle with a woman with such a dubious past, who had been born out of wedlock and had lived with several men before marrying.

Duty, naturally, prevailed over principle. The distinguished ladies decided to follow tradition and offer the post to the Bimbo—as they called her in their catty gossip—while at the same time laying down so many conditions that she would be unable to accept.

They visited her one Saturday, at the presidential residence. Evita had agreed to meet them at nine a.m., but at eleven she still wasn't up. The night before, agents from State Control had sent her a copy of the letter that one of the ladies on the board of directors of the association had sent to the writer Delfina Bunge de Gálvez. "We're hoping you'll come to the residence with us, Delfina dear," the letter said. "We know that you have a very delicate palate and that the visit will make you sick to your stomach. But if you feel queasy in the presence of the b—— (excuse us, but only *le mot juste* ought to be used when writing to a poet), just keep in mind that you are offering a sacrifice to the Lord that will earn you countless plenary indulgences."

Evita came downstairs looking so elegant she left them stunned. She was wearing a tailored black-and-white-checkered suit with velvet trimmings. Although her vocabulary was still shaky, she already had a quick, sharp, fearsome tongue.

"What brings you here, ladies?" she asked, seating herself on a piano stool.

One of the ladies, dressed in black, with a hat from which birds' wings soared, answered haughtily:

"Exhaustion. We've been waiting over three hours."

Evita gave an innocent smile:

"Only three hours. You're lucky. There are two ambassadors upstairs who've been waiting for five hours. Let's not waste time. If you're tired, you'd no doubt like to leave as soon as possible."

"A sacred obligation brings us here," another of the ladies, with a fox stole draped around her neck, said. "Out of respect for a tradition nearly a century old, we are offering you the presidency of the Charitable Association . . ."

"Despite the fact that you're too young," the lady with the feather hat put in. "And perhaps, inasmuch as you were an actress, you may not be familiar with the work we do. There are eighty-seven of us ladies."

Evita rose to her feet.

"You must understand that I am unable to accept," she said cuttingly. "This isn't the sort of thing I go in for. I don't know how to play bridge, I don't care for tea and petits fours. I'd embarrass you. Find someone like yourselves."

The lady with the stole held out, with relief, a gloved hand. "If that is your decision, we'll leave."

"You're forgetting tradition," Evita said, ignoring the farewell. "How will you get along without an honorary president?"

"Would you care to suggest someone?" the lady with the fox said superciliously.

"Appoint my mother. She's fifty. She isn't a b———, as this letter phrases it," she answered, spreading the copy of it out on the table, "but she is better spoken than all of you are."

And turning around, she gracefully climbed the stairs.

In a few weeks, charity disappeared from Argentina, replaced by other theological virtues that Evita baptized "social aid." The Charitable Society vanished from sight, and the distinguished ladies retired to their country estates. All the victims still on the calle Florida were placed in vacation camps, where they played soccer from morning to night and sang hymns of thanksgiving: *We will all be Peronists as one / in the new Argentina of Evita and Perón.*

To satisfy her passion for weddings, the first lady rounded up fiancés for the homeless girls taken in at El Buen Pastor and the other one thousand three hundred girls confined there on the grounds that they were tarts, pickpockets, runners for gambling rings, smugglers, or madams who kept brothels, redeeming them by way of collective nuptials at which she herself served as matron of honor.

Everybody was happy. On July 8, 1948, two years after the meeting with the distinguished ladies, an official decree proclaimed the birth of the María Eva Duarte de Perón Foundation for Social Aid, authorized to offer "a life of dignity to the less favored social classes."

The worst part of this story is that victims never stop being victims. Evita didn't need to be president of a charitable association. She wanted all charity work to bear her name, period. She worked day and night for that immortality. She gathered up the troubles that were lying around loose and made a bonfire of them that could be seen from afar. She did the job too well. The fire was so thoroughgoing it also burned her.

4. Perón loved her madly.

Love does not have units of measurement, but it is obvious that Evita loved him very much. Haven't I said this before?

In *My Mission in Life*, Evita described her meeting with Perón as an epiphany: she believed herself to be Saul on the road to Damascus, saved by a light from heaven. Perón, however, evoked the moment without attributing any particular importance to it: "When she came to me, she was a young girl with little education, albeit hardworking and with noble feelings. I diligently practiced with her the art of guidance. Eva must be seen as a product of mine."

They met each other amid the confusion of the San Juan earthquake. The catastrophe happened on a Saturday, January 15, 1944. The following Saturday there was a benefit in Luna Park for the victims. In the National Archives in Washington I have seen film footage from that night: clips from newsreels shown in Singapore, Cairo, Medellín, Ankara. They add up to three hours and twenty minutes. Although at times the same shot shows up again and again—the French newsreel and the Dutch one, for instance, are identical—the effect of shattered, broken, disjointed reality resembles the chaos, brought on by hashish, that Baudelaire describes. The people shown are suspended in their past, but they are never again the same: the past shifts with them, and when a person least expects it, the facts have changed places and mean something else.

Strange as it may seem, Evita is less Evita in the São Paulo newsreel than in the Bombay one. The Bombay one shows her looking self-assured, wearing a box-pleated skirt, a light-colored blouse decorated with a big cloth rose, and an ethereal brimmed hat; in the São Paulo one Evita never smiles: she seems upset by the situation. The skirt and blouse look like a dress in that one, perhaps because the light has no shading.

The meeting took place at 10:14 p.m.: at the top of the gymnasium are two clocks showing the exact time. Evita and a friend were in the first row of seats next to a man in a stiff-brimmed felt hat whom certain commentators—the one in Medellín, the one in London—identify as "Lieutenant Colonel Aníbal Imbert, head of the Postal and Telegraph Services." He was an important figure, to whom Evita owed the immense favor of being offered the contract by Radio Belgrano to play the roles of eighteen heroines of history. That night, however, Imbert didn't interest her. The man she was really dying to meet was the "colonel of the people," who promised a better life to the insulted and injured like herself. "I am not a man of sophisms or of halfway solutions," she had heard him say on the radio two weeks previously. (What could *sophisms* mean? Perón's odd language sometimes confused her, and she was afraid she wouldn't understand him when they saw each other. It didn't matter: he would understand what she would say to him, and maybe there wouldn't even be any need for words.) "I am only a humble soldier," Perón often said, "who has been granted the honor of protecting the working masses of Argentina." How beautiful those few phrases were, how profound! Later on, if she could, she would repeat them, almost word for word: "I am only a humble woman of the people who offers her love to the workers of Argentina."

Long lines of people with Indian features got off the trains every afternoon at Retiro station to beg for the help of the colonel who promised bread and happiness. She had not had the good fortune of having someone like that waiting for her when she arrived in Buenos Aires ten years before. Why not take her place at his side now? It wasn't too late. On the contrary: perhaps it was too early.

The colonel was just a little over forty-eight; she was just under twenty-five. Ever since Evita had recited Amado Nervo's verses over the loudspeakers in Junín, still wearing her school apron, she had dreamed of a man like that, sympathetic and at the same time possessed of boundless strength and wisdom. The other girls settled for a man who was hardworking and good-hearted. Not her: she wanted him to be the best as well. In recent months, she had followed Perón's every move and felt that nobody but him could protect her. A woman must choose, Evita said to herself, not wait for a man to choose her. A woman has to know from the beginning who suits her and who doesn't. She had never seen Perón except in photographs in the newspapers. And yet she sensed that they were meant to be together: Perón was the redeemer, and she the downtrodden victim; Perón knew only the compulsory love of his marriage with Potota Tizón and hygienic couplings with casual lovers; she, being predictably chased after by male leads on the radio, editors of scandal sheets, soap salesmen. The flesh of their two bodies needed each other; the moment they touched, God would set them afire. She trusted in God, for whom no dream is unreal.

When the MC at the benefit announced over the loudspeakers that Colonel Juan Perón was making his entrance into Luna Park, the audience stood up to applaud him: Evita did too. She rose from her seat trembling, bending the brim of her hat a little farther back, and draped her face with a smile that never faded for a moment. She saw him walk over to the seat next to her with his arms upraised; as she greeted him she felt with her gloved hands the warmth of his firm ones, dotted with freckles, whose caresses she had so often dreamed of, and came close to inviting him, with an irrepressible nod, to occupy the empty seat to her right. She had been pondering for a long time what she would say to him once he was close beside her. It had to be a brief, direct sentence that would hit him right in the middle of his soul: a sentence that would plague his memory. Evita had practiced in front of her mirror the cadence of each syllable, the slight movement of her brimmed hat, the timid expression, the ineffaceable smile on lips that ought perhaps to tremble:

"Colonel," she said, riveting her dark brown eyes on him.

"What is it, my girl?" he answered, without looking at her.

"Thanks for existing."

I have reconstructed every line of that exchange more than once at the National Archives in Washington. I have read it on the lips of the characters. I have often stopped the images in a freeze-frame in search of sighs, of pauses cut out at the editing table, of syllables hidden by a profile that glides past or by a gesture that I fail to see. But there is nothing else, apart from those words that can't even be heard. After uttering them, Evita crosses her legs and lowers her head. Perón, surprised perhaps, pretends to look toward the stage. Hugging the microphone, Libertad Lamarque sings "Madreselva" in a voice that survives, soppy and saccharine, in almost all the newsreels.

"Thanks for existing" is the phrase that splits Evita's destiny in two. In *My Mission in Life*, she doesn't even recall that she said it. The ghostwriter of those memoirs, Manuel Penella de Silva, chose to attribute to her a much simpler and much longer declaration of love: "I sat down beside him," he writes (pretending that it is Evita writing). "Perhaps it attracted his attention, and when he was able to hear me, I managed to say to him, in my most eloquent words, 'If, as you say, the cause of the people is your own cause, no matter how far the sacrifice leads, I shall be at your side until I faint from exhaustion.' He accepted my offer. That was the day the miracle happened to me."

That version is too wordy. The simple images of the film show that Evita said only "Thanks for existing" and that afterward she was a different person. Perhaps the machine-gun burst of those few syllables suffices to explain her immortality. God created the world with the single phrase: "I am." And then he said: "Let there be." Evita has endured through time with as few words.

There are sixteen newsreels reporting the earthquake and the meeting that took place a week later. Only one of them, the one shown in Mexico, allows the story to go on to its predictable end. It allows the actresses María Duval, Felisa Mary, Silvana Roth, to parade across the stage. Then as Feliciano Brunelli's musicians are packing up their music stands, it shows Evita walking off down the center aisle of Luna Park. One of her hands is pushing (or so it seems) Perón's back, as though she were someone who has taken possession of history and is leading it wherever she chooses.

5. For many people, touching Evita was touching the stars.

Fetishism. Ah, yes; that has been of enormous importance in the myth. Evita's aides used to drop off rolls of bills when she passed through towns on the train. The scene has been recorded in almost all the film documentaries on her life. Every so often, Evita herself picked up a bill between two fingers, kissed it, and threw it to the four winds. I knew a family in La Banda, Santiago del Estero, who displayed one of the "kissed bills" in a frame. They refused to spend it, even at times of dire want, when they had nothing to eat. Now that the bill is out of circulation, the family keeps it as a religious object, on a shelf in the dining room, alongside a color photo of Evita in a long black satin dress. There is always a bunch of flowers next to the photo. In the popular cult of Evita, the wildflowers and the lighted candles are offerings that are inseparable from the photos of her, which are venerated as though they were saints or miraculous virgins. And with the same religious fervor, neither more nor less.

I know that there are some hundred—at least a hundred—articles used, kissed, or touched by the Lady of Hope that have served as objects of worship of her. I shall not cite the complete list here, but, rather, a few samples from it:

• The embalmed canary that Evita gave Dr. Campora as a gift when he was President of the Chamber of Deputies.

• The lipstick mark that she left on a champagne glass during a gala evening at the Colón Theater, before her departure for her tour of Europe. It was kept in the museum of the theater for several years.

• The bottle of Gomenol that Américo Cali, a professor and poet from Mendoza, bought in the middle of 1936 to enable Evita to clear her nasal passages. In 1954 it was displayed inside a little sandalwood box by the "Immortal Evita" Museum Committee of Mendoza.

• The locks of her hair that were cut off when she died. Strands or curls of it are still sold in several jewelry stores on the calle Libertad. They can be mounted in silver, crystal, or gold reliquaries, and prices vary according to the mounting chosen by the purchaser.
• The autographed copies of *My Mission in Life* that are sold at auction at the San Telmo Fair, and then used as missals.
• A timeworn, off-white coat, with a V neck and short sleeves, that between 1962 and 1967 was exhibited in a house, known at the time as the Museum of the Shroud, on the corner of the calle Irala and Sebastián Gaboto, on Isla Maciel.
• The mummified body of Evita herself.

6. What could be called "the story of the gifts."
In every Peronist family a story is told: The grandfather hadn't seen the ocean, the grandmother didn't know what sheets or curtains were, the uncle needed a truck to deliver cases of soda, the cousin wanted an artificial leg, the mother didn't have the wherewithal to buy a bridal trousseau, the neighbor with tuberculosis couldn't afford a bed in a sanitarium in the Córdoba Mountains. And one morning Evita appeared. In the set design of the stories, everything happens one morning: a sunny one, in spring, not a cloud in the sky, the sound of violins. Evita arrived and with her great wings filled the space of desires, fulfilled dreams. Evita was the emissary of happiness, the gateway of miracles. The grandfather saw the sea. She took him by the hand, and both of them wept on sighting the ocean waves. That is how the story goes. The oral tradition is passed down from generation to generation; the gratitude is infinite. When the time comes to vote, the grandchildren think of Evita. Although some people say that Perón's successors sacked Argentina and that Perón himself betrayed them before he died, they hand in their votes at the sacrificial altar nonetheless. Because Grandfather asked me to before he died. Because my mother's trousseau was a present from Evita. Full of hope, people seek the path for their yearnings that dreams promised to open before them.

7. The unfinished monument.

In July 1951, Evita conceived the idea of a Monument to the Descamisado. She wanted it to be the tallest, the most massive, the most costly one in the world, one that could be seen from a long way off, like the Eiffel Tower. This is what she told the deputy Celina Rodríguez de Martínez Paiva, who was to present the project in Congress. "The work must serve to rouse the fervor of Peronists and be an outlet for their emotions forevermore, even when none of us is still alive."

At the end of that year, Evita approved the model. The central figure, a muscular worker one hundred eighty feet high, would stand on a pedestal two hundred fifty feet high. There would be an enormous square, three times larger than the Champs de Mars, surrounded by statues of Love, Social Justice, Rights of the Elderly, and Children: The Only Privileged. In the center of the monument a sarcophagus would be constructed, like Napoleon's at Les Invalides, but made of silver, with a recumbent image in relief. The immense structure, almost the same size as the Statue of Liberty, was to be placed in an open space between the law school and the presidential residence. Evita was so excited by the model that she gave orders that the figure of the muscular worker be replaced with a statue of herself. Congress hastened to approve the idea twenty days before she died, and Evita herself refers in her last will and testament to that illusion of eternity: "I will thus feel forever close to my people and will continue to be the bridge of love linking the *descamisados* and Perón."

After the funeral rites, the euphoria occasioned by the monument gradually waned. The foundations began to be dug at a pace whose slowness was fraught with meaning. When Perón fell, there was still nothing but a huge hole in the ground, which the new authorities filled in one night. To disguise the empty expanse, children's playground equipment and lighted fountains were improvised. But the funereal memory of Evita has not left that site. The enormous square is still empty, with its spell intact. At the end of 1974, José López

Rega, the former chief of police and master of occult sciences in the service of Perón's third wife—who was president of the Republic at the time—tried to erect on the same site an Altar of the Fatherland that would serve to reconcile mortal enemies. They began to dig the foundations again, but the adversities of history—as on the previous occasion—interrupted the project.

Every so often Evita reappears there, on the branches of a lapacho tree. The *descamisados* sense her glow, hear her dress rustle, recognize the murmur of her hoarse, impassioned voice, discover the servitude of her lights in the beyond and the fussing of her nerves, and as they place votive candles at the site where her catafalque should have lain, they question her about the future. She replies in ellipses, variations of black, clouding over of the light, announcing that future days will be dark. Since they have always been dark, the credulity of the devout is assured. Evita is infallible.

Myth is constructed on one plane, and human writing, at times, flies off in another. The image of Evita that literature is leaving behind, for example, is only that of her dead body or that of her unfortunate sex. The fascination for her dead body began even before her illness, in 1950. That year, Julio Cortázar finished *The Test,* at the time an unpublishable novel in more than one sense, as he himself declares in the introduction written three decades later. It is the story of a brutish multitude from every corner of Argentina that suddenly appears in the Plaza de Mayo to worship a bone. People await heaven only knows what miracle, have their hearts broken by a woman dressed in white, "her very fair disheveled hair drooping down to her breasts." She is good, she is very good, the blackies who invade the city keep saying, then finally turn into fungi and poisonous mists. The fear floating in the air is not mortal fear of Perón but of her, the woman who dredges up from the immortal depths of history the worst detritus of barbarism. Evita is the return to the horde, the anthropophagous instinct of the species, the ignorant beast that bursts blindly into the glassware shop of beauty.

"A Woman Reaches Her Eternity"

In the Argentina of the years in which Cortázar wrote *The Test*, its Spiritual Head, still in good health, with sharp fangs and cruel talons thirsting for blood, inspired a sacred terror. She was a woman who came out of the darkness of the cave and ceased to embroider, to starch the shirts, to light the fire in the kitchen, to brew the maté, to bathe the kids, and installed herself in the halls of government and lawmaking, which were domains reserved for men. "That strange woman was different from almost every other white woman," the *Black Book of the Second Tyranny*, published in 1958, says of her. "She lacked education but not political intuition; she was vehement, dominating, and spectacular." In other words, unforgivable, indecent, with gifts of "passion and courage" unnatural in a woman. "Her tastes must run to females," Martínez Estrada conjectures in his *Orations against Catiline*. "In bed she is no doubt as shameless as a fallen woman, who takes her pleasure as readily with an habitué of the brothel as with a pet or any of the other whorehouse strumpets."

The sumptuous spectacle of her death was an affront to Argentine decency. The intellectual elite imagined her dying with the same gestures with which, perhaps, she made love. She breathed her last, disappeared into another body, went past the limits, making love when she was deader than anybody, dying to all love, soulless but surrendering her soul, putting her pleasure out to pasture in the fields of death. Nothing by herself; everything had to be done openly, shamelessly, intimidating the elite by her intimate, exaggerated, strident privacy, Evita the lowlife, Evita the woman who's been around.

Some of the best stories of the fifties are a parody of her death. Writers needed to forget Evita, to exorcise her ghost. In "She," a story he wrote in 1953 and published forty years later, Juan Carlos Onetti dyed the corpse green, made it disappear in a sinister greenness: "Now they were waiting for the rotting to spread, for a green fly to come down, despite the season, and alight on her open lips. Her forehead was turning green."

Almost at the same time, Borges, more oblique, more elusive, denigrated the burial in "The Simulacrum," a brief text whose only char-

acter is a man dressed in mourning, with Indian features, who ex-
hibits a doll with red hair in a wretched funeral chapel. It was
Borges's intention to bring out the barbarism of the mourning and
the falsification of grief by exaggerating them: Eva is a dead doll in
a cardboard box, venerated in all the slums. What the story turns
out to be, however, without this being his conscious intention—for
literature is not always a voluntary act—is an homage to Evita's
immensity: in "The Simulacrum," Evita is the image of God made
woman, the female God of all women, the female Man of all the
gods.

Those who have best understood the historic link between love
and death are homosexuals. They all imagine themselves fornicating
wildly with Evita. They suck her, they bring her back to life, they
bury her, they bury themselves in her, they idolize her. They are her,
her till they waste away to nothing. In Paris, many years ago, I saw
Eva Perón, a comedy—or a play?—by Copi. I don't remember now
who played the part of Evita. I believe it was Facundo Bo, a trans-
vestite. During one of the rehearsals I recorded, or copied from
Copi, a monologue in French that he then translated for me with the
residua of language he still had left: "A grotesque text," he said to
me, "as tarty and as tender as Eva herself." Something on the bor-
derline of pure sound, interjections that spanned the entire spectrum
of feelings. It went like this, more or less:

EVITA (to the group of gays—of undetermined gender—who sur-
round her as she embraces them one by one): *Hey, listen, they let me fall
down to the bottom of cancer all by myself. They're stupid jerks. I've gone nuts,
I'm all alone. Look at me dying like a cow in the slaughterhouse. I'm not who
I was once. I even had to go through the whole death bit all by myself. They
let me do whatever I wanted. I went to shitty shantytowns, gave out wads of
bills, and left everything to the little greasers: my jewelry, the car, my dresses. I
came back like a mad thing, bare naked in the taxi, sticking my ass out the
window. Like I was already dead, like I was only the memory of a dead
woman.*

Yes, of course, it's a portrait of her going to pieces, but an imperfect one. Copi didn't have the street life that Evita had had, and it shows in this text. The language tends to be onomatopoetic and hysterical, mimicking the desperation and the insolence with which she gradually created a style and a tone that haven't been repeated since in Argentine culture. But Copi wrote with good manners. He can't free himself from his powerful family or his rich-kid background (Copi's grandfather, remember, was the Great Gatsby of Argentine journalism), his turds stink of the place Vendôme and not of the sewers of Los Toldos: he's a long way away from Evita's tough, illiterate street language.

He loved her, of course. The comedy—or the play?—*Eva Perón* is an outpouring of compassion for the darns in her dress; no one who sees it can doubt that for Copi the work was a patient and undisguised labor of identification: *Evita c'est moi.* That did not keep a pack of Peronist fanatics from burning the Epée-de-Bois Theater down the week after the premiere. The stage sets, the dressing rooms, the wardrobe department, everything burned down. The flames could be seen from the rue Claude Bernard, two hundred yards away. The fanatics didn't like it that Evita showed her ass. In the work, she offers her love as best she can or as best she knows how. She surrenders her body to be devoured. "I am the Christ of erotic Peronism," Copi has her say. "Fuck me however you like."

What a lack of respect, what an outrage, the arsonists protested in the leaflets they flung about the day after they burned down the Epée-de-Bois Theater. Almost twenty years later, when Néstor Perlongher published the three short stories that came out under the title *Evita Lives (in Every Call-House),* other fanatics, when they filed a suit against him, again quoted words from Discépolo's tango: *What a lack of respect, what a display of insolent depravity.*

Perlongher wants desperately to be Evita; he looks for her amid the folds of sex and death, and when he finds her, what he sees in her is the body of a soul, or what Leibniz would call "the body of a monad." Perlongher understands her better than anyone else. He speaks the same language of Indian encampments, of humiliation and the abyss. He doesn't dare touch her life, so he touches her death: he fingers the body, he decks it with jewels, he puts makeup on it, he removes the down from her upper lip, he undoes her chignon. Contemplating it from below, he deifies it. And since every Goddess is free, he unbridles her. In "The Corpse of the Nation" and in the two or three other poems in which Perlongher pillages her, she does not speak: what speaks are the jewels of the dead body. The stories of *Evita Lives*, on the other hand, are an epiphany in the meaning that Joyce gave the word: a "sudden spiritual manifestation," the soul of an avid body coming back to life.

This is how the second of the three stories begins:

> We were there in the house where we got together to smoke, and the cat that brought the shit that day turned up with a blonde who must have been thirty-eight, looking really beat, wearing tons of warpaint and her hair done up in a bun. . . .

The ones who brought suit against Perlongher because of his "sacrilegious writing" didn't understand that his intention was precisely the opposite: to clothe Evita in a sacred writing. Read the story of the Resurrection in the Gospel according to Saint John: the parodic intent of *Evita Lives* then leaps to the eye. In the story, nobody recognizes her in the beginning, nobody wants to believe that she is who she is. The same thing happens to Jesus in John 20:14, when he appears to Mary Magdalene for the first time. Evita offers proofs, signs of who she is to the police officer who wants to arrest her, just as Jesus does to Thomas the Twin. Evita sucks a wart, Christ asks his disciples to touch him: "Bring here thy finger . . . and bring here thy hand, and put it into my side" (John 20:27).

When he wrote the last version of *Evita Lives*, Perlongher was submerged in a wave of mysticism; he had learned a few weeks before that he had AIDS, and was dreaming of resurrection. Writing to Evita in the language that Evita might have used in the eighties was his strategy for saving himself and enduring in "The Corpse of the

Nation." He did not say to himself, as Copi had done: *Evita c'est moi.*
Instead he asked himself: And what if God were a woman? What if
I were the Goddess and on the third day my body came back to life?

Literature has seen Evita in a way precisely the opposite of the
way she wanted to see herself. She never spoke of sex in public and
perhaps not in private either. Perhaps she would have freed herself
from sex if she had been able to. She did something better: she
learned it and forgot it as it suited her, as though it were just another
character in a radio soap opera. Those who knew her intimately
thought that she was the least sexy woman in the world. "You
wouldn't get turned on by her even on a desert island," a leading
man in one of her films said. What turned on Perón then? There is
no way of knowing: Perón was a dark sun, an empty landscape, the
wasteland of nonfeeling. She may have filled him with her desires.
Not sex, but desires. Eva had nothing in common with the wanton
hetaera of whom her vehement critic Martínez Estrada speaks, and
nothing in common with the "whore from the slums" whom Borges
slandered. In Evita's discussions of women, which take up all the
third part of *My Mission in Life*, the word *sex* does not appear even
once. She does not speak of pleasure or of desire; she refutes them.
She writes (or dictates, or lets the words be put in her mouth): "I am
the same as any woman in any of the countless homes of my people . . . I like the same things: jewels, furs, dresses, shoes . . . But like
her, I prefer everyone in the house to be better than me. Like her,
like all of them, it would please me to be free to stroll about and
amuse myself . . . But I am tied down just as they are, by household
tasks that it is no one's responsibility to take on in my stead."

Evita wanted to efface sex from her image in history, and she has
partially succeeded. The biographies written after 1955 maintain a
respectful silence on the subject. Only the madwomen of literature
set it on fire, strip it naked, make it wiggle its ass, as though it were
a poem by Oliverio Girondo. They take it over, they paw it, they sur-
render to it. In the last analysis, isn't that what Evita asked the public to do with her memory?

* * *

People construct the myth of the body however they please, read Evita's body with the grammatical declensions of their gaze. She can be anything and everything. In Argentina she is still the Cinderella of television serials, the nostalgia for having been what we never were, the woman with the whip, the celestial mother. Outside the country, she is power, the woman who died young, the compassionate hyena who declaims from the balconies of the beyond: "Don't cry for me, Argentina."

The opera, the musical (what's it called?), by Tim Rice and Andrew Lloyd Webber has simplified and condensed the myth. The Evita who *Time* claimed in 1947 was indecipherable has now been turned into a sing-along article out of *Selections from the Reader's Digest*. In the suburb where I am writing this story, which goes by the suggestive name of Middlesex County (or Middling Sex? or Medium Sex?), Evita is a figure as familiar as the Statue of Liberty, which, to top it all off, she resembles.

Sometimes, to get away from the word processor, I go out for a drive, wandering aimlessly up and down the deserted back roads of New Jersey. I go from Highland Park to Flemington or from Millstone to Woods Tavern with the radio on. When I least expect it, Evita sings. I hear her coming out of the rasping throat of the razor-shorn Sinéad O'Connor. The dead woman and the singer have the same hoarse, sad voice, about to burst into a sob. They sing, both of them, "Don't cry for me, Argentina," with drawn-out, ruminant *r*s, they pronounce *Aryentina* as though the *y* were an *r* of my native province. Am I looking for Evita or is Evita looking for me? There is so much silence here, in this stifled breathing of the song!

I drive along, approaching Trenton or taking off toward Oak Grove, the soot in the air doesn't move, the sky keeps on showing the same scars, and in a deserted mall, amid the flashing signs of Macy's, Kentucky Fried Chicken, Pet Doktor, the Gap, Athlete's Foot, between a billboard showing Clint Eastwood and another showing Goldie Hawn, Evita's image towers like a queen's, alone against the powers of heaven and earth, beyond the reach of the suburb, the rain, anyone's tears, Don't cry for me, with the raised halo of the Statue of Liberty at the crest of her beauty.

In this Middlesex County, in New Jersey, Evita is a familiar figure, but the story that people know about her is the one in the opera, the one by Tim Rice. Nobody, perhaps, knows who she really was; most of them suppose that Argentina is a suburb of Guatemala City. But in my house, Evita floats about: her wind blows there; she leaves her name in the fire every day. I write in the lap of her photographs: I see her with her hair in the wind on an April morning; or disguised as a sailor, posing for a cover of *Sintonía* magazine; or sweating in a mink coat, standing next to the dictator Francisco Franco, in the iron summer of Madrid; or stretching her hands out toward the *descamisados;* or falling into Perón's arms, with dark circles under her eyes, nothing but skin and bones. I write in her lap, listening to the pathetic speeches of the last months of her life, or fleeing from these pages to look once more at videos of the films that nobody here has seen: *The Prodigal Woman, The Circus Parade, The Unhappiest Man in Town,* in which Evita Duarte moves awkwardly and speaks her lines with atrocious diction, a terrible actress, a beauty: *May the beautiful be only the beginning of the terrible?*

So I go on, day after day, advancing along the razor-thin edge between what is mythical and what is true, slipping between the lights of what was not and the darknesses of what might have been. I lose myself in those folds, and she always finds me. She never ceases to exist, to exist me: she makes her existence an exaggeration.

A few miles from my house, in New Brunswick, a black soprano, whose name is Janice Brown, revived, a while back, the hit songs from the musical *Evita.* Two nights a week she sings "Don't cry for me, Argentina." She wears a blond wig and a long bell-shaped skirt. The rundown theater, with seats upholstered in threadbare velvet, is always full. Almost all the audience is black, they eat enormous amounts of popcorn during the hour and a quarter the show lasts, but when Evita is on her deathbed, they stop chewing and they too cry, like Argentina. Evita never would have imagined herself reincarnated in Janice Brown or in the raw, razed voice of Sinéad O'Connor. She would not have thought of herself as being shown on billboards of a far-off country where she is a character in an opera. She would, however, have liked seeing her name in lights on the marquee of a theater in New Brunswick, even though it is a theater that since 1990 has been about to be torn down and the site made into a parking lot.

9

"Grandeurs of Misery"

As long as the truck with its funereal guest remained stationed next to the sidewalk of the Intelligence Service, the Colonel couldn't sleep a wink. He ordered guards posted day and night and the remains of the flowers and candles cleared away. He looked in the afternoon papers for a story about the damage done by the fire that had kept him from leaving Evita amid the cisterns of the Waterworks building: he didn't find a single word. A warehouse full of fats and oils had burned down, but over a mile to the south of the Waterworks. What was happening to reality? Was it possible that certain facts existed for some people and were invisible to others? The Colonel didn't know how to get over his restlessness. At times he walked taciturnly along the corridors of the Service and stopped in front of the desks of the NCOs, staring at them. Or else he shut himself up in his office to sketch domes of imaginary cities. He was afraid of losing his hold on everything if he allowed sleep to overcome him. He couldn't close his eyes. His insomnia was also his inferno.

At nightfall on the first day, the guards on the second watch discovered a daisy in the radiator of the truck. The officers came out to see it and concluded that they had overlooked the flower when they made their morning inspection. Nobody would have been able to weave it into the radiator grille without being seen. Pedestrians had been constantly coming and going by; the guards hadn't taken their eyes off the vehicle. And yet they had failed to notice the long-stemmed daisy, its corolla filled with pollen.

Another surprise was forthcoming the following morning. On the street, underneath the running boards of the truck, two tall, lathe-turned candles were burning. The breeze blew them out, and then after giving off one swift spark they began burning again. The Colonel ordered them removed immediately, but after nightfall there were flowers scattered underneath the chassis again, next to a bunch of candles that gave off barely visible light, like desires. Alongside the back of the truck, several crude mimeographed leaflets were whirling in the wind, with an explicit caption: *Commando of Vengeance.* And at the bottom: *Give Evita back. Leave her in peace.*

It's a warning; the battle is about to begin, the Colonel thought. The enemy could steal the corpse that very night, right from under his nose. If that happened, he was going to have to kill himself. The world would fall in on him. The president of the Republic had already asked: "Have you finally buried her?" And the only thing the Colonel could tell him was: "Sir, we still don't have the answer." "Don't delay any longer," the president had insisted. "Take her to Monte Grande cemetery." But that couldn't be done. Monte Grande was the very place that their enemies would go looking for her.

He decided he was going to guard the coffin himself that night. He would stretch out inside the back of the truck, on a field blanket. He would order Major Arancibia, the Madman, to stay with him. Just for a few hours, he said to himself. He felt afraid. But what did that matter, as long as nobody knew it? It wasn't fear of death but fear of luck: fear of not knowing from what quarter of the darkness the lightning bolt of bad luck would descend on him.

He posted the guards in such a way that chance could not sneak up on him: he left one man in the cab of the truck, at the wheel; two guards on the sidewalk opposite, dressed in civvies; two more on the corners; one underneath the chassis, lying between the wheels. He ordered one of the officers, posted at the windows inside the Service, to watch the area through binoculars and report any unusual movement. The guards were to be relieved every three hours, from nine p.m. on. Things that go wrong have a limit, the Colonel kept telling himself. They never happen a second time.

It was shortly after midnight when he and the Madman installed themselves in the truck. They were wearing fatigues. The vague presentiment that they would do battle before dawn drove all thoughts from their minds save the hollow, desolate idea of waiting. "Death will come and it will have her eyes," the Colonel had read somewhere. Whose eyes? The hardest part of waiting was not knowing who the enemy was. Anyone could come out of nowhere and confront them. A secret adversary was, perhaps, preparing himself in their very own heart of hearts. The Madman was armed with the Ballester Molinas that he had used to shoot hundreds of dogs to death. Moori Koenig had, as always, his Colt. Inside the back of the truck, in the dense, stuffy air, there floated a faint fragrance of flowers. No street noises could be heard: only the panting of time, marching on. They lay in silence in the dark. After a while, they heard a piercing, high-pitched buzzing whose keen edge seemed to be cutting through the silence.

"It's bees," the Colonel surmised. "The smell of the flowers is attracting them."

"There aren't any flowers," Arancibia observed.

They looked in vain for the bees, until everything was silent once again. Every so often, they asked each other pointless questions, just to hear each other's voice. Neither of them felt sleepy. Sleep grazed their consciousness and then went away, like a weary cloud. They heard the first changing of the guard. At intervals, the Colonel knocked three times on the floor of the truck and someone—the man stretched out underneath the chassis—answered with three identical knocks.

"Do you hear that?" the Madman said all of a sudden.

The Colonel sat up. The silence was everywhere, waking up and stretching in the boundless dark. "There's nothing."

"Listen to her. She's moving."

"There's nothing," the Colonel repeated.

"What we buried were the copies," the Madman said. "This one is her, the Mare. I realized right away, on account of the smell."

"They all smell: the corpse, the copies. They've all been treated with chemicals."

"No. This body's breathing. Maybe the embalmer put something in her insides, so she'd get some life back in her. She might have a microphone."

"It's not possible. The government doctors saw the X rays. The Deceased is intact, like a live person. But she isn't alive. She can't breathe."

"Then it's her?"

"How should I know?" the Colonel said. "We buried the bodies at random."

"Listen, there it is again. She's there. Listen to her breathing," the Madman insisted.

If a person listened carefully, sounds came flowing by, as in a dream: choirs of monks in the distance, the crackling of dry leaves, the beating wings of a bird rowing against the wind.

"It's the air, down below," the Colonel said.

He knocked on the floor three times with his bayonet shaft, varying the rhythm: two rapid drumrolls, and then after waiting a few seconds, another long, challenging knock. The man who was lying underneath the chassis answered in precisely the same rhythm. It was the countersign.

They remained motionless again, smelling the acrid residues of time passing by. The darkness went on devouring itself and moving deeper inside its mole's tunnel. They were sweating from tension at the thought of the imminent battle. Would there be a battle? The Madman's voice leapt up like a spark:

"It seems to me the Mare isn't there any longer, sir. I think she's gone."

"Stop talking nonsense, Arancibia."

"I haven't heard her for quite a while."

"You never did hear her. It was hallucinations. Calm down."

The Madman's anxiety went back and forth from one side of the truck to the other. It could be heard bumping into the benches and the canvas sides.

"Why don't we see if she's still there, sir?" he proposed. "That woman's strange. She can do anything. She always was strange."

The Colonel thought that perhaps Arancibia was right, but he refused to admit it. Of course she's strange, he said to himself. In just one night, just lying there, not lifting a finger, she'd unhinged heaven only knew how many lives. Even he wasn't the same now, just as the navy captain had said. He couldn't make another mistake. He must rule out every possible wrong step. He cleared his throat. The voice he spoke in wasn't his either.

"We've nothing to lose if we take a look," he said. He aimed the flashlight beam toward the coffin. "Take the lid off slowly, Arancibia."

He heard the Madman's eager panting. He saw his hands lifting up the wooden lid with a desire that was searching for something more, something that was no longer within anyone's reach. He couldn't recall what the scene resembled, but it must be something he had already witnessed and perhaps lived many times, something as basic and fundamental as thirst or dreams. In the narrow beam of light, Evita's profile suddenly stood out in the emptiness.

"It's like the moon," the Madman said. "You'd think it was cut out with a pair of scissors."

"Keep calm," the Colonel ordered. "Be alert."

He crouched down until his line of sight coincided with the Deceased's horizon line. And then, pretending disdain, he lifted up the lobe of her ear that was still intact and examined the tiny star-shaped brand he had marked her with. It was still there, indelible. Only he could see it.

"Cover her up again, Arancibia. It isn't good for her to be exposed to the air."

The Madman ventured a quick, sharp whistle, like a bird's. He couldn't help himself.

"Look at that. It's her all right," he said. "This is how she's ended up. The Spiritual Head, the Standard Bearer of the Humble. And now she's lonelier than a dog."

They waited once again in the desert of darkness. Every so often, they could hear their own quiet breathing. Later on, the going and coming of the patrols outside served as a diversion. Around dawn it rained. The Colonel gave in to sleep or to the sensation of no longer being anywhere at all. They were awakened by the sound of footsteps trotting down the sidewalk on the double and the voice of Captain Galarza shouting out an order:

"Don't touch anything! The Colonel must see this catastrophe."

Someone knocked on the door of the truck. Moori Koenig smoothed down his hair and buttoned his jacket. The watch in the night had ended.

The bright daylight dazzled him. Through the narrow slit in the door that had just been opened he caught a glimpse of Galarza, his arms akimbo. He was telling him something, but he didn't catch what it was. He simply followed the line of Galarza's index finger that was pointing to one corner of the truck, underneath the chassis. He found there what he had been afraid of finding, all night long. He saw a row of lighted candles, immune to the breeze and the misty rain. He saw the gusts of daisies, sweet peas, and honeysuckle that accompanied the Deceased as though they were the angels of her death, except that now there were many flowers, two round heaps of them. And between the wheels he saw Sergeant Gandini, who had been assigned to the last watch of the night, his head bleeding, still alive. They had beat him cruelly. There was a bunch of papers stuffed in his mouth. The Colonel didn't need to read them to know what they said.

He frantically climbed the stairs to his office. He drank a long swallow of brandy. He looked out the window at the endless city: the flat, even roofs, from which there stood out, at intervals, the birds' necks of domes. Then he remembered that he could still use the phone. He made a couple of calls and sent for the Madman.

"Our troubles are almost over, Major," he said. "We're going to

194

take the coffin to a movie theater. I've already arranged things. They're waiting for us."

"A movie theater?" Arancibia said in surprise. "The president is going to be upset by the news."

"The president isn't going to know anything about it. He thinks we've already buried her at Monte Grande."

"When are we taking her?"

"Right now. We have to act fast. Tell Galarza and Fesquet to get a move on. This time we're going to work alone."

"Alone?" the Madman asked. The whole situation seemed like a delirium in which no piece fitted together with any other. "A movie theater is a public place, sir. Where are we going to put her?"

"In plain sight of everyone," Moori said arrogantly. "Behind the screen." Wasn't that what she wanted? Hadn't she come to Buenos Aires looking for a bit part in a movie? Now she was going to be in all of them.

"Behind the screen," Arancibia repeated. "Nobody's going to think of a thing like that. Which movie theater is it?"

The Colonel took his time answering. He was looking up at the purple sky.

"The Rialto," he said, "in Palermo. The owner is an Intelligence officer who's retired now. I asked him what there was behind the screen. Rats, he told me. Nothing but rats and spiders."

His eyes had turned yellow and slanted from having looked for so long at the lighted coals of projectors. They were veiled by a cloudy membrane, like dirty glass, and tears slid down his cheeks if he wasn't careful. If it hadn't been for Yolanda, his daughter, he might have killed himself. But the baby girl's shy affection and the films he projected at the Rialto—two at the evening showing, three at the late afternoon matinee—kept him from thoughts of suicide.

In a school run by friars he had been taught that life is divided by a fold—a before and an after—that turns men into what they will be forever. The friars called that moment an "epiphany" or "the encounter with Christ." To José Nemesio Astorga, also known as el Chino, the Chinaman, the first undulation of the fold began on the afternoon he met Evita.

He remembered the exact day and hour. At 12:10 on Sunday, September 5, 1948, the owner of the Rialto had ordered him to go to the presidential residence on the calle Austria where he was to project a couple of films. "There's a miniature movie theater there," he told him. "It has brand-new, deluxe equipment." The film industry labor unions were out on strike and movie theaters had been closed for three days, but el Chino Astorga couldn't refuse to work. He was under the owner's thumb seven days a week. This was how he paid for the two rooms with flaking paint where he lived, in the back of the movie theater, with Lidia, his wife, and their daughter, a year and a half old.

An official car came by to pick him up at three. Fifteen minutes later he was dropped off at the residence on the calle Austria and was shown into the cramped booth of the microtheater, in which reels of film were already piled up in two tall columns. The air was stifling, and the sweetish odor of celluloid dragged itself along the carpets like an old servant. Eight of the reels were of a movie Astorga had never heard of; three were editions of *Events in Argentina.* Through the peephole he peered out at the empty screening room with twenty armchairs. José Nemesio Astorga was a methodical man, who trusted the wisdom of precise figures.

A butler told him to dim the lights and begin the showing without waiting for anyone to come. Amid the stammers of the opening titles he saw a shadow slip in and take a seat at one end of the room, next to the exit. The unknown film was called *The Prodigal Woman,* and the stars of it were Juan José Míguez and Eva Duarte.

There was a world of difference between the Evita of the film and the one everybody knew. The one in the movie was a hieratic matron, with dark hair and intense black eyes, who was always dressed in mourning, with towering lace mantillas. Within the confines of what the matron called "my country estate" a dam was being built. An endless river of villagers bowed low as she passed, kissing her rings and calling her the "little mother of the poor." The woman re-paid this great veneration by giving away jewels, blankets, spindles, small herds of cattle. In a hoarse voice she declaimed impossible phrases such as "Give me an arrow and I shall bury it in the heart of the universe" or "Forgive the archbishops, my Lord God, for they know not what they do." Both because of its subject and because of its language, *The Prodigal Woman* was a film made in another century, before movies were invented.

During the showing, the shadow didn't move from its armchair. Astorga watched it through the peephole, but he couldn't make out its features. He heard it cough every so often or accompany the downfall of the heroine with sighs and moans. The vague image of a suicide appeared on the screen: the matron bade farewell to the world with either a dagger or a bottle of poison. A broken voice then came from the armchair in the screening room:

"Hey, you, don't turn on the light. Go ahead and show the news-reels."

He recognized the voice. It had spoken in the same harsh tone as Evita's speeches, with the same diction that wavered between the slums and tackiness. In the pitiless light of *Events in Argentina* he could finally see her, as she was in a reality that the films of her failed to capture: with her tousled locks caught up in a simple hair band, her agile tapered hands above her skirt, her thin torso under-neath her housedress, her long straight nose above the promontory of her lips. It was her. The image to which his wife prayed each night before going to bed. She was there, a few steps away.

El Chino knew by heart all the installments of *Events in Argentina* that came out weekly, yet he had never seen the one he was now projecting. It did not have an edition number or a release date, and the takes were irregular in length: sometimes they were very long and showed whole conversations, or else they were quick shots of crowds, faces, details of dress. In the first sections of the newsreel, Evita was alone at a writing desk, with papers that she disarranged and then put back in order again. An enormous curl fell over her forehead. "My countrywomen, comrades, and friends," she recited.

197

Her voice was strident and pompous. "I have come to speak to you, on behalf of women's suffrage, with the heart of a provincial girl, brought up in the rugged virtue of work . . ." The Evita of the screening room moved her lips, repeating the words of the film, as her fingers moved back and forth with an emphasis different from the script: the pantomime transformed the meaning of the words. If the Evita of the screen said: "I wish to contribute my grain of sand to this great work that General Perón is carrying out," the Evita in the screening room bowed her head, raised her hands to her bosom, or held them out toward the invisible audience with such eloquence that the word *Perón* got lost on the way, and only the sound of the word *Evita* could be heard. It was as though, by going over the speeches of the past, she were rehearsing those of the future in front of the strange mirror of the screen, where what was reflected was no longer what she could do but what would never be again.

The images jerked from one official ceremony to another. At times, the deputies in the opposition appeared in fleeting scenes protesting against "that woman who pokes her nose into everything, though no one has elected her to any office." From her seat, Evita shooed the words away with a disdainful wave of her hands. At the end she was seen in the Plaza de Mayo, on a sunny day, waving papers at the crowd and peering dubiously at a script whose rhetoric made her feel as uncomfortable as a corset. "Women of my country," she was saying. "I have just this moment received directly from the government of the nation the law that establishes the right of all Argentine women to vote." The other Evita, from her armchair, went on repeating that same phrase with other gestures, as in stage rehearsals.

The images of the European tour began almost immediately after that. Evita was walking on the beach at Rapallo, wearing a long cape, platform shoes, and dark harlequin glasses, like Joan Crawford's. She was walking by herself beneath a leaden sky in which seagulls were sputtering. A herd of bodyguards was following her. The camera soon moved away for a long shot and caught her distant image from a balcony overshadowed by a sign that perhaps showed

the name of the hotel: EXCELSIOR. She left the cape on the sand and
dove into the sea. Her legs appeared every so often amid the curling
waves. A white bathing cap disfigured her head. Not a soul was to
be seen on the beach, but on the other side of the dunes the horizon
was filled with beach umbrellas.

How lonely she looks, el Chino thought. What use to her is
everything she has?

The next newsreel repeated the images that had been distributed
in torrents during her trip to Rome: the majestic entrance of the first
lady by way of the via della Conciliazione in a coach drawn by four
white horses, the open-eyed astonishment of her entourage at the
sight of the columns of St. Peter's and the obelisk of Caligula in Vatican Square, the reception by the papal courtiers in the courtyard of
San Damaso, the walk to the Pio Clementino Museum amid guards
wearing doublets and carrying lances, as an old papal knight in
black breeches, with a patch over one eye, pointed out in passing the
tapestries by Raphael, Bacchus's sarcophagus, the marble figures of
animals. Enveloped in a mantilla, Evita smiled without understanding a word. The entourage halted before a tall door in carved wood.
Behind the dignitaries the vague geometry of gardens with fountains could be glimpsed. Everyone suddenly fell silent. Pius XII appeared beneath an arch of shadows and introduced himself with his
hand outstretched. Evita knelt and kissed the boss of the ring that
the camera, daringly, zoomed in on for a close-up. All the newsreels
usually ended with that shot.

The entourage now entered the papal library and halted before
Coptic manuscripts, books of hours, Gutenberg Bibles. The first lady
walked with lowered head, and unlike what had happened on all the
other stops of the European tour, this time she didn't open her
mouth. In the center of the library was a black-and-white-checkered
table with two straight-backed chairs. At a gesture from the pontiff,
both of them seated themselves: she timidly, knees together, not
leaning back.

"Parla, figlia mia. Ti ascolto," Pius XII said.

Evita recited, as in radio soap operas:

"I come from beyond the sea with humility, Holy Father. Allow me to tell you about the bases of the Christian society which General Perón is constructing in Argentina through the inspiration of our Redeemer and Divine Master."

"Our Lord will bless this work," Pius XII answered in Spanish. "I pray each day for my dearly beloved Argentina."

"I am deeply grateful," Evita said. "A prayer of the Holy Father's ascends to heaven more swiftly."

"No, my daughter," Pius XII explained with a Cheshire-cat smile. "The Lord listens to the prayers of all mankind with the same attentiveness."

Standing next to the doors of the library, the Swiss guards held their halberds upright. A starched brotherhood of cardinals, ambassadors, nuns of the papal household, and ladies of honor awaited alongside the shelves, behind the papal knights in ruffs and knee breeches, wearing decorations even on their shirt cuffs. With a secrecy that the camera clearly caught, the pontiff raised one of his little fingers: in the pitiless beam of the spotlights, the finger darted out, as long and slender as a viper's tongue. It must have been a signal. Two nuns trotted from the other end of the library carrying a gilded chest brimming over with gifts. One of the cardinals announced in a loud voice:

"His Holiness is offering the first lady of Argentina a rosary from Jerusalem with relics of the Holy Crusade . . ." Pius XII showed the audience one of the boxes, already freed of its wrapping by the nuns, as Evita held out her hands and assayed an awkward curtsy. "His Holiness also wishes to decorate the Señora with the Medaglia d'Oro del Pontificato . . ." Evita bowed her head, perhaps believing that the pope was going to hang a ribbon around her neck, but the latter displayed to the delegation of ambassadors and cardinals a coin with his own effigy and placed it offhandedly in the hands of the visitor, who stammered: "I thank you in the name of my people." Her words were lost, for one of the nuns took a canvas from the bottom of the chest and handed it to the pontiff, who adroitly unrolled it before the audience. "This"—the cardinal who was serving as master of ceremonies continued—"is an almost perfect reproduction of the work of Jan van Eyck, *Il matrimonio degli Arnolfini,* painted on wood in 1434. The copy, done in oil on canvas, by Pietro Gucci, dates from 1548 and belongs to the Vatican collection. I should say *belonged,* since it will be donated to the Argentine government . . ." The ladies of honor applauded, thus perhaps violating protocol; Evita kept her eyes lowered. "The husband and wife in the painting are Giovanni di Arrigo Arnolfini and Giovanna Cenami, the daughter of a merchant of Lucca. Round about them are symbols of matrimony: a candle, a pair of clogs, a dog."

Not moving from her armchair, with her legs crossed, Evita watched the scene, hypnotized. Pius XII had risen to his feet, and holding the canvas out to the Evita of the film, was saying: "This painting, my daughter, is the perfect image of matrimonial bliss. Young Arnolfini reflects strength and protection, as do good husbands. Despite her feeling of fulfillment, Giovanna seems somewhat discomfited, embarrassed." The Evita in the screening room took off one of her shoes and loosened her hair band. She looked uncomfortable, bemused, as though she had lost a day out of her life. Meanwhile, the Evita of the film was saying clearly: "She ought to be embarrassed, Holy Father, seeing she's in the family way, around seven months along, I'd say." A wicked smile played over the face of Pius XII. The Argentine ambassador ran his hand over his balding pate, slick with pomade. A couple of cardinals coughed in unison.

"The marriage had not yet been consummated, my daughter," the pope corrected her, in an understanding tone of voice. "When van Eyck painted her, Giovanna was a virgin. What is misleading you is her high girdle, which makes her belly protrude, as was the dictate of fashion for young ladies of that era. But the Lord blessed the Arnolfini with numerous offspring. It is my heartfelt wish that he may bless you as well."

"Let us hope so, Holy Father," Evita answered.

"You are still young. You can have all the children you like."

"I would like to have some, but they haven't come. I have many others, thousands. They call me Mother and I call them my little greasers."

"Those are children of politics," the pope said. "I am speaking of children sent by the Lord. If you wish to have them, you must seek them with love and prayer."

In the solitude of the screening room, Evita began to cry. Perhaps not really weeping but only a sudden tear, yet el Chino, who was a past master at deciphering signs given off by the backs and the napes of the necks of filmgoers, read Evita's sadness in the slight trembling of her shoulders and in her fingers which, furtively, stole up to her eyes. The camera, meanwhile, had begun to move through Raphael's bedrooms and the Borgia Apartments, but Evita had already left, leaving behind only the heavy sorrow of her body clad in tulle: she was not onscreen or in her armchair but in some secret landscape of herself.

El Chino saw her walk to one corner of the screening room and heard her speak over the phone. Her orders mingled with the voice of the newsreel commentator, and he could make out only a few words:

". . . these bedrooms were part of the apartments where Julius II lived from 1507 on . . . If you have the negatives, burn them, Negro . . . the paintings on the ceiling, which represent the glory of the Most Holy Trinity, were executed by Perugino . . . What gets burned up doesn't exist, Negro, what doesn't get written down or filmed is forgotten . . . the ceiling of the chapel is divided into nine fields that Michelangelo separated over time with pillars, cornices, columns . . . I don't want one single frame left, you hear? . . . The eighth field represents the Flood, Noah's ark can be seen in the distance, don't crane your necks, everything is reflected in mirrors . . . Don't you worry, nobody's going to say anything, if anybody blabs, they're going to have me to reckon with . . . in the ninth field Noah's drunkenness . . . Burn them and that's the end of that."

The light of the screening room went on before el Chino could make out where she was. Suddenly he caught sight of her, standing next to the door of the projection booth, giving him the once-over.

"Are you a Peronist? I don't see Perón's emblem in your lapel," she said to him. "Maybe you're not a Peronist."

"What else can I be, señora?" el Chino answered, upset. "I always wear the emblem. I always wear it."

"You'd better. We have to get rid of everybody who isn't a Peronist."

"I didn't do it on purpose, señora. I swear. I left my house without thinking. I always wear it, señora, believe me."

"Don't call me señora. Call me Evita. Where do you live?"

"I'm a projectionist at the Rialto Theater, in Palermo. I live right there, in some rooms behind the stage."

"I'm going to see that you get better housing. Come by the Foundation one of these days."

"I'll come, señora, but who knows whether they'll let me in."

"Say that Evita sent for you. You'll see how quickly they let you in."

He didn't sleep a wink that night thinking of what a house created by Evita's express wish and power would be like. He discussed with his wife, Lidia, what they ought to say when they were given the title deed to the house, and they finally agreed that it would be best not to utter a single word.

Around eleven a.m., José Nemesio Astorga tried to reach the offices of the Foundation to get what Evita had promised him. He couldn't even get close. The line of people seeking favors stretched all the way around the block twice. To make the wait seem shorter to them, some Peronist volunteers were handing out propaganda leaflets for them to read, and now and again they offered folding chairs to mothers who bared their enormous breasts in full flower and nursed children who could already stand up by themselves. "Evita hasn't arrived, Evita hasn't arrived," the volunteers, dressed in stiffly starched uniforms and nurses' coifs, kept announcing.

Going over to one of them, el Chino informed her that the Señora in person had told him to come see her. "What I don't know is what day or what time," he explained without her asking.

"Then you're going to have to stand in line like everybody else," the woman said. "There are people lined up who have been here since one o'clock this morning. What's more, nobody ever knows whether the Señora is going to come or not."

Astorga presented himself at precisely one o'clock the next morning, after having taken Lidia and Yolanda, their baby girl, to the home of his parents-in-law, who lived in Banfield. "I'll be back around three this afternoon," he told them. "Wait for me at the theater."

"By that time, you'll surely have good news," Lidia conjectured.

"I hope it'll be good news," he said.

On arriving in front of the doors of the Foundation, he discovered that twenty-two people had gotten there ahead of him. The sheep of the mist stretched their legs in the deserted streets, and you could hear them bleating down inside your bones. People were coughing and complaining of their rheumatism. It was ironic that the name of the city meant "Good Air."

El Chino had found out that Evita never came (when she did come) before ten a.m. She had toast and coffee for breakfast at the presidential residence between eight and nine, she spoke on the phone to ministers and governors, and on her way at last to the Foundation, she dropped in briefly at Government House, where she chatted for a quarter of an hour with her husband. They saw each other only at that time of day, because she didn't get back from her work until eleven at night, and by then he was asleep. Evita gave very long audiences, during which she quizzed those seeking favors about their lives and hard times, inspected their false teeth, and diverted herself by commenting on the photographs of their children. Each audience took her at least twenty minutes; at that rate—el Chino calculated—it would be seven and a half hours before his turn came.

Before daybreak, the wailing of the children became intolerable. From time to time little kerosene stoves were lighted, on which people heated milk for baby bottles and water for maté. El Chino asked the families in line behind him if they had waited for hours like this before.

"This is the third time we've come, and we still haven't been able to see Evita," a young man with a drooping mustache said, holding a denture that was too loose in place with his finger as he spoke. "It took us more than ten hours to get here by train from San Francisco. We arrived at midnight and were given number twelve, but when they got to ten, the general sent for the Señora to come at once, and they told us to come back the next day. We slept in the street. We woke up at around three in the morning. This time they gave us number one hundred four. You can never tell with Evita. She's like God. She either comes or she disappears."

"She promised me a house," el Chino said. "And why are you people here?"

A skinny girl, with bird legs, hid behind the young man with the mustache, her hand over her mouth. She didn't have any teeth left either.

"We want a bridal gown," the man answered, moving forward. "We've already bought the bedroom suite and I have the suit they were going to bury my papa in. But if she doesn't get a wedding dress, there's no way the priest is going to be willing to marry us."

El Chino would have liked to cheer them up, but he didn't know how.

"Today's our day," he said. "We're all going to get in today."

"I hope God hears you," the girl answered.

Although the line already went around the corner and the last heads couldn't be seen in the dark, the crowd respected the order of importance of their misfortunes. El Chino heard tell of sufferings so unbearable that no human power, not even Evita's, could relieve the burning ardor of those desires. There was talk of children with rickets who were wasting away in ditches dug at the foot of garbage heaps, of hands severed by knife-sharp train tracks, of raving madmen who lived chained up in squalid hovels with zinc roofs, of kidneys that had failed, of perforated duodenal ulcers, and of hernias about to rupture. And what if those sorrows are unending? Astorga said to himself. What if the end of those sorrows is longer in coming than the end of Evita? What if it turns out that Evita isn't God, like everyone thinks?

Daybreak left him perplexed, because its streaks of light were the same as those at night: damp and ashen. The volunteers served coffee with rolls, but el Chino refused to eat. The list of human misfortunes had made his gorge rise, and he couldn't swallow. He let his mind wander aimlessly, and during the hours that followed he lost all sense of reality, for he was afraid to look it in the face.

At one moment the line began to move. The doors of the Foundation opened, and the visitors climbed slowly up stairways of polished wood hung with banners bearing the Peronist emblem. Upstairs, grasping the handrails, amanuenses with hair shiny with brilliantine and women volunteers with pencils behind their ears came and went. The line went up the stairs between velvet curtains and reached an enormous salon, lighted by teardrop chandeliers. It looked like a church. There was a narrow aisle down the middle, flanked by wooden benches, on which families who had not stood in line like the others were waiting. The air reeked of excrement of newborn babies, unwashed diapers, and sick people's vomit. The odor was stubborn, like the dampness, and its splinters stuck in one's memory for whole days afterward.

At the far end of the room, at the head of a long table, Evita in person was stroking the hands of a peasant couple, bringing her ear closer to their tremulous voices and throwing her head back every so often, as though she were searching for the unforgettable words that those humble people had come seeking. Her hair was pulled back into a knot, and she was wearing a checkered tailored suit, like in photographs of her. Every now and then she removed, in annoyance, a ring or one of her heavy gold bracelets and left them lying on the table.

There followed one upon the other, in a completely natural way, stories that would have been impossible anywhere else. Two men with straw-colored hair who had climbed up on benches were delivering speeches in a language that nobody could make any sense of. From behind the curtains families appeared with tableaux of live bees making their hives inside a garden of tulle: they wanted Evita to accept their gift before the bees finished their work. In the ante-rooms children were waiting, the survivors of the latest epidemic of polio, ready to file past Evita in wheelchairs donated by the Foundation. In the face of that endless torrent of misfortunes, Astorga thanked God for the humbleness of his life, which had not been tainted by any great unhappiness.

An unexpected incident interrupted the morning's routines. After the peasant couple, Evita had attended to triplets who were acrobats eager to marry the prepubescent contortionists of the same circus and needed a special permit for the premature nuptials. As she dismissed them, a big woman with untamable tangled locks complained at the top of her lungs that an employee of the Foundation had taken her apartment away from her.

"Is that true?" the first lady said.

"I swear on the soul of my dead husband that it is," the woman answered.

"Who was it?"

A name was stammered out. The Señora rose to her feet, with her hands on the table. The whole roomful of people held their breath.

"Have Chueco Ansalde come here," she ordered. "I want him here this instant."

The doors behind the Señora opened immediately, revealing a storeroom piled full of bicycles, refrigerators, and trousseaux. From between the boxes a thin, gangling man came forward, the veins of his forehead so swollen that it looked like a map of the circulatory system. His legs were parted in a perfect oval. He was pale, as though he were being taken to the scaffold.

"You took this poor woman's apartment away from her," Evita declared.

"No, señora," Chueco said. "I gave her a smaller apartment. She was living all by herself in three rooms. I have five children who were sleeping one on top of the other in the living room. I paid for

207

her moving expenses. I installed her furniture for her. Unfortunately I broke one of her wicker chairs, but I bought her another one that very same day."

"You had no right," Evita said. "You didn't ask anyone's permission."

"Please forgive me, señora."

"Who gave you the apartment you had?"

"You did, señora."

"I gave it to you, and now I'm taking it away from you. Give the apartment back to this comrade right now and put all her things back where they were."

"And where am I to go, señora?" Chueco turned to the crowd, looking for support. Nobody said a word.

"You're going to hell, a place you never should have left," she said. "Next."

The big woman knelt to kiss Evita's hands, but she impatiently pulled them away. Standing next to the door of the storeroom, Chueco Ansalde was reluctant to leave. Butterflies of tears appeared in his eyes, but shame and uncertainty did not allow them to brim over.

"One of my kids has bronchitis," he pleaded. "How am I going to get him out of bed?"

"That's enough of that," Evita said. "You knew what you were getting into. And now you'll know how to get out."

The intensity of that indignation disconcerted el Chino. People gossiped about the first lady's bad moods, but the newsreels offered only benevolent, maternal images of her. He realized now that she could be ferocious. Two deep wrinkles formed, one on either side of her nose, and at such moments no one could withstand her gaze.

He now regretted being there. The farther the line moved forward, the more afraid el Chino was of revealing his desire. It was going to seem like an insult amid the undertow of tragedies that people were leaving behind. What could he say to her? That he had projected a few films for her on Sunday, in the presidential palace? It was ridiculous. Why not forget about the whole thing and go back home? He didn't have time to go on thinking. A volunteer motioned to him to come forward. Evita smiled at him and took his hands in hers.

"Astorga," she said with unexpected gentleness, consulting a piece of paper. "José Nemesio Astorga. What is it you need?"

"Don't you remember me?" el Chino asked.

Evita didn't have time to answer him. Two nurses burst into the salon, shouting:

"Come, señora! Come with us! There's been a terrible catastrophe!"

"A catastrophe?" Evita repeated.

"A train was derailed as it was entering Constitución. The railway cars turned over, señora, they turned all the way over." The nurses were sobbing. "They're removing the bodies. A tragedy."

All of a sudden, Evita lost all interest in Astorga. She let go of his hands and stood up.

"Let's go then, right away," she said. She turned to the nurses and ordered: "Note down what these comrades need. Arrange for them to come back tomorrow. I am going to receive them early in the morning. I don't know if I'll come back here later. When there's been a tragedy like that how can I come back?"

It was all happening as if in a dream. Without knowing why, el Chino's attention was attracted by the labyrinth of little blue veins trembling beneath Evita's throat. The salon filled with voices that seemed like flotsam from a shipwreck. Amid the uproar and confusion, the smell of dirty diapers kept elbowing its way in and settling down invincibly.

Evita disappeared into an elevator as el Chino was dragged along to the stairs by a sudden stampede. Next to one of the doors, the toothless bride was sobbing, her hands tightly gripping the bridegroom's waist. Dusk fell. The city was stained by a viscous sun, but people studied the sky and opened their umbrellas as though protecting themselves from other suns that were about to fall.

El Chino took the Lacroze subway, got off near Centenary Park, and walked along the streets of Palermo Antiguo, amid the fleshy

shadows of the paradise trees and the rubber trees that bowed po-
litely before the coolness of the entryways. He nosed about the
pocked passageways of the tenements to while away a bit of time
and then turned down the calle Lavalleja, heading toward the Rialto.
His father had told him that before dying people's memories and
feelings of a lifetime all return with the same vividness as the first
time, but now he discovered that it wasn't necessary to die for that
to happen. The past returned to him with the clarity of a long present: the Sundays doing penance in the orphanage, the celluloid bits
cut from filmstrips that he played with next to the entrance to movie
theaters, the first time he kissed Lidia, the boat rides along Rosedal,
the waltz "From the Soul" that he danced on their wedding night,
Yolanda's little mossy face burying itself for the first time in her
mother's trembling breast. He felt that his life did not belong to him
and that, if it did happen to belong to him someday, he wouldn't
know what to do with it.

From a distance he caught sight of a crowd of neighbors in front
of the closed doors of the Rialto. The mechanics from the Armenia
Libre garage, who did not come out of their grease pits even when
the loud crash of an accident reached their ears, came and went, the
legs of their overalls rolled up, among the matrons who had come
downstairs in house slippers and with knitted shawls over their
shoulders. Even the owner of the movie theater was there, talking
with extravagant gestures to a squad of police officers.

Astorga heard his daughter Yolanda crying, but it seemed to him
that things were happening on another shore of reality and that he
was merely looking at them, indifferently, from a distance. If nothing had ever happened to him, it seemed to him that nothing could
happen to him now either.

He ran to the movie theater, not feeling his body. Amid the confusion of the afternoon he made out Yolanda, with her dress torn
and her little face frozen in a surprised expression that he was never
to forget. A neighbor woman was holding her in her arms and rocking her. Suddenly there entered his awareness the terrifying images

of Lidia and the little girl riding on the train from Banfield and the derailment of the railway cars on Constitución. He felt the air change color and fall into a faint from the weight of the bad omens. The owner of the theater came out to meet him.

"Where's Lidia?" Chino asked. "Has something happened?"

"Lidia was in the last car," the owner answered. "She broke her neck against the window, but nothing happened to the little girl, see? She's perfectly all right. I spoke to one of the doctors. He said your wife didn't have time to suffer. It all happened very fast."

"They took her to Argerich," one of the neighbor women broke in. "Your in-laws are there, Chino, waiting for the autopsy. It seems that Lidia almost missed the train in Banfield. She had to run to catch it. If she'd missed it, nothing would have happened. But she caught it."

He had difficulty recognizing Lidia in the hospital bed, with her head wound in bandages like a silkworm. The blow had wrecked her insides, and her face was the same as always, but her yellow features had bird shapes: fleeting curves. She was her and had forever ceased to be her: a stranger, from somewhere else, whom he had never fallen in love with.

From the way the nurses were rushing around and the fuss the police were making, he realized that Evita was still at the hospital, visiting the injured and consoling the families of the dead. When she came into the room where Lidia was, el Chino was weeping, with his face between his hands, and he didn't see her till she put her hand on his shoulder. Their eyes met, and for a moment he had the impression that she had recognized him, but Evita smiled at him with the same sympathetic expression that had been glued to her face since the beginning of the afternoon. One of the nurses handed her Lidia's identification card. The Señora glanced at it and said:

"Astorga. José Nemesio Astorga. I see that you're a Peronist and are wearing the emblem in your lapel. That's what I like to see, Astorga. You needn't worry. The general and Evita are going to pay for your girl's schooling. The general and Evita are going to give you a house. When you've recovered from this cruel blow, drop by the Foundation. Explain what's happened to you and say that Evita has sent for you."

It was at that moment that el Chino felt, in his most secret inner being, the vibration that the friars of his school used to speak of: the epiphany, the fold that separated life into an after and a before. He felt that things were beginning to be what they would always be from now on, but none of all that remade the past. Nothing took the past back to the point where the story could begin all over again.

10

*"A Role
in the Movies"*

At the end of 1989 I set out in search of el Chino Astorga not knowing if I'd find him dead or alive. After forty years, only the Rialto
movie theater had survived the ravages of video-game arcades and
upheld the tradition of continuous showings. An ominous billboard
on the facade announced, however, that it was to be torn down. I
asked about Astorga at the film industry's labor union. They told me
that the records for the fifties had been lost and that no projectionist remembered his name.

I didn't give up after these failed attempts. I decided to call my
friend Emilio Kaufman, whom I hadn't seen for years. The back of
his house and the back of the Rialto were adjacent, and his memory
was prodigious. I had been taken to the house once or twice by
Irene, Emilio's eldest daughter, with whom I had been in love at the
end of the sixties. Irene was married shortly thereafter to someone
else and went, as I did, into exile. In 1977, the unexpected news of
her death plunged me into a depression that lasted for weeks. At the
time I wrote many grief-filled pages meant for Emilio to read; I
never sent them. I felt ashamed of my own feelings. One is free to
feel as one chooses, but people rarely dare to obey the call of that
freedom.

I met Emilio in a café on the calle Corrientes. He had put on weight and had a crest of gray hair, but once he smiled I noted that the depths of his being were still intact and that there was no past separating us. We spoke of what we would do the following week, as though life were about to begin again. It rained outside and then cleared up, but inside us there was no change in the weather. One story kept leading us to another and from one city we leapt to the next, until Emilio mentioned a mangy hotel in the Marais, in Paris, not knowing that Irene and I had also lived there for a few tempestuous weeks. This brief image was enough to make me break down and tell him how much I'd loved her. I told him that I still dreamed of her and that, in my dreams, I promised her never to love another woman.

"Are you going to turn into a necrophiliac?" he said to me. "I've suffered more than you because of Irene and I'm still alive. Hey, enough of that, what was it you wanted to know about the Rialto?"

I asked him about Astorga. I heard, to my relief, that Emilio remembered down to the last detail the accident that Lidia had been killed in. For several months, he told me, the only thing people in Palermo talked about was that tragedy, perhaps because el Chino's in-laws had also died shortly afterward, asphyxiated by gas from a brazier. He knew that Yolanda, the daughter, spent her days all by herself, setting up cardboard theaters behind the stage and conversing in an invented English with the little figures that stood out against the light from the screen.

"I happened to run into el Chino and his daughter at the entrance to the movie theater two or three times," Emilio said. "Being shut up in the dark with no sun had made their skin turn pale. They disappeared a little while after that. Nobody ever saw them again. That must have been shortly after Perón's fall from power."

"They left on account of the corpse," I said, knowing the story.

"What corpse?" Emilio said, thinking I'd gotten the sequence of events wrong. "Lidia died in '48. They took off somewhere seven or eight years after that."

"Nobody ever saw them again," I said, feeling discouraged.

"I saw el Chino again," he corrected me. "One Sunday, in San Telmo, I stopped to buy cigarettes at a tobacco shop. The old man who waited on me struck a lost chord within me. 'Aren't you Chino?' I asked him. 'How are things with you, Emilio?' he greeted me in answer, showing no surprise. I saw a colored photograph of Lidia behind him. 'I see you haven't married again,' I said. 'Why would I?' he replied. 'The one who got married is my girl, remember her? She lives with me, just around the corner. She was lucky. She found herself a robust, hardworking man: somebody better than me.' We went on talking for a while, warily, as though we were both afraid of words. I don't think we shared any confidences. The only thing we had to give each other was empty time."

"How long ago was that?" I asked him.

"Who knows? Some years ago. I went by the shop several times more, but I always found it closed. There's a telephone and fax business there now."

"In San Telmo?" I said. "I live there."

"I know," Emilio said. "The tobacco shop was opposite your house."

That same afternoon I started looking for el Chino, and I don't think I've ever had such a hard time finding someone who was so close by. The shop had passed from one owner to another at the same pace as bouts of inflation and national misfortunes: people's past vanished at a much faster rate than the present arrived. I followed a series of false trails. From a warehouse in Mataderos I drifted to another in Pompeya and from there to an old people's home in Lanús. Finally, someone remembered a slant-eyed man who lived in a tenement on the calle Carlos Calvo, around the corner from the tobacco shop where it had all begun.

More than once I've told my friends what happened after that, and I've always encountered the same signs of disbelief: not because the story is implausible—it isn't—but because it seems unreal.

I didn't know if el Chino was alive or dead, as I said. He'd been seen on the second floor of a rundown building, whose balconies overlooked a flagstone courtyard. I went inside it one spring morn-

215

ing. The towels, the sheets, and other belongings of some twenty families hung from the balcony railings.

When I knocked on his door—on what was perhaps his door— it must have been around eleven. Through the windows darkened by cretonne curtains I made out several plastic chairs. A woman with broad hips like crinoline petticoats, bovine eyes, and copper-colored hair being tortured by a helmet of curlers answered the door. In the background I heard a tango by Manzi being sung off-key by Virginia Luque and the sound of hammering. I told her who I was and asked her about José Nemesio Astorga.

"He was my daddy," she said to me. "God rest his soul. He died from a perforated ulcer last summer. I won't tell you what sort of Christmas we had."

I reassured her by explaining that all I needed was to confirm a story and that I wouldn't waste much of her time. She hesitated and then stepped aside to let me in. It smelled of freshly sliced onions and cigarette butts inside. I sat down on one of the plastic chairs and bore without complaint the cruel sunlight that was pouring through the skylights.

"You must be Yolanda," I said to her.

"Yolanda Astorga de Ramallo." She nodded. "My husband is in the other room, repairing a sideboard," she said, pointing toward the darkness at the far end of the room. "Nobody sets foot inside here unless he's somewhere around."

"That's the right thing to do," I said, to reassure her. "You have to be careful these days. You may remember something that happened at the Rialto, between November and December of 1955. You must have been just a little girl—"

"Very little," she interrupted, covering a mouth in which there were only a few stubby brown teeth left. "I've always looked older than I really am."

"Between November and December," I repeated, "some men brought a big box, about five feet long, made of polished wood, to the Rialto. They left it behind the movie screen. Did your father ever say anything to you about it?"

She sighed with impossible coyness. Then she lit a cigarette and took two deep drags on it. She was taking her time, and all I could do was wait.

"Sure, I saw the box. They brought it one afternoon, before the matinee. The movies that day were *Road to Bali, Rear Window*, and *Abbott and Costello in the Foreign Legion*. I've got a positively torrid memory for the programs at the Rialto. Men remember soccer teams, but what I never forget are the movies that were showing."

Yolanda's conversation easily drifted off the subject.

"How many days was the box there?" I asked her.

"Two weeks, three, less time than I would have liked. One morning, when I got out of bed, I saw it. I thought it was a new tabletop and they'd be bringing the trestles for it later. I tried it out. I made some drawings. The wood was very soft. I didn't realize it, but my pencils left marks in it. I was afraid Daddy would be mad and I locked myself in the room. Daddy never noticed the marks, God rest his soul."

"Did your father tell you what was inside?"

"Of course he did. It was Sweetie. I knew what it was from the beginning. Daddy and I were on the same wavelength. We told each other everything. When that night's show was over, he came to see if I was asleep. He could tell I wasn't, so he sat down on the edge of the bed and said to me: Yoli, you're not to go near that box. What's in it, Daddy? I asked him. A big doll, he told me. The theater owner bought it in Europe and he wants to give it to his granddaughter for Christmas. It's a very expensive doll, Yoli. If anybody finds out we have it here they're going to try to steal it. I understood right away, but I couldn't help being curious. I walked round and round the box as I watched the films from the other side."

"That's what I was told. That you played in back of the screen, that you set up theaters with dolls."

"They told you that? You can't imagine how mad I was about dolls. The screen was made of transparent canvas, so I got used to seeing films from the other side. When I saw them from the real side, they never seemed the same to me. I spent all my time telling the stories of the movies to my dolls. I must have told them over and over, more than ten times, the story of how the mansion of Rebecca, the unforgettable woman, burned to the ground."

"So you never saw the big doll," I interrupted her, putting the conversation back on course.

"What do you mean I never saw it?" The hammering in the next room stopped and the sighs of a carpenter's plane were heard. "Didn't I tell you I was dying of curiosity to know what it looked like? One afternoon, once the matinee had started, I discovered that the lid opened all by itself, maybe because it was already loose or because I forced it without realizing it. Then I saw my Sweetie for the first time, all dressed in white, barefoot, with each toe clearly outlined, as soft as she could be, as though she'd been made out of real skin. They don't make dolls like that anymore. They're all plastic ones now, mass-produced, to be played with and then thrown away."

"That one was unique," I murmured.

"You can say that again. They were showing *Imperial Violets* for the first time that day, a movie that later turned out to be one of my favorites, but I didn't watch it. I was hypnotized by Sweetie. I couldn't keep my eyes off her. I don't know how many hours went by before I worked up my nerve to touch her. What a surprise I got. She was as soft as could be. My fingertips came away smelling of lavender."

"You told her the stories of the movies, the way you told the other dolls."

"I told her a lot of them later. But that day I could see she was so sound asleep that I said to her, Sleep as long as you like, Sweetie. I'm never going to wake you up. Then I put my hands on her forehead and sang to her. After that I straightened her lace and muslin costume very carefully and left her just the way she'd been."

Yolanda couldn't have been lying. That didn't make any sense at all. She was the survivor, I told myself, of a reality where the only true thing is desires. In 1955, when these stories had taken place, she must have been eight, maybe nine years old. She lived completely apart from the world, on the edge of a landscape haunted by ghosts.

"You didn't tell your father about it," I said to her.

"I didn't dare. I knew that Sweetie wasn't mine and that sooner or later they were going to take her away. I wanted to spend all the time I could with her, but Daddy had forbidden me to go near her, like I told you. It was an innocent game: a child's game, though I felt guilty too. I handled Sweetie very carefully, as though she were made of glass. I tied ribbons in her hair and painted her lips with powder from a red crayon. One night, before going to sleep, I began to tell her the films. I remember it all very clearly, you see. The first one I told her was *Viva Zapata,* with that ending that's so sad and so beautiful, with the white horse galloping through the mountains as though it were Zapata's soul, while the townspeople say he isn't dead. What are you laughing at?"

"I'm not laughing," I said to her. It was true. I too was moved.

"I don't know why I'm telling you these things just because you came and asked me about Sweetie. You'd best leave. You can see I haven't finished my cooking."

I sensed that if I lost her now I wasn't ever going to get her back. From the next room came the whisper of sandpaper.

"Let me stay while you cook," I said. "Just ten or fifteen minutes more. What you're telling me is important. You've no idea how important it is."

"What do you want me to tell you?"

"About their taking her away," I answered.

"Don't make me talk about that. The closer it got to Christmas the more on edge I was. I couldn't sleep at night. I think I even got sick. Since I didn't want any neighbor woman coming in to take care of me, I got up out of bed as though nothing was wrong, I did the shopping, I cleaned the rooms, and around two-thirty, when Daddy was beginning the first show, I pulled the lid of the box back and began to play with Sweetie. And what had to happen finally happened. One day my fever went up and I fell asleep in my doll's lap. When Daddy got off work, he found me there. He was speechless. I never knew what he said or what he did. I fell into bed, with a fever of over a hundred and two. Sometimes, in my delirium, I asked if

219

they'd already taken my Sweetie away. Calm down, Yolanda, Daddy would say to me, she's right where you left her. Christmas went by, and by the grace of God I began to get better. When the bells rang in the New Year, I went to give my Sweetie a kiss and I prayed to God that that great happiness in my life would never end. As you may already know, God didn't hear me."

"He couldn't hear you. What's more, your father had warned you: sooner or later, the theater owner was going to take the box away."

She finished slicing the onions and fried them in a skillet, with her lips clamped around a cigarette that she took a drag on every so often. The smoke got in her eyes and I saw them fill with tears. I sensed a shadow in the doorway to the kitchen following a sudden silence in the next room, and it seemed to me that a man poked his head in, but when I tried to say hello to him, he vanished. Perhaps I just imagined it. Everything I was experiencing seemed to be suspended in a cloud of unreality, as though Yolanda and I were talking to each other from places that were all wrong and far away. She said:

"That January was an oven. There was never a breeze. The movie theater was damp and cool, so all sorts of creepy-crawly bugs took refuge there. It was vacation time, but I didn't go anywhere. The Rialto was my whole life. I didn't need anything else."

"Nobody visited you?" I asked her.

"Sometimes, in the morning, a tall man with thick eyebrows came, with another quite bald man, with eyes set very far apart and a neck like a bull's. I was struck by how little the tall man's feet were, like a woman's. People called the other one Colonel. Daddy took me to the furniture store on the corner and left me there to play, I never understood why. One night in January the weather changed for the worse and one of those southeasters that break all the records blew in. Daddy had to stop the last show because nobody could hear the soundtrack on account of the thunder. We made sure the doors of the theater were shut tight, but the wind beat furiously at them. I clung to Sweetie and sang her the music from *Neptune's Daughter,* which we both liked very much. I don't know if you remember the words. *Pretty dolly, with golden hair, pearly teeth, ivory skin.* That song is the very picture of my Sweetie. That's exactly how she looked. Look what it does to me just telling you that."

I offered her a handkerchief.

"They took her away that very night," I said.

"No. It was worse. I can't tell you how it made me feel to leave my Sweetie all by herself behind the screen, with all those violent flashes of lightning, but Daddy dragged me off to bed by the ear. It was very late. As you can imagine, I hardly slept a wink. The next morning I got up very early, heated the water for the maté, and the silence surprised me. The trees were bare, with no birds in them, and neither the tramways nor the cars could get through the streets strewn with broken branches. I was scared and ran to see if anything had happened to my Sweetie. Thank heaven she was the same as always, there in the box, but somebody had left her little body uncovered. The lid was standing upright, leaning against the crossbeams of the screen. I saw all sorts of flowers on the floor, sweet peas, violets, honeysuckle, who knows how many. At the head of the big box a row of stubby candles was burning, and that was what made me realize that it wasn't Daddy who'd lit them: lighting candles was irresponsible, you see. The first thing he taught me in life was that I couldn't set anything alight in a place full of wood, canvas, celluloid."

"The owner had a key, didn't he?" I asked.

"The owner? He was the one who had the worst scare. When I discovered the candles and let out a scream, the first thing Daddy did was phone him. He came over right away, with the man with the thick eyebrows and the other one they called the Colonel. They took me to the furniture store on the corner with strict orders not to budge from there. That was the longest morning of my life. You can see that lots of things have happened to me, right? But none of them were as bad as that. I sat waiting for hours in a wicker chair, suffering because Sweetie wasn't mine and sooner or later they were going to take her away from me. How could I have had any idea that at that very moment I was losing her forever?"

Yolanda burst out crying for all she was worth. Feeling embarrassed, I made for the door. I wanted to get out of there, but I couldn't leave her like that. In the next room all movement ceased. A man's voice said:

"What time are we going to eat, Mommy?"

"In five more minutes, Daddy," she said, regaining her composure. "Are you starving?"

"I want to eat this minute," he said.

"Okay," she answered. "We call each other Daddy and Mommy on account of the kids," she explained to me in a confidential tone of voice.

"I understand," I said, even though I didn't care if I understood or not. I went on, relentlessly: "When you came back, the box was no longer there."

"They'd taken it away. You wouldn't believe how I reacted when I found out. I never forgave Daddy for not calling me so I could say goodbye to my Sweetie. I got sick again, I think I even took it into my head that I wanted Daddy to die, poor thing, so I'd be all by myself in the world and people would feel sorry for me."

"It was the end," I said. I didn't say it to her but to myself. I wanted the last dregs of the past to disappear and that to be really the end.

"The end," Yolanda agreed. "I loved that doll as you can only love a person."

"She was a person," I told her.

"Who was?" she asked, distractedly, with the cigarette between her lips.

"Your Sweetie. She wasn't a doll. She was an embalmed woman."

She burst out laughing. There were still dying embers of tears in her eyes: she put them out with the water of a hearty, defiant laugh.

"How do you know?" she said. "You never saw her. You just wandered by this morning to see what you could find out."

"I knew the corpse had been at the Rialto," I said. "I didn't know for how long. Nor did it ever enter my mind that you'd seen it."

"A corpse," she said. She repeated: "A corpse. That's all I needed. Go away. I opened the door out of curiosity. Now leave me alone."

"Think," I said to her. "You've seen the photographs. Try to remember. Think."

I don't know why I insisted. Maybe I did so out of the perverse, morbid desire to do away with Yolanda. She was a character who had already contributed everything she could to this story.

"What photos?" she said. "Go away."

"The ones of Evita's body. They came out in all the newspapers, remember? They came out when the body was returned to Perón in 1971. Search your memory. The body was embalmed."

"I don't know what you're talking about," she said. I had the impression she did know but was refusing to let the truth enter her mind and tear her to pieces.

"Your Sweetie was Evita," I said to her, cruelly. "Eva Perón. You yourself noticed the resemblance. In November 1955 the body was hijacked from the CGT and hidden at the Rialto."

She walked over closer to me with her hands outstretched and pushed me away. Her voice was as strident and shrill as a bird's as she spoke:

"You heard me. Go away. What did I do to you for you to tell me what you're telling me? How did you ever get the idea that my doll was a dead woman? Daddy!" she called. "Come here right away, Daddy!"

Before that I had thought that I was nowhere. Now I felt that I was outside of time. I saw the husband in the crack of the door that led to the other room. He was a husky man, with stiff crew-cut hair.

"What did you do to her?" he said to me, as he took Yolanda in his arms.

"Nothing," I answered, like an idiot. "I didn't do anything to her. I just came to talk to her about her doll."

Yolanda burst into tears again. This time her tears overflowed her body and drenched the air, dense and salty, like a damp mist from the sea.

"Tell him to go away, Daddy. He didn't do anything to me. He scared me. He's sick in the head."

The husband riveted his gentle dark eyes on me. I opened the door and went out into the vast midday sun, without remorse or pity.

That very afternoon I called Emilio Kaufman and asked him to come to my place. I wanted to tell him everything I knew about Evita and have him listen to the cassettes with the voices of the embalmer, of Aldo Cifuentes, and of the Colonel's widow. I wanted him to see the photographs of the corpse, the brittle yellow papers attesting to the departure of Evita, and the copies of her for the ports of Genoa, Hamburg, Lisbon. I wanted to get the story off my chest, just as thirty years before I had given vent to my unhappiness at my misfortunes in the lap of Irene, his daughter.

Emilio hadn't the slightest intention of speaking of the past, or at least of a past that had stopped moving. At the time—not so long ago, only the eternity of the few years that have gone by since the Berlin wall fell and the Rumanian dictator Ceauşescu was shot to death in front of television cameras and the Soviet Union disappeared from the map, the explosion of a present that fell headlong into the abyss of the past—at the time, people also thought that Evita was crystallized forever in a pose, in an essence, in a breath of eternity and that, like everything that is peaceful and quiet, everything that is predictable, she would never again awaken passions. But the past always returns, passions return. No one can ever get rid of what he or she has lost.

I remember every detail of that day but not the exact date: it was a warm, silent spring, and the air smelled whimsically of violin wood. I was listening to the "Goldberg Variations" in Kenneth Gilbert's clavichord version. At some point in Variation 15, halfway through the andante, Emilio appeared with a bottle of cabernet. We drank it almost without realizing as we fixed mushrooms with scallions and sour cream, boiled spinach noodles, and spoke of the pitched battles between the president of the Republic and his wife, who had never loved each other and proclaimed the fact on the radio.

"Now we can talk about Evita."

I understood him to say: "We can talk about Irene." More than once I have heard words that moved not in the direction of their meaning but in that of my desires. "Irene," I felt or heard. I said to him:

"I wish we'd talked about her some time ago, Emilio. Nobody told me she'd died. The news took so long in arriving that when it reached me my grief was unreal."

He turned pale. Every time a feeling appears on his face, Emilio looks elsewhere, as though the feeling were someone else's and the person who'd lost it was somewhere around.

"I wasn't with her when she died either," he said. He was speaking of Irene. We understood each other without the need to speak her name.

He told me that after the military coup in 1976 she had not been able to stand the horror of the kidnappings and the senseless slaughter. She decided to go into exile. She said she was going to seek refuge in Paris, but she kept sending letters from South American cities that didn't appear on maps: Ubatuba, Sabaneta, Crixás, Sainte-Elle. She wasn't guilty of anything, and yet she dragged the world's guilts around with her, like all Argentines in that era. She stayed just a few weeks in those places in the middle of nowhere, where it rained a lot all the time, Emilio told me, and when a strange face came her way on the street, she caught the first bus and fled. She felt terrified: all her letters spoke of her terror and of the rain. At one point she came through Caracas, but she didn't call me. She had my telephone number and my address, but I was the salt in her wounds and she didn't want to see me again.

A year after leaving Buenos Aires she arrived in Mexico, rented an apartment in the Mixcoac district, and began to haunt book publishers in search of translations to do. She got Joaquín Mortiz, the publishing house, to give her a novel of Beckett's to translate, and even struggled with the fundamental music of the first pages, when all of a sudden she felt a terrible burning sensation in the middle of her brain and was left blind, deaf, and mute, like the mother in *Mol-*

loy. She could hardly move. She took one step, and the wrenching pain pinned her to the floor. She thought (though in the rare moments of lucidity that she had later on she never again said "I think"), she nonetheless thought that the violent onset of her affliction was directly related to the altitude of Mexico City, the volcanoes, the temperature inversions, retrospective sorrow over her exile, and never consulted a doctor. She believed a couple of days in bed and six aspirins every twenty-four hours would save her. She took to her bed only to die. She had contracted a staphylococcus aureus infection. She underwent a series of devastating illnesses: purulent meningitis, pelvic nephritis, acute endocarditis. In a week's time she was another being, deeply wounded by the world's cruelty. A horrible death was consuming her.

We remained silent for a while. I poured myself some cognac and spilled a few drops on my shirt. My hands were clumsy, my being was in another place, in another time, and perhaps also in another life. I sensed that Emilio wanted to leave and the look in my eyes begged him not to. I heard him say:

"Why are we beating around the bush? Talk to me about Evita."

I did so for almost an hour without stopping. I told him everything that all of you already know and everything that there has been no place for in these pages as well. I stressed the mystery of the flowers and the candles, which reproduced themselves as though they were another miracle of loaves and fishes. I told of the series of accidents that had enabled me to meet Yolanda and learn of the long summer the doll had spent behind the screen at the Rialto. I told him that the body had apparently been taken from the movie theater to Major Arancibia's house, where it remained for another month.

"It was Arancibia who unleashed the worst of the tragedies," Emilio said. "Have you checked the newspapers?"

"I read them all: the daily papers, the magazines that reconstructed the corpse's calvary. Whole forests of documents were published when Evita's body was handed over to Perón in 1971. Nobody, as far as I recall, mentioned Arancibia."

"Do you know why nobody did? Because in this country when a madness can't be explained, people would rather it didn't exist. They all look the other way. Have you seen what Evita's biographers do? Every time they stumble on a fact that seems crazy to them, they don't report it. To her biographers, Evita had no odors or fevers or tricks up her sleeve. She wasn't a person. The only ones who occasionally penetrated her defenses were a couple of journalists you may not remember, Roberto Vacca and Otelo Borroni. They brought their book out in 1970: just think of how much water has gone under the bridge since. It was called *The Life of Eva Perón, Volume I.* No second volume was ever published. In the final pages, I remember, they devoted a paragraph to the dramatic story of Arancibia. They speak of unconfirmed versions, of rumors that may or may not be true."

"They're true," I interrupted him. "I checked."

"Of course they're true," Emilio said, overwhelming me with another Mexican cigar. "But they don't interest her biographers. That part of the story is beyond their ken. It never enters their head that Evita's life and death are inseparable. It always amazes me that they're so scrupulous about setting down facts that don't interest anybody, such as the list of novels that Eva read over the radio, while at the same time they don't bother filling in any number of gaping holes. What happened to Arancibia, the Madman, for instance? History swallowed him up. What did Evita do in that blind gap in her life from January to September 1943? It was as though she'd vanished. She didn't act in any radio serials; nobody saw her during that time."

"Listen, there's no point in exaggerating either. Where do you expect them to get their facts from? Don't forget that at the time, Evita was a poverty-stricken second-rate actress. When she had no work on the radio, she made ends meet as best she could. I've already told you about the photos that Alcaraz, the hairdresser, saw at a newspaper stand in Retiro station."

"A witness always turns up if you start looking," Emilio insisted.

He got up and poured himself another cognac. I couldn't see his face as he said: "You don't have to look any farther. I knew Eva in those months of '43. I know what happened."

I wasn't expecting that. I haven't smoked for over fifteen years, but at that moment I heard my lungs crying out for cigarettes with suicidal voracity. I took a deep breath.

"Why didn't you tell anybody?" I said to him. "Why didn't you write about it?"

"First of all, I didn't have the courage," he said. "If you told a story like that you had to leave the country. Later on, when it was possible to tell it, I no longer felt like it."

"I'm going to be merciless with you," I told him. "You're going to tell it to me this minute."

He stayed till dawn. At the end we were so exhausted we understood each other by way of signs and stammers. When he finished, I went with him to his house in Centenary Park in a taxi, I saw the fossils in the Museum of Natural Sciences wake up and stretch, and I told the taxi driver to wake me up when we got to San Telmo. But I couldn't sleep. I've never had a peaceful night's sleep till now, when I've finally reached the point where I can repeat the story without fear of betraying either its tone or its details.

It must have been July or August 1943, Emilio recounted. General Patton's army was advancing on Messina, the Fascist hierarchy had voted against the Duce and in favor of a constitutional monarchy, but the outcome of the war was still uncertain. Emilio went from one editorial room to another and from several simultaneous love affairs to none at all. That winter he met an actress with no talent named Mercedes Printer, and she finally managed to get him to settle down. She wasn't a beauty out of this world, Emilio said, but she was different from the other women in his life because she didn't look out for him but for herself. All she wanted to do was dance. Every Saturday she went out with Emilio to make the rounds of the night-clubs open to the public and the private neighborhood clubs where Fiorentino attuned his tenor voice to Aníbal Troilo's accordion, or Feliciano Brunelli's orchestra got involved in fox-trot variations that awakened the dead. Mercedes and he didn't talk with each other about anything: words didn't have the slightest importance. The only thing that was important was to make sure that life flowed by like a stream of fresh water. Sometimes Emilio, who was the layout editor at *Noticias Gráficas* at the time, amused himself by explaining to her what a great time he had combining twelve-point pica, half rounds, and reglets; she got even for those technical tongue twisters by telling him about the last-minute corrections that the scriptwriter Martinelli Massa had made in the dialogues of *The Hand of Fate,* the soap opera that was the big hit of the moment. When they were alone they told each other everything, examined the tunnels of each other's body with flashlights, promised each other a love for the present only because the idea of a future, Mercedes said, is the death of all passion: tomorrow's love is never love. In one of those conversations as day was dawning Mercedes talked to him about Evita.

"What can I tell you? I feel sorry for her," Mercedes had told him. "She's frail and sickly; I took a liking to her. Do you know how we became friends? The two of us were acting in Rosario. In addition to men, we shared food, a dressing room, all the rest, but we hardly ever talked to each other. She went her way and I went mine. She was interested in impresarios, men with dough, even if they were old and potbellied, and what I liked was partying. Neither she nor I had a cent to our names. A friend of mine had given me some silk stockings that I handled as carefully as a treasure. You can't imagine what real silk stockings are like: they fall to pieces if you so much as breathe on them. One night I couldn't find them. I had to go onstage and they weren't anywhere. At that moment Evita appeared, her face caked with makeup. Hey, have you seen my stockings? I asked. Oh, I'm sorry, Mercedes, I'm wearing them, she said to me. I could have killed her, but when I took a look at her legs, I saw that she wasn't wearing my stockings. The ones she had on were cheap cotton ones. You're mistaken, those aren't mine, I said to her. The thing is, I've put them here, she answered, pointing to her bosom. Since she had little tits and had a complex about the size of them, she was using my stockings as padding. At first I was hopping mad, but then I got hold of myself and burst out laughing. She showed me my stockings. They were all in one piece, with not even a run in them. The two of us went onstage laughing, and the audience couldn't understand why. From that time on we saw a lot of each other. She used to come to my pension to make maté and we'd chat for hours. She's a good kid, very reserved. She's just getting over a long illness. She goes around looking sad, really down in the mouth. Why don't you invite a friend and we'll all go out together."

Emilio invited a surgeon, who wore his hair slicked down with pomade, a stiff collar, and a very proper felt Orion hat and collected photos of actresses. Emilio resigned himself in advance to a dull night, he told me, the kind of night that leaves you feeling empty and drained. If it hadn't been for the meaning that events were to take on later, in the light of history, Emilio would have forgotten the whole thing. He didn't know—he had no way of knowing—that, with time, that kid was going to be Evita. Evita didn't know it either. History lays traps like that. If we could see ourselves inside history, Emilio said, we'd be terrified. There wouldn't be any history, because nobody would want to even move.

They agreed to meet at the Munich restaurant on the promenade on the south bank of the river. Evita was wearing a diadem of white flowers and a thick tulle veil down to the tip of her nose. She seemed vapid to Emilio, invulnerable to the pain of illness and sorrow. What impressed him most about her, he told me, was how white she was. Her skin was so pale that you could see the maps of veins and smooth stretches of thought through it. There was nothing attractive about her physically, he said, no electric power for either good or ill.

On the other side of the street, behind the enclosure of poplars and tipa trees, was the dock from which Vito Dumas, the solitary seafarer, had begun his voyage around the world the year before in *Lehg II,* a sailboat ten meters long. The city was awaiting his return from one moment to the next. The surgeon, who had followed each one of Dumas's endless skirmishes with the monsoons of the Indian Ocean and the walls of foam off Cape Horn, tried to interest Evita by describing to her the biting winds and the hailstorms that the navigator had encountered in his three hundred days of unrelieved solitude, but she listened to him with a faraway look in her eyes, as though the surgeon were speaking in a remote tongue and the sound of his words were falling far away, into the invisible river of the sidewalk across the street.

Mercedes wanted to go dancing, but Evita seemed unresponsive to all wishes, her own and those of others. She lowered her head and answered: "Later, in a while," without moving, with a contagious sadness. She perked up only when Emilio proposed going to Fantasio, in Olivos, where producers of Argentina Sono Film and big-name actresses got together every night.

Not for a moment, Emilio told me, did I have the sensation that Evita was the helpless creature Mercedes had told me about. She looked more like one of those alley cats that will survive cold, hunger, the cruelty of human beings, and the rash mistakes of nature. When they got to Fantasio she sat down at the table with her antennas up, keeping a sharp eye on who was with whom and urging Emilio to introduce her. He took her by the hand to the corner where the producer Atilio Mentasti was having dinner with Sixto Pondal Ríos and Carlos Olivari, minor poets who turned up in anthologies and also successful scriptwriters. I was an old friend of all three, Emilio told me, but I was embarrassed to be seen like that, with that woman who was a nobody. I was so uptight I stammered as I introduced her:

"Eva Duarte, a second lead on the radio."

"Hey, what do you mean, 'a second lead'?" she contradicted him. "At Radio Belgrano they've put me under contract as head of the troupe."

She made a move as if to sit down at that other table, but Mentasti, whose manners were glacial, stopped her.

"I've already shaken hands with you, kid. Now beat it."

A lightning flash of hatred traversed Eva's eyes, Emilio told me. Ever since she'd come to Buenos Aires, she'd been snubbed and humiliated so many times that nothing surprised her anymore: she'd stored up in her memory a long catalog of insults that she was intending to take her revenge for sooner or later. Mentasti's was one of the worst. She never forgave him, because she was of no mind to forgive anybody. If Eva managed to become somebody, Emilio told me, it was because she resolved never to forgive.

They walked back across the room, which had now filled up with couples. The orchestra was playing a fox-trot. They saw Mercedes entwined with the surgeon on a shore far distant from the dance floor. She was dancing defiantly, happily, her mind focused only on the fire of her body. Evita, however, didn't even open her mouth once she returned to her seat.

Emilio didn't know what to do. He asked her if she was feeling sad, and she answered him that women were always sad, but she didn't look at him. Maybe, Emilio said, she didn't even speak to me. After so long a time, that night seemed to him more imagined than real. The couples were dancing in an empty space in the dark to the rhythms of Gershwin and Jerome Kern. They heard the rustle of dresses, the sizzle of shoes, the gabble of gossip. As the sounds came and went, Evita's voice suddenly filtered through them, as though it were following the thread of something she was thinking:

"What would you do, Emilio, if Mercedes got pregnant?"

The question took Emilio so completely by surprise that it took him a while to understand what it meant. The orchestra was playing "The Man I Love." The surgeon was rocking Mercedes back and forth as though her body were made of tulle. Pondal Ríos was smoking a Havana. Emilio remembered (he said, half a century later, that he had remembered at that very instant) some sadistic verses by Olivari: *"What pleases me most about your sickly body / is seeing how it comes beneath my riding crop, so quickly, so quickly."* He answered, distractedly:

"I'd take her to get an abortion, right? Can you picture the two of us having a kid?"

"But she could have the baby without your knowing it. What would you do if she had it?" Evita persisted. "I'm asking you because I've never been able to figure men out."

"How should I know? How in the world do you come up with

things like that? I'd like to see my baby, it seems to me. But I'd never want to see Mercedes again."

"That's how men are," Evita said. "They feel differently from women."

It was a pointless conversation, but everything seemed to be drifting about aimlessly in the dense air of that place called Fantasio. The orchestra left for the night, and the surgeon came back to the table with Mercedes. Perhaps Evita was waiting for them, because she stopped smoothing her skirt like a teenager and said:

"I'm leaving. I don't want to ruin your night, all of you, but I don't feel well. I shouldn't have come."

And that was almost all there was to it, Emilio recounted. We took her to an apartment that she was renting in the pasaje Seaver, and I went with Mercedes to the cheap hotel on the avenida de Mayo where I was staying in those days. Maybe she and I were about to break up, Emilio told me, even though we didn't finally separate till more than a year after that. Maybe she was offended because we hadn't danced even one number together. At that point I'd given up trying to understand her, though neither then nor now have I ever been able to understand a woman. I don't know what they think or what they want; all I know is that they want just the opposite of what they think. She sat down in front of the triple mirror in that hotel room and began to remove her makeup. That was always the sign that we weren't going to make love and that when we switched off the light we'd turn our backs to each other without touching. As she wiped a piece of cotton with cleansing cream across her face, she said, as if in passing:

"You didn't realize what bad shape Evita was in, how desperate."

"What do you mean, 'desperate'?" Emilio said. "She's crazy in the head. She asked me what I'd do if you got pregnant."

"And what would you do? What did you answer her?"

"How should I know?" Emilio lied. "I'd probably marry you. I'd probably make you unhappy."

"She's been pregnant," Mercedes said. "Evita. But that was no problem. Neither she nor the father wanted to have the kid. He

233

didn't want one because he was already married, and she because it would ruin her career. The problem was that the abortion ended in disaster. Butchery. The bottom of her uterus got perforated, the ligaments, the tubes were badly torn. In half an hour, drenched with blood, she collapsed with peritonitis. She was taken to a clinic as an emergency case. It took her more than two months to recover. I was the only person who came to see her in all that time. She nearly died. She was on the brink. She nearly died."

"And what about the man who got her pregnant?" Emilio asked. "What did he do?"

"He did right by her. He's a decent sort. He even paid the bill for the clinic, down to the last cent. He didn't let the midwife who did the abortion down either. He wasn't the one who'd chosen her."

"Those things can happen to anybody," Emilio said. "They're terrible, but they can happen to anybody. She ought to be thankful to be alive."

"In those days she would rather have been dead. When the guy finally knew for sure that she was out of danger, he beat it to Europe. She almost missed out on her career. Imagine. She didn't appear in the magazines, nobody called her. She was saved by a providential note in *Antena*, that pictured her as a little star enjoying a life of leisure. 'If Eva Duarte isn't working it's because she isn't offered roles worthy of her talent,' the note said. People swallow stuff like that. Later on, the military coup saved her again. The lieutenant colonel in charge of radio broadcasting fell in love with her."

"So she doesn't need you to protect her any longer," Emilio said.

"Of course she does, because she doesn't love anybody now. She doesn't love anything," Mercedes said. "The lieutenant colonel who's chasing after her is married, like all the guys she's ever taken up with. One of these days Evita is capable of knocking on the door of his house and shooting herself right there in front of his eyes."

Emilio turned out the light and lay there staring into the darkness. Outside, the wind shook the trees and carried off the splinters of voices that had been left adrift in the street. Later, since none of it mattered anymore, he forgot the whole thing.

"A Role in the Movies"

He met Evita again seven years later, at an official ceremony.

"She didn't recognize me," Emilio said, "or else she pretended she didn't recognize me. She was different. She seemed full of light. It was as if instead of having one soul she had two, or many. But sadness still stalked her. When she least expected it, sadness tapped her on the shoulder and reminded her of the past."

I was faithful to what Emilio Kaufman told me, but I don't know if he was faithful to what he knew about Evita. There were a few names and dates in his story that didn't fit, and I corrected them when I checked them against the memories of other people. I was able to verify that Evita had been admitted to the Otamendi and Miroli clinic in Buenos Aires, under the name of María Eva Ibarguren, between February and May of 1943. The clinic hasn't kept the files from that period, but the Colonel copied the record of her admittance and left it, along with his other papers, at Cifuentes' house. I wasn't able to find Mercedes Printer, even though I know that she's been living somewhere in Mexico since 1945. Stories get lost or distorted. The world's memory passes by without stopping and moves farther and farther into the distance. The world passes by and memory seldom finds the place where it went astray.

11

*"A Wonderful
Husband"*

The Colonel had been torturing himself for months for allowing
Evita to go away. Nothing had any meaning without her. When he
drank (and every night of loneliness he drank more), he realized it
was foolish to go on taking her from one place to another. Why did
he have to hand her over to the care of persons unknown? Why
didn't they allow him to be responsible for her, when he would defend her better than anyone else? They kept him away from her
body, as though she were a virgin bride. It was stupid, he thought,
to take so many precautions with an adult married woman, who had
been dead for more than three years. Good heavens, how he missed
her. Was he the one who gave the orders, or was it others? He was
lost. That woman or alcohol or the fate of being an army officer had
been his downfall.

Good heavens, how he missed her. He had visited her only three
times that summer and spring, and never alone. Arancibia, the Madman, was always there, watching for subtle signs of change in the
body. "Just look, Colonel, she's darker today," he would say. "Look
how inflamed her plantar artery is, how the tendons of the extensors
in her fingers stand out. Who knows if this woman is still alive?" He
felt terribly thirsty. What was happening to him? He was thirsty all

236

the time. There was no fire, no alcohol, that relieved the thirst of his insatiable insides.

He'd been through the worst of it, he thought. Nothing, however, was ever the worst. He had suffered when he saw her lying amid dolls, behind the screen at the Rialto movie theater. Every so often the thin layer of dust that licked at the coffin drifted down to the body: on raising the lid, the Colonel had found a faint trace of dust on the tip of her nose. He cleaned it off with his handkerchief and before leaving advised the projectionist: "Air out this pigsty. Put poison out and get rid of the mice. See if bugs are still eating away at the Deceased without your noticing." The following week what he had feared most happened: one morning the body was surrounded with flowers and candles. He didn't find threatening letters: just a couple of matches alongside the coffin. It was a nightmare. Sooner or later they were going to discover her. Who? In what numbers? The enemy wasn't giving up: it appeared to be driven by an obsession even more deeply rooted than his own.

Between one transfer and another, he had recourse, very reluctantly, to the embalmer. He called him in to determine whether the body was still intact. They scarcely spoke to each other. Ara put on his white coat and rubber gloves, shut himself up with the Deceased for two or three hours, and when he came out offered the same opinion as ever: "She's safe and sound, just the way I left her."

Every morning, on entering his office, the Colonel noted on file cards the peregrinations of the corpse. He wanted the president to know how much he had done to protect it from adversity, fanaticism, and fires. He kept a record of the hours in which the nomad wandered all through the city, with no starting or stopping points. There was no safe place for her. Every time he anchored her somewhere, something terrible happened.

The Colonel studied his file cards once again. From December 14, 1955, to February 20, 1956, the Deceased had been behind the screen at the Rialto: they had left her there on a night when a sudden rainstorm came up, and they had had to take her away, in broad daylight, after another storm. The truck in which they moved her stalled in the deep water on the calle Salguero, under the railroad bridge. A mule cart had towed it out. "The driver charged me sixty pesos," the Colonel noted on one of the file cards. "I waited for the carburetor to dry out and left Person on the corner of Viamonte and Rodríguez Peña on the nights of February 20 and 21." On the file cards he sometimes referred to her as Person, at times as "Deceased," at times "ED" or "TW," standing for "Eva Duarte" and "That Woman." She was becoming more and more Person and less and less Deceased: he could feel it in his blood, which was becoming diseased and changing, and in others such as Major Arancibia and First Lieutenant Fesquet, who were no longer the same.

From February 22 to March 14—he read on the cards—Evita had lain in peace in the military storeroom in the calle Sucre, number 1835, on top of the cliffs of Belgrano. "The box with the body, which among ourselves we call 'the gun chest,' is on the second row of shelves, at the back of the shed, amid hammers, hammer handles, bolts, safety latches, and discarded firing pins from a consignment of Smith & Wesson pistols. Nobody has touched the boxes for at least four years." Between March 10 and 12, Security discovered two NCOs, First Corporal Abdala and Sergeant Llubrán, closely examining the coffin. "On the morning of the thirteenth," the following card said, "I appeared in person at the storeroom on Sucre for the routine inspection. I noted a nick in the box or a mark made with a jackknife in the shape of a half-moon or the letter *c*, and to the right a diagonal stripe, the lower end of which touches the base of the *c*, and may be the unfinished half of a letter *v*. Commando of Vengeance? Galarza and Fesquet suppose that the nicks are accidental scratches. Arancibia, on the other hand, shares my opinion: the Deceased has been detected. I order NCOs Llubrán and Abdala to be arrested immediately and subjected to the severest interrogation. They say nothing. Now we must transport the Deceased in a new box, since the previous one is marked."

From that time on, the nomad had been continually moved, at shorter and shorter intervals. Wherever the body migrated, it was followed by its escort of flowers and candles. They would suddenly appear at the guards' first lapse of vigilance: sometimes a single flower and a single candle, never one that had gone out.

The Colonel remembered very well the morning of April 22: the nomad looked exhausted after three weeks of wandering about in vans, army buses, cellars of battalions, and district mess kitchens. He had already resigned himself to burying her in Monte Grande cemetery when Arancibia, the Madman, offered a providential solution: How about keeping her at his house?

The Madman lived in the Saavedra district in a two-story house: downstairs were the living room–dining room, the service room, and the kitchen, with a door that led downstairs to the garage and the garden; upstairs was the master bedroom, the guest room, and a bath. Opposite the first of the rooms there was a door leading to the attic: that was where the Madman kept his files, the maps from the War College, a sand table with lead soldiers that were still fighting the interminable battle of the Ebro, and his cadet's uniform. That attic, he thought, was the ideal place to hide Evita.

And what about his wife? The Colonel examined the medical report: *Elena Heredia de Arancibia. Age: 22. Eight weeks pregnant.* He could no longer recall the order in which events had occurred. The body was transferred to Saavedra early on the morning of April 24, between three and four a.m. It was lying in a box of dark, plain, unpolished walnut wood, with official seals burned into the wood: ARGENTINE ARMY. Beneath a feeble light, a forty-watt bulb, he and the Madman had worked until six in the greasy garage, which smelled of mold and cheap tobacco. At intervals they heard overhead the muffled footsteps of the wife.

They were just two tired men when they took the heavy box upstairs to the attic, stumbling on the narrow curves of the stairway and bumping into the stair rails that were too high. The Colonel heard the wife going and coming in the bedroom, heard her moaning and calling out in a muffled voice, as though she had a handkerchief over her mouth:

"Eduardo, what's going on, Eduardo? Open the door, please. I'm feeling ill."

"Don't pay any attention to her," the Madman murmured in the Colonel's ear. "She's a spoiled brat."

The wife went on moaning as they finally got the box all the way up the stairs and left it among the maps. The pale light of dawn was entering through the slits in the window shutters. The Colonel was surprised at the meticulous order that Arancibia kept his things in, and recognized the precise moment at which he had interrupted the battle of the Ebro on the sand table.

It took them more time still to cover the Deceased with piles of dossiers and files. As the documents gradually began to bury it, the body defended itself by giving off faint signs: a very slender thread of chemical odors and a reflection that, as it floated in the still air, seemed to raise a fine net of little gray clouds.

"Do you hear?" the Madman said. "The woman moved."

They removed the papers and looked at her closely. She lay there not moving, impassive, with the same treacherous smile that so perturbed the Colonel. They stood looking at her until morning and eternity became one to them. Then they covered her up again with her shroud of papers.

Now and again the wife's moaning reached their ears. They heard tattered phrases, syllables that might have said "Thirsty, 'duardo. Thirsty, water": nothing clear. The sounds bumbled about like a blowfly, unwilling to give up and leave.

There were two locks in the heavy walnut door leading to the attic, at the foot of the stairway. Arancibia held up the long bronze keys to show them to the Colonel before inserting them in the keyholes and turning them.

"They're the only ones," he said. "If they got lost, someone would have to knock down the door."

"It's an expensive door," the Colonel ventured. "I wouldn't like to damage it."

That had been all. He had left the house, and at that very moment, he had begun to miss her.

During the weeks that followed, the Colonel made serious efforts to forget Evita's loneliness and helplessness. She's better off the way she is now, he kept telling himself. She is no longer being attacked by enemies nor does she need to be protected from the flowers. The light from the window glides over her body in the late afternoon. And what had he for his part gained thereby? Evita's absence was a sadness difficult to bear. At times he happened on remains of posters showing her face, glued on walls here and there in the city. In shreds, stained, the Deceased smiled mindlessly from that nowhere. Good heavens, how he missed her. He cursed the hour when he had accepted Arancibia's plan. If he had studied it a little more carefully he would have found shortcomings in it. And she would be hidden in a corner of his office. He could raise the lid of the coffin at that very instant and contemplate her. Why had he not brought her there? Good heavens, how he hated her, how he needed her.

He noted on his index cards the nothings that transpired: *May 7. Order my boots and spurs polished. Nothing happened. / May 19. Met Cifuentes at the Richmond. Had seven pilsners. Did not speak of anything together. / June 3. Went to 10 o'clock Mass at Socorro. Saw General Lonardi's widow. Found her looking rather depressed. Made as if to greet her. She turned her face away. Sunday, at the Service: no one there.*

On June 9, shortly before midnight, he heard a squadron of transport planes flying south. He looked out the window and was surprised not to see lights in the sky: only the din of the propellers and the glacial darkness. Then the telephone rang. It was the minister of the army.

"The tyrant has risen up in arms, Moori," he said.

"Has he come back?" the Colonel asked.

"What gave you that idea?" the minister replied. "That one is never coming back. A few lunatics who still believe in him have started an uprising. We're going to decree martial law."

"Yes, General."

"You have a responsibility: the package." The president and the ministers called the Deceased "the package." "If someone tries to take it away from you, don't hesitate for a moment. Shoot him."

"Martial law," the Colonel repeated.

"That's right: don't hesitate."

"Where have they staged the coup?" the Colonel asked.

"In La Plata. In La Pampa. I don't have time to explain to you. Get a move on, Moori. They're bearing her on a flag."

"I don't understand, sir."

"The rebels are carrying a white flag. There's a face in the middle of it. It's her face."

"A mere detail, General. Are there any names? Have you identified the guilty parties?"

"You should know who they are better than I do, and you don't. Pamphlets have been found in a public square in La Plata. They're signed by something called the Commando of Vengeance. That explains quite clearly what people they are. They want revenge."

Before going out, he heard the battle orders. They were reading them over the radio every five minutes: "The laws governing the nation in wartime will apply. Any officer of the security forces can order a summary trial and sentence those who disturb public security to be executed by firing squad."

The Colonel put on his uniform and ordered twenty enlisted men to accompany him to Saavedra. His throat was dry and his mind in a tangle. He saw the wounds of stars in the clear sky. He raised the collar of his cape. It was frightfully cold.

He set up a guard post at the entrance to the houses and ordered three-man platoons to patrol the few streets in the district. He hid on a street corner, underneath a balcony, and watched the night go by. Between two white roofs he spied the silhouette of the attic. Evita was there and he didn't dare go up and look at her. They must be following him. Wherever he goes—those in the Commando of Vengeance are no doubt saying—there she must be. What were they calling her? The Colonel was intrigued by the countless names people referred to her by: Señora, Saint, Evita, Beloved Mother. He too called her Beloved Mother when despair alighted in his heart. Beloved Mother. She was there, a few steps away, and he couldn't touch her. He walked past the Madman's house twice. There was a light upstairs: blue, veiled, a light of vapors. Or of ideas? A river of sounds reached his ears from somewhere, he couldn't say where:

"This is the light of the mind, cold and planetary. The trees of the mind are black. The light is blue."

At dawn someone took him by the arm. It was the Madman. He looked freshly bathed. His hair shone beneath a cuirasse of newly applied pomade.

"I'm going to relieve you, sir," he said. "It's all over."

"What are you doing here, Arancibia? You should be at home, taking care of her."

"She can take care of herself. She doesn't need anybody. She's more alive by the day."

It wasn't the first time he'd said it: "She's more alive by the day." Sentences like that are peculiar to this country, the Colonel thought. They aren't heard anywhere else. "She's more alive by the day." "She sings better by the day."

"How do you know it's all over?" he asked.

"I called headquarters. There's no resistance. They've already shot fifteen to death. Not one is going to be left alive. The president wants it to be a lesson."

"That's best. Kill them all," the Colonel said.

He put his hands into the pockets of his cape. He felt the weight of the darkness in his parched throat. He had almost no voice left when next he spoke: "We might have to move the body, Arancibia. They might know it's here."

"Nobody knows," the Madman said. "This is the first time in months they haven't found it. There hasn't been a single flower, a single candle."

The Colonel was silent for a moment.

"You're right," he finally said. "They don't know where it is."

How much time had gone by since then: a month, forty days? He was sick at heart from missing her so badly. And all for what: such desolation was pointless. Events had taken a horrendous turn when he least expected it.

More than once he had tried to resign himself by reading what

survived of that story in the account of Margarita Heredia de Arancibia, the Madman's sister-in-law twice over: two sisters married to
two brothers. He went on reading what he already knew almost by
heart. Margarita or Margot had testified for more than three hours
before the military judge, and the résumé of the typed version was
there, in the files. The Colonel had noted in the margins of the first
page a detail that had attracted his attention: whenever she spoke of
herself, the witness referred to herself in the third person. Where the
written words read "Margot and her sister," they were to be read as
"I and my sister," or "I and Elena." It was very odd. Only in the last
sentences of the deposition did Margarita slip back, with a certain
sense of shame, to her own self, as though she felt no regret at the
idea of being herself again.

DOCUMENT 1

"Margot and her sister Elena come from a very upright family, the
Heredias. Both are direct descendants of Alejandro Heredia, one of
the distinguished federal governors of Tucumán. They have been
brought up to fear God, to love their country, and to defend home
and fireside above all else. Only in the light of these values can the
reason for what happened be understood.

"Margot was the first of the two to marry. She chose a handsome,
cultivated army officer, a native of Santiago, with whom she was
very happy for the first two years of their marriage. The only blight
on the couple's bliss was the fact that the husband, Ernesto Arancibia, a captain at the time, refused to have a family. Very unhappy,
Margot became suspicious and made certain inquiries. She learned
that two of Ernesto's maternal uncles were mentally defective and
had been sent to an asylum. She also found out that Ernesto's
younger brother, named Eduardo, had contracted meningitis at the
age of seven months and that he still suffered nervous sequelae. She
then deduced that if Ernesto did not want children it was out of fear
that they would be born with hereditary defects.

"Margot had unfortunately learned these details after her sister

Elena had already become engaged to Eduardo Arancibia, and the wedding was only two months away. Not knowing what she should do, Margot sought the advice of her mother, to whom the two sisters had always been very close. With Christian wisdom, the mother said that it was too late to make such a grave revelation, and that they should avoid creating enmity between the Heredia family and the Arancibia family. 'I do not see any reason to deny Elenita the destiny that has already come Margot's way,' she said.

"Eduardo also held the rank of captain at this time and was two years older than his fiancée. He had had no difficulty passing the medical examinations at the military college, and the only sign of meningitis was his moody, almost mad disposition, which Elena put up with good-humoredly. The two of them shared a fervent Catholicism. They took Communion every Sunday and were members of the Angelic Militia, which is very demanding as regards orthodoxy and precepts. Margot feared that her sister, Elena, would sooner or later become pregnant. That misfortune soon befell her."

DOCUMENT 2

"On April 10 Elena informed Eduardo that she was pregnant. Upset perhaps by the news, the husband had terrible convulsions that same afternoon: the muscles of his left eye became rigid. He was diagnosed as suffering from a slight irritation of the dura mater, stemming from the infantile meningitis."

"Although Eduardo promptly recovered from his ailment, Margot noticed that his left eye became rigid when he was nervous. He also became taciturn and behaved oddly.

"We thus arrive at the end of April. Margot's sister, who had been vomiting and suffering from minor disorders, had an alarming loss of blood. Total rest was prescribed. Her mother insisted that she wished to remain with her, but Eduardo was opposed. He argued that he was to receive some officers from the Intelligence Service at home and sort through with them certain confidential documents that were going to be kept in the attic. He seemed very anxious, and

Elena, with her woman's sixth sense, suspected that something peculiar was going on.

"Although Eduardo had promised he would come home for dinner that night, he failed to appear. Elena's discharges of blood grew worse, and she tried to reach Margot or her mother by phone to have an ambulance sent for her. She did not want to stay home, alone and helpless, for one minute more. It can well be imagined how upset she was when she discovered that the telephone was out of order. She tried two or three times to get out of bed, but she felt very weak and was afraid she would have a miscarriage. Between ten and eleven p.m. she finally was able to get to sleep. Hours later she was awakened by very loud sounds coming from the garage. She heard her husband's voice and also identified Colonel Moori Koenig's. She called out to them several times and even began to pound on the floor of the bedroom with a chair, but neither had the consideration to answer her."

DOCUMENT 3

"Then she heard them coming upstairs. They were carrying something heavy and stopped every two or three steps. Elena decided to leave the bedroom. She moved slowly, clutching her belly to hold back the blood, and reached the door that way. She tried to open it, and with a desperation that can be imagined, discovered that it was locked from the outside.

"Weakness overcame her. Not knowing what to do, she peeked through the keyhole. Margot's sister had always been most discreet but that was a case of force majeure. She saw her husband and Colonel Moori Koenig taking up to the attic, with the greatest of difficulty, a box that looked like a coffin. Elena pleaded in vain with them to bring her a glass of water. She felt extremely weak and her throat was parched. Finally she fainted.

"Neither Margot nor her mother had any way of knowing how many hours the poor thing lay there unconscious. At around ten a.m., Eduardo called them from the military hospital. Elena had been admitted with a mild case of dehydration and, despite the fears of the Heredia family, by the grace of God both she and her child were out of danger.

"Alarmed by the state of total prostration in which she found her, her mother gradually wrung from her the story of the terrible night she had had. As she learned the details, her indignation mounted. Nonetheless, when Elena told her that she did not want to live with Eduardo any longer and begged to be allowed to return to the bosom of her family, her mother reminded her of the duties she had pledged at the altar to fulfill."

DOCUMENT 4

"Eduardo's behavior was becoming stranger and stranger as the weeks went by. He remained in the attic for many hours at a time, with the door locked, and when he saw Elena he didn't even ask after her health. She too had changed. Anxiety had aroused in her an incessant desire to eat sweets. She was so fat she looked almost like a different person.

"In May Eduardo took up Egyptology. He filled the house with treatises on the mummies in the British Museum and began to get up in the middle of the night to underline passages in a copy of the *Book of the Dead*. Elena noticed that the marked section gave instructions on how to feed and adorn with jewels bodies that were already in the other world. Eduardo became stranger still during the week and a half that he spent reading *The Egyptian*, Mika Waltari's novel that had been highly popular two or three years before. One Sunday morning, shortly before going to Mass and while her husband was taking a shower, Elena dared to leaf through it. On one of the pages, Eduardo had written 'Exactly! Exactly!' in red pencil.

"And now, Your Honor, Margot wishes to read you a few lines from that novel, in order to acquaint you with the abysses of madness into which Eduardo Arancibia had fallen."

DOCUMENT 5

"From *The Egyptian*, book four, entitled 'Nefernefernefer,' chapter 4: *The jubilation of the embalmers reached its height when they received the corpse of a young woman . . . They did not throw her into the dungeon immediately. They cast lots for her and made her spend the night in the bed of one of them . . . They justified themselves by recounting that once upon a time, during the reign of the great king, they had taken to the House of Death a woman who awoke during the treatment, which was a miracle . . . For the embalmers there was no more pious duty than to try to repeat the miracle by lending the heat of their frightful bodies to the women who were brought to them."*

DOCUMENT 6

"Embarrassed and worried, Elena told Margot of the sacrilegious readings that were occupying her husband's mind. Her sister concluded immediately that the key to the secret lay in the attic and offered to go up there with her to see what was going on. Elena explained to her that that was impossible: Eduardo had placed a double lock on the door and only he had the keys. Moreover, he had strictly forbidden her to go up there. 'Perhaps he's taken up with another woman,' Margot told her sister, not thinking what those words might mean. 'Perhaps he's hiding love letters or who knows what other despicable things up there.' That insinuation caused Elena great pain, but also awakened her desire to get to the bottom of the secret as soon as possible. 'Margot, help me,' she said to her sister. 'All sorts of ideas are running through my head. I'm even afraid Eduardo is a Bluebeard.'

"Margot decided to call in a locksmith from the Army College, and with his aid made molds of the two locks. The keys were large, heavy ones, with curved indents, and it took the worker nearly a week to get them to fit properly.

"The sisters were ready to go up to the attic on July 2 or 3. In her confession on Sunday, which was the first day of the month, Elena decided to tell the whole story to her spiritual guide, a Salesian father far along in years. The priest insisted that she obey her husband and not violate so important a secret. Elena left the confessional rent by doubt and that same Sunday sought her mother's advice. It was a long discussion. Her mother concurred that it was imperative to ascertain the truth because Elena could endanger her pregnancy if she continued to be under such great nervous strain. Margot, who agreed with her mother, insisted that her sister was not able to go up to the attic by herself and offered once again to accompany her. Elena went on weeping and repeating over and over the order that the confessor had given her."

DOCUMENT 7

"Many secrets came to light in the course of the conversation that the Heredia family had that Sunday. Margot learned that Eduardo had been visited once or twice by Dr. Pedro Ara, a Spanish diplomat and physician who was world famous as an embalmer. The two of them would shut themselves up for several hours in the attic and on one occasion they even boiled syringes and medical instruments. She was extremely alarmed when she heard this story. No matter how often she turned the subject over in her mind she could not imagine what was afoot.

"Finally, heeding her family's pleas, Elena agreed to look into what was going on, but she imposed one ironclad condition: she would go up to the attic alone. She wanted to decide for herself, with only the aid of her confessor, how to confront Eduardo if she discovered that he had a mistress.

"The following days were ones of terrible anxiety for Margot. She had ominous presentiments. One night she said to Ernesto, her husband: 'It seems to me that things aren't going at all well between Elena and Eduardo these days.' But he did not ask any questions.

"So we arrive at Friday, July 6, 1956. That night Eduardo was scheduled to stand guard at the Service as he regularly did once a week. It was a twelve-hour watch, which began at seven p.m. Hence Elena had all night to go up into the attic. She had hidden the keys in her brassiere and even slept with them. That was the best place, for she had not had conjugal relations with her husband once she had had definite confirmation that she was pregnant. She felt afraid nonetheless. More than once Eduardo had unexpectedly turned up at home during his watch and had shut himself up in the attic without saying a word. Elena intended to act quickly. It would not take her more than an hour to look through the old maps and the strange wooden crate. That was what she told Margot the last time that the two of them talked together on the telephone."

DOCUMENT 8

"That midnight will never be erased from Margot's memory. She was sleeping at her house on the calle Juramento, where she still lives, when she was awakened by the phone ringing.

"It was Eduardo, speaking in a sick-sounding, broken voice. 'A tragedy has happened,' he told his brother. 'Come over to my house right away. Don't let anyone come with you, no one.'

"Margot, who had her ear glued to the receiver too, went half crazy. 'Ask him what's going on,' she said to her husband.

"'Elena, Elenita, a tragedy, she's wounded,' Eduardo said, weeping. And he hung up.

"Naturally, Ernesto immediately informed Colonel Moori Koenig, who was Eduardo's superior, and got dressed. With a heavy heart, fearing for her sister's life, Margot insisted on going with him. The trip to Saavedra seemed to last forever. When they arrived, they thought they might well have dreamed the phone call, for the house was dark and there wasn't a sound. But two people never dream the same dream, even if they are husband and wife. The street door was open. Upstairs, Eduardo was inconsolably embracing Elena's already lifeless body.

"What had actually happened is a secret that Margot's sister took to her grave. The neighbors thought they had heard a violent argument, screams, and two shots. But in Elena's body there was only one bullet, which had pierced her throat. Eduardo admits that he fired the shots. He has said that in the dark attic he took Elena for a thief. His remorse appears to be sincere and the Heredia family has forgiven him. But what Margot saw that night is so incredible that she has doubts about everything: doubts about her feelings, doubts about her emotions, and, of course, doubts too about the man who is still her brother-in-law."

DOCUMENT 9

"As Ernesto was comforting Eduardo, Margot saw a blue glow in the attic and tried to extinguish it. She was unable to: although she clicked the light switch off and on several times, the glow was still there. She then decided to go upstairs to the attic. The stairway was awash with blood, and Margot had to cling to the wall so as not to slip and fall. At that moment she thought that her first duty to her dead sister was to clean up the blood, but what she saw in the attic made her forget altogether her well-meant intention.

"The blue glow was coming from the wooden crate, projecting a transparent and very elaborate shape, which looked like a piece of ghostly lace or a leafless tree. Dr. Ara, who visited Elena at her home that very day, deduced that I had seen, that Margot had seen, not a light but the map of the illness known as cancer, but he was unable to explain what sort of force held that image in the air. Around the crate thousands of papers and folders were scattered about, and there were blood stains on all of them. Terrified, I drew closer. I remember that my mouth was dry and that I suddenly lost my voice. Then I saw her. I saw her for only a moment but it is as though I were still seeing her and God had doomed me to see her forever.

"The moment I saw her I knew it was Evita. I don't know why they had taken her to Elena's nor do I want to know. I no longer know what I want to know and what I don't. Evita was lying in the box, still and calm, with her eyes closed. The body, stark naked, was blue, not a blue that can be explained in words but transparent, a neon color, a blue that was not of this world. Alongside the box was a wooden bench that could only have served to watch over the dead woman. There were also horrible stains, heaven only knows what filth, God forgive me: Eduardo had been with the cadaver for all those weeks.

"Reality is a river. Events come and go. It all happened like a flash, in a few seconds. I fell into a faint. I mean: Margot fell. When she came to the room was dark, the blue light had disappeared, her hands and her clothes were soaked with blood.

"So she went downstairs and cleaned herself up as best she could.

She didn't have a dress to change into and put on one of Elena's, a flannel one with velvet appliqués. From the bathroom she heard Colonel Moori Koenig arrive. She also heard Ernesto, her husband, say: 'This story mustn't go any farther. It mustn't go beyond army circles.' And she heard Moori Koenig correct him: 'This story must not go *beyond this house.* Major Arancibia shot a thief. That was all: a thief.' Eduardo was sobbing. When he saw me in his wife's dress, he turned pale. 'Elena,' he stammered. And then he said: 'Elita.' I went over to him: 'Eva, Evena,' he repeated, as though he were calling me. His eyes were staring into space; his being had left him. He repeated this litany all night long: 'Evena, Elita.'

"Colonel Moori Koenig asked me to wash my sister's body and I readied it for the funeral chapel, the shroud. I wept as I did so. I caressed her belly, her swollen breasts. Her belly sagged from the weight of the dead child. She was already nearly rigid and I had difficulty opening her fingers so as to be able to intertwine them. When I finally succeeded, I noted that she was clutching in her fist the keys to the attic; both keys were bloodstained, as in the story of Bluebeard."

In the weeks of surveillance and investigations that followed, the Colonel's body changed. Dark pouches appeared underneath his eyes and stars of varicose veins at his ankles. As they took the Deceased from one part of the city to another, he had dizzy spells and attacks of heartburn that kept him from sleeping. Whenever he saw himself reflected in the windows of his office he asked himself why. What can possibly be happening to me? he said. On January 22 I'll be forty-two. If a man is old at my age it's because he doesn't know how to live or because he wants to die. I don't want to die. That woman is the one who wants to see me dead.

During the entire night of July 6 he had tried to conceal the crime. At dawn he realized that he would not be able to. The neighbors had heard Elena and Eduardo arguing and then the shots. They all spoke of two shots, but the Colonel saw the trace of only one: the bullet buried in Elena's throat.

"Nobody ever knew the true story of what had happened," Aldo Cifuentes told me almost thirty years later. "Moori Koenig had had some idea, but he was missing pieces of the puzzle. It was a mistake to have left the Deceased in Arancibia's attic. The motionless body had gone on seducing the Madman day after day. He thought only of returning home so as to be able to contemplate it. He had undressed it. Alongside the big box he placed a little wooden bench where heaven only knows what he did. He must have sat there studying the details of the body: the eyelashes, the delicate curve of the eyebrows, the toenails that were still painted with transparent enamel, the protruding navel. If he had heard her moving before, when he was alone with her he perhaps believed that she was alive. Or hoped that she had come back to life, as is indicated by his readings of *The Egyptian*."

The neighbors stated that between nine and ten p.m. there had been a loud argument, with shouting and screaming. A retired major who lived opposite the Arancibias heard the Madman say: "I caught you, you bitch!" And Elena, who was weeping: "Don't kill me, forgive me." At six a.m. the military judge arrived. At seven, the minister of the army ordered Dr. Ara to examine the corpse. The embalmer noted nothing irregular. He had been in the house a week before, injecting solutions of grayling into its femoral artery. Moori Koenig was indignant with Ara for having touched the Deceased without his permission or knowledge. "Major Arancibia told me that you were the one who requested it," the embalmer explained. "He told me that the body shifted position when it was left alone and that none of you knew why. I made a meticulous examination of the corpse. It has small nicks in it; it has obviously been badly jolted. But, essentially, it hasn't changed since they took it away from me." His tone of voice was, as usual, self-important, mordant. Moori Koenig contained himself to keep from punching him. He left the scene of the crime feeling terribly depressed. At ten a.m., he phoned

Cifuentes to invite him to have a drink with him. His voice was slurred from alcohol and in the middle of a sentence he put the phone down and stammered nonsense syllables: "Evena, Elita."

During the wake for Elena and the nine nights of prayer for the repose of her soul, Eva Perón's body remained in the attic, protected by the piles of dossiers and documents. There were two dead women in the house, but no one was allowed to say anything about either one. Events drifted onward, as though looking for a place and finding no room. On July 17 and 18, Eduardo Arancibia was put on trial before an army tribunal. His defense attorneys urged him in vain to throw himself on the mercy of the court: he did not speak; he did not offer apologies; he did not answer the judge's impatient questions. Only on the afternoon of the second day did he complain of flames in his head. He shouted irreverently: "My flames hurt! Evina, Evena, where have you gone?" He was forcibly removed from the courtroom. He was not present when he was sentenced to life imprisonment in Magdalena penitentiary. Out of a sense of propriety or a scrupulous concern for secrecy, the judge decided that the case would be filed in a dossier with a false title page: *Accidental Homicide*.

During those days the Deceased resumed the wandering that was causing her so much harm: from one truck to another, down streets that were never the same. They moved her at random through the flat, endless city: the city without a weft or folds. Since the Colonel did not stray from his inferno of alcohol, Captain Milton Galarza took over the reins of the Service: he planned the transfers of the Deceased, he bought her a new tunic, he changed the order of the watches. At times, when he saw the truck containing the body beneath the windows of his office, he greeted it with a clarinet beat that would have driven Mozart or Carl Maria von Weber mad. He was informed one morning that candles had been found near the ambulance where the body was confined. It could have been mere chance: the three stubby lighted candles had been set at the foot of a monument in the plaza Rodríguez Peña. The soldiers on guard, who recognized the signs by now, had heard nothing out of the ordinary. Galarza decided that, in any event, the moment had come to change the "gun chest." He ordered that a rough pine box, with no adornments and no handles, be purchased, and had the sides of it labeled in large painted letters like a packing crate: RADIO EQUIPMENT. LV2 THE VOICE OF FREEDOM.

Alone in his office, the Colonel surrendered, more and more, to sadness, to the feeling of loss. Ever since he'd begun receiving anonymous letters and threatening phone calls at home, he hadn't gone near Evita. He couldn't. "If we see you with her we'll snatch your balls off," the voices said. They were never the same. "Why don't you leave her in peace?" the letters repeated. "We are following you day and night. We know that where you are she is going to be." They gave him orders. "We are giving you until October 17 to hand the body over to the CGT"; "We forbid you to take her to the Army Intelligence Service." He couldn't bear to obey and yet he obeyed. He missed her. If I had her near me, he thought, I wouldn't feel so parched. Nothing satisfied his thirst.

He'd changed his phone number three times, but the enemy always found him. Early one morning a woman's voice called, and still in a daze, he handed the phone to his wife. She let go of it, screaming.

"What did they say to you?" he asked. "What do those bastards want?"

"She says that today, at noon, they're going to blow our house up. That they've poisoned the children's milk. That they're going to lop my nipples off."

"Don't pay any attention to them."

"She wants you to give that woman back."

"What woman? I don't know anything about any woman."

"The Mother, she said. Santa Evita, she said. Beloved Mother."

At twelve a stick of dynamite went off on the landing. The windows, the vases, the dishes, were blown to pieces. The shards of glass wounded the cheekbone of their eldest daughter. She had to be taken to the hospital: twelve stitches. She could have been hope-

255

lessly disfigured. Person had done him more damage than anybody, and yet he missed her. He couldn't stop thinking about her. Just remembering her made him feel breathless, gave him chest spasms. In the middle of August a storm came up that ushered spring in ahead of time, and the Colonel decided that his long submission to fate no longer had any meaning. He shaved, soaked in the bathtub for more than two hours, and dressed in the last new uniform he had. Then he went out in the rain. The Deceased was still parked in the calle Paraguay, in front of the Carmen Chapel: two soldiers were watching the street; two others were safeguarding the coffin, inside the ambulance. The Colonel ordered them to get inside and drove it to the corner of Callao and Viamonte. He left Person there, within sight, below his office.

Now, he said to himself, no enemy could confront him. When Cifuentes visited him that afternoon, the Colonel told him in confidence that he had surrounded the ambulance with a barricade of fifteen men: six of them were covering that number of angles from the windows of buildings, one was hidden underneath the chassis, waiting with his regulation firearm drawn, the others were posted on the sidewalk, inside the vehicle, in front of it, and behind it.

"I thought he'd gone mad," Cifuentes told me. "But he wasn't mad. He was desperate. He told me he was going to tame the Mare before she did him in."

So he waited. In uniform, sitting next to the window, with his eyes fixed on the ambulance and without drinking a drop of alcohol: he waited the entire night of August 15 and the peaceful day that followed, without anything happening. He waited, missing her and at the same time hating her, certain that in the end he would get the better of her.

By late afternoon on Thursday, the sixteenth, the clouds had already scattered, and there alighted on the city a stiff, icy air that crunched when people crossed through it. Shortly before seven, the procession in honor of the feast day of San Roque paraded down the avenida Callao. The Colonel was standing in front of the window when the police patrols diverted the traffic eastward, and he heard the sacred music of the trombones. The effigy of the saint and his dog barely rose above the surge of black and purple habits. The worshipers were carrying tapers, garlands of flowers, and great silver viscera. "What an ardent desire to waste time," the Colonel said. And he hoped it would rain.

It was one of those moments when the setting sun can't make up its mind, according to what Cifuentes told me: its light wavers between gray, purple, and orange, like an oblivious cow. Moori Koenig returned to his desk to go over the file cards on Margot Arancibia once again when a din of honking horns stopped him short. Outside, Galarza was shouting hoarse orders, not a single word of which the Colonel could make out. The men on guard were running blindly down the street. A bad omen stuck in his throat, Cifuentes recounted. Moori Koenig had always felt the omens in the caverns of his body as being like needles or burns. He hurried down into the street. He reached the corner of Callao in time to see, in the sudden darkness, a row of thirty-three stubby candles burning at the foot of the facades of the buildings. From a distance they looked like sea foam or the wake of a ship. Inside one entryway he found a funeral wreath of sweet peas, pansies, and forget-me-nots, with a ribbon inscribed in gold letters across it. Resignedly, he read the almost predictable message: SANTA EVITA, OUR MOTHER. COMMANDO OF VENGEANCE.

Half an hour later, Captain Galarza had completed his brief interrogation of the priests who had been at the head of the procession and the devout women in brown habits following them. The hypnosis of the prayers and the drifting clouds of incense had blinded all of them. They recalled nothing out of the ordinary: no funeral offering or any candles except those sold in parish churches. On the avenida Córdoba, a few devotees in violet habits had fallen behind the others to aid an exhausted nun, but such mishaps abound in processions. Nobody remembered anybody's features.

The Colonel was beside himself. He went inside the ambulance twice and confronted Person in a loud voice choked with rage: "You'll pay me for this, you'll pay me for this." Fesquet heard him repeat curses in German, but remembered only one question that seemed to be a plea: "Bist du noch da?" And then: "Keiner geht weiter."[8]

He paced about with his hands behind his back, his wrists gripping each other with an icy firmness, as he pretended not to notice the cold, which was also implacable. Finally he halted. He summoned Galarza.

"Take that woman up to my office," he ordered.

The captain looked at him in amazement. He had a crack in the middle of his lower lip: The cold perhaps, Moori Koenig thought, surprised that in moments of stress that sort of thought should occur to him, the clarinet perhaps.

"What about secrecy, sir?" Galarza asked. "We're going to break the regulation."

"To hell with secrecy," Moori Koenig answered. "Everybody knows by now. Take her upstairs."

"They're going to be annoyed at headquarters," Galarza warned him.

"I couldn't care less. Think of all the harm she's done us. Think of Arancibia's poor wife."

"She can do us more harm if we let her inside."

"Take her upstairs, Captain. I know what I'm doing. Take her up this minute."

The box was light, or seemed lighter than the pine boards it was made of: it stood upright in the elevator cage as it went up four flights to the Colonel's office. They left it underneath a Gründig hi-fi which was also the color of light honey. The three objects that found themselves together on that side of the room didn't know what to do with each other, like someone who wants to clap and can't find his other hand: the sketch in pencil and tempera of Kant in Königsberg up above, below it the Gründig that had yet to be turned on, and at the foot of it the box marked LV2 THE VOICE OF FREEDOM, in which she lay, with her inaudible, but resounding, fatal

---

[8] "Are you still there?" And then: "No one will go farther."

voice, freer than any live voice. The Colonel stood for a long time contemplating that bright outline of the room as the brandy went down his throat in rapid cascades. Yes, it all went together, at first glance nothing seemed amiss, except that every so often a wisp of a chemical smell that he knew so well escaped. Who was going to notice? He felt thirsty to see her, thirsty to touch her. He locked the door and moved the big box to a spot in the room that had always been empty. He opened the lid and looked at her: somewhat rumpled and hunkered down from the trip in the elevator, but even more frightening than four months before, when he had left her in the Madman's attic. Although she was ice-cold, Person managed to give a devious smile, as if she were about to say something at once tender and terrifying.

"You're a shit," the Colonel said to her. "Why did you go away for such a long time?"

He felt bitter: an untimely sob was mounting in his throat, and he didn't know how to stop it.

"Are you going to stay, Evita?" he asked her. "Are you going to obey me?"

The blue gleam from the depths of Person blinked, or he thought it blinked.

"Why don't you love me?" he said to her. "What did I do to you? I spend my life taking care of you."

She didn't answer. She seemed radiant, triumphant. A tear escaped the Colonel, and at the same time a gust of hatred overtook him.

"You're going to learn, Mare," he said to her, "even though I have to teach you by force."

He went out into the hallway.

"Galarza, Fesquet!" he called.

The officers came on the run, sensing disaster. Galarza stopped short next to the door and and wouldn't let Fesquet by.

"Look at her," the Colonel said. "Shitty mare. She won't let herself be tamed."

Cifuentes told me years later that nothing had impressed Galarza

259

as much as the acrid smell of drunkard's piss. "He felt a terrible urge to vomit," he said to me, "but he couldn't. It seemed to him that he was inside a dream."

The Colonel stood there looking at them, not understanding. He raised his square jaw and ordered:

"Pee on her."

Since the officers just stood there, he repeated the order, syllable by syllable:

"Come on, what are you waiting for? Line up. Pee on her."

12

"Shreds of My Life"

And now he was a prisoner. They had come to get him at six a.m., as he was trying to shave. His hands were trembling. He had cut his chin with the razor: a deep gash that wouldn't stop bleeding. They had arrested him in that wretched state.

"You have half an hour to say goodbye to your family," they had told him. And so he had climbed into a military van: three days of journeying blindly, along a smooth, endless road, with no curves. The captain who was escorting him wouldn't or couldn't offer any explanations.

"Don't be impatient," he said. "You'll soon find out what's going on when we get there. It's a secret order from the minister of the army."

He had no idea where they were taking him. At dawn on the second day the van had stopped on a horizon of thistles. The sky was dark and freezing cold. The surge of the sea could be heard. The men dressed in civvies who were escorting him began to cover the windowpanes and the chassis of the van with close-woven barbed wire.

"I'm going to file a complaint," the Colonel said. "I'm not a crim-

261

inal. I'm a colonel in the nation's armed forces. Remove those prison bars."

"It's not because of you," the captain answered indifferently. "It's because of the stones. We're about to enter a road with stones as big as ostrich eggs. If we don't protect the van, they're going to pound us to pieces."

As soon as they started up again he heard them. They were punishing the metal panels with a maddening clatter. As they went slowly on, the tall curtains of wind could be heard: incessant, frenzied.

At midnight on the third day they drove down a row of square cement buildings, with iron doors and transoms above them. The captain left him in front of an entrance and handed him a key.

"There's everything you need inside," he said. "They'll be coming for you early tomorrow morning."

In the room were a camp cot, a large table with pencils and notepads, a standing lamp, and a wardrobe with two mirrors. He saw, with relief, his colonel's uniforms hanging inside. They were clean, with new gold stars sewn on the epaulets. The air smelled of a stubborn, eternal dust. He tried to go out into the night, but the wind outside, in the vast darkness, did not allow him to go a single step. It blew dust and shards of silica over his exhausted flesh, fanned his body as though there were no space or light or anything save the madness of the wind blowing to itself. He thought he could make out a cone-shaped hill in the distance. Birds, seagulls perhaps, were cawing in the darkness, a phenomenon that was incomprehensible. He felt a terrible thirst and also knew that nothing could satisfy it. So he returned to his room (or to that emptiness that he now called his room), knowing that the loneliness had begun and that it would have no end.

There was a knock on his door before dawn. A retired colonel, whom he didn't know, informed him that the minister of the army had confined him to that rim of the desert because he hadn't obeyed orders from his superiors.

"What orders?" the Colonel asked.

"They told me you knew."

"I don't know anything. For how long?"

"Six months. It's a confinement, not an arrest. When you get out of here, this incident won't show on your service record."

"Confinement, arrest," the Colonel said. "It makes no difference to me."

The whole situation seemed odd to him. He had sat halfway up on the cot, leaning on a thin burlap pillow, as the other colonel spoke without looking at him. A gray light filtered in through the transom, but it took eternities to advance across the room: the gray didn't want to move, as though that indecision constituted the real nature of the day.

"You may stroll about wherever you like," the other colonel said. "You may bring your wife and daughters here. You may write them letters. The dining room is close by, in the next building. Breakfast is served from six to eight, lunch from twelve to two, dinner from eight to ten. The climate is healthful; we're on the seaside here. It's going to be like a vacation, a rest."

"Who are my neighbors?" the Colonel asked.

"For the moment you don't have any. You're alone. I've been here ten months and haven't seen a soul outside of my assistant and the commander of the barracks. But someone else may turn up at any moment." He suddenly fell silent and stood there for a moment stroking the lapels of his greatcoat. He was an elderly colonel with a round, inscrutable face. He looked like a peasant. Heaven only knew how long he had been retired before Perón's fall from power had brought him back into the army. Who could tell whether, all things considered, he was really a colonel. "If I were you," he said, "I'd have my wife come. A person can go mad here. Listen to that wind. It never dies down. It blows like that twenty-four hours a day."

"I don't know how to phone my wife," the Colonel said, over-whelmed. "I don't even know where we are."

"I thought you'd realized. Facing the Gulf of San Jorge, in the south. What good does it do you to know? With this wind, a person can't go very far."

263

"Is there by any chance a place where one can buy a bit of gin?" the Colonel hinted. "I'm going to need a couple of bottles."

"I don't advise it. Alcohol is very expensive. They sell it in the dining room, but each bottle costs an arm and a leg."

"I have my pay."

"Only a third of it," the round-faced colonel explained. "The army gives the rest of it to your family. Your third barely covers the cost of meals, which are also expensive. Nothing is grown or raised here. Provisions have to be brought in from a long distance away."

"In that case, I won't eat."

"Don't say that. The sea air gives a person an appetite."

At noon he went out and began walking against the wind. The dining room was less than fifty yards away, underneath a big sign that read CANTEEN, but every step cost him an enormous effort, as though his feet had anchors tied to them. A short, muscular man, with a boxer's nose, served him some pea-flour soup.

"Bring me some gin," the Colonel ordered him.

"We sell alcohol only on Friday and Saturday nights," the man said. It was Thursday. "Before you order anything to eat, you'd better have a look at the prices."

He studied the menu. The only items that didn't cost an exorbitant sum were pea soup and lamb.

"How about salt?" he asked. "How much does salt cost?"

"Salt and water are free," the man said. "You can help yourself to all you want."

"Give me some salt then," the Colonel said. "That's all I need."

Outside the air was still murky. The wind blew so hard that it seemed to comprise a brotherhood of many winds that never died down. It was damp and healthful, with fringes of sea air and piercing needles of sand that perhaps came from the desert. The ungainly silhouette of the cone-shaped hill that the Colonel had glimpsed the night before stood out on the horizon. It now seemed about to fade away altogether.

When he returned to his room he found the cot made up with

clean sheets. His shaving gear had been laid out neatly on the bathroom shelf. His clothes were all carefully hung up on the hangers or placed in the drawers of the wardrobe. He was indignant that someone had taken the liberty of opening his valise and putting his belongings away without permission. He began, frantically, to write a letter of complaint to the minister of the army, but left it half finished. The desolation and forlornness all about him seemed irremediable, and he supposed that the best thing to do would be to wait for the six months' confinement to be over. The only thing that preyed on his mind now was the Deceased. He had tried to tame her, and she hadn't let him. Sooner or later, when she got out of hand, the ruling authorities would have to summon him. He was, after all, the only one who knew how to handle her. The embalmer too had attained a certain skill at it, but they weren't going to take any notice of him: he was a foreigner, a civilian, and was perhaps secretly conniving with Perón.

A dark suspicion slowly crept into his mind until it filled it completely: his secrets had been violated. Whoever had emptied his valise already knew that it contained the manuscript of *My Message* and the sheaf of school composition books that Renzi, the butler, had entrusted to the mother of Person, those which she, Person, had written between 1939 and 1940 and which bore, on the odd-numbered pages, titles such as *Nales, Hare, Legs, Makup, Nose, Esercises,* and *Hospittle Espences.* The intruder had also found, doubtless, the file cards on which the Colonel noted down the activities of the Service. In the scant half hour that he had been given to say goodbye to his family, he had spent less time kissing his daughters and piling up his clothes to pack than he had gathering those papers without which he became vulnerable, washed up, a nonentity. What he now possessed was nothing, and at the same time it was everything: secrets that could not be shared, loose strands of stories which did not mean very much by themselves but which, on being woven together by someone who knew how to do so, were enough to set the country on fire.

If they had touched a single document of his, he would kill the first human being he met. It didn't matter to him which of them had entered his room: all of them must be accomplices. They had left him his Smith & Wesson with six bullets in it, perhaps with the hope that he would commit suicide. He didn't intend to do so: he would use the weapon to kill anyone who got in his way. He would wreak havoc before he disappeared in the wind or in the vast expanses there outside. Sick with rage, he inspected the valise. It was strange. It looked as though nobody had touched the packets. They were all still tied up with the German knots in the shape of a figure eight that only he knew how to tie and untie.

He spread the file cards from the Service out on the cot and took a look at them: it was unlikely that anyone could figure out what they said just by reading them. He had written them in a simple, almost primitive key, but if the sentence that afforded access to them was not known, they were meaningless. He had left a copy of the key for decoding them in his safe-deposit box in the Banco Francés, along with instructions that if he died or disappeared it should be given to his friend Aldo Cifuentes. It was Cifuentes who showed me the sentence, written in the Colonel's angular, slanting handwriting:

I've learned that the harm being done me is quite just
abc dcefgch ijei ijc jefk lcagm hngc kc ao pqaic rqoi

And then: s = ñ; t = y; v = w; w = c; x = f; z = p. The numbers: 0 = 1, 2 = 9, 3 = 4, 8 = 3, 5 = 5. The coded message is written backward. The text is the mirror.[9]

"For some time I thought that Moori had composed the key of the cryptogram on one of the desperate days that he must have spent on the shores of the Gulf of San Jorge," Cifuentes said to me. "I thought the sentence was a penitent portrait of himself. I was wrong: he had adapted it from a book by Evita. You can find it in the

[9]The Colonel's cryptogram resembles the one in Jules Verne's "The Raft," where the message, once coded, must likewise be read backward, letter by letter.

edition of *My Message* sold at newsstands.[10] Moori changed the sentence, so as to introduce several more letters, I suppose. Evita says: 'Illness and pain have brought me closer to God. *I have learned that everything that is happening to me* and that is making me suffer is *not unjust.*' Moori, however, speaks of 'the harm being done me' as 'quite just.' Perhaps he was also thinking of himself, as I believed in the beginning. Perhaps the idea of a curse was already preying on his mind."

But when he spread out the file cards on the cot, the Colonel only wanted to check that the order had not been changed. He read the notes that he had written after marking Person with a star behind her ear. *What happened after her father died in 1926?* And he deciphered the last line of the report: "She went with her mother and her brother and sisters to Chivilcoy on the bus."[11] Everything was in the right place. He went over the card that read: *During the first seven months of 1943, the Deceased disappeared. She did not act either on the radio or in the theater, and the magazines covering the entertainment world scarcely mention her. What happened during this lapse of time? Was she ill, on a blacklist, back in Junín?* He decoded, halfheartedly, the last line: "Mercedes Printer, who accompanied her to Otamendi and Miroli, has told . . ."

He spent the remainder of the morning stretched out on the cot, pondering how he would go about recovering Evita. He wanted to

[10]Cifuentes was referring to a ninety-six-page volume, published under the imprint Ediciones del Mundo, with a prologue by Fermín Chávez. On the cover, under the title *My Message: The Book That Disappeared for 32 Years,* Evita is smiling, with a bonfire behind her.
[11]Does it suffice to copy the key of this sentence to understand the work that the Colonel took upon himself? Cifuentes told me that even in his last days of total ruin, Moori remembered by heart the equivalents of each letter and could translate any sentence into his code:

She went with her mother and her brother and sisters to Chivilcoy on the bus
ojc vcgi vaij jcf knijcf egh jcf lfnijcf egh oaoicfo in wjabadwnt ng ijc lqo

By reading the letters backward and omitting the blanks, the last line read:

oqlcjigntnwdabajwniofcioaohgefcjinflfcjhgefcjinkfcjjiavigcvcjo

267

have her there. In that remote place, alone with him, she would be better off than anywhere else. Someone could bring her to the Gulf of San Jorge. He needed, once again, a plan, an officer he could trust, and some money. Maybe he could sell the story of the Deceased to a magazine and disappear. Cifuentes had put the idea into his head: "Think, Colonel, think. *Paris Match, Life,* five thousand dollars. Ten thousand. Whatever you like." But if he gave away his secret, he would no longer be who he was. He would be worth nothing.

A trickle of sunlight slowly came through the curtain over the transom. He ran his eyes over the austere interior of the building, in search of a hiding place for the documents. They were solid, impenetrable walls. In the cement the only irregularities to be seen were those in the hardened surface: lumps and craters like the ones on the moon. Outside, the wind kept howling and the inexplicable seagulls shrieked. At around three, hunger drove his drowsiness away. He was lying motionless on the cot when he thought he saw someone steal into the dark room. He groped for the Smith & Wesson underneath the pillow and calculated how long it would take him to leap out of bed and fire. He did not loosen his grip on the trigger even after he realized that the intruder was an incredibly tiny woman—it was easy for him to tell it was a woman: a pair of enormous breasts gave her away—with her hair in a bun and dressed in a short skirt. He saw her come over to the table with a smoking plate of food that gave off an aroma of olives, nutmeg, and a strong sauce, from which wispy specters of wine escaped. When the woman rolled up the wicker curtain covering the transom, the same gray light as in the morning—strong now, as though it were made of steel—invaded the room and, oddly enough, made it darker.

"We thought you were sick," the woman said. "I've brought you a potato pie. It's a gift to welcome you."

"Did you open my valise?" the Colonel asked.

He could see her now. She was a miniature of a woman: no taller than a nine- or ten-year-old, with deep wrinkles above her lips and those breasts like planets, which made her bend forward as she walked.

"The room must be kept in order," she said. "The rule must be obeyed."

"I don't want you to touch anything. Who are you? The colonel didn't tell me anything about a woman."

"I'm Ersilia," she murmured, without setting the plate down, "Ferruccio's wife. He never mentions me, so as to put on airs. I'm the one who does everything around here. Without me this place wouldn't exist. Have you heard the wind?"

"I'd hear it even if I were deaf. I can't imagine how these huts ever got built."

The Colonel wanted the woman to leave, but she stood there holding not the pie but the breath of wine of the pie.

"They brought the blocks of cement in trucks and put them in place with winches and cranes. The first windows didn't last a month. The frames, the panes of glass, went flying off. One morning they found the cement walls bare. The wind had swallowed up everything. Then they replaced the windows with transoms."

"Leave me the pie and be off with you. Tell the colonel . . . what's his name?"

"Ferruccio," the dwarf answered.

"Tell Ferruccio that I forbid anyone to touch my things. Tell him that I'm going to take care of keeping the room in order myself."

The dwarf left the pie on the table and stopped to look at the closed valise. She rubbed her hands on the apron that barely covered her legs and belly—a minuscule bit of cloth hidden beneath the unbelievable globes on her chest—and said, with a smile that made her look almost pretty:

"You're going to let me read the notebooks you have here, all right? One of these days. I learned to read from notebooks like that. When I saw them, it made me nostalgic."

"They're not mine," the Colonel said. "It's not possible to read them. They belong to the army."

"So it's not possible to read them," she said in surprise.

She had left the door ajar. The wind blew down in capricious waves, gentle at times, fierce at times: it raised clouds of dust and scattered them all over the horizon. The dark swell of dust also entered the room and made rancor, feelings, words, fade: it made everything that dared oppose it fade.

"It's going to rain," Ersilia said as she left. "Ferruccio has a radiogram for you. It came early this morning."

He stood there motionless for a long time, contemplating the slow waning of the light, which lingered on in a pale tone of orange from four until six and then turned unhurriedly to violet until after seven: a majestic, cheerless twilight that no one could look straight at and that perhaps was not made for human beings. Shortly after seven a fine, ice-cold rain fell that quenched the insolence of the dust. The wind went on blowing nonetheless, stronger than ever. He shaved, bathed, and put on his useless uniform. Then he undid the knots of the packets to reinforce them with a new kind of knot and, almost unintentionally, opened one of the notebooks. What surprised him was not the untidy handwriting, in big letters, that seemed to be doing acrobatics on the wires of the horizontal lines of the paper, but, rather, the phrases that he read:

> dont make noise when eating soup dont lean over the plate too far dont bite the bread so as to eat a mouthfull of it brake it off with your fingers instead dont put bread in soup dont raize your nife to your mouth

Was it a notebook of rules of etiquette? All the pages headed by the title *Esercises* repeated *dont . . . you mustnt . . . you shouldnt . . . eat . . . drink . . . use . . .* Only at the end had Evita copied something that appeared to be a thought or the words of a tango:

> The other night as I made my way
> from the theater to the pension where I stay
> I felt the knife edge of a pain
> that stole in from my side
> and treacherously tried
> to slash my heart in twain.

Intrigued, the Colonel leafed through the *Hospittle Espences*. On the first page, underlined in red pencil, Person—the mistreated adolescent of the days of the notebook who was the rough draft of Person—had defined an illness. Chicha's pleurisy: *it beggins with a hi fever and bad chest panes sharp panes in the side rather.*[12] The following pages contained a travel diary written almost like a grocery list:

Roun trip to Junín	$ 3.50
Box of asperins	$0.25
Hot water botal	$ 1.10
Ampulles of codene	$0.80

When I get there I find her alredy quite a bit better poor Chicha with the biggest circles under her eyes so that in a cupple of days I'll be back dont worry Pascual you had to try Rosa out in my role sooner or later and if shes playing it badly pull her out without feeling sick about it and put Pampín in so to make a long story short when I come back Im leaving the pencion which is a filthy hole as you know full of cockroches and nasty things.[13]

He closed the notebooks and the darkness or shame gnawed at him inside—not the wind now, which had perhaps been banished by the

---

[12]Cifuentes, who copied a few pages of the notebooks in 1956, assured me that he had scrupulously respected the original spelling errors. I owe to him the description of Evita's handwriting, of the notebooks, and of the knots the Colonel used to tie them together.

[13]Cifuentes deduced that this was the rough draft of a letter to Pascual Pelliciotta, the actor with whom Evita headed a company of radio actors. From May 1939 on Pelliciotta and Duarte played in *The Gardens of the Eighties,* a serial novel by Héctor Pedro Blomberg. Chicha (Erminda Duarte, Evita's sister) suffered the attack of pleurisy between July and August, when the company put on a stage version of Blomberg's novel in Rosario. Evita's part was then played by Rosa del Río—with whom she shared a room in her pension—in the afternoon and evening performances on Thursday, August 3. In the performances on Saturday, August 5, the leading role was played by Ada Pampín.

rain, but the shame of having set foot in a past that wasn't worth the trouble: it was a past that vanished the moment the Colonel set eyes on it. What was Person doing in those years? He could read it on his own file cards:

January 1939: *Within weeks after breaking off with the director Rafael Firtuoso (a two-month romance) ED fell in love with the owner of* Sintonía *magazine. She moved from a pension in the calle Sarmiento to an apartment in the pasaje Seaver.* May: *She appeared on the cover of* Antena *magazine but when she went to thank the editor, he refused to see her. She had roles in four radio serials by Héctor Pedro Blomberg.* July: *Her brother Juan, who was a soap delivery man, introduced her to the owner of Radical Soap. She posed as a model in two Línter publicity ads.* November: *She fell in love with the owner of Radical Soap but continued to be seen secretly keeping company with the owner of* Sintonía. January 1940: *Pampa Films put her under contract as a feature player in* The Charge of the Valiant, *whose leads were Santiago Arrieta and Anita Jordan. On the film set, near Mar del Plata, she met Julio Alcaraz, the hairdresser. She was just under twenty-three. She had a sickly pallor, a garden-variety beauty; she aroused not passion but pity. And yet she was determined not to let anything stand in her way.*

He tied the packages up with complex, delicate knots, and went out into the vague night light. The cold was relentless. He walked on through the drizzle and the wind and felt once more that he was making his way through nothingness. In the canteen a fire of artificial logs was burning on the hearth. Ferruccio had his back turned. The short man with a boxer's nose was working behind the counter. The Colonel clicked the heels of his boots with a pointless martial air and sat down at Ferruccio's table.

"Glad you came," Ferruccio said. "We were waiting for you. My wife has cooked something for you. Stuff yourself, since this is going to be your last free meal."

He glimpsed the silhouette of Ersilia, the dwarf, in the kitchen, moving about quickly, like a mosquito.

"Order that man," the Colonel said, pointing toward the counter with his chin, "to bring me a gin. In two hours it'll be Friday."

"Parientini," the boxer said. "My name is Caín Parientini."

"I don't care what it is," the Colonel said. "Bring me a gin."

"It's not allowed," Ferruccio broke in. "It's a pity. The rule is very strict here. If they catch us, we'll all land in the cooler."

"Who's going to catch us? There's nobody here."

"There's no gin either," Ferruccio said. "They bring a bottle on Friday night and take it away on Sunday morning. The bottle's stayed the same ever since I've been here. It comes in and goes out untouched."

"Tomorrow, then," the Colonel shouted to the boxer. "Tomorrow at this same time. Ask them to leave several bottles. We won't get anywhere with one." He turned to Ferruccio. "Your wife told me that there's a radiogram for me."

"Ah, yes. Bad news. Captain Galarza had an accident."

He took the crumpled paper that Ferruccio held out to him. The message was written out in long strips pasted together, and no one had even taken the precaution of encoding it. He read that Galarza had been transporting TW Radio Equipment in the Intelligence Service van. He had orders to give it "a Christian burial" in Monte Grande cemetery. As the van turned down Pavón toward Llavallol, it hit the shoulder and turned over. Galarza's right cheek had a gash across it that required thirty-three stitches. He escaped with his life by a miracle but was going to be disfigured. The top post at the Service was vacant again, and Fesquet had had to take over. He didn't make a move without the approval of the higher-ups. Unharmed, TW Radio Equipment was again lying in the niche that she was becoming accustomed to, below the Gründig. The minister of the army was going to appoint the new head of the Intelligence Service at any moment and determine once and for all the final destination of TW. There was talk of burning her body to ashes at Chacarita or burying her in the potter's field on Martín García Island. Colonel Tulio Ricardo Corominas's name was insistently being put forward for the post of head of the Service. The radiogram was signed by Fesquet, Gustavo Adolfo, first lieutenant of infantry.

The Colonel read the text again in disbelief. Since it was not in code, anybody could read it. For months, he had supervised, down to the last detail, a secret operation in which the peace of the nation was at stake, and now a junior officer, a bungler, was weakening the web that had been so skillfully woven. So Plummy had ended up at the head of the Service. He was the fourth in the line of command and the only one who had not yet fallen victim to Person's curse. The only one? Perhaps the curse had long been weighing heavily upon him. A despicable fairy: bad luck in the simon-pure cadres of the army. How long would they leave him there? A week, two? If Corominas was the man chosen by the minister, he was not in any condition to take over the post. He had just been operated on for a herniated disk and was still walking around in a plaster cast. Galarza was out of action now for heaven only knew how long: thirty-three stitches in his face. A stitch for each year of Evita's life: it was the curse, as sure as shooting. Arancibia, meanwhile, was rotting away in Magdalena prison, in solitary, not allowed to see or speak to anyone. How far had the insanity that ran in the family led him? And what if the Madman were the only sane one? What if the Madman, to keep the curse from getting to him, had chosen to get to it first? Heavy sweats, a dryness in his throat, the sensation that reality was going off somewhere and he was unable to follow it, tormented him once again.

"Galarza was a victim of the curse," he said. "The Mare."

"A terrible accident," Ferruccio agreed.

"Not all that terrible. His face is split in two, but he's going to come out all right."

"The Mare," Parientini repeated, like a tardy echo.

"We should have burned her with acid. I was in favor of their burning her," Ferruccio said. "In the beginning they wanted to bring her here. We refused. I was firm. Where Ferruccio is that woman doesn't get in, I told them."

The Colonel was astonished. Nobody had told him of those details, but they were doubtless true. In Argentina there was no more closely guarded secret than the destination of the Deceased, and yet those three nobodies knew it. What Ferruccio had just said was more than what almost any general in the nation knew at that moment.

"Who wanted to bring her here?" he asked, pretending it was an offhanded question.

"The minister, Ara, all of them," Ferruccio said. "We're far away here, but we're up on everything that's happening."

"You be careful, Colonel," Ersilia shouted from the kitchen. "You don't know how lucky you are to be with us. If you were with her, you'd be dead now."

"Nobody wants that Mare here," the boxer repeated.

"I do," Ersilia said. "I wanted them to bring her. She and I would have gotten along well together. Evita had no problems with women. I would have taken care of her. I would have had somebody to talk to. I wouldn't feel so lonely."

"I don't know why it is that all women always feel lonely," Ferruccio said.

"That Mare isn't running here," Parientini said emphatically. "We gave her the chance when she was alive and she turned it down. We invited her to come, we begged her, and she never showed her face. She can go fuck herself now."

"That was in 1951. She was sick," Ferruccio said.

"So what if she was? It didn't matter to you because you didn't live here."

"That's neither here nor there. Everything matters to me. I know the whole story. She didn't come because she'd just been operated on for cancer. She was nothing but skin and bones. She could hardly stand up. Imagine her in this wind. She'd have blown away."

"She traveled all over in those days," Parientini said. "She gave money away in every last hovel, but she gave us the brush-off. I can't forgive her."

Ersilia came in with a pot with bay leaves, lamb, potatoes, and slices of baby corn on the cob floating in it. She was wearing her

275

hair done up in a fine net and again looked almost pretty. Even though she was amazingly small, she had a well-proportioned body; only her breasts were outsize. Her miniature feet, her graceful bird's thighs, her warm, smiling face, put one in mind of a cherub by Tintoretto. The weight of the pot doubled her over. No one made a move to help her.

"I wanted them to bring Evita's body here," she said to the Colonel as she served him a ladleful of stew. "I would have liked washing her and caring for her. What got her back up wasn't women but men, because they treated her so badly."

"If they'd brought her, I would have left," Parientini said. "I could never stand that woman. She had a chip on her shoulder. She put on airs with other people's dough. Whose cash was it she handed out, may I ask? It was the people's own money, right? She took it out of one pocket and put it in another. She was dying to be somebody. Look where she came from. She was nobody, she didn't know how to do anything. She got a license as an actress, she balled Perón in bed, and then she turned into the great benefactor. Anybody could do that."

"She didn't have to do what she did," Ersilia said, sitting down at the table. "She could have lolled around in the lap of luxury and lived it up, like other first ladies. But she didn't. She wore herself out for the poor. She killed herself. You'd better shut your mouth, Caín. You were a Peronist till last year."

"I don't feel well," the Colonel said. He left his knife and fork on the plate, took off the napkin tucked between two buttons of his uniform jacket, and made a move to leave. He was tired, lost, as though there had been too many places in that place without anybody.

"Stay," Ferruccio begged him. "We'll shut up and eat."

"I'm coming down with something," the Colonel said. "I need a drink of gin. I take it as medicine. My blood pressure's going up."

"Too bad. We don't have any," Ferruccio said. "There's nothing to be done about it."

They ate in silence for a while as the Colonel sat resignedly in his chair, without the strength or the will to get up. What sense was there in going back to solitude? He still had six months to be alone. In such a dreary place, why not take advantage of what little life these people gave it? Parientini was shaking his head in annoyance and muttering every so often, like a litany: "That Mare, that Mare." Ferruccio was eating with his mouth open, spitting out the nerves and splinters of bone of the lamb. The only one who looked ill at ease was the dwarf. She craned her neck and looked inquisitively at the others. They all went on through the silence as though crossing a plateau until finally she could bear it no longer and turned to the Colonel.

"You can't imagine how much Evita's handwriting touched me," she said. She had a calm voice with no innuendos: the voice of someone who has never left innocence behind. "Who would ever think that a woman with such guts would have handwriting like a six-year-old kid's?"

The Colonel went rigid. There had been so many surprises that night that they hadn't even left him room to be bewildered. What those idiots didn't know they found out, and what they couldn't find out they guessed.

"Where did you see that handwriting?" the Colonel asked.

"In the notebooks," Ersilia answered guilelessly. "I didn't open them, see? I hope you don't think I did. I only read what's written on the covers: *Don't make noise while eating soup. A line of mascara underneath and brown shadow on the lids is best for dark brown eyes.* That was Evita. Those sentences couldn't have been anybody else's."

"They weren't hers," the Colonel heard himself say. He was speaking against his will. His mind was full of fires and blank spaces. When he couldn't put them out with gin they filled up with words. "She copied them from somewhere. Or someone dictated them to her, who knows? Those notebooks are from long ago. They must be twenty years old."

"Seventeen," Ferruccio corrected him. "They can't be more than seventeen years old. That kind of notebook began to be sold in 1939."

"We're very up on things here," Parientini said. "Nothing gets past us."

"Shut up once and for all, Caín," Ersilia ordered him. She had a hoarse, imperious voice, reminiscent of Evita's.

"We know something," Ferruccio said. "But we never know everything we'd like to. Before you came, they ordered me to decipher this document. I've spent six, seven hours at it every day. I can't do it."

He stopped eating and took out of his shirt pocket a button and a wrinkled sheet of paper, with the army's letterhead. The button was the red rosette of officers on the general staff. The Colonel tried to recall: Ferruccio, Ferruccio. He couldn't remember his name or what class he'd belonged to in officers' school, nor which branch: artillery, engineers? Those nagging details annoyed him like a speck in his eye.

"I guessed one word," Ersilia said. "If it's in capitals and has five letters, there's no mistaking it. *EIABC* is 'Evita.'"

The Colonel gave a start. "You all read my file cards," he said, forcing himself to appear calm. His hands were trembling. In all truth, they had been trembling for days.

"No, we didn't," Ferruccio explained. "Why would we? They made copies of all her papers at the Ministry and sent them to me. All I have to do is decipher them. But I'm right where I started. Take the question on that page there: *Did she take off from Junín with the singer Agustín Magaldi . . . ?* And just look at the tongue twister of an answer. If the five capital letters mean 'Evita,' the way Ersilia thinks, the *E* is an *E*, and the *I* is a *V*. Let's suppose that the coded message is backwards. Then the *C* is an *E* and the *B* is a *V*. But that doesn't get us anywhere. I haven't been able to understand any of the other words."

"You have to help us, Colonel," Ersilia pleaded.

"I can't," the Colonel said. "I don't have the key."

They poured him a glass of water that he refused to touch. The wind blew wearily.

"You know what those messages mean," Ferruccio insisted. "Try to remember. When we get out of this fix we're in, life is going to be easier for all of us."

"I don't know. I can't," the Colonel repeated. "Whatever I do, my life is never going to be easy."

"Think," Ersilia said. "You're going to be here six months, re-member."

"So what? If I could remember the key would they reduce my sentence?"

"No," Ferruccio said. "Nobody can shorten the time you serve. But the army is going to give you all the gin you like. That helps. The six months will fly by."

The Colonel rose from the table with dignity.

"I don't know anything," he said. "And furthermore, who cares what's in those papers? What can the army gain by knowing the story of a poor kid fifteen years old who dreamed of being an actress?"

"You're right. What's to be gained?" Ersilia conceded.

"You always gain what you don't lose," Ferruccio interrupted her. "The Mare fucked up everybody. She fucked me up. Even though it's too late, we have to make her pay for it." He stopped, out of breath. His round face looked like a caricature of the moon. "Hundreds of people are investigating her, Colonel. They aren't finding anything new; not one story that hasn't already come out in the magazines. Fights in backstage dressing rooms, screwing with some guy who helped her on her way up. They're dregs that arouse compassion, but not hatred. And what we need is hatred: something that'll slan-der her outrageously and bury her forever. They checked to see if she had bank accounts in Switzerland. Not a one. If she bought her-self jewels with the State's dough. No. They were all gifts. They wasted months trying to prove she was a Nazi agent. What kind of Nazi agent would she have made if she didn't even read the news-papers? Now they're about to publish all that shit in a book. It's called *The Black Book of the Second Tyranny*. It's over four hundred pages long. And do you know how many of them are about the Mare? Two. A measly two. The only thing they accuse her of is not having written *My Mission in Life*. That's real news for you. Even cloistered nuns already knew that. You've got a lot more there on those file cards. If you give me the key, we can destroy the Mare forever. Let her body go on existing without rotting as long as it likes. We're going to trash the memory of her."

"No," the Colonel answered. He was tired. He wanted to go far away. If tomorrow or the day after he was unable to escape the madness they'd confined him in, he'd go deep inside the wind and let God do whatever he pleased with him.

"Stop screwing around and give me the key," Ferruccio demanded. "You're a high-ranking officer in the Argentine army. What you found out doesn't belong to you."

"I can't," the Colonel said. "I don't know what it is. I can't give you what I don't have."

He went to the door and opened it. The wind whirled round and round, whipping up the emptiness. An enormous moon shone in the frozen sky. He thought that if they had condemned him to die in that desolation he would await death proudly, unscathed. After all, only in death could a person be, like Evita, immortal.

13

*"A Few Hours
Before My Departure"*

In the ten years that followed the hijack, nobody published a single line about Evita's corpse. The first one to do so was Rodolfo Walsh in "That Woman," but the word *Evita* doesn't appear in it. The text prowls about it, alludes to it, invokes it, and yet nobody ever utters it. The word left unspoken was at that moment the perfect description of the body that had disappeared.

As soon as Walsh's short story appeared, in 1965, the press took to making countless conjectures about the corpse. *Panorama* magazine announced, in a triumphant ten-page story: "Here lies Eva Perón. The truth about one of the great mysteries of our time." But the truth was lost in a rhizome of replies. An anonymous navy captain declared: "We burned the body at the Naval School of Mechanics and threw the ashes into the Río de la Plata." "She was buried on Martín García," Cardinal Copello reported from the Vatican. "She was taken to Chile," a diplomat hypothesized.

Crítica spoke of a cemetery on a walled island: "Coffins wrapped in red velvet rock in the water, like gondolas." *La Razón, Gente,* and *Así* published vague maps that promised an impossible discovery. All Peronist young people dreamed of finding the body and covering themselves with glory. El Lino, Juan, La Negra, Paco, Clarisa, Emilio,

281

died beneath the army's machine guns believing that Evita was waiting for them on the other side of eternity and would there reveal her
mystery to them. What has happened to that woman? we wondered
in the sixties. What has become of her, where have they put her?
How, Evita, have you been able to die so much?

More than fifteen years went by before the body turned up, and
more than once it was thought to be lost. Between 1967 and 1969
there appeared in print interviews with Dr. Ara, with Navy officers
who had been guarding the CGT building when the Colonel took
the body away, and with the Colonel himself, of course, who no
longer wanted to speak of the subject. Ara too preferred mystery. He
received the journalists in his office in the Spanish Embassy, showed
them the embalmed head of a beggar he kept amid bottles of
chamomile tea, and then bade them goodbye with a pompous statement: "I am a deputy cultural attaché of the Spanish government. If
I were to speak, I would unleash many storms. I cannot do so. I can
serve as a lightning rod, but not as a cloud." At the end of the sixties, the mystery of the lost body was an idée fixe in Argentina. As
long as it failed to turn up, any speculation seemed legitimate: that it
had been dragged over the pavement on Route 3 until it had no skin
left, that it had been embedded in a block of cement, which had
then been thrown into the lonely depths of the Atlantic, that it had
been burned, dissolved in acid, buried in the saltpeter deposits on
the pampas. It was said that, as long as it was missing, the country
was going to be cut in half, unfinished, defenseless against the vul-
tures of foreign capital, stripped bare, sold to the highest bidder. *She
will come back and she will be millions,* they wrote on the walls of
Buenos Aires. *Evita is coming back to life. Death will come and it will have
her eyes.*

I was living in Paris in those years, and it was there that I met
Walsh by chance one August morning. The sun was whistling above
the tops of the horse-chestnut trees, people were walking along happily, but in Paris the memory of that woman was covered with blood
(or at least that was what Apollinaire said in "Zone"): it was a memory taken by surprise in the middle of its fall from beauty. The verses

of "Zone" were running through my mind as I sat with Walsh and Lilia, his companion, under the awnings of a café on the Champs-Elysées, near the rue Balzac: *Aujourd'hui tu marches dans Paris / cette femme-là est ensanglantée.*

I had just come back from Gstaad, where I had interviewed Nahum Goldman, the president of the World Jewish Congress. In one of those indiscreet asides that have nothing to do with one's conscious will, I began to tell Walsh and Lilia stories with which on several occasions Goldman's secretary had helped me pass the time as I waited for him. The last of them, which was also the most trivial, deeply interested Walsh. For at least ten years the Argentine Embassy in Bonn had been closed all during the first weeks in August for remodeling. They tore down the coal shed and planted a garden, and the next year, the garden was dug up so the coal shed could be rebuilt. That was all: the story of a stupid wastefulness at the embassy of a poor country.

Walsh leaned forward and said to me with a conspiratorial air:

"Evita is in that garden. So that's where they're keeping her."

"Eva Perón?" I asked, believing I'd misunderstood.

"The corpse." He nodded. "So they took it to Bonn, then. I always presumed so, and now I know."

"It must have been the Colonel," Lilia said. "Only he could have taken it there. In 1957 he was the military attaché in Bonn. That was thirteen years ago, not ten."

"Moori Koenig," Walsh confirmed, "Carlos Eugenio de Moori Koenig."

I remember his glasses with tortoiseshell frames, the solitary wisp of hair growing above his bulging forehead, his lips as thin as a knife cut. I remember Lilia's big green eyes and her happy smile. A quartet of street musicians disguised as harlequins clouded over Vivaldi's "Summer."

"So the colonel of 'That Woman' really exists," I said.

"The Colonel died a few months ago," Walsh answered.

As he had put the reader on notice in a brief foreword, "That Woman" was written not as a short story but as the transcription of

283

a dialogue with Moori Koenig in his apartment on the corner of Callao and Santa Fe. During that tense meeting, Walsh had managed to get only a couple of things out of him: the corpse had been buried outside of Argentina, standing up, "in a garden where it rains every other day." And the Colonel, sitting alongside the corpse during his endless watches, had allowed himself to be carried away by a necrophiliac passion. Everything in his account was true, but it had been published as fiction, and we readers also wanted to believe that it was fiction. We thought that in Argentina, which prided itself on being Cartesian and European, there was no place for any delirious notions of reality.

"I suppose they rebuild the coal shed so that the wood of the coffin won't decay," Walsh continued. "Then after that, out of fear that the body will be discovered, they redo the garden and bury it again."

"Evita was naked," I said, citing the story. "'That woman was naked. A goddess, and naked, and dead. With all of her exposed to death.'"

"Precisely," Walsh said. "The Colonel exhibited her. He spit on her one time. He spit on the defenseless, mutilated body, can you imagine? He had cut one of her fingers off to prove that she was her. Finally, an officer from the Service informed on him. Only then did they arrest him. They should have discharged him, but they didn't. He knew too much."

"He was held for six months," Lilia said. "He lived in the worst solitude, in the wilderness, north of Comodoro."

"He almost went mad," Walsh went on. "He wasn't allowed to drink alcohol. That was the worst part of his punishment. He had hallucinations; he attempted to escape. At daybreak one morning, a month and a half after his arrest, they found him half frozen to death near Punta Peligro. It was lucky for him, because the wind there is fierce and the dust covers and uncovers objects in a matter of seconds. A month later he was luckier still. They found him in a bar in Puerto Visser. He'd been on a bender for two days. He didn't have a cent, but he threatened the bartender with his pistol and forced him to serve him. If they'd found him half a day later, his liver would already have burst. He had galloping cirrhosis and infections in his mouth and legs. He spent the last part of his detention being detoxified."

"You forgot the letters," Lilia said. "We were told that every week he wrote to one of the officers in the Service, a certain Fesquet, demanding that Evita's body be brought to the wilderness. I don't think that not drinking was the worst part of the punishment. It was Evita's absence."

"You're right," Walsh said. "To the Colonel, the absence of Evita was like the absence of God. The weight of such total solitude unhinged his mind forever."

"What is beyond all understanding is how Moori Koenig came to be the military attaché in Bonn," I remarked. "He was an undesirable, dangerous, an alcoholic. First they punish him for exhibiting Evita, and the next year they hand her over to him. It's not logical."

"I've often wondered what happened, and I haven't been able to come up with any explanation either," Walsh said. "I always believed that the corpse was in an Italian convent, and that Moori Koenig was sent to Bonn to put people off the track. But when I visited him in his apartment on Callao and Santa Fe, he assured me that he had buried her. He had no reason to lie."

The harlequins had withered the last flowers of Vivaldi's "Summer," and were passing their berets around the tables. Walsh gave them a franc, and the woman with a viola thanked him with a solemn, mechanical bow.

"Let's go look for the body," I heard myself say. "Let's leave for Bonn tonight."

"Not me," Walsh said. "When I wrote 'That Woman' I put myself outside of history. I've already written the story. And that's the end of it for me."

"You wrote that you were going to look for her someday. If I find her, you said, I'll no longer feel lonely. The time has come."

"Ten years have gone by," he answered. "I've moved on to something else now."

"I'm going anyway," I said to him. I felt disappointed and sad as

285

well. I felt that I was living something like a memory, but from the reverse side, as though the events in the memory had yet to take place. "When I find her I don't know what I'm going to do. What's to be done with a body like that?"

"Nothing," Lilia said. "Leave it where it is, and then report it. You're the only one who knows who it is you're going to have to notify."

"A body that size," Walsh repeated in a low voice.

"Maybe I'll load it into the trunk of the car and bring it here," I said. "Maybe I'll take it to Madrid and hand it over to Perón. I don't know if he wants it. I don't know if he ever wanted that body."

Walsh contemplated me inquisitively from far behind his opaque glasses. I sensed that my obstinacy took him by surprise.

"Before making the trip, you should know what she looks like," he said to me. "She's changed a lot. She doesn't look like the photographs of her or shots of her in newsreels. Incredible as it may seem to you, she's more beautiful."

He opened his wallet. Underneath his identity card was a yellowish, wrinkled photo. He showed it to me. Evita was lying in profile, with her classic chignon below the nape of her neck and a crooked smile. It surprised me that Walsh carried that image around like an amulet, but I didn't tell him so.

"If you find her," he went on, "that's how she should look. Nothing can corrupt her body: neither the dampness of the Rhine nor the passage of the years. She would have to look the way she does in this photo: asleep, imperturbable."

"Who gave it to you?" I asked him. My breath had been taken away.

"The Colonel," he said. "He had more than a hundred of them. There were photos of Evita all over the apartment. Some of them were striking. In them she was shown suspended in the air, on a silk sheet, or on a crystal vase, framed in flowers. The Colonel spent his afternoons contemplating them. At the time I visited him, he had almost no way of occupying himself other than examining the photos with a magnifying glass and getting drunk."

"You could have sold them for publication," I said to him. "You would have been paid whatever you asked."

"No," he replied. I saw a quick smile cross his face, like a cloud. "That woman isn't mine."

I drove to Bonn that same night. I found the Argentine Embassy deserted, with almost all the staff on vacation. I happened by sheer chance to have known for a long time the only embassy employee left behind to guard the place. Thanks to him, I was able to visit the garden. At the end of the tulip beds I discovered a pile of planks. My friend confirmed that they were the remains of the coal shed.

We had lunch in a beer garden in Bad Godesberg and instinctively, after downing two or three steins, I decided to tell him why I had come. I saw him look at me in surprise, as though he no longer knew who I was. He agreed that the capricious cycle of digging up and replanting the garden was unusual, but he didn't have a clue about Evita. What I conjectured couldn't possibly be true, he said. Perhaps the body had passed through there, but not to stay. I asked him to study the records in the accounting files for 1957 and 1958 nonetheless, no matter how trivial they might seem to him: repair bills, travel allowances, moving expenses. Any detail might prove useful.

Before dusk fell, we went through the house that the Colonel had lived in on Adenaueralle 47, across from the embassy. It was unoccupied and half torn down. It had been condemned because of excavations for the subway. The windows of the upstairs bedrooms overlooked an inhospitable garage, on whose north side weeds and shrubbery were growing. In the kitchen I saw, on the floor where it had fallen, the door to an attic. I took a look into the empty space, in the vain hope that the corpse might be there. I heard the hissing of rats and the moaning of the wind. Dust was piling up in the hallways.

The next morning I received from my friend a shoe box full of old papers, with a brief, unsigned note: "After looking at what I'm sending on to you, throw it away," it said. "If you find something, I didn't give it to you, I don't know you, you never came to Bonn."

287

I found nothing. At least I believed for years that there was nothing, but I kept it all anyway. I found a receipt for a white Volkswagen bus, made out to Colonel Moori Koenig. I found an invoice for the purchase of some two hundred pounds of coal, delivered to the embassy in an oak box. I read that two other oak boxes had been sent to Signor Giorgio De Magistris, in Milan. It seemed odd to me, but I didn't know why. I couldn't manage to fit one piece of the puzzle together with another.

I saw a notebook with black binding and a label that proclaimed, in flowery handwriting: *Property of Prof. Dr. Pedro Ara Sarría.* The pages were dirty and torn. Some of the notes had survived. I managed to read:

November 23. Eleven p.m. Remember me darling . . . When they come to get you you will have everything you lacked in this worl . . . toris? I made a gash in her, grilles to enable her to feel . . . new lips . . . When science goes wrong, prescience comes along . . . science today is classified according to deliriums . . . rather than write theorems, it takes leaps . . . science is a system of doubts. It hesitates. On stumbling upon the herbarium of your cells, I too hesitated, did you notice? I felt my way along amid the lights of the protoplasm eating away the scars of the metastasis. I reconstructed you. You were new. You were different . . . so read the inscriptions that I put on your wings luciola tineola archangelic butterfly . . . What you are no longer is what you are going to be . . . listen to them they're coming to get you. Don't accept their authority. You must impose your will again as you did when you were a child.

At the bottom of the box I found a page from a notebook, on which someone had written, in a shaky hand:

More for My Message. *Can an entire people be happy? Or is it only humans who can be happy, one by one? If a people cannot be happy, who is going to give me back all the love I have lost?*

On the way back to Paris I stopped at a roadside hotel in Verdun. Over my head I saw an enormous butterfly, suspended in the eternity of a sky with no wind. One of its wings was black and was beating backward. The other one, which was yellow, was trying to fly forward. All of a sudden it took off and disappeared in the fields of blue. It did not obey the will of its wings. It flew upward.

Twenty years later I too began to fly, though toward the past. In a collection of *Sintonía,* "the magazine of the heavenly stars and of movie stars," which had been Evita's favorite reading, I found an item that intrigued me. It mentioned the plans of the top radio celebrities for the end of 1934: "The ever-lucky Mario Pugliese (Cariño) will be touring the province of Buenos Aires with his comic orchestra. On November 3 and 4 he will perform in Chivilcoy, on the fifth in Nueve de Julio, on the tenth and eleventh in Junín. A full house is expected in the latter two cities, because there Cariño's Bohemians will be sharing the bill with the incomparable Magaldi-Noda duo."

There was no need to be particularly clever to deduce that Magaldi had met Evita on that tour and that Cariño had perhaps witnessed the scene. I had always had my doubts: it seemed unlikely to me that an idol of popular song, who was used to having hordes of women throw themselves at his head, would have introduced a fifteen-year-old girl from the provinces, ignorant and not very attractive, around at Buenos Aires radio stations. In 1934, Evita was far from being Evita. Magaldi, on the other hand, was enjoying a fame comparable only to Gardel's. He had a melancholy face and a voice so hurt and so sentimental that his audience left his concerts drying their tears. While Gardel's repertory abounded in unrequited love, suffering mothers, and stories of defeat, Magaldi's condemned the underhanded deals of politicians and extolled the working class and the humble. Not only in that respect was his image in perfect harmony with Evita's. He was also a generous, impassioned man. He earned more than ten thousand pesos a month, which was more than enough money to buy a palace, and he didn't even have a house of his own. He supported, without ostentatious luxuries, his mother and six grown-up brothers. Several magazines constantly assured their readers that his money went for aid to prisoners and orphans. Other magazines hinted that he lost it at gambling casinos and poker tables. In the thirties he was the dreamboat of every teenage girl in Latin America. Evita's cousins, who lived in Los Toldos at that time, recounted how they slept with their arms around Magaldi's photo as though he were their guardian angel. If someone wanted to round out Evita's legend by attributing to her a youthful romance that would be on a par with the one with Perón—"the man of my life"—that person would find no one more suited for the part than Magaldi. That exaggeration of the workings of chance was what led me to have my doubts.

Those historians devoted to Evita have always believed, however, that she came to Buenos Aires alone, with her mother's permission. "That version is more provincial and more normal," Fermín Chávez, one of her devotees, presumes. And Evita's sister, Erminda, is indignant at the mere idea that Magaldi—or anyone else—could have attracted her more than the peace and happiness of her family home: "Who out of tedious small-mindedness indicated that you had abandoned your home? What nonsense to suppose that you left us just like that, in such an untimely way!"

It was Evita herself who told her first friends at the radio station, in confidence, that Magaldi had brought her to Buenos Aires, and they were the ones who passed the story on and started the ball rolling: Elena Zucotti, Alfonso Pisano, Pascual Pelliciotta, Amelia Musto. But the only one who knew the real truth was Mario Cariño. It took me several weeks to find him.

In 1934, Cariño's reputation was as vast as Magaldi's, though of another sort. Disguised as Chaplin, he was the leader of a comic orchestra that wreaked havoc with the most popular waltzes and foxtrots of the day by grafting onto them sounds of the jungle, chains creaking, babies bawling, and sweethearts sighing. Thirty years later, having gone steadily downhill, he turned into a chiromancer, an astrologer, and an adviser of the lovelorn. It was those skills that allowed me to locate him. In his neighborhood, near Rivadavia Park, he was still earning a living by reading palms and drawing up astrological charts for the people there. He could hardly move: a fall in the bathtub had shattered his hipbone.

When he received me he was pale, wasted away, as though he had died and nobody had noticed. His gaze was easily distracted toward vague regions of the air and rarely landed on any particular object. We spoke together just a little over two hours, until his attention wandered and he was unable to bring it back to the subject at hand. His memory of the past remained intact and pure within him, like an old house without doors or windows where the air and the dust have never settled. Only as he moved on to the present did his memory turn to ashes. I don't know how much of what I am going to recount now is faithful to the truth. I do know that it is as faithful to his memories and to his sense of decorum as it is unfaithful to his sly, indirect language, which struck me as being from another century.

Cariño began by describing his first dull afternoon in Junín: the earsplitting sambas being broadcast over the loudspeaker till ten at night; the cloud of flies in the Hotel Roma, where he was staying with the musicians of his orchestra; the deafening shunting back and forth of locomotives in the Pacífico station; the girls circling arm in arm around the plaza San Martín, and as they looked at the musicians out of the corner of their eye, talking about them with their hand over their mouth. He told me vaguely (or perhaps led me to think) that such a monotonous reality finally came to resemble eternity, and that any eternity is maddening. In the dining room of the Roma they ate rancid ham and greenish offal for dinner. The musicians got indigestion. None of them slept well.

Magaldi arrived the following morning on the ten o'clock train with Pedro Noda, his stage partner. They left their baggage in another inhospitable room in the Roma, and then whiled away the rest of the morning with Cariño at the Crystal Palace movie theater, where they were to give the performance that night. The dressing rooms were bare bathrooms with cement floors. The only spotlight onstage went out three minutes after it was turned on, or else it condescended to blink. Magaldi was of the opinion that it was preferable to sing in the dark.

His naturally somber mood was about to plunge straight down into depression. Lunchtime came. Cariño didn't want to go back to the hotel, where the midday menu was as forbidding as the one at night. At a general store they were advised to go to the pension run by doña Juana Ibarguren de Duarte, who served meals only to permanent boarders, but who would not allow lunch guests as famous as they to get away.

The pension was on the calle Winter, three blocks from the main square. From the entryway they could see an enormous dining room, on the far side of which they glimpsed a patio with climbing vines and wisteria. Magaldi knocked on the door and asked if they would accept ten more people for lunch. A robust woman in glasses, with a kerchief over her head, nodded, showing no surprise. "There are three courses," she said, "and each of them costs seventy centavos. Come back in half an hour."

A memorable lunch awaited them, with tamales and chicken stew. Cariño remembered that they shared the table with three stiff-necked guests, who wore gaiters and wing collars: one of them was, he believed, an officer from the local garrison; the others introduced themselves as lawyers or schoolmasters. Doña Juana's daughters ate in silence, without lifting their eyes from their plates. One of the older ones, however, lamented, in passing, the fact that their only brother was so far from home. Nobody, she said, imitated Cariño's imitations as well as he did.

Magaldi monopolized the conversation. The company and the wine had put him in a better mood. He entertained the girls by explaining to them in detail the secrets of making recordings in soundproof studios, where the singers project their voices into a gigantic horn, and captivated the guests by telling them about the great Caruso, whom he had taken for a walk through Rosario. The only one who appeared to be immune to Magaldi's spell was the youngest daughter, who scrutinized him with a serious expression, not smiling even once. Such indifference troubled the singer. "I noticed," Cariño told me, "that by the end of the lunch he had forgotten the others and was speaking only to her."

Evita was fifteen years old. She had pale, translucent skin and long plucked eyebrows that she made longer still by penciling them almost to her temples. She had fine, somewhat oily hair, cut in a boyish bob. Like almost all the adolescents in town, Cariño noted, she was scruffy and demurely flirtatious. I don't know how much of the image that he passed on to me was colored by the Evita that he saw a good deal of later, during the early months of 1935. Memory has a propensity for betrayal, and all in all, what is important in this story is not her vapid beauty of those years but her brazenness.

Before dessert was served, a calandria lark alighted on one of the platters and pecked at a grain of corn. Doña Juana regarded this as a sign of good luck and proposed another toast. The lawyer or the schoolteacher insisted that it wasn't a calandria lark but a thrush. One of them put on a pair of glasses with dark tortoiseshell frames to study the bird from close up. Evita stopped him with a brusque gesture.

"Stay still," she said to him. "When you frighten them, calandria larks don't sing anymore."

Magaldi sat there lost in thought and from that moment on stopped talking. People were in the habit of calling him, and Gardel and Ignacio Corsini as well, either "the Creole thrush" or "the Argentine nightingale" (*nightingale* is the other name for the calandria lark). He was superstitious, and must have felt that if by chance he found himself at the same table with a surly bird that lets itself be seen only if it has been caught and tamed, it was because both of them shared the same nature. Magaldi believed in reincarnation, in symbolic apparitions, in the determining power of names. That Evita should unwittingly mention his most secret terror—not being able to sing—made him suppose that between himself and her there was also an invisible tie. Cariño told me this in a more esoteric language, and I fear that in my eagerness to clarify his ideas what I am doing is making them sound strange. He spoke of Ra, Urni, astral journeys, and other landscapes of the spirit whose meaning I did not understand. One of his images, however, remained engraved on my memory. He said that, after the incident involving the calandria lark,

Evita's gaze and Magaldi's met at intervals. She never looked away. He was the one who lowered his head. After dessert, she said, in a voice that brooked no argument:

"Magaldi is the best singer there is. I am going to be the best actress too."

Before they left, the mother beckoned to Magaldi and took him to one of the bedrooms. The rhythm of the woman's *ss* could be heard from the dining room, but not her words. The singer murmured something that sounded like a protest. When he came back out, he had taken on his melancholy air again. "Let's talk some more about it tomorrow," he said. "Remind me of it tomorrow."

The Crystal Palace was full that Saturday night. Cariño's orchestra performed by the light from chandeliers. Magaldi, who preferred semidarkness, lit two candelabra onstage and created the gloomy effect that suited his songs of misfortune. The women of the Duarte family occupied half a row of seats, at the back, and applauded enthusiastically. Only Evita seemed distant and impassive. Her big chestnut-brown eyes were riveted on the stage and reflected nothing, as though she had withdrawn her feelings from them.

At the exit, they were met by six or seven truck farmers who had been waiting with their families, whom they had brought to prove to them that Magaldi was made of flesh and bone and was not just an illusion created by the airwaves. The mothers of some prison inmates approached Pedro Noda with petitions for the alleviation of the horrors of the cells in Olmos. At the curb, leaning on the door of their voiturettes, were the impresarios of the Crystal Palace, who had organized a banquet at the Social Club. They were wearing white suits and shirts with stiff collars. They seemed impatient and honked their horns every so often. Doña Juana stepped between them and Magaldi, her arms folded, imperturbable. She was very elegant, with a big organdy rose in her décolletage. She waited for a few minutes, then went over to the singer. She grabbed him by the arm and took him aside. Cariño, who was all ears, heard the brief, curt exchange between them.

"Remember what you promised me: you'll be having lunch at my place again tomorrow, isn't that right? You and Noda will be my guests."

"I don't know if we're going to be able to," Magaldi said evasively. "It's a late matinee performance. That leaves us very little time."

"The performance is at six. You have plenty of time. Why don't you come at twelve and stay till three?"

"Very well. At twelve-thirty."

"And do me one last favor, Magaldi. Stop by the plaza at eleven, can you? They've given Evita fifteen minutes to recite poems over the loudspeaker. She's dying to have you hear her. Have you had a good look at her?"

"She's pretty," Magaldi said. "She has promise."

"She is pretty, isn't she? I told you so. This town is too small for her."

The voiturettes honked at them impatiently. Magaldi freed himself from her grasp as best he could and climbed into one of the cars. He spent all evening buried in thought, giving out a few monosyllables in agreement. He ate almost nothing, drank only a couple of grappas, and when they asked him to tune his guitar and play, he claimed he didn't feel like it. Noda had to sing alone.

They went back to the hotel shortly before dawn. They killed a little time in the lobby listening to the vibrations of the express train as it came in across the desert. Cariño proposed that they take a turn around the block, and before anyone could answer he corralled Magaldi, who resignedly followed his lead. It was November, the sky was clear, and sparkling drops of dew floated in the air. They went down a block of houses that were all alike, where they could hear the cackling of hens. They crossed a vacant lot, a tenement yard, the uneven paving stones of a livery stable. They walked with their hands in their pockets, not looking at each other.

"What are you waiting for before you tell me what's going on with you?" Cariño said. "Let's see if you can learn to trust somebody."

"I'm okay," Magaldi answered.

"Don't hand me that baloney. I was born knowing how people are feeling."

They stopped underneath a lamppost. The light traced a tremulous circle. "I sensed," Cariño told me, "that the dikes inside him were tumbling down. He was at his wit's end and needed to unburden himself."

Doña Juana, Magaldi recounted, had asked him to act as Evita's sponsor in Buenos Aires, after she'd spent months opposing her going there. She didn't want her daughter to go off all by herself, at the age of fifteen, when she had barely finished elementary school. But Evita, she said, wouldn't give in. She was so insistent that she broke doña Juana's will. She was fatherless, she had no other relative there except for a brother who was an army conscript, and she dreamed of being an actress. Dramatists such as Vacarezza, singers such as Charlo, poetry readers such as Pedro Miguel Obligado, had passed through Junín. She had asked all of them for help, and all of them had refused her on the grounds that she was still just a girl and needed to grow up. Magaldi, on the other hand, was more farsighted than any of them. He was more famous, had more contacts, more material means. Nobody would turn down someone he recommended. That girl has talent, he had said. And he couldn't back out. Moreover, there was the calandria lark. It had alighted on the table to point to a destiny. To disregard the counsel of a calandria lark was to bring bad luck.

It was rapidly getting light. On the other side of the railroad tracks, the sky was stretching and yawning amid long streaks of orange-colored vapor. As they turned the corner, they spied the hotel. Magaldi halted. He said he'd hesitated all night long but that their conversation had cleared his mind. He finally knew what to do. He would take Evita with him to Buenos Aires. He would pay for her to stay in a pension; he would introduce her at the radio station. It was now either too late or too early, and Cariño didn't have the strength left to dissuade him.

"She's fifteen years old," was the only thing he said. "She's only fifteen."

"She's already a woman," Magaldi answered. "Her mother told me so: she became a woman overnight."

A dull, endless Sunday followed, one of those a person prefers to forget. Evita recited a poem by Amado Nervo over the loudspeakers of the music store with an excess of little warbles and disastrous diction. She said "dead" and "shadows," Cariño remembered, in a vulgar drawl that was an imitation of Gardel's. "Wheyere do the deyad go, Lawrd, wheyere do they go? Perhaaaps to a palanet baethed in shahadohws. . . ." They applauded her. She crossed the square with her sisters, as a village soprano murdered Schubert's "Ave Maria." Magaldi removed the white carnation he was wearing in his lapel and offered it to her. According to Cariño, he was seduced by Evita's aloofness, by the disdain with which she expressed something that was perhaps admiration.

That night, after the performance, they took the train that came from the Pacific. Doña Juana and her daughters bade Evita a tearful goodbye on the platform. Beneath the yellow lights of the station, she seemed childish and half asleep. She was wearing knee socks, a cotton skirt, and a linen blouse, and a little straw cloche hat, and was carrying a worn suitcase. Her mother slipped ten pesos down the neckline of her blouse and remained at her side the whole time, stroking her hair, till the train pulled in. It was a scene out of a radio drama, Cariño told me: the knight in shining armor rescued the poor and not very attractive little provincial maiden from her misfortune. Everything happened in more or less the same way as in the opera by Tim Rice and Lloyd Webber, though without castanets.

The railway car was nearly empty. Evita chose to sit by herself and leaned her forehead on the little windowpane, contemplating the swift shadows of the landscape. When the train stopped in Chivilcoy or in Suipacha, an hour later, Magaldi came over to her and asked her if she was happy. Evita didn't look at him. She said to him, "I want to sleep," and turned her head toward the darkness of the plain.

From that night on, Magaldi was a man divided. He spent the morning and part of the afternoon in the pension on the avenida Callao where Evita was living. He composed his prettiest love songs there, "Who You Are" and "Whenever You Want Me," sitting in an armchair upholstered in colt hide. Cariño, who visited him a couple of times, remembered the iron bed like a nun's; the chipped wash-basin; the photos of Ramon Novarro and Clark Gable pinned to the wall with thumbtacks. The cramped room was invaded by the over-whelming stench of a public urinal and of bleach, but Magaldi, sur-rendering to the felicity of his guitar, sang on in a low voice, oblivious to everything. Evita too seemed beyond all wretchedness. She walked about in her slip, with a towel on her head, touching up the polish on her nails or plucking her eyebrows in front of a pitted mirror.

When dusk fell, Magaldi whiled away his time with Noda at the radio station, going over the five or six songs they were going to sing on the program at nine p.m. Afterward, he got together with musicians and librettists from other orchestras at 36 Billares or La Emiliana, leaving every day at one in the morning. He never gave up spending the night at the enormous family house on the calle Alsina, where his windowless bedroom was shaded by bougainvillea and jasmine. His mother waited up for him, made him maté, and told him about the day's happenings. Evita's name did not come up in these conversations. According to Cariño, Evita weighed heavily on the singer's life, like a sin or like an inavowable sense of shame. He was eighteen years older than she was; in this respect Perón was to outdo him by seven years. To Magaldi, however, being that much older seemed like taking unfair advantage of her.

It was during those months that luck began to snub him. At the end of November, he had an altercation with don Jaime Yankelevich, the radio czar: in one and the same day he lost his contract for 1935 and the chance for Evita to have the audition that had been promised her. Magaldi reluctantly agreed to perform on Radio París, but a violent liver attack held up his debut. These setbacks damaged his friendship with Noda and infuriated Evita, who spent days at a time without saying one word to him.

From the beginning, the dates in Cariño's story bewildered me. Evita's biographers agree that she left Junín on January 3, 1935. They don't know whether she made the trip with Magaldi or without him, but they stubbornly stick to the January 3 date. I told Cariño this. "What proof can they show to be so certain?" he asked me. "A train ticket, a photograph?" I admitted that I had seen no proof at all. "There can't be any proof," he told me. "I know it because it's part of my life. Historians have no call to correct my memory or my life."

According to Cariño, Evita spent Christmas of 1934 with him. Her brother, Juan, was on guard duty at Campo de Mayo that night; the auditions at Radio Stentor and Radio Fénix had been a failure; not a cent of the money that her mother had given her was left. She complained that Magaldi was abandoning her. He was, she told Cariño, a man who was dominated by his family, who didn't like having a good time or dancing. Cariño suggested to her then that she go back to Junín so as to throw a scare into him by being gone. "You're mad," she answered. "I'd have to be dead for anybody to get me out of Buenos Aires."

Once Magaldi recovered from his liver attacks, Evita turned into his shadow. She waited for him in the control room of the recording studios or in a café on the corner of Cangallo and Suipacha, across from the radio station. He began to give her the slip and very seldom visited her in the pension, although he went on paying for her board and room. It had been more than a week since he'd seen her when *The Soul of the Accordion* had its premiere at the Monumental. She was in the crowd in the lobby of the movie theater, asking Santiago Arrieta and Dorita Davis for their autographs. She had put makeup on her legs to look as though she were wearing silk stockings. Magaldi felt an overwhelming sense of shame once again and slipped through the mob with his head down, but the applause, the magnesium flashes, and the screams of his fans cleared the way for him. He was preceded by Noda and big-nosed Discépolo, who had composed the music for the film. Behind him, elbowing their way through the crowd, came Cariño and Libertad Lamarque. Evita spied Magaldi from a distance and grabbed his arm. "What are you doing here?" he managed to ask her. She didn't answer. She came on ahead with him, determined, triumphant, her face turned toward the photographers' flashes.

It was the end. Magaldi got up from his seat as soon as the lights went down. She followed him out, teetering on heels that were too high. They had a fierce argument. Or rather, she spoke to him fiercely, he listened resignedly, as always, and left her chewing on her rage in the hostile night. They never saw each other again.

"She seduced him with her disdain and lost him by carrying her brashness too far," Cariño said to me. "Magaldi had been bored with her for some time. His love was made of foam, like that of all Don Juans, but if Evita had been patient with him, he would have put up with the relationship until the end, out of a sense of responsibility or guilt. Perhaps he would never have let her have her rightful place, because a woman gains a man's respect from the first day or else she never does, but Magaldi was a man of his word. Without the quarrel at the Monumental, he wouldn't have left her as alone and helpless as he did."

Cariño had to help her out more than once in the ill-fated evenings of that autumn. He paid for three days' board and room for her in a pension on the calle Sarmiento, he shared croissants with her at lunchtime at the marble tables of El Ateneo several times, and he invited her to a matinee performance at a neighborhood movie theater. She was always anxious, chewing her nails, just waiting for a chance to come her way to play a part on the radio. She didn't want to send sorrowful letters to Junín for fear that they would make her come back home, nor did she accept the pennies that her brother, Juan, offered her, because she knew that he was in debt up to his neck. Several biographers believe that it was Magaldi who got Evita her first job in Eva Franco's comedy troupe. That's not how it was: he never even saw her act. The one who straightened her life out was Cariño. He told me that happy ending to the story on the one afternoon that I saw him. I remember the exact moment: the birds warbling in the leafless trees, the rusty kiosks that sold second-hand books and rare stamps in the park across the way.

"One night, in mid-March, I found her in a coffee bar on the corner of Sarmiento and Suipacha," he said to me. "She had circles under her eyes, everything made her sick to her stomach, her legs were covered with scabs and scratches. At fifteen, she had already come to know life's blackest moments. We were about to say goodbye to each other when she burst out crying. Tears from that kid who was so strong, who never let misfortunes get the better of her, made a deep impression on me. I don't think she ever cried in front of anyone else until much later, when the loss of her health made her so sad and her voice broke on the balcony of the Plaza de Mayo. I took her home with me. That same night I phoned Edmundo Guibourg, the columnist of *Crítica,* someone all of us performers respected. I knew where to find him, because he usually stayed up till dawn writing the story of the origins of theater in Argentina. I described Evita to him and asked him as a favor to get her some kind of work. I presumed he could get her a job as a prompter, a makeup girl, or an assistant seamstress. Nobody knows by what twist of fate she ended up appearing as an actress. She made her debut on March 28, 1935, at the Comedia. She played the part of a maid in *The Lady of the House,* a three-act play. She came out of the shadows of the wings, opened a door, and walked to the center of the stage. She was never to leave it.

"After Gardel's death," Cariño told me in a distant voice, diluted by fatigue or sleepiness, "we Argentines had only Magaldi. His fame never faded, not even when he drifted toward bad taste or started composing songs alluding to the horrors of Siberia, which no listener of his identified with. He often came down with some ailment that he cured himself of with poultices and cupping glasses, hidden away in the big rundown house on the calle Alsina, refusing to accept any other company than his mother's. Onstage, he acknowledged the applause with a fleeting bow, and more than once he got confused, mixing up words of one song and music of another. I believe he was cured when he married a girl from Río Cuarto and announced that he was going to be a father. But that happiness killed him. A fulminating flux of bile carried him off overnight. Evita was working in Rafael Firtuoso's company at the time. On the night of the wake for him, after the performance, the people in the company filed through Luna Park to say goodbye to Magaldi. She refused. She waited for them by herself, in a nearby bar, disdainfully drinking a coffee with milk."

There were other things said that afternoon, but I don't want to repeat them. I sat next to Cariño in silence for a long time, and then I walked to the hostile park, carried along by a tide of questions which no one could answer now, and which perhaps were of interest to no one.

14

*"The Fiction
I Performed"*

By the sixth day out, the cramped cabin was stifling him. The crew's pity, however, was more unbearable. Early every morning, the officer with whom he went down to the hold greeted him with the same question:

"Are you feeling better, señor De Magistris? Did you rest well?"

"Yes," he would answer. "Mi sento bene."

He was suffering but didn't want to say so. The burning pain of his injuries awoke him in the night. And the vision in his left eye grew worse: if he covered the good eye, the world turned into a network of shifting clouds, of agitated points of light, of shadows with yellow streaks. He could allow no weakness to show, however. Once they saw how weak he was, the enemy was going to deal him the final cruel blow. The enemy could be hiding anywhere: aboard the ship, in the ports of call of Santos and Recife, among the stevedores in the port of Genoa. He could hear muffled breathing on the other side of the door, and on the way to the hold he was startled by the sound of footsteps disappearing. Someone was watching his every move: that he was certain of. They hadn't attacked him yet, but they would: the voyage was far from ended.

He went down to the hold between four and six a.m.: never at the same time, never along the same passageways. Maria Maggi's coffin was resting on top of an iron pedestal, next to the hull, in the bow. It was hidden by a diplomat's furniture and Arturo Toscanini's archives, which had been put aboard in Santos. He stood in front of the coffin for ten or fifteen minutes, with bowed head, and then left. Each dawn he was a little more vigilant. It seemed to him that the Deceased's body was secretly, slyly, calling to him. Had he been a believer, he would have been able to say that it was a supernatural call. The moment he approached the coffin, a lightning flash of icy breath grazed him. He fearfully opened the combination locks and raised the cover: those were the orders. She was never the same: the strange body was having a restless, unstable eternity. Since the coffin was enormous and she had a tendency to drift about in it, they had immobilized her with bricks: the dust gave a slight red tinge to her hair, her nose, her eyelids. And yet she shone. The embalmer, in the port, had warned him with a cockeyed phrase: "That woman shines as brightly as the moon with its right-hand voice." Whether a moon, seaweed, or misfortune, in the deep shadows of the hold the Woman was phosphorescent.

At times, to banish the nightmares of the descent, passenger De Magistris stood talking with the officer who accompanied him to the entrance to the hold. On the first day, the officer asked him about the death of his wife. He answered with the version which had been cooked up in the Intelligence Service and which he had rehearsed endlessly, in front of the minister of the army and in front of his new superior, Colonel Tulio Ricardo Corominas. "We were driving along," he said, "in a new Chevrolet, heading south. It was daybreak. My wife had fallen asleep. As we reached Las Flores a tire blew out, and the car went out of control. We hit a telegraph pole. Her skull was fractured: she died instantly. I was thrown through the windshield."

De Magistris was tall, imposing, slightly stoop shouldered. A long wound ran across his forehead, his left eye, his cheek. It looked as though the crack in his lower lip was a prolongation of the scar, but it wasn't: it was his only consciously acquired disfiguring mark.

He had gotten it from playing the clarinet. He still had one of his arms in a cast, and the bridge of his nose was broken. However, no suffering, he said, was comparable to that of the loss of his wife. They had been born in Genoa. Their families emigrated to Brazil on the same boat. They grew up together, in Berazategui. Both dreamed of returning someday to the city they had never seen, although they knew they would recognize each of its public squares, each monument: the chapel of San Giovanni Battista, the valley of Bisagno, the bell tower of Santa Maria di Carignano, from which there was a view of the fortifications, the port, the blue of the Tyrrhenian Sea. He had decided to bury her there, amid those vistas.

De Magistris repeated the story in a grief-filled, convincing tone of voice. The accident had happened, of course, although it was not the work of chance but, perhaps, of the Commando of Vengeance. The true facts involved none of the love that he made mention of: they involved only hatred.

After the embarrassing arrest of Moori Koenig, Evita's destiny had kept the military government on tenterhooks. If someone were to publish the story of the profanations, the advisers warned, the country could be blown apart. It was necessary to bury that powder keg of a body as soon as possible.

The order reached Captain Galarza's desk one night in November. It was handwritten by the president, on notepaper that bore the national seal. "I will not tolerate further delays," it said. "Kindly bury that woman as soon as possible in Monte Grande cemetery."

That, Galarza thought, was going to be the assignment of his life. At two in the morning he ordered the coffin taken to an army truck. He brought along a platoon of six soldiers to guard it. Fesquet had offered to go with him, but he refused. He preferred solitude, secrecy. He drove slowly, with extreme caution, avoiding the dips and unexpected humps in the pavement. He went past the meat-processing plants, the switchyards of the railway to the south, the deserted suburbs of Banfield and Remedios de Escalada. He calculated that at the end of the year, his fate would be different: he would be promoted to the rank of major, he would be transferred to a distant regiment. He would never live anything comparable to what he was living now, and yet he would be unable to tell about it. History was in his hands, but his hands were going to leave no trace.

Near the Lomas railway station, a tank truck came out of the darkness and bore down on him. All he felt was the sudden blow, which ripped off the back bumper and drove the front end of his vehicle into a utility pole. He managed to take his revolver out of its holster and sit up. If they took the Deceased away from him it would be the end of him and perhaps the end of Argentina. Blood blinded his eyes. The fear that the pain would finish him off led him to go around to the back door of the truck. He opened it, out of desperation or by instinct, and lost consciousness.

He came to in the hospital. Two of the soldiers, he was told, had been killed. Two others had injuries worse than his. Person, just to give the story variety, was unharmed: without a single injury, lying impassively amid the starched veils of the shroud.

He met up with her again in the office of the head of the Service, where she had been taken, with no attempt to keep the transfer secret, on the night of the accident. She was lying below the Gründig in the same rough pine packing crate marked RADIO EQUIPMENT. LV2 THE VOICE OF FREEDOM in big letters. Daylight no longer entered the office. In order to discourage an attack, Corominas had ordered the windows overlooking the street to be sealed with steel plating. The desk was flanked by two large flags. Instead of the pencil and tempera sketch of Kant strolling about Königsberg, myriad portraits of national heroes hung on the walls in a long frieze. In order to avoid the temptations of his imagination, the new chief never stayed alone with the corpse: one of his sons studied or drew battle maps at the conference table. If an officer came to receive orders, the teenager withdrew to the next room. Methodical and tidy, Corominas scented the office with Atkinsons lavender to rid it of the persistent odor of the hidden body, and exorcised the blue glow that seemed to emanate from the coffin with a five-hundred-watt spotlight that poured an imperious yellow light down on the Gründig.

Between December and February, Galarza had had to undergo

several consecutive operations. His plaster casts and bandages had not yet been removed when Coróminas summoned him to the Service one Sunday. Autumn was announcing its approach with a tide of reddish leaves and violent rainstorms. The city was melancholy and beautiful. The melancholy was its beauty. Nobody was out walking along Callao or Viamonte, always so full of people. On an island unto itself off Buenos Aires, he was surprised to hear a ship's siren.

In the sudden accident, Galarza had lost, at one fell swoop, his career, his health, and his self-confidence. The glass shards of the windshield had disfigured him. A deep cut in the flexor muscles of his left hand kept him from being able to move it. His wife, whom he had pitied and looked down on, now pitied him. None of the destinies that he had dreamed of had been fulfilled: he had not been promoted to major, he was obliged to retire from the army, the ghosts of the Tobas and Mocobís that he had killed in Clorinda tormented him at night. He had hated Perón even before he was Perón; one shameful day in 1946 he had joined a conspiracy to kill him. He no longer thought about him now. He hated only Person, who had woven the net of his misfortune.

He was surprised that the meeting included Fesquet. He hadn't seen him since the eve of the accident. The lieutenant had lost a lot of weight, was wearing glasses with metal frames, had grown a wide mustache. Coróminas stood leaning on a cane. A cuirass of plaster made his uniform blouse taut.

He unfolded a map. Three European cities were marked with red dots. Another one, Genoa, was circled in blue. The colonel—this colonel—had heavy-lidded eyes with a lynxlike gaze.

"We're going to bury the Deceased forever," he said. "Her time has come."

"We already have," Galarza said. "We've tried to bury her more than once. She won't let us."

"What do you mean she won't let you? She's dead," Coróminas said. "She's a dead woman, like any other. The Order of Saint Paul has readied a final resting place for her a long way off from here."

307

"In any event, there are still copies of the corpse left," Fesquet pointed out. "Three copies. They're identical."

"There are two copies left," Corominas corrected him. "The navy exhumed the one in Flores cemetery and took it out of the country."

"That one was mine," Galarza said. "It was the one I buried."

"At this juncture it must be in Lisbon," the chief went on, pointing to one of the dots on the map. "The second one is going to be leaving for Rotterdam at the end of the month. Like the first one, it has a false but plausible identity. Its papers are in order. In each port there are relatives waiting for one of them. This time there won't be any mistakes, any superstitions."

"We still don't know what the Commando of Vengeance will do," Galarza said.

"Two individuals from that Commando came by in Lisbon," Corominas informed them. "They wanted the coffin, not knowing that the dead woman inside was a copy. They too had papers that were in order. The Portuguese police discovered them. They got away. They're never going to bother us again. They're following a false trail."

"Don't be so sure," Galarza said. "Those men know what they're looking for. They're going to find it sooner or later."

"They're not going to find it. The body you see over there is the Deceased's," Corominas said. He stretched one of his arms out and turned off the dramatic light that was falling on the Gründig. "The real body. It hasn't budged from here since the accident on the avenida Pavón. Day before yesterday, the embalmer examined it from head to foot. It took him over an hour. He injected acids into it and put new enamels on it. He was so thorough he discovered an almost invisible mark, in the shape of a star, behind its right ear. I saw it. It was made after she was embalmed."

"Colonel Moori Koenig," Galarza surmised.

"It has to be him. His obsession for the Deceased hasn't abated, but he's a long way off now. He left for Bonn in February. The government appointed him to the post of military attaché in the German

Federal Republic. There are still generals who support him or are afraid of him. He's a dangerous sort. The sooner we get him out of the operation the better. If he starts screwing things up again, Fesquet and I are going to see to it that he toes the line."

Ill at ease, Fesquet crossed and uncrossed his legs. The colonel lit a cigarette. The three of them began smoking in the empty, awkward, Sunday silence.

"Moori Koenig is sick," Fesquet said. "Being so far away from the Deceased has made him ill. He keeps threatening me. He wants me to take the body to him."

"Why don't you tell him to go to hell?" Galarza said.

"They're very serious threats," Corominas explained. "Blackmail. Past weaknesses that he wants to bring to light."

"Don't let him scare you, Fesquet."

"I'm going to finish this assignment and then I'm going to put in for retirement," the lieutenant said. A sudden pallor clouded his face. His whole life was there, out in the open, between those two men who were perhaps implacable, and from whom he expected no forgiveness. He didn't need it. All he wanted to do was clear out.

"That's best," Corominas said. "You'll be leaving with your head held high."

That was how the voyage had begun. Galarza was to board the *Conte Biancamano* with the corpse on April 23. He would pretend to be Giorgio De Magistris, the grief-stricken widowed husband of Maria Maggi. Fesquet would leave the following night on the *Cap Frio* for Hamburg. He would give his name as Enno Köppen and the false dead woman—the last copy of Person—would be smuggled aboard, in the crate of radio equipment in which the real dead woman was now lying. They would cover her up with cables, microphones, reels of tape recordings. Or Ara would duplicate in the vinyl and wax body the star-shaped mark in her ear and would tattoo a very short capillary on the nape of her neck.

Person was perfect, but what happened to her seldom was. The coffin bought for her for the crossing was immense and was late in arriving at the Service. It had two combination locks, and there was no way to replace it. The body kept shifting amid the sumptuous lengths of fabric lining the coffin.

"High seas are going to toss her back and forth constantly," Galarza observed. "She's going to be terribly battered when she arrives."

They tried to keep her from moving about by stuffing newspapers and wrapping paper around her, but as Fesquet pertinently noted, that coffin was the last one: she would lie in it, unknown, in a permanent mausoleum. Galarza then ordered the NCOs on guard duty to bring rocks and paving stones from any storage shed that contained building materials. There weren't any within ten blocks. They finally resigned themselves to surrounding the body with a clumsy padding of small logs and bricks. Corominas, who was still convalescing from a spinal operation, contented himself with carefully supervising the weight distribution. Fesquet finished the work alone, awkwardly, not knowing how to plug up the empty spaces and the airholes that his jerrybuilt construction was leaving.

"It beggars belief," Corominas said. "This Service is the pride of the army, but when there's an important job at hand three invalids have to turn to and do it."

The fine red powder from the bricks invaded the new chief's office and took days to settle. The slow rain of minute, irritating particles of dust reminded them that she had left at last, perhaps forever.

It was almost seven at night when Galarza arrived alone at the port, in a hearse. The Italian consul and a priest, wearing the stole bordered in black for reciting the Prayer for the Dead, were nervously awaiting him.

"Si tratta di suo padre?" the consul asked, pointing to the coffin.

"My wife, may she rest in peace," Galarza answered.

"Ma, accidenti, que grossa era!" he observed.

The ship's watch bells rang, and the siren gave a quick, deep-pitched wail. Two customs inspectors ordered the coffin weighed, and as there was scarcely any time left, the priest recited the Prayer for the Dead as it was being hoisted onto the scales. The pointer showed a weight of almost a thousand pounds.

"That's too much," one of the inspectors said. "These coffins seldom weigh more than five hundred. Was he very fat?"

"Yes, she was fat," the consul replied.

"More suspicious still if it was a woman. It will have to be opened."

The priest rolled his eyes and raised his arms toward the tall iron domes of the dock.

"You can't do that," he said. "It would be a profanation. I knew this lady. The Holy Mother Church will act as guarantor."

"There are rules," the inspector insisted. "If we don't follow them, they kick us out. Perón and Evita aren't running the country anymore. There's no way to bend the rules anymore."

The ship's siren gave out with another lament, higher pitched, longer. All the lights on board went on. On the pier, a number of people were waving handkerchiefs. Hundreds of passengers came out on deck. The *Conte Biancamano* appeared to be about to depart, but the stevedores were still carrying trunks into the hold.

"Don't open it," the priest repeated, in a melodramatic tone of voice. "I beg you in God's name. It would be a sacrilege. You'll be excommunicated as punishment."

He spoke so emphatically that he could only be an agent of the Service, Galarza surmised: perhaps the same one who had made the secret arrangements with the Paulist fathers for the body to be buried "a long way off from here, on the other side of the world."

"Don't worry, Father," the passenger said. "The inspectors are understanding."

He walked with them to a ramshackle counter and handed them the shipping permit for the crossing: number 4, final destination via Mercali 23, Milan. Underneath it, he had slipped two thousand-peso bills.

"To repay you for your trouble," he said.

The inspector who ruled the roost around there pocketed the bills and said, not turning a hair:

"All right then, go ahead. Just this once, we'll let you through."

"There won't be a second time," Galarza said, unable to resist the temptation to make one last joke. "My wife isn't going to die again."

As he went up the gangplank, the thought came to him that Evita had undergone a number of deaths in the last sixteen months, and had survived all of them: the hijackings, the movie theater where she'd been a doll, the Colonel's love and his insults, Arancibia's insane fits of delirium in the attic in Saavedra. She died almost every day, like Christ in the sacrifice of the Mass, he thought. But he didn't intend to repeat that to anyone. All the irrationalities of faith, he believed, had served only to make the world a worse place.

He woke up each morning now with lingering claustrophobic nightmares. The only relief of the unbearable routine of the crossing was the captain's record collection, a potpourri of fireworks by the Boston Pops and little airs by Purcell that Galarza had now and again played on the clarinet. Every afternoon, on the rickety record player that had been brought to his cabin, he listened to the allegretto of Beethoven's Seventh Symphony. When the melody died away he listened to it again, finding it neither boring nor wearisome: like the body lying down below, the ceremonial flight of that music aroused passions within him, grew first louder and then softer, and shivered with the same majestic insolence.

When the ship called at Santos, a delegation from the Wagnerian Society deposited on board a long wooden chest full of manuscripts by Toscanini. They were notes and portraits that the maestro had left behind when he passed through Brazil, seventy years before. There was a hurried ceremony on deck, alongside the entrance to the hold: an improvised orchestra played the funeral march from the *Eroica* and Verdi's "Libera me." Standing in front of Evita's coffin, Galarza didn't miss one detail of the homage. He was carrying a Beretta in his pocket and intended to use it without a second thought if anyone approached the coffin with a lighted candle or a bouquet of flowers. He was fed up with the tricks that the Commando of Vengeance had employed to honor the Deceased. He closed his hand around the pistol when the musicians opened their instrument cases and studied their faces, in search of any suspicious sign. Nothing happened, however. The melodies, left unfinished, died away quickly in the stifling air.

Once the visitors left, Galarza was pursued by the idea that they had hidden an incendiary bomb in the chest full of manuscripts. The captain was obliged to come down in person and open it, as the boat was heading for Rio de Janeiro. Annotated scores, adolescent letters, and yellow photos were all they found.

Toscanini had been buried with great pomp on February 18, the captain related over dinner that night. More than forty thousand people awaited the passage of the funeral procession in front of La Scala in Milan. "I was one of them," he said. "I wept as though it were my father." After the Prayer for the Dead, the doors of the opera house were opened and the orchestra of La Scala played the second movement of the *Eroica,* the same one the musicians of Santos had played to render him honor. An imposing procession had then followed the hearse, adorned with palms and black mourning plumes, to the vaults of Monumental cemetery.

"Do you remember how much the coffin weighed?" Galarza asked out of the blue.

One of the guests at the table protested. That was not a proper subject for dinner conversation, she said. Not taking it personally, the captain answered gravely:

"Three hundred eighty pounds. The figure was published in all the newspapers. I haven't forgotten it because I have three children and eighty was my street address."

"He must have been very thin," Galarza commented.

"Skin and bones," the captain said. "He was nearly ninety years old when he died, remember."

"At that age a person can no longer even think," one of the ladies commented.

"Toscanini thought so much," the captain corrected her, "that he had a cerebral thrombosis. Nonetheless, madame, he regained consciousness. As he lay in the throes of death, he spoke to imaginary musicians. He said to them: 'Più morbido, prego. Ripetiamo. Più morbido. Ecco, bravi, così va bene,' the way he did when he used to direct the *Eroica*."

After crossing the equator, Galarza began, for no reason, to feel less lonely. He didn't like to read, the seascapes didn't divert him, he hated the sun. His only way of making time pass was to go down to the hold and talk with Person. He arrived before dawn and more than once stayed on till after sunrise. He told her of his wife's countless ailments and the unhappiness of a loveless life. "You should have separated," Person said to him. "You should have asked for forgiveness." He heard her voice flow from amid towers of cargo or from the other side of the hull, from out of the sea. But when he returned to his cabin he kept telling himself that the voice could only be within him, in some depth of his being that he knew nothing of. And what if God were a woman? he then thought. What if God gently moved his breasts and was a woman? Who cared? God could be whatever He or She pleased. He had never believed in Him, or in Her. And this was no time to begin.

On the second Saturday in May they spied in the distance the coast of Corsica. The voyage was coming to an end. Shortly after midnight, Galarza took the record player to the hold, left it at the foot of the pedestal with the coffin, and lay down in the same position as the Deceased, with his fingers intertwined on his chest. The music of the allegretto flooded over him with a peace that compensated for all the sadnesses of the past; the music sketched plains and havens and rain forests in the desert of his feelings. He loved her, he said to himself. He loved Person, and hated her. There was no reason for there to be the slightest contradiction in that.

The *Conte Biancamano* docked in Genoa at eight in the morning. The San Giorgio Palace was decked with countless rosettes and pennants; the great lighthouse had its beacon pointlessly lighted. As the gangplank was let down and the passengers' baggage unloaded, Galarza spied, in the square with the customs office, a military formation. Two horsemen in uniform and wearing plumed two-cornered hats were brandishing swords or batons alongside a horse-drawn carriage. The bersaglieris' band was playing the "Va, pensiero," from the opera *Nabucco,* sung by an invisible chorus. Groups of nuns in stiffly starched wimples were coming and going amid the statues in the square. An alarmingly pale priest was scrutinizing the deck of the ship through opera glasses. When he caught sight of Galarza, he pointed at him with his index finger and handed the glasses to one of the nuns. Then he ran to the pier and shouted a sentence at him that was lost in the din being raised by the porters. Perhaps he said, "Noi siamo dell'Ordine di San Paulo"; perhaps "Ci vediamo domani a Rapallo." The traveler was dizzy, confused. He had been prepared for the crossing but not for the surprises of the arrival. He suddenly heard drumrolls. There was a moment of silence. The priest stood stock-still. The horsemen in two-cornered hats raised their batons with a martial air. One of the ship's officers, who was walking past Galarza, halted and greeted him with a nod.

"What's going on?" the passenger asked him. "Why all this commotion?"

"Zitto!" the officer said. "Can't you see they're about to unload the maestro's manuscripts?"

An avalanche of trumpets played the triumphal march from *Aïda.* As though obeying the signal of the first bars, Evita's coffin slowly glided from the hold to the pier on a conveyor belt. A salvo of rifle shots was fired. Eight soldiers in mourning shakos lifted the coffin up and laboriously deposited it in the carriage, where it was draped in the Italian flag. The horsemen grabbed the reins and the carriage began to draw away. Everything happened so fast and the music was so all-enveloping, so deafening, that no one saw Galarza's desperate gestures or heard his protests:

"Where are they taking that? That's not Toscanini's! It's mine!"

The priest and the nuns had also disappeared in the crowd. Held prisoner on deck, surrounded by wheelchairs, boxes, and trunks that were being moved toward the gangplank so slowly it made his heart sink, Galarza couldn't manage to clear a path for himself. He spied the captain, much too far away, on the bridge bidding a flock of passengers goodbye, and tried to shout at him to attract his attention. Not a sound came out.

After three or four endless minutes, the coffin reappeared amid the dockside warehouses. A few bunches of flowers adorned it, but other than that everything was the same as before, as though it were returning from a harmless outing. Only Galarza was beside himself, sick with panic. Just one of the horsemen was guiding the carriage; the other one was trotting behind, with his baton still upraised, alongside the priest and the cortege of nuns. As they stepped onto the pier, all the figures obediently positioned themselves in the same places that they had occupied as the ship was arriving: the bersaglieri band, the soldiers, the stevedores. Only a few of the passengers, paying no attention, were going off with their families. There was an odd parenthesis of silence and, before the triumphal march from *Aïda* was thunderously struck up, one of the ship's officers was heard to exclaim:

"Guarda un po! Che confusione!"

"A monumental error," a member of the crew standing behind Galarza agreed.

Ten or twelve sailors obligingly removed Evita's coffin from the carriage. They took the flag off it and disdainfully deposited it on the paving stones of the pier, as the chest with Toscanani's manuscripts slid slowly along the conveyor belt. Galarza took advantage of the chaos that followed the rifle salvos to run down the gangplank.

Before Galarza could reach the coffin he had almost lost, the priest came out from a spot that was hidden by the carriage and clapped a hand on his shoulder. Galarza pushed it off with his good elbow, and when he turned around, he was met with a beatific expression.

"We were waiting for you," the priest said. "I'm Father Giulio Madurini. What do you make of what happened? It almost ruined everything."

He spoke with an impeccable Argentine accent. Galarza's suspicion was aroused.

"God?" he asked him. The agents in the Service had decided to use the same countersign as the Colonel, which was also the one that had been used during the coup against Perón.

"Is just," the priest and the nuns answered in chorus, in the tone of voice used to recite litanies.

The nuns too must have been part of the plot hatched by Corominas, because they took charge of everything. They got Galarza's baggage off the ship and hired a team of stevedores to transport the coffin to a parish bus. Despite its volume, Person was placed without difficulty in the vast space underneath the seats.

"So large sized," the priest said admiringly. "I didn't imagine her as being that big."

"It's not her," Galarza explained. "We had to stuff the coffin with stones and bricks."

"All the better. She could be taken for a male. A grown man."

From close up, Madurini bore a surprising resemblance to Pius XII: the same cerulean complexion, the same long, slender fingers that moved in slow camera shots, the same aquiline nose above which round glasses in metal frames were perched. He slid behind the wheel of the bus and gestured to Galarza to sit in the seat alongside him. The nuns milled about in the backseats. They seemed excited. They never stopped chattering.

"I thought they'd robbed me," Galarza said with relief. "My throat went dry."

"It was a stupid mix-up," the priest commented. "Nobody was to blame. With a chest that size, anybody could make a mistake."

"I didn't lose sight of it once during the entire voyage. Who would ever have thought that owing to a moment's distraction, in the end . . ."

"Don't let it bother you anymore. The sisters stopped the people in the carriage and explained everything to them."

After they had traversed the steep passes through the Apennines, the priest turned off on a dirt road. Stretching out on either side of it were fields of wheat and flowers. In the distance a few mills ground their own skeletal shadows.

"Did anyone follow you, Father?"

"Call me Alessandro. The Service sent me false identification. Until this story ends my name is Alessandro Angeli."

"De Magistris," Galarza said. "Giorgio De Magistris."

"I recognized you immediately, because of the scar. It's impressive."

They reached Pavia shortly before twelve. They stopped for half an hour at a tourist hotel next to the train station, where the priest urinated amid sighs and devoured two outsize plates of noodles with mushrooms. Then he disappeared into a rice field with the bus and came back looking hot and tired.

"There's no danger," he said. "Did anybody shadow you on the boat, Giorgio?"

"I don't believe so. I kept my eyes open. I didn't see anything out of the ordinary."

"There isn't anybody now either. We have twenty-five miles to go yet, on the flat. We have to go through a wood."

"Where are we headed for now?" Galarza asked. "I want to be sure."

"The loading permits say that the Deceased is to be delivered to Giuseppina Airoldi, at via Mercali 23, Milan. Sister Giuseppina is here in the back, and she lives in this bus. We can take the body wherever we like."

It was a warm Saturday. In the narrow streets near the Garibaldi Gate, in Milan, women in housedresses were walking about, dragging their feet shod in thong sandals, their breasts quivering with little fans of wrinkles. The birds screeched madly and dived on the bus from the tops of monkey puzzle trees. A little after two they stopped in front of the columns of Monumental cemetery. Through the grilles they could see the tombs in the Temple of Fame; in the middle of it, the statue of Manzoni sighed amid black angels with broken wings.

They walked between rows of cypresses to the west end of the cemetery. The splendor of the monuments fell off, degenerating from marble to stone and from presumptuous Gothic cupolas to unpretentious crucifixes. In plot 41 there were only gravestones. Madurini had put his cassock and the objects for burial rites in the bus and was now reciting, in a monotonous voice, the Latin words of the Prayer for the Dead. One of the nuns was swinging the censer. Person was let down with great effort into the cement-lined grave of her next eternity. As the grave diggers struggled with the coffin, Madurini whispered in Galarza's ear:

"You must weep, Giorgio. You're the widower."

"I can't do it. Not just like that, all of a sudden."

Atop the adjoining grave was the gray marble headstone that they were going to place on the new grave. Galarza read: MARIA MAGGI DE MAGISTRIS 1911–1941. GIORGIO A SUA SPOSA CARISSIMA.

It's all over, Galarza thought. I'm not going to see her again. He felt relieved, he felt sad, and the sobs mounted effortlessly to his throat. He hadn't wept since he was a child, and now that the tears were invading his eyes with a harsh, painful thirst, it seemed a blessing to him.

The Colonel had been waiting for the body for almost a month now. One Sunday night, Fesquet and two NCOs had recovered the copy buried in the churchyard at Olivos, substituting the original for it. "On April 24, that woman is leaving on the *Cap Frio*," he informed the lieutenant in a coded radiogram. "She is arriving on May 20 at the port of Hamburg. She is consigned to Karl von Moori Koenig, an amateur radio operator. It's a pine crate, remember, labeled LV2 THE VOICE OF FREEDOM." But the message that followed perturbed him: "Embarking on the *Cap Frio*. Bringing the body myself."

On the one hand, he was happy that his threats had brought results. More than once he had written Fesquet that he was prepared to bring him before a court-martial and accuse him of being a fairy. He was not boasting: he would have done it. On the other hand, things had gone too far. Fesquet had deserted. If not, with whose permission was he traveling aboard the *Cap Frio*? Perhaps desperation had driven him mad. Or he was malingering. Who knows, who knows? the Colonel said to himself in despair. He couldn't even stop him and order him to return now: Fesquet had placed himself beyond his reach. Who could say whether, in such extreme despair, Fesquet's reflexes were still intact? He sent a couple of telegrams to the *Cap Frio* asking him, in code: *Have you watched to see whether someone is following you? Have you taken precautions so that no one gets near the coffin, down in the hold? Do you want me to get you a medical report that will enable you to return to the Service?* He repeated the telegrams for three days, but there was no answer.

His whole life was on that ship. Bonn, on the other hand, seemed to him a waste of time. He had rented the two top floors of a stately building that had survived the war. His neighbors on the lower floors were also on the embassy staff: he lived in a closed world, with no way out, in which everyone knew beforehand exactly what phrases the others would utter. At times, the Colonel eased off on his duties—which consisted, first and foremost, of translating military news items from the German newspapers so as to send them on to Buenos Aires as though they reflected his own investigations—by meeting in secret with arms dealers and confidants of the countries of the Eastern Bloc. They drank together and talked of long-lost battles, not remembering when they had taken place. They talked of everything, except the truth.

For lack of other distractions, the Colonel resignedly attended the parties given almost daily by diplomats. He entertained the ladies with risqué stories about the "runaway tyrant," whom he imagined putting on weight in the heat of Venezuela. It seemed incredible to him that the man still aroused passions: the latest woman in his life had caught up with him in Panama and was still chasing after him in Caracas. She was a flamenco dancer, thirty-five years younger than he, who played duo piano with Roberto Galán.

The Colonel couldn't bear the thought that Evita had loved that old duffer madly. *He is my sun, my sky, everything that I am belongs to him,* her last will and testament said. *Everything is his, beginning with my own life, that I gave to him with love, forevermore, totally.* How blind she must have been, the Colonel said to himself, how blind or forsaken or defenseless to have licked so thirstily the one hand that had caressed her without humiliating her. Poor thing, how stupid and how grand, he kept telling himself. *I want you to know at this moment that I loved and love Perón with all my soul.* And what good had that done her? He had betrayed her, had left her in the hands of the embalmer when they toppled him from power; he was the one responsible for her body's nomad wanderings all over the world, coveted, unburied, with no identity or name. What was Person now aboard the *Cap Frio*? A piece of trash. The Spiritual Head of the Nation was radio equipment. If the ship went down, nobody would think of saving her. She would be the eternal execration of the ex-despot. These thoughts tormented the Colonel, but he did not give voice to them. At parties, he wanted only to appear to be someone without a care in the world.

On Sundays, to escape scoldings from his daughters, he took shelter in the embassy, where he received reports from the agents who were shadowing doña Juana in exile. Wearing mourning, forced to live a cloistered life in Santiago, Chile, the mother went out only to visit the casino at Viña del Mar, where the croupiers, recognizing her from a distance, would make a place for her at the gaming tables. She had bleached her hair white with slight blue glints and spent her mornings consulting fortune-tellers in the Providencia district. Two mysteries kept her from getting a good night's sleep: the whereabouts of Evita, and how many times the second series of twelve numbers would come up again during that night's game.

One of the seers was an informant of the Colonel's. He had won doña Juana's confidence by reading, in two aces of clubs and a queen of diamonds, that Evita was lying in hallowed ground at last. "Your daughter is lying beneath a marble cross," he had told her, in a trance. A few hours after that prophecy, the president of Argentina broke an inconsiderate silence of almost two years' duration and answered the mother's pleading letters: "Dear señora. You no longer have anything to fear. You are free to return to Buenos Aires whenever you wish. No one is going to bother you. I give you my word."

But the reports in code that the Chilean spy sent to the embassy in Bonn were all dull and unnecessary. They were transcriptions of doña Juana's monologues about Evita's early childhood in Los Toldos, because the mother's memory had stopped at that strip of life, and there was no incentive for it to move beyond it. There was mention of fig trees and paradises where Person was pretending that she was a trapeze artist in a circus, and of the frames full of mulberry leaves where she was growing silkworms. Why so many stories? the Colonel said to himself. What she was is not to be found in those pasts. It is not in any past because she is spinning herself anew each day. She exists only in the future: that is the only thing about her that doesn't change. And the future is approaching aboard the *Cap Frio*.

The first thing the Colonel did in the mornings was to follow the ship's course on a map. He had lost track of it in João Pessoa and had found it again in the Azores. He underlined in red the days it was in port loading and unloading cargo, and in green the ones when it was at sea. He drove consuls mad with telegrams and requests for reports on the Argentine passengers who were aboard and on the knots per day the *Cap Frio* made as it sailed from one port to another. He was almost sick with anxiety when the ship put in at Vigo for three days to repair a dent in the propeller and when it lost a morning in Le Havre because of a mix-up about customs permits. On May 18 he received, finally, the following radiogram in code from Lieutenant Fesquet: "The *Cap Frio* docks at Hamburg Tuesday 21 at three p.m. I will be waiting for you from five-thirty on at St. Pauli pier number 4. Take precautions. I am being followed."

Instead of the anxiety attack he was expecting, a deep peace came over him. Person is within my reach now, he said to himself. Never, for any reason whatsoever, will we be separated from now on. He didn't even stop to think about what he would do with her, what sort of life as nomads or steppe dwellers the two of them would find themselves involved in. He wanted only to possess her, to see her again.

He rented an Opel ambulance for three months, with metal tracks on the floor in the back and a folding seat on which he could sit and contemplate the coffin for as long as he liked. Between the building where he lived and the embassy building was a no-man's-land where diplomats and police officers sometimes parked their cars. The Colonel ordered the space below his bedroom window marked off with stripes of white paint and put up a warning sign: KRANKEN-WAGEN. PARKEN VERBOTEN. (AMBULANCE. NO PARKING.) Late one night, his wife asked him how they were going to meet the many expenses entailed.

"People don't allow themselves luxuries like that," she said to him. "An ambulance. What do we need it for? We're in good health."

"It's none of your business," the Colonel answered. "Go to sleep."

"What's going on, Carlos?" she persisted. "Why don't you tell me what you're up to?"

"Nothing that's any concern of yours. They're my secrets: they have to do with my job."

He left for Hamburg on Monday morning, the twentieth. He wanted to arrive at his destination early, study the roads out of the city, the topography of the port, the traffic patterns. He registered under the name of Karl Geliebter at a modest hotel in Max Brauer Allee, opposite the Altona station. He signed the registration book in a hand that curved amorously to the right, and the desk clerks repeated his name in surprise: Geliebter, "the Lover." It was spring, and even in the blind tunnels of the subway people breathed in the riots of pollen and the glories of laurel and chestnut trees. The city smelled of the sea, and the sea smelled of Person: of her salty, chemical, domineering life.

"Take precautions. I am being followed," Fesquet had radioed him. The Colonel had never been as well prepared to confront his adversary as he was this time. He already knew by heart his strategies for outwitting him. He was wearing a Walther automatic in his belt and carrying two spare cartridge clips in his pocket. If Fesquet had been traveling unarmed, he would give him a Beretta.

When night fell, he got lost in a labyrinth of narrow little streets named Path of Virgins, Sea of Pleasures, Mount of Venus. Sailors, tourists in shorts, and elderly men poured out of the cavernous

depths of the houses and lifted their noses up toward the windows
streaked with shafts of neon light. He came out without realizing it
at the vast Reeperbahn, along which women and dogs were strolling. The women dropped their cigarettes and bent down to pick them
up, leaving their sentiments exposed. Whores, the Colonel said to
himself. Let's see if I can get out of this seething cauldron of lust.
But their paths kept crossing and they kept calling out to him:
Schätzchen, Schätzchen!

Finally he found the Hans Albers Platz, and leaning back on a
stone bench, caught his breath. The shadows were cool, and in an
entryway somewhere a stew was cooking. Around the square were
fading signs identifying old hotels, with windows that gave off a red
light. Alongside the door of the Hotel Keller, three women were indifferently leaning their feet against the baseboard outside. The
three were brandishing empty cigarette holders and gazing disdainfully into space. They weren't moving, but the Colonel sensed that
their big eyes were keeping close watch on the goings and comings
of their victims. They looked as if they had come out of one and the
same placenta, defeated perhaps by one and the same life. From a
distance, they bore a vague resemblance to her: they reminded him
of her. Perhaps he could speak with them, find out what misfortunes
had brought them there.

To the left of the Keller was a store window flooded with yellow
lights. On display were studded gloves, whips, battery-powered dil-
dos, and mechanical devices for artificial pleasures. A Volkswagen
drove by the Keller and braked to a sudden stop. The Colonel hid
behind a tree and watched.

The man driving the Volkswagen was young, with his hair in a
short, round cut, like an open umbrella. He stuck one arm out and
signaled to the tallest of the women. She didn't even deign to look
at him. She remained submerged in her silence, with one foot raised
onto the baseboard, baring her spindle-shaped knees. Two obese
characters, who must have been pimps, went over to the car. A dialogue began, one of few words, that came and went like slaps in the
face. None of the women took any interest in this interchange: they

simply stood there, indifferent to the night dew and to the passions they aroused. Finally, the man with the umbrella haircut handed the pimps an outsize roll of bills and got out of the car. He briefly examined the woman he'd bought, tugged at her skirt, and straightened her bent leg as a father might. Then he picked her up in his arms and effortlessly laid her down in the backseat. It had all happened so fast, was so charged with an invisible violence, that the Colonel was afraid he was wasting the night and strode off at a rapid pace.

It was time now to go back to the hotel, he told himself. He would ask to have a light dinner sent up to his room and go over the next day's movements. If everything went well, he could be back in Bonn before midnight. He would wait inside the ambulance for Wednesday to dawn. He would never leave Evita again.

He wanted to go back to the Reeperbahn but couldn't find the way in the delta of dark streets. He saw a high wall with a hidden wrought-iron gate in it. Through this entrance strode a giant who, despite the warm breeze, was wearing a raincoat and a bowler hat. He called to the Colonel several times in a low voice:

"Komm her! Komm her!" He had a delicate little contralto voice that seemed to have been placed in his throat by mistake.

"I can't," the Colonel answered apologetically. "I need to get to the Reeperbahn as quickly as possible."

"Come in," the giant said. "There's a shortcut through here."

On the other side of the gate was a narrow street, the Herbert-strasse, lined with balconies and windows like aquariums. Behind the glass panes floated women with their breasts exposed. All of them were busily sewing lace edgings onto the minuscule panties beneath which they hid their charms, and paid attention to those passing by only when the latter, as they walked away, half closed their eyes and studied the women's anatomies. When that happened, the ghostly figures slowly turned their heads and held their hands outstretched in a pleading or a threatening gesture. Ultraviolet lights and Lutheran hymns in Old German poured down on the aquariums. Alles geht und wird verredet, the Colonel thought he heard.

Alles geht. If a passerby came up closer to the windows to say some-thing, the women opened little invisible doors in the windowpanes and ghostly lips or fingers appeared.

After walking the entire length of the street, the Colonel tried to go through a second gate, but another giant barred his way. He too was wearing a raincoat and a bowler hat. Except for the fact that the bridge of his nose was deep set, he looked exactly like the first one.

"Du kannst nicht," he stopped him, in the same contralto voice.

"Why can't I go through? I'm on my way to the Reeperbahn. I was told that this is the shortest way."

"We don't like voyeurs," the giant said. "People come here to take their pleasure, not to gawk."

The Colonel looked him up and down, fearlessly, and, heedless of the consequences, pushed him aside with a scornful gesture. He feared for a moment that the giant would hit him in the back of the neck, but nothing happened: only the neon lights along the avenue, the surges of sailors landing on the beaches swarming with whores, and inexpressible happiness that the next day was just around the corner.

He slept so peacefully that he dreamed again one of the lost dreams of his adolescence. He was walking in ashen moonlight un-der a sky in which six or seven enormous moons, also ash gray, were shining. At times he was crossing a city with minarets and Venetian bridges, at other times he was running through narrow gorges of sil-ica and caverns full of bats and flashes of lightning, never knowing what it was he was looking for but longing to find whatever it was as soon as he possibly could.

He got up before daylight, bought the daily papers, and read them in a café in the train station. In the section on ship arrivals and departures there was an announcement of the arrival of the *Cap Frio,* but the hours given in the various papers had nothing to do with each other: one gave the time as 7:55, others 4:20 or 11:45; none of them clearly stated whether a.m. or p.m. was meant. It couldn't be that the ship had already arrived, but at the same time the idea of a chance disaster kept preying on his mind. He hurried back to the hotel, paid the bill, and drove the ambulance to the port. Calm had vanished from his heart.

He parked in the Hafenstrasse, across from pier 4. He had a hard time getting his bearings on that horizon crisscrossed with cranes and masts in constant motion. He hurried toward the tall Romanesque arches of the entrance to the pier, in search of offices where someone could decipher the timetable that had put him in mind of a juggling act. Two drowsy officials were talking together alongside the shelves full of tools, contemplating the river's placid current. Day had dawned swiftly, and the white light of the Elbe was everywhere, but the sun, once it had reached its imperial position, was standing still in the sky, not allowing the morning to continue on its way. The Colonel asked whether they knew anything about the *Cap Frio*. One of the men answered curtly, "It's due to dock at three," and turned his back on him.

He went back to the ambulance. Time was still fixed in its socket, indifferent. Police patrols alerted him several times and asked him to leave. The Colonel showed them his diplomatic credentials.

"I have to be here," he told them. "I'm waiting for a dead man to arrive."

"At what time?" they asked.

"At twelve," he lied the first time. And the second: "At a quarter past twelve."

He then downed his entire supply of gin. Thirst tormented him, but he had no intention of moving. At one point, he was so exhausted he dozed off. Ships came and went amid the flocks of gulls, and every so often the tops of smokestacks appeared above the domes of the pier. In his drowsy stupor, he glimpsed a mast as arrogant and fierce as summer in Buenos Aires and heard the wail of a siren. A blue Opel marked with ambulance crosses braked to a sudden stop in front of pier 4. Two robust men, who were also wearing bowler hats, left the rear doors wide open and picked up from the loading area a long bundle, which they carefully placed in the back of the ambulance. Things happened slowly, as though they were undecided whether to happen or not, and the Colonel saw them go by without knowing in what dimension of his being he was, whether in his being of the day before or that of the next day. He saw one-thirty come on the clock of the Hafentor and spied Fesquet at the same time, standing underneath the Romanesque arch of the pier. First Lieutenant Gustavo Adolfo Fesquet looked up one side of the street and down the other with a lost or defeated expression. People and time were not in the right place; the Colonel too felt out of place, on a downward slope of reality where he might not belong. He hurried toward the pier with his memory full of useless images: bones, schoolroom globes, veins of metal.

"What are you doing here so early, sir?" Fesquet greeted him. He was thinner; his hair was dyed blond.

The Colonel didn't answer his question. He said:

"You came on another ship, Lieutenant. You didn't come on the *Cap Frio*."

"The *Cap Frio* is at dockside. See for yourself. It came into port an hour ago. Everything has turned out badly."

"It can't have turned out badly," the Colonel said. "Where is she?"

"They took her away," Fesquet stammered. "A disaster. What are we going to do now?"

The Colonel put his hands on the lieutenant's shoulders and in an icy, strangely pure voice said to him:

"You can't have lost her, Fesquet. If you did, I swear I'll kill you."

"You don't understand," the lieutenant answered. "I had nothing to do with it."

Someone must have been planning everything for some time, Fesquet explained to him, because unforeseen events had taken place as though on schedule. The captain had ordered the cargo unloaded before the passengers were let off the ship. What had come out of the hold first were two large wooden chests and the crate with the radio equipment. Nobody knew who had carried the crate off or how. And the officers of the *Cap Frio* could help only after they'd finished with the red tape of landing.

"We have to be patient," Fesquet said, "and wait for the captain."

The Colonel fell into a sudden stupor that presaged the worst tortures. He watched the slow-moving line of old people descending the gangplank of the ship, the stuttering flight of the seagulls, the rust of the siesta hour, and every so often he repeated, in a tired voice that did not flow toward the outside but inside his body:

"You lost her. You lost her. I'll kill you."

It was a stupid scene, of the sort that reality never wants to happen: the Colonel leaned his heavy body against the pillars of the pier, and Fesquet looked at him with a compassion he doubtless did not feel, standing there motionless, his hands in his pockets.

Finally the captain came over to them and told them to come with him to the offices. On the way upstairs he repeated, testily:

"Radio equipment, radio equipment. The Mafia carried it off."

They arrived at a glassed-in shed with iron beams that smelled of dried fish. The captain led the way amid the counters piled high with cargo manifests of the ships that were arriving. It was a nightmare of papers badly marked up by the meticulous handwriting of the Germans. It took them a long time to find the customs declarations of the *Cap Frio* and even longer to find that of the impostor: "Herbert Strasser, consignee authorized by Karl von Moori Koenig."

"I'm Moori Koenig," the Colonel said, "but I don't know any Strasser."

The name rang a bell, however. He had heard it somewhere, not long before.

"This is all we can find out here," the captain said. "Go to the police station now and report a theft."

The Colonel pulled his head in like a tortoise. He had to accustom his thoughts to this hostile reality. He said:

"Why waste time? I know who took the crate."

Fesquet looked at him mistrustfully. "Who?" he asked.

"It was a blue Opel. It had white crosses painted on the doors, like an ambulance. If one thinks with logic, they are now on a journey for the border."

He was speaking in German and in Spanish at the same time, with a syntax that was not that of any language. Heaven only knew how much of it the captain of the *Cap Frio* and Lieutenant Fesquet understood: nothing mattered to the Colonel now.

"We have to catch up with them," Fesquet said.

The ship's captain repeated:

"Herbert Strasser. Maybe it isn't someone's name. Maybe it's a town, in Westphalia. Or a street, in Germany."

"A street in Hamburg," the Colonel suddenly said.

"Was nimmt man hinüber?" the captain observed. "What would bring a man to a place like that: Herbertstrasse? Whores, dolls. Nobody wants radio equipment there."

The Colonel stood there looking at him. He felt the cold of the Walther against his ribs. He said:

"I know where that street is. I'm going to go look for them. Are you coming, Lieutenant? Bring your baggage."

It took the ambulance a long time to get going. Above the river, the yellow sun turned red. It was still early but on all the street corners the slow streams of whores were already flowing by: the ones that afternoon were tough and defiant and not afraid of the punishing light. The Colonel drove through the narrow streets that in no way resembled those of the night before: the Reeperbahn, which only a few hours before had proved so elusive, now lay ahead at every street crossing. He finally found the Hans Albers Platz. The enemy Opel, the blue one, was parked opposite the Hotel Keller.

"It's them," the Colonel said.

"Maybe they're in the hotel," Fesquet remarked.

"No. They're in the Herbertstrasse. They've left the Opel here because there's no parking in that street. It's like the courtyard of a house. At the entrance, there's a weight lifter. Do you want a gun? We may have to shoot it out."

"Do you think the Commando of Vengeance took her?"

"I'm sure they're the ones who did. The guys who disembarked in Rotterdam. We'll have to hurry."

Fesquet stopped in the middle of the square and looked at the Colonel with his big sad eyes.

"Why do you hate me?" he said to him all of a sudden.

"I don't hate you. You're a weakling, Lieutenant. There's no place for weaklings in the army."

"I'm strong. I brought her here. Nobody else would have."

"You're not all that strong. They took her away from you," the Colonel said. "What do you want now?"

"Letters, photos, proof of what you're accusing me of."

"There isn't any proof. There's just the eyewitness statement against you made by a private first class, in Tucumán, a long time ago. It's in your service record, Lieutenant, but I'm the only one who asked the questions that had to be asked. Are you coming or aren't you?"

"Give me the gun," Fesquet said.

The Colonel was readying himself to confront the giant guarding the entrance to the Herbertstrasse, but there was nobody there. The gate was open and a few downhearted men were strolling past the picture windows, where life wasn't wholly awake yet. A few aquariums still had their curtains drawn and most of the johns were watching a duo of androgynes, dressed in leopard skin, who were cracking studded rawhide whips. The Colonel was tense and stood contemplating the scene disdainfully. Fesquet kept saying, dumbfounded:

"It's unbelievable. It's like another world."

As they walked toward the exit they quickened their pace. The Colonel sniffed about in the entryways and brought his face close to the enormous glass theaters as though he were trying to get through the thick pane to the other side. There were no onlookers in front of the last windows. In one of them, the women were knitting baby smocks and booties, with their breasts exposed. In the one opposite a Valkyrie with a bull neck was listlessly dancing, while another blond woman, dressed in a long white tunic, was letting herself be carried away by the rhythm of the music. Both of them had their eyes closed and looked like ghosts in the ultraviolet light.

The Colonel stopped short.

"It's her!" he said in a choked voice.

It wasn't easy to recognize her in that perverted, alien aquarium.

331

They had stretched her out on a divan in the shape of an Egyptian boat, with crocodile feet: lying on her side, in an improper position for dead people, with her face turned toward the jeers from the street, with her fingers intertwined at her waist. The Colonel knocked loudly on the glass. Inside, the Valkyrie moved across the room with exaggerated slowness and opened the imperceptible little door in the glass halfway.

"Where are the ones who brought that woman here?" he asked in German, putting one hand in the opening to keep her from closing it.

"It's a doll," the Valkyrie answered. "I don't know anything about it. The men who sell them haven't arrived yet."

"I want that one," the Colonel said.

"That one isn't for sale. They keep it for a sample. There are lots of them like it in the back. Chinese ones, African ones, Greek goddesses. I'm better. I know things they don't."

The Colonel pointed his Walther at her.

"Open the door," he said. "I want to have a look at that woman from close up."

"I'll open it," the Valkyrie said. "But if they catch you, you're going to be in for it."

The buzzer rang to open the door and the Colonel spied a narrow entry hall, with walls upholstered in black velvet. The living room of the aquarium was to the right.

"Come on, Fesquet!" the Colonel called. "Help me carry her!"

But Fesquet wasn't in the Herbertstrasse or anywhere in sight.

With his pistol at the ready, the Colonel leapt out of the entryway into the aquarium and landed smack in the middle of the outlandish ultraviolet light. Taken aback, the Valkyrie retreated to one corner. The Colonel felt lost too, now that Person was finally within reach. Everything that had happened in Hamburg seemed unreal to him, as though he were someone else. Not forgetting to guard his flanks and his back, waiting for them to attack him at any moment, he examined the identifying marks on the body: the missing joint of the middle finger of its right hand and its mutilated left earlobe. Then he lifted up the other ear and searched anxiously for the star-shaped scar. It was her. The mark was there.

He lifted the body up and slung it over his shoulder, the way the man in the Volkswagen had done the night before. He headed for the gate leading out of the Herbertstrasse, but one of the giants, with the bowler hat and that raincoat he knew well by now, barred his way and shouted to him, in his strange contralto voice: "Komm her! Du kannst nicht!" ("Come here! You can't go through!") Everything happened twice: the reality that had never happened was nonetheless copying itself, the life that would live tomorrow was living itself out for the second time. He retreated then to the Hans Albers Platz, where Fesquet might be waiting for him, but he didn't see Fesquet or the other giant: only the first one was at his heels. The Colonel turned around and faced him, with her on his shoulder (her weight was that of tulle, of air: he recognized her by her lightness), threatening him with the Walther. He saw his pursuer hide, quickly, in an entryway, and that was all he cared to see. He fired in the air. The sharp report made time stand still, and the sun disappeared. The Colonel tenderly laid Person down in the white Opel, started it, realized that Fesquet wouldn't be coming and had perhaps parted company with him forever.

He reached Bonn, as he had anticipated, shortly before midnight. On the Autobahn, he stopped twice to contemplate her: she was his conquest, his victory, but there was no telling whether or not he was rescuing her too late, poor thing, my saint, my darling, they've taken such bad care of you that they've stripped you of almost all your light, you've lost your fragrance, what would I do without you, my blessed one, my Argentine.

That night he never once left her side. In the cab of the ambulance, he went through the baggage that Fesquet had left behind: he found nothing but two dirty shirts and a couple of physical culture magazines. Before dawn, he went silently upstairs to his apartment, shaved, and bathed, without taking his eyes off the ambulance. The apartment was a perfect observatory: except in the living room, the garage could be seen from all the windows. Two police cars were parked near the Weberstrasse; the Volkswagen belonging to the guard at the embassy was all by itself, getting damp, off to one side on the Bonngasse.

He didn't know whether to go to work in his inhospitable office that morning or not. On the one hand, he didn't want to be apart from her; on the other hand, he feared that such a long absence from work would raise questions at the embassy that he was unable to answer. He peered at himself in the mirror. He didn't look well. He was suffering from a dull, stubborn pain in his back muscles that forced him to walk doubled over: his body was taking its revenge for the torture it had gone through at the wheel. He made himself a strong cup of coffee as the sun came up over the rough waters of the Rhine.

He didn't need to see his wife to sense that bad news awaited him. He heard her bare feet, the swish of her nightgown, her raw, raging voice.

"You disappear like a ghost and you don't even know what's happening to your family," she said to him.

"What can happen?" the Colonel replied. "If anything serious had happened, you wouldn't be getting up so late."

"The ambassador phoned. You have to go back to Buenos Aires right away."

Something collapsed inside his head: love, anger, faith in himself. Everything that had to do with feelings fell and shattered to bits. Only he heard the deafening roar.

"What for?" he said.

"How should I know? I packed your bag. You have to leave tomorrow, on the night plane."

"I can't," he said. "I'm not going to follow those orders."

"If you don't leave tomorrow, next week we'll all have to leave."

"Shit," he said. "Life is shit. What it gives you here it takes away there."

He phoned the embassy and reported that he was sick. "I had to take a trip up north," he explained. "I had to stay sitting down for hours. When I got back I was paralyzed. I can't move." In an impatient voice, the ambassador answered: "You have to leave for Buenos Aires tomorrow, even if it's on a stretcher, Moori. The minister wants to see you right away." "What's happened?" the Colonel asked. "I don't know. Something terrible."

It's Person, the Colonel thought as he hung up. They've discovered that Fesquet took the original and left them a copy. They're going to put me in charge of the investigation, he said to himself. There's no doubt about it. But this time I can't give them what they're expecting.

He would have to leave, cross the ocean. When he left, what would become of her, who would take care of her? He hadn't even had time to dress her and buy her a coffin. In the last analysis, that was the least of it. The hard part would be to hide her while he was gone. He imagined her all alone in the storerooms of the embassy, in the basement of his building, in the ambulance that could be locked till he got back. Nothing convinced him. In the desolation of that dark, sealed space, sadness would snuff her out, like a candle. Suddenly he remembered a trapdoor in the kitchen ceiling. His wife used the space up above for storing trunks, suitcases, winter clothes. That was the place, he said to himself. There was a sky there that tapped on the roof with its knuckles; the sunlight fell obliquely; the gentle, companionable rain of humans could be heard. The one drawback was that she, his wife, would have to know about it.

"There's something you must know," he said to her.

They were in the kitchen, with the rectangle of the trapdoor above their heads. His wife was dipping a croissant in her coffee.

"I've brought a package with me from Hamburg. I'm going to put it up above, among the suitcases."

"If it's explosives, forget it," she said. That had happened before.

"That's not what it is. Don't worry. But you're not going to be able to go up there till I get back."

"The girls go up there all the time. What am I to tell them? What am I to do?"

"Tell them not to go up there and that's that. They have to obey."

"Are you going to store a gun up there?"

335

"No. A woman. She's dead, embalmed. The woman who was the cause of those threats against us. Remember? The Señora."

"That Mare? You're out of your mind. If you bring her, I'm leaving, and I'm taking the kids with me. And if I leave, I'm not going to keep my mouth shut. Everybody's going to hear what I have to say."

He had never seen her like that: fierce, indomitable.

"You can't do that to me. It's only for a few days. When I get back from Buenos Aires, you won't see any more of her."

"That woman, here in my house, above my head. Never."

"It's all over between us," he said. "You've screwed yourself."

"Okay then, it's all over," she said. "It's best that way."

The Colonel could hardly move, his midriff strangulated by dejection and helplessness. He shut himself up in his studio, avidly finished what was left of a bottle of gin, and took a couple of aspirins. Then, paying no attention to the protests of his vertebrae, he took out of the closet the bundle of school composition books that Renzi the butler had entrusted to doña Juana and the originals of *My Message,* which Evita had written shortly before she died. He put them in an overnight bag, with a change of underwear and a clean shirt. Bag in hand, he went out into the light of day again. He opened the door of the ambulance. It seemed amazing to him that she was still there and that she was his.

"We're leaving," he told her.

The Opel crossed one of the bridges over the Rhine and took off for the south or for nowhere.

15

"A Postcard Collection"

He drove all that morning through the aimless desolation of the Autobahns, turning off at Mainz to buy a bottle of gin and at Heidelberg to refill the gas tank. I'm an Argentine, he said to himself. I am a space with nothing in it, a timeless place, that has no idea where it's going.

He had told himself over and over: she is guiding me. Now he felt it in his very bones: she was his way, his truth, and his life.

When he was six years old, his father and mother had taken him to Eichstätt, in Bavaria, to meet his grandparents. He remembered the furrowed faces of the two ever-silent old people; the tombs of bishop-princes beneath the flagstone floor of churches; the calm of the Altmühl River at dusk. Before he returned to Buenos Aires, his grandmother showed him the cabin by the river where she had been born. The earth was damp and soft, and clouds of thirsty insects were flying just above the ground. He heard the howling of animals that he was unable to identify and a long, deep-pitched lament that sounded as if it came from a woman. "They're cats," his grandmother told him. "They're in heat." He had always remembered that moment as though his life had begun only then and before that there had been no reality or horizon, only a closed door that led nowhere.

Since he had to go on in one direction or another, he decided to head for Eichstätt. Near Dombühl a patrol car stopped him.

"Are you transporting someone critically ill?" they asked him. "What hospital are you going to?"

"I'm not going to a hospital. I'm transporting the body of a countrywoman of mine. I have to take her to Nuremburg."

"Open up the back of the ambulance," they told him. "You can't drive on the Autobahn that way, with a dead body. You need to have a permit."

"I have credentials. I'm a diplomat."

"It doesn't matter. Open the rear door."

Resignedly, he got out of the ambulance. After all, the only lie he'd told was the one about the city of Nuremburg, but if the police forced him to he could change his destination. Freedom afforded him the advantage of being able to turn lies into truths and to tell truths in which everything appeared to be a lie.

One of the policemen climbed into the ambulance as the other one kept a close watch on the Colonel. The sky clouded over and after a while an imperceptible drizzle fell.

"This isn't a dead woman," the policeman inside the Opel said. "It's a wax doll."

For a moment the Colonel was tempted to be arrogant and explain to them who she was, but he didn't want to waste any more time. He felt a sudden cramp in his midriff again.

"Where did you get it?" the man said as he got out of the ambulance. "It's very lifelike."

"In Hamburg. In Bonn. I don't remember."

"Enjoy her," the other police officer sarcastically bade him farewell. "And if you're stopped again, don't say you're transporting a dead woman."

When he reached Ansbach he left the Autobahn and took Route 13 heading south. On the horizon a network of little blue lakes and rivers had appeared, their waters mingling in a complex pattern in the drizzle. Near Merkendorf he bought a coffin and, farther on, a spade and a hoe. He felt the threats of darkness, of loneliness, of the elements, but before going on he needed to speak to her, to know whether the unhappiness of discovering that she was about to be abandoned would flood her with tears and wash her body away. He stopped the Opel alongside a field of barley. He laid her down gently in the coffin and began to speak to her. Every so often, he raised the bottle of gin, looked at it in amazement in the dimmer and dimmer light, and took a swallow. "My butterfly," he said. Never in his life had he used that word before. "I am going to be obliged to leave you." His chest felt empty, as if everything he still was and every-thing he had ever been had drained out of him by way of the wound of that awful certainty: "I'm going to be obliged to leave you. I'm going away. If I stay, they're going to come looking for me. The agents from the Intelligence Service, the Commando of Vengeance: they're all after me. If they find me, they'll find you too. I'm not go-ing to leave you by yourself. I'm going to bury you in my grand-mother's garden. She and her husband are going to take care of you. The two of them are kindly dead people. When I was little, they said to me: Come back if you miss us, Karle. And now I miss them. Oma, Opapa. Person is going to stay with you. She's well mannered, calm. She knows how to look after herself. Just think of how she fooled the policemen patrolling the Autobahn. You've transformed yourself, Butterfly. You've hidden your wings and turned back into a chrysalis. You've erased your scent of death. You didn't allow them to see the star-shaped scar. Don't get lost now. As soon as I can, I'll come back to get you. Don't suffer anymore. It's time for you to rest now. You've wandered far and wide in these months. A nomad. How much earth and water, how many flat expanses you've been scattered over."

As he entered Eichstätt, he felt the unexpected joy of being on his way back to a home that, nonetheless, he scarcely knew. The steep, deserted streets, the imposing convent buildings: everything seemed familiar to him. Heaven only knew how many times he'd been in the town in his dreams, as he realized only now. His grandparents' cabin was somewhere on the banks of the Altmühl, to the east, toward Plunz. He crossed two or three bridges that weren't the right ones before he found it. It was in ruins: only the logs of the facade and the skeleton of a cookstove were left. The land now belonged, perhaps, to other owners. The landscape wasn't the same as in his memory: in the distance he saw the ungainly shadows of cows and a tall windmill. Night was falling swiftly, hungrily. He sank the hoe in alongside the cookstove, and immediately began to dig, so furiously that the sound muffled the complaints of his vertebrae, but he knew that once he'd finished the pain in his back would be frightful. He might not even be able to move. Perhaps he couldn't even go back to Buenos Aires. He could hear, a few steps away, the murmur of the dense black current of the river. The rain kept falling. Since the earth was soft and easily worked, it took him less than an hour to dig a five-foot trench, which he shored up with old boards and stones. You're going to be comfortable here, Person, he said again and again. You're going to hear the snoring of the harvests and the bleating of springtime. I'm not going to leave you waiting, wandering. I'll go and come.

Around midnight he kissed her on the forehead, placed beneath her bare feet the packet of school composition books and the manuscript of *My Message,* and hammered the lid of the coffin shut with a row of nails so as to protect her from the vermin underground and from the curiosity of the cats. At first, when he left her in the grave and began to cover her with the debris from the cookstove—rotten logs, bricks, tires, and even a set of false teeth that might have been his grandfather's—he felt like weeping and apologizing one last time. But then an oasis of relief appeared within him. Now that he could no longer go on defending her, Evita was going to be better off. Now only he knew where she was hidden, only he would know how to go about rescuing her, and that knowledge could serve to shield her. If they wanted to see her back in Buenos Aires again, they would have to beg him on their knees.

At dawn he arrived in Koblenz, south of Bonn. He took a motel room, bathed, and changed clothes. The sharp pains in his back were beginning to miraculously disappear, and the sunlight that came through the window was of an unfamiliar, innocent, otherworldly color. When another day dawned and the sunlight was different, he would be in Buenos Aires. Heaven only knew what the city would be like. Heaven only knew whether the city was still where he'd left it. Perhaps it had left its humid plain and was now growing alongside a cookstove, on the banks of the Altmühl.

It was Aldo Cifuentes who recounted to me those last movements of the story. One Sunday morning, at his place, we spread out Moori Koenig's file cards and papers on the desk and studied his goings and comings in a 1958 Hammond atlas that Cifuentes had bought at the San Telmo book fair. When we traced the Colonel's itinerary in red pencil, I was surprised to see that he had driven along the highways and byways of Germany for more than twenty hours without giving in to the torments of lumbago.

"Nothing mattered to him anymore," Cifuentes said. "He had ceased to be what he was. He had turned into a mystic. When we met, in later years, he would say to me: 'Person is a light that no one can reach. The less I understand, the more I believe.' The phrase wasn't his. It's Saint Teresa's."

"He died without knowing, then, that he hadn't buried Evita but one of the copies."

"No, he knew. They told him everything. They were cruel to him. When he arrived in Buenos Aires, Corominas, Fesquet, and an emissary from the Ministry of the Army were waiting for him. They took him to one of the offices at the airport and informed him there that he'd fallen into a trap. For a few moments, Moori Koenig lost his composure. He nearly fainted. Then he decided not to believe them. His conviction gave him the courage to go on living."

"What was Fesquet doing there?" I asked.

"Nothing. He was simply a witness. He'd been the Colonel's victim: he ended up being his nemesis. Once he'd made his escape from the Herbertstrasse, he caught the first plane for Buenos Aires. He was already back here when the minister of the army sent Moori the cablegram ordering him to return."

"I don't understand why they kept shilly-shallying. Why they didn't boot the Colonel out for good and be done with it. Why they sent him the doll."

"They needed to unmask him. Moori had woven a net of complicities within the army. He knew many compromising things and kept threatening to bring them to light. At the airport, Corominas told him that they'd discovered the scar behind the Deceased's ear and that Ara had tattooed that same mark on one of the copies. At that point, Moori couldn't tell whether they were lying to him or not. He was exhausted, bewildered, sick with humiliation and hatred. He wanted to take his revenge, but he didn't know how. He needed to know the truth first."

"Maybe they were wrong," I said. "Maybe the body the Colonel buried at the cabin was Evita's, and that's the end of the story. Hey, what are you laughing at? It'd be a typical Argentine mix-up."

"Corominas couldn't make such a serious blunder. It would have cost him his career. Imagine the scandal: Evita's corpse abandoned by the army in a show window for whores, on the other side of the Atlantic. Moori Koenig's belly laugh would be heard till Judgment Day. No, that wasn't how it was. Corominas staged a comedy of intrigue, but not the one you think. Who knows why he did? Who knows what secret accounts with the Colonel he settled at that point? Neither of the two ever once bad-mouthed the other."

"I'm like Saint Teresa: I believe you, but I don't understand. What happened to the others: the Valkyrie and the giants in bowler hats?"

"They were all actors in the same performance: the man who pretended to be the captain of the *Cap Frio,* the thieves in the blue Opel, the men guarding the Herbertstrasse. They were all hired for a few marks."

"The Colonel could at least find consolation in the fact that they'd defeated him by a tour de force of the imagination. Who wrote the script?"

"Corominas. But Moori was never willing to admit it. He stubbornly held to his belief that Evita was the one on the Altmühl and that, once again, he'd lost her. After the incident at the airport he had to go back to Bonn, having been dismissed from his post, to retrieve his papers and move out of his apartment. He then lived one last moment of dignity and perhaps of grandeur. He spoke to no one. He gave his wife the instructions and the money she needed in order to come back, put the documents that you now see in this room into a trunk, and returned to the cabin that had belonged to his grandparents, between Eichstätt and Plunz, in search of Evita. He didn't find her."

Cifuentes rose to his feet.

"Evita's elusive body," I said. "The nomad body. That was the Colonel's fate."

"Perhaps," Cifuentes said. "But that wasn't her body, don't forget. He didn't find the place either. He was condemned, rather, to cling to places that disappear. When he arrived, nothing was left of his grandparents' plot of land: only mud and mosquitoes. The waters had washed away all signs of the cabin, except for the logs of the facade and the rusted legs of the cookstove. A tire full of stones led him to surmise that that was the place where he had dug the grave. He then dug down a second time, in desperation, until he struck the underground current of the Altmühl. The coffin was lying there submerged, without its lid and, naturally, without the body. When he tried to disinter it, the trench that he'd dug caved in. The skeleton of the coffin was standing straight up, with the curved end sticking out above the tree roots and the mire."

Cifuentes had left me alone at his place, and I was able to spend the remainder of the morning reading the reports that the Colonel's spy—also referred to as "the seer"—had sent to Bonn from Santiago, Chile. The first thing I noticed was that there was a story in those papers. That is to say, the source of a myth: or, rather, an accident on the road at the place where myth and history fork and in the middle is the indestructible and defiant domain of fiction. But that wasn't fiction: it was the beginning of a true story that nonetheless seemed like a fable. I understood then why the Colonel had nothing but disdain for factual reports: he didn't believe them, he didn't *see* them. The only thing that interested him was the dead woman, not her past.

"Remember doña Juana's thin lips, Colonel," the seer wrote. "Imagine her speaking. Remember her white hair with blue glints, her lively round eyes, her sunken cheeks: not the remotest resemblance to Evita, none at all, as though the daughter had been her own sole procreator."

I put the papers in order and began to copy them. It was an endless task. In addition to the reports from Santiago, Chile, Moori had collected croupiers' gossip, birth, death, and marriage certificates from city halls, and research into the past by journalists in Los Toldos. In the end, I copied only a few paragraphs word for word. I made summaries and rescued bits of dialogue. Years later, when I wanted to make a fair copy of those notes and turn them into the beginning of a biography, I kept straying off into the third person. When the mother said: "As soon as Evita came into the world I suffered a great deal," I fell into the habit of writing: "As soon as Evita was born, her mother, doña Juana, suffered a great deal." It was not the same. It was almost the opposite. Without the mother's voice, without her pauses, without her way of looking at the story, the words no longer meant anything. I have seldom fought as hard against bringing into being a text that cried out to be narrated in the feminine as, meanwhile, I cruelly insisted on contorting its nature. Nor have I ever failed as miserably. It took me a long time to accept the fact that only when the mother's voice made me give in was there a story. I allowed her to speak, then, through me. And only in that way did I hear myself write:

"As soon as Evita came into the world I suffered a great deal. Duarte, my husband, who until then had been an obliging, considerate man, became cagey. We had, as you know, four other children, and I was the one who insisted on having that last child, not him. 'She didn't come out of love,' I said. 'She came out of habit.' Maybe I was too submissive, too eager to keep him. Maybe he didn't love

344

me anymore or they'd made him believe he didn't. He would only drop by Los Toldos now and again, on a business trip. He would ask permission to come into the house as though he were a stranger and accept, without a word, a couple of matés. After a while he'd let out a sigh or two, hand me an envelope with some money in it, and go off shaking his head. The same thing, over and over. He saw so little of Evita that if he'd happened to meet her somewhere in the countryside he wouldn't have recognized her.

"He had another household in Chivilcoy: a very attractive lawfully wedded wife and three children. The wife was from a wealthy family, with cattle ranches and flour mills. She suited Duarte, because poverty terrified him. I had nothing to offer him but responsibilities and expenses. Happiness doesn't count when it comes to things like that. Happiness is something men always forget.

"One Friday in November, Duarte came by Los Toldos with a herd of sorrel horses. They were going to shoe them on the ranch he was managing, La Unión, and as they were inviting people for a barbecue, it seemed like a good time to baptize Evita, who was already ten months old, and Juan, who was over five years old. I sent word to him to come to the parish church at eleven, but he never showed up and didn't send his apologies. At noon, the parish priest hurriedly performed the baptismal rites, because afterwards he was to celebrate a betrothal Mass. I asked him to allow me to stay. 'It's not possible, Juana,' he said to me. 'It would be a scandal. Decent people don't want to have anything to do with a woman who lives with a man as his concubine.' 'That's unjust,' I answered. 'We are all equal in the sight of God.' 'That's so,' the priest said. 'But when people see you, their minds are diverted from God.' Though the insult pierced my soul, I burst out laughing. 'So that's how it is,' I answered him. 'I would never have thought that people find me more entertaining than God.'

"I left the church intending never to set foot in it again. I went on my way on foot with my children to La Unión, to get Duarte to account to me for his not being at the baptism, but he refused to see me. I'd fallen in love with him when I was hardly more than a child and didn't realize what I was doing. Later on the price I had to pay for my ignorance was a lifetime of unhappiness.

"There was another fateful morning, in 1923. The sky was burning hot. I put oil on the fire to fry some potatoes, and the heat was mind numbing. I allowed myself to be carried away by the current of my thoughts. The earth had swallowed Duarte, and other men, who could see that I was living by myself, were beginning to chase after me. I didn't know what was going to become of my life, I didn't know what curse was causing me to waste my youth, and I wanted to go far away, but I didn't know where or what I'd use for money. I was lost in bitter thoughts like that, when all of a sudden I heard a scream. Evita, I thought. It was her. Attracted by the sputtering of the boiling oil, she had come closer to look. The pot tipped over on top of her, goodness only knows how, and that lava covered her entire body. The pain of the burns made her faint. I ran to the welfare clinic. I almost didn't dare touch her because no matter how gently my fingers brushed against her, her skin came off in strips. They treated her with oil that had calx in it and bandaged her. I asked if the burns were going to leave marks. 'Keloidal tissue,' the nurse told me. 'Keloidal tissue may form.' I asked what that was. 'She's going to look like a tortoise,' she answered me, without the slightest pity. 'Skin in folds, crisscrossed with wrinkles, full of scars.'

"After a week they removed her bandages. I had my saints that I was particularly devoted to, and my virgins: every night I knelt on corn husks and prayed that they would give her back her health and a beauty that it seemed impossible that she would ever have again. The red scabs covered her whole face and drew maps on her chest. When the torture of the burns abated, itches like those of a person possessed kept Evita from sleeping. Since the scabs were driving her mad and she kept trying to scratch them off, I had to tie her hands down. She stayed tied up that way for more than a month, as the scabs turned from red to black. She looked like a caterpillar spinning itself a mourning cocoon. One morning, before daylight, I heard her get up out of bed. It was raining outside and the wind was blowing hard, in gusts, like a fit of coughing. I was afraid she might come down with something even worse and looked out the window. She was standing there motionless in the yard, with her face upraised, embracing the rain. Her scabs had fallen off. Instead of being covered with scars, she had that delicate, translucent, alabaster skin that so many men were later to fall in love with. There was not one streak or mark left. But every miracle has its price. The one Evita had to pay for being saved was enduring other of life's insults, other deceptions, other misfortunes.

"I thought that in 1923 we'd already paid the debt of bitterness we owed. The year 1926 was even worse though. Blanca, my oldest daughter, had just received her diploma as a schoolteacher. I needed to get some relief from the exhaustion of sewing and began to help her look for work. Early each morning, the two of us went knocking on the doors of schools in that desolate backwater: San Emilio, El Tejar, La Delfina, Bayauca. It was nothing but dust, wind, and killing sun. In the afternoons, I'd sit in the hammock out in the yard, exhausted, with my ankles all swollen. My varicose veins burst, and no matter how often I told myself, Lie still, Juana, don't walk anymore, each new day always brought a hope that made me go on walking. We went up and down those dirt roads hundreds of times, and it was always useless. It was only when Duarte died that they finally took pity on us.

"It happened, as I may already have told you, one Friday in January. At vesper time we heard galloping. A bad sign, I thought. When the heat is like an inferno and people urge their horses on like that it's only because they're bringing bad news. And that's exactly what it was. The horseman was one of the farm laborers from La Unión. He was coming to bring the news of Duarte's death. He'd died at dawn, he said. Duarte was driving from Chivilcoy to Bragado to have a look at some cornfields, and in the dim light his Ford went off into the ditch at the side of the road. An animal had crossed his path, apparently. Or perhaps he'd fallen asleep at the wheel. That wasn't what happened at all, I said to myself. It was sadness that killed Duarte. A man who gives up his desires the way he did

347

doesn't want to go on living. He either lets one illness or another carry him off or else he falls asleep while he's driving.

"I'd stopped loving him a long time before that. My heart was empty of love for him and for anybody else except my children. I felt that death could overtake me at any moment too, and I imagined the terrible life my orphans would have, enslaved by hostile store-keepers and mad priests. I was so overcome with anxiety I couldn't breathe. Facing the yard, in the bedroom, was a wardrobe with a mirror. I saw myself reflected in it, as white as a sheet, as my legs gave way. I let out a scream as I fell. Blanca lifted me up. My boy, Juan, God rest his soul, ran to the pharmacy. They wanted to give me a shot to calm me down so I could sleep, but I wouldn't let them. 'Absolutely not,' I said. 'If Duarte has died, my family's place is with him.' I asked whether they'd be holding a wake for him at La Unión. 'No,' the farmhand told me. 'They're going to bury him in Chivilcoy early tomorrow afternoon.'

"I felt the rush of an unknown energy. It's always been hard for me to give up. Neither sorrows nor illnesses nor disappointments nor poverty have broken my spirit. But at that moment I had no way of putting up a fight.

"I bought a mourning dress and black stockings on credit. I sewed a black band on Juancito's shirtsleeve. The older girls were crying. Evita wasn't. She went on playing as though nothing had happened.

"We took a bus from Los Toldos to Bragado and then another one that left at dawn from Bragado for Chivilcoy: a twenty-league trip. The life that lay ahead was dark, empty, and I didn't know what ha-treds I'd have to confront. I didn't care. As long as my children were with me, I felt invincible. None of them had been conceived through wiles of mine or cheating on the side, but because the father they'd just lost wanted them. I wasn't going to allow them to grow up feel-ing the shame of being nobody, living in secret, as though they'd come into being by chance.

"I reached the Duarte house around nine in the morning. The bells of the Holy Rosary were tolling, and flower pollen was drifting in the stifling air of Chivilcoy. The funeral wreaths could be seen from a long way away. They had lined them up on the walk, on purple cardboard stands. On the ribbons were the names of normal schools, Rotary clubs, the town council, and parish associations that Duarte had never mentioned in my presence. Even though I was in a daze as I arrived, I realized that I didn't recognize that dead man as the father of my five children. With me, he had always been untalkative, unassuming, unimaginative. His other life revealed, though, that he'd been a powerful, sociable man.

"Someone must have recognized us and told us to go on ahead because, at the corner of the house, two old men came to meet us, and they made me feel ill at ease. The one dressed in deepest mourning, with a handlebar mustache, took off his straw hat, revealing a sweating bald head.

"'I know who you are and where you're coming from, señora,' he said, without looking me in the eye. 'I understand your grief and your children's. But be aware too of the grief that Juan Duarte's legitimate family is feeling. I am the deceased's first cousin. I beg you not to approach the home of his family. Don't make a scene.'

"I didn't let him go on.

"'I have come with these children from a long way off. They too have a right to say goodbye to their father. When we've done what we came to do, we'll leave. Don't worry. I won't make a scene.'

"'I don't believe you understand me,' the cousin persisted. He was sweating hard. A handkerchief soaked in scent relieved him. 'His death was sudden and the widow is badly shaken. Knowing that all of you have entered her own home is not going to be good for her. I advise you to go to the church and pray there for Juan's eternal repose. And kindly take this money to buy him some flowers.'

"He held out a hundred-peso bill to me, which in those days was a whole lot of money. I didn't deign to answer him. I pushed him aside and went on ahead. When he saw how determined I was, the other old man gave a scornful smile and asked, disparagingly:

"'Are these the bastard children?'

"'Their mother's bastard children,' I answered, emphasizing the word *mother's,* to return the insult. 'And Juan Duarte's. That's how it is. The pot always calls the kettle black.'

"I was able to go on only a few steps. A girl just a little older than Blanca came out of the house. You could tell from her eyes that she'd been crying, and her lips were pale. She rushed down the rows of the funeral wreaths so fast that two or three of them fell from their stands. She was enraged. I thought she was going to hit me.

"'How dare you?' she said. 'We've suffered all our lives on account of you, señora. Clear out of here, go away. In heaven's name, what sort of woman are you? What a lack of respect.'

"I didn't lose my composure. I thought: this is one of Duarte's daughters. She, too, in her own way, must be feeling defenseless.

"'I came here out of respect for the deceased,' I said to her. 'As long as he lived, he was a good father. I don't see why things should be different now that he's dead. Don't do my children the harm that they wouldn't do you.'

"'Clear out this very minute!' she answered. I didn't know whether she was about to attack me or burst into tears.

"Who knows why there came to my mind at that moment the train station where I'd waited in vain for Duarte so many times, my father's cart making its way amid the mirages of the parched fields, the birth of my first daughter, Evita's face disfigured by the burns. Among these many images I also found that of a pale, thin gentleman. He was dressed in black and had approached us without our noticing, since he was walking against the light. It seemed to me that he was another person out of my memories, but he wasn't: he was there in the reality of that day that was so different for me, standing motionless, witnessing the hysterical fit of the girl who, in fact, was my children's half sister. The thin gentleman put his hands on her shoulders and by that simple gesture put an end to her anger, or at least made her contain it.

"'We're going to allow them to come in for a moment, Eloísa,' he said to her. 'There is no reason for these people to take back to Los Toldos the same grief that they came with.'

"The girl went back into the house sobbing. The man then said to me, with neither anger nor pity:

"'Everything about this death has taken us by surprise. It would have been better if you hadn't come. But here you are in Chivilcoy, and the fewer people who know it the better. In Los Toldos Duarte could do whatever he pleased. Here we must keep up appearances. If anyone asks who you are, I'm going to say that you're the cook at La Unión. Don't contradict me. Either you come in with that proviso, or you leave. No one is going to speak to you. Nor do I want you to speak to anyone. I shall give you five minutes to say goodbye to the dead man, pray, and leave. The widow is going to be in another part of the house during that time, and perhaps everyone who has come to offer condolences will also want to be far from the scene. There will not be anyone in the room where he's laid out. Except me, to see to it that you live up to this agreement.'

"'There's still the cemetery,' I said. My throat felt dry, but I didn't want to show any sign of weakness. 'I promised Duarte that when he died his children would be in the funeral procession and leave him flowers.'

"The man stood there for a time in silence. His silence was more intimidating than his words.

"'There are still three hours left before the funeral. I don't know what the lot of you intend to do meanwhile, but there is no reason for you to stay here. The funeral cortege will necessarily include relatives, high-ranking police officers, town councilmen, teachers from the normal school, and estate managers who had business dealings with the deceased. That is too many people, and you don't know any of them. I can't keep you from walking behind the procession. But nobody is going to make room for you to join it.'

"The thin gentleman disappeared into the house where the deceased lay and in a few moments beckoned to us with a contemptuous crook of his index finger. I remember that, as we walked past the double row of funeral wreaths, I didn't know who I was and didn't know the names of anything I saw. Candles, grilles, eyes, flat stones—reality was elsewhere. My body as well. I no longer felt my varicose veins. In the funeral chapel was a grand piano and, along-side the piano stool, two stuffed hunting dogs.

"I am sorry to say, however, that the deceased was not departing from this world with a very impressive air about him. It had been nearly two years since we had last seen each other, and in that time he had not been careful about what he ate. He was fat. He had such a bulging belly that when I saw his shadow projected on the wall, it looked as if there were another piano there, but one with the top raised. His head was battered from the accident, and there were trickles of dried blood in his nostrils. I thought they'd left him that way on purpose, so no one would remember him as having been handsome. We went up to him to kiss him, but we didn't know where. They had tied a handkerchief around his jaw so that it wouldn't hang down, and it covered almost his whole face. Blanca stroked the translucent tip of his pointed nose. I took his hands, which were clutching a rosary. I wondered what his thoughts had been as his car overturned on the shoulder of the road. He was a coward and probably didn't dare think about anything. He doubt-less felt only astonishment and the terror of meeting his end.

"Evita wasn't tall enough to see the body, and I had to lift her up in my arms. When I brought her close to the coffin, I noted that she had her lips pressed tightly together and a blank look in her eyes. 'Your papa,' I said to her. She turned to me and hugged me, her face expressionless, only because she needed to hug someone and didn't want to touch the last remains of a stranger.

"The thin gentleman saw us to the door. I believe he handed me a card, but I wasn't able to read it. The sun had unsheathed a merci-less heat that morning, and everything I remember is yellow.

"We took refuge in a cheap restaurant near the bus station, and around one o'clock we headed for the cemetery. I arrived as the fu-neral procession was entering. I saw Duarte's other wife weeping on the shoulder of the girl who had insulted me; I saw the thin man car-rying the coffin, alongside a captain who in that piercing heat had bundled himself up in his long full dress cape and stripes. I felt sorry for the deceased, who was taking his leave of this world surrounded by people who knew nothing of his life and hadn't loved him just as he was. We were left all by ourselves, and it seemed to me, because of the children, that it wasn't worth following the funeral procession. There was no reason to stay now nor any reason to come back another time."

The mother's voice went on speaking, but my writing no longer heard it. Among the things I allowed to escape me were some verses that Evita recited on the patio of the coeducational public school in Los Toldos, the pedal of the Singer moving swiftly back and forth, two photographs of a sad, unsmiling little girl, and that morning when she said: "I'm going to be an actress." They were postcard images that should perhaps be included here. But I was deafened by the flight of a single yellow wing in the air of the page. I saw the wing fly backward, and when I bent closer, I no longer saw it. That's the way the light of the past goes out, I said to myself. The past keeps coming and going, not caring what it leaves behind.

"You can imagine the terrible times the Colonel went through when he returned to Buenos Aires," Cifuentes said to me. We were together again, early in the afternoon on that same Sunday. I was eating an apple; he was smoking avidly, arrogant and slender. "Whatever remained of his pride, instinct, strength, and desire had been left behind, in Germany. He was living alone, in a pension on the corner of Arenales and Coronel Díaz: with nothing to do, nothing to think about, brooding over the images of the lost corpse. At the end of that year I was summoned by the army hospital because he had been admitted in a hepatic coma, and the doctors thought he wasn't going to live to tell the tale. They tormented him with intestinal irrigations and drip injections of glucose. His poor tortured body had swellings, stigmata, contusions from having been carelessly handled. I called his wife from the telephone at the hospital and asked her to help him. 'Who knows if he'll want to see me,' she said. 'Come,' I replied. 'He's not going to reject you. He's using the little breath he has left trying to survive.'"

"He survived," I said to him. "I've never heard of anybody who fell down and got back on his feet as many times as he did."

"You don't know how many things he survived."

Cifuentes and I sat motionless for a long time that same Sunday. Outside there were mists, drizzles, gusts of wet wind: all the bad moods of the climate of Buenos Aires came and went without making any difference to us at all. As was his habit, Cifuentes took a few tiny bread crumbs out of his pocket and ate them. The last little bits stuck in his pointed beard.

"Before the end, Moori was reconciled with his wife again," he said to me, "and came back to live in the apartment on Callao and Santa Fe. He had hopes they'd take him back into the army and promote him to general, but his friends had lost their pull by then, and the army itself was too unhinged by the factions within its ranks to take any interest in him. It was during those months that Rodolfo Walsh visited him, and the Colonel told him that he'd buried Evita standing up, in a garden where it never stopped raining. He supposed that the Deceased was still wandering all over the world, in the hands of some occult power. One day he said to me: 'Let's go get her, Tom Thumb.' I tried, for the only time in our lives, to make him listen to reason. 'The body you buried in Eichstätt was a copy, Moori,' I told him. 'They put one over on you. Heaven only knows what's become of Eva. Maybe they've buried her at sea.' I immediately regretted having spoken out like that. We had a violent argument. I saw him lift a hand toward the Walther. He was, I am persuaded, about to kill me. He didn't speak to me for months. To the Colonel, there was no other reality except Evita. Without her, the world seemed unbearable to him."

At times we went for long intervals without saying a word, until the silence felt completely at home within us. At times we agreed to speak and repeated what we had already said as though we'd forgotten what it had been. I still think that that Sunday was not just one day but many, and that when night came Cifuentes departed from my life.

But I still haven't finished telling several stories that, since that time, have remained inside me.

As was perhaps inevitable, Cifuentes said to me, the Colonel allowed himself to be consumed once more by his addiction to alcohol and fell into fits of delirium tremens again. Hordes of butterflies buried him beneath a shroud of lighted candles and wildflowers. Rats out of a nightmare dislocated his bones and seared his eyes. His wife had him put in the hospital twice, and twice he went back to his old ways. The Commando of Vengeance kept sending him threatening letters and asking him where Evita was. *I returned the Saint's body to the people,* he wrote them. *We're going to cut your ear off, the way you cut Hers off. We're going to pluck your eyes out. Where did you hide the sacred relics of our Beloved Mother?*

At daylight one morning, he appeared at Cifuentes' studio, bringing with him two trunks stuffed full of letters, documents, and file cards with reports in code. He told Cifuentes he'd come back for them when the past quieted down.

"They're right at my heels, Tom Thumb," he explained. "They're going to kill me any moment now. Maybe it'll be a relief. Maybe it's best."

He left the trunks there for good. When he needed to consult one of the texts, he entered his friend's studio, by day or by night, held the pages up to the light, and examined them with the aid of a magnifying glass in search of notations written on them in invisible ink. No one thought of him as a living being anymore, Cifuentes told me. "In the end, Moori ceased being the Colonel: he was his illness, his vices, his torments."

In 1965 he left his wife for the last time and also stopped drinking for a while. He set up a "Transamerican Press Agency" that spread rumors about barracks conspiracies and factory strikes. He wrote the news items himself and copied them on a 1930s mimeograph machine, which continually coughed or stuttered. He found ways to bring his name back to life in the daily papers. Early in 1967 he was interviewed by the famous magazine *Primera Plana*. In the photograph he looks fat and bald, with the red, knobby nose alcohol had left him with and a ghostly, toothless smile. He was asked if it was true that he had "buried Evita's corpse in darkness." "I'm not going to answer that trick question," he said. "I'm gathering material for a book on the whole affair. Do you know who's helping me? Surprise: Dr. Pedro Ara and señora Juana Ibarguren de Duarte."

He was lying, of course, without knowing that he was lying. He had invented a reality, and within it he was God. He imitated God's imagination, and in that virtual kingdom, in that nothingness that was full only of itself, he believed himself to be invulnerable, invincible, omnipotent.

Sooner or later, the bubble was bound to burst. It happened one night in August. The Colonel had made arrangements to meet with an informant at the Liniers train station. As he went out onto the platform, he thought he was having one of his old nightmares again. Petitioners with crossed arms were marching past the wooden benches and the closed ticket windows, holding thick lighted candles and wreaths of daisies. Some of them were bearing on portable platforms the effigy of an unidentifiable saint, frozen in the gesture of distributing plastic loaves of bread and imitation coins. Others were venerating the triumphant photo of Evita, dressed in the Marie Antoinette–style skirt she had worn on gala evenings at the Colón Theater. The hymns "Come Christians," "Saint Cayetano Pray for Us," *Eva Perón, / the one we adore, / your heart is with us / forevermore,* intermingled. The scent of desperation, of patchouli, and of aromatic smoke blended. Opposite the vault of the ticket window, a woman wearing a long coat that reached to the ground handed the flabbergasted Colonel a bunch of sweet peas and pushed him toward the altar where she smiled down from her long-ago gala evening.

"Go on," the woman said. "Give her a hundred pesos."

"Who are you?" the Colonel said, using the familiar form of address as she had done. "You're from the Commando of Vengeance."

"Who would I be?" she replied, perhaps without understanding.

"I'm an Evitist, from the Angelic Militia. But here, in these celebrations, any faith is as good as another. Give a hundred pesos."

The Colonel handed her back the bouquet and, appalled, went out into the night. Around the station altars had proliferated everywhere, like honeycombs. A sea of candles blurred the silhouettes of praying petitioners and pilgrims. Evita's profile bestowed her blessings from the banners raised on high. On the balconies were other Evitas, in plaster, adorned with Virgin Mary veils. All of them were wearing a smile that was trying hard to appear benevolent but instead looked deceitful, cunning, threatening.

He made his escape as best he could. As he walked along the street, every so often he heard them say from the entryways: "We're going to kill you. We're going to cut your balls off. We're going to pluck your eyes out." In the first grocery store he found open he bought a bottle of gin, raised it to his lips, and drank the whole of it, right then and there, with a thirst that for two years he had been unable to satisfy. Then he shut himself up in his office and went on drinking without stopping until Evita took her leave of his hallucinations and other more terrifying shades kept him pinned to the floor, in a swamp of urine and feces.

That time it was the cleaning crew who saved him. His body was so ravaged that it was six months before the doctors would release him from the hospital. Fate willed that when he arrived as a convalescent at the offices of the Transamerican Press Agency—where he now lived—someone should slip a sealed envelope underneath the door, with the sealed message: *Your hour is at hand. Commando of Vengeance.*

In desperation, he went out into the street, shirtless. It was early autumn, and a hard rain was falling. The writer Tununa Mercado, who was in the habit of walking her dog late at night, met him in the plaza Rodríguez Peña. "I took him for an inmate who'd escaped from a poorhouse," she told me many years later. "I thought: He can only be a poor wretch who's sick. Till I recognized him from the photos of him in the papers. He ran to the statue of O'Higgins and

357

stopped in front of the pedestal, with his arms crossed. I heard him shout: 'Why don't you come once and for all and kill me?' He kept saying over and over: 'Why don't you come?' I didn't know who he was talking about. I looked all around. There wasn't anybody there. Just the silence and the milky light from the street lamps. 'What are you waiting for, you sons of bitches?' he shouted again. 'Kill me, kill me!' All of a sudden, something made him go all to pieces. He started to cry. I came closer to ask him if he needed help, if he wanted me to call a doctor."

Tununa had always been touched by the homeless men who live out in the open, exposed to the elements, in that plaza. She was about to cross over to the Pizzurno building to ask the night watchmen for help when a bald man, with an aquiline nose and a musketeer's beard, appeared.

"It was Cifuentes," I said to her. "Aldo Cifuentes."

"Who knows?" Tununa answered me; she trusts her feelings blindly, but not her senses. "The little bald man was looking for him. With incredible tact, he said to him: 'Let's go, Moori. You don't have anything keeping you here.' 'Don't ask me to do that, Tom Thumb,' the Colonel begged him. I was surprised that someone so rough spoken, who looked so animal-like, should speak the name of a character out of the storybooks of my childhood. 'I want to die.' The Colonel's friend covered him with a blanket and dragged him, on his back practically, to a car. I stood for a long time, not moving, there in the drizzle, and I couldn't sleep that night."

Selflessly, stubbornly, Cifuentes guided the Colonel about until the very eve of his death, in 1970. There are beings who, for no reason, protect others with a compulsive pity, as though keeping watch over those destinies of others allows them to expiate past derelictions and unfulfilled duties. Cifuentes devoted himself to this work of compassion without making a show of it. In his posthumous memoirs he devotes a dispassionate paragraph to the subject: "Moori Koenig was my soul brother. I tried to save him and was unable to. He fell into disgrace for obscure reasons. His home broke up. Shadows darkened his mental clarity. Many people may speak of his drunken binges, of his little tricks and lies. The only thing that mattered to me was his dreams."

I am going to allow this last cadence of the story to come to rest, then, on the bosom of a dream.

As I have already said, the Colonel dreamed of the moon almost every night. He saw himself walking through the cracked white deserts of the Sea of Serenity, above which six or seven grim, threatening moons shone. He sensed, in the dream, that he was searching for something, but each time he glimpsed a promontory, a tremor of the landscape, the illusion dissolved before he could reach it. Those images of nothingness and silence lingered within him for hours, and faded away only with his first swallows of gin.

When it was announced that three NASA astronauts were going to land on the moon, the Colonel thought, with relief, that that repeated dream would lose its reason for being—like all dreams which, after much persistence, finally make their appearance somewhere in reality—and that he would then be free to dream of other things. He and Cifuentes decided that they would watch together on television the final hours of the long journey in space. And that was how they came to settle themselves comfortably in front of the television set one Sunday night, with a dice box to entertain them as they waited, plus a generous supply of cigarettes. The broadcast overdid the number of images transmitted from the Houston control center and interviews with the technicians who were teleguiding the spacecraft. These digressions made them drowsy.

They had promised each other to resist the temptation of gin until the adventure was over. Finally, an amazing round, gleaming disk appeared in the vastness. It was not there long. The belly of the disk sank immediately, and little by little a concave, waning sickle shape appeared in empty space.

"The moon," the Colonel said.

"It's the earth," Cifuentes decided. "It's us. It looks as though our forehead has strips of cloth across it, like a nun's coif."

For hours, nothing more happened. The air outside was full of urban sounds, but the sounds gradually became farther and farther apart, and all that remained was the emptiness of the hard winter. The apartment grew intolerably cold, yet the Colonel felt only warm and thirsty. In the middle of the night he broke his promise and went to have a drink of gin. When he came back, melancholy overcame him. The lunar module, having taken off from the main spacecraft, was placing its tentacles on a dusty crater. The human species had just reached the moon, but the Colonel was aware of nothing except the drumrolls of his own inferno.

"Who do you think made off with her, Tom Thumb?" he said.

"With Evita? How should I know? What odd thoughts you come up with at a time like this."

Cifuentes was upset with him. The air was saturated with the smell of gin.

"Who knows whether they're taking care of her, Tom Thumb. Who knows what they may be doing to her."

"Don't think about that anymore. You promised me."

"I miss her. I miss her. I'd like not to think, but I miss her."

They slept right there, in the armchairs. When Cifuentes woke up, early the following afternoon, the Colonel had already drunk more than half a bottle of gin and was weeping as he watched the endless images of the ashen plain. Buses could be heard braking in the street. Everything seemed to have returned to normal, although at times surprising parentheses of silence opened. The entire screen then went dark, as if the world were holding its breath as it awaited an extraordinary, Pantagruelian birth.

On Monday night, at eleven o'clock, Neil Armstrong set foot on the moon and uttered the lofty sentence that he had so often rehearsed: *That's one small step for a man, one giant leap for mankind.* The image on the screen froze on the print of a boot, the left one, in the gray dust.

"How strange: so many black spots," the Colonel said. "Maybe there are flies up there."

"There isn't anything," Cifuentes said. "There's no life."

"There are flies, butterflies, blowfly larvae," the Colonel insisted. "Look at them on the screen. They're everywhere."

"Come off it, Moori. It's the gin you drank. You've had enough. I don't want us to end up in the hospital again."

Armstrong was leaping from one crater to another, and all of a sudden he disappeared on the horizon, carrying a small spade. He said, or the Colonel thought he heard him say: "I can't see what I'm doing when I go into the shadow. Bring the machine, Buzz. Send me the machine."

"They're going to work with machines," the Colonel said.

"It was in the papers." Cifuentes yawned. "They're going to dig. They have to collect some rocks."

Armstrong and the man named Buzz seemed to be flying above that soft, dead world. They lifted their winged arms and rose above fragile cordilleras and seas impossible to cross. The camera lost sight of them, and when they came back into view, they were floating together, holding on to a metal box with blurred contours by the handles.

"Look at that box," the Colonel said. "A coffin."

"They're tools," Cifuentes corrected him. "You'll see when they set to work."

But the camera left the astronauts at the exact moment when they leaned down over something that looked to be a riverbed, a crevice, and amused itself filming more views of the landscape. In the terrifying whiteness, rings, dark circles, squalls of feathers, stalactites, plagues of sunlight, appeared. Then space was occupied by a merciless silence, until Armstrong, seen all by himself in profile, digging, returned to the screen.

"Did you see that?" the Colonel said. He was standing up, with one hand on his forehead, deathly pale amid the reverberating images.

"What?" Cifuentes answered wearily.

"Just look what they're doing."

"It's the flag they brought," Cifuentes said. "They're going to plant a flag."

"Don't you realize?"

Cifuentes took him by the arm. "Calm down, Moori. Nothing's happening."

361

"What do you mean nothing's happening? They took her up there, Cifuentes! They're burying her on the moon!"

"You can see the flag," one of the Houston technicians announced. "So beautiful!"

"She's beautiful all right," the Colonel said. "She's the most beautiful person in this world." He collapsed on the sofa and repeated disconsolately, hundreds of times, the revelation that would consume what was left of his life: "She's up there. The sons of bitches buried her on the moon."

16

*"I Must Write
Again"*

*History can take us anywhere,
provided we leave it.*

CLAUDE LÉVI-STRAUSS, The Savage Mind

At the end of June 1989, overcome by an attack of depression, I took
to my bed, determined not to get up until my melancholy went away
by itself. So I was in bed for a long time. Solitude, little by little, enveloped me like a chrysalis. One Friday, shortly before midnight, the
telephone rang. In my confusion, or my lethargy, I answered.

"What is it you want?" I asked.

"Nothing," a sharp, commanding voice said. "Weren't you the one
who was trying to find out something? We're all together finally and
can talk now."

"I don't want to talk to anyone," I said. "You have the wrong number." I almost hung up.

The voice stopped me. "Tomás Eloy?"

There are few people who call me by that name: only close
friends, fellow exiles, and also, on occasion, my children.

"Yes," I said. "But I'm not trying to find anyone."

"You wanted to write about Evita."

"That was a long time ago. I've already put what I wanted to say in a novel. It came out four years ago."

"We read it," the voice insisted. "There were lots of mistakes you let slip past you. We're the only ones who really know what happened."

In the background, splinters of sound could be heard: indecipherable conversations, a deafening clatter of glasses and dishes. They sounded like the insomniac echoes of an all-night restaurant.

"Who is this speaking?" I asked.

"We'll wait for you till one o'clock, at the Tabac on the corner of Libertador and Coronel Díaz. It's about the corpse, you know what I mean? We took charge of looking after it."

"What corpse?"

In those days, Evita was a historic, immortal figure. I never thought of her as a corpse. I knew, of course, about the vicissitudes that her dead body had undergone after it disappeared and about its return to her widower, in Madrid, but I had banished the knowledge from my memory.

"What a question. Eva Perón's."

"Who is this speaking?" I repeated.

"A colonel," the voice said. "Army Intelligence Service."

On hearing that name, all the hyenas of the past sank their teeth into me. Only six years had gone by since the military had left power in Argentina, leaving in its wake the traces of a terrible bloodbath. The military was in the habit of phoning its victims at their homes and then, five minutes later, swooping down on them to strip them of their possessions in God's name and torture them for the good of the country. A person could be innocent of any crime, save that of thought, but that was reason enough for people to expect, every night, that the Horsemen of the Apocalypse would knock on their door.

"I'm not going to come," I said. "I don't know you. I have no reason to come."

Time had gone by. Such outright refusals were possible now.

"As you like. We've been discussing the matter for months. We finally decided, just tonight, to tell the whole story."

"Tell it to me over the phone."

"It's a very long one," the voice persisted. "It's a story that went on for twenty years."

"Then call me tomorrow. Do you realize what time it is?"

"Not tomorrow. Tonight. You're the one who doesn't realize what we're talking about. Eva Perón. Imagine. The corpse. A president of the Republic said to me: 'We are all that corpse. It's the country.'"

"He must have been crazy."

"If you knew what president I'm talking about, you wouldn't say that."

"Tomorrow," I said again. "Maybe tomorrow."

"Then the story is going to be lost," he said.

I had a feeling that now he was the one who was going to hang up. I've spent my life rebelling against powers that forbid stories or cut chunks out of them and against the accomplices who distort them or allow them to be lost. To allow a story like that to get away from me was an act of high treason against my conscience.

"All right," I said. "Wait for me. I'll be there in less than an hour."

The moment I hung up, I regretted having told him that. I felt naked, defenseless, vulnerable, the way I'd felt the night before my exile. I was afraid, but the humiliation of being afraid freed me. I thought that if I was afraid I was accepting the fact that death squads were invincible. They weren't, I told myself. *The silent sun / the beauty of the vanquished / untouched by anger / had vanquished them.* I looked at the city through the venetian blinds. Thin splinters of ice were falling. I put on my raincoat and went out.

One of the advantages of the Tabac is that next to the windows inexplicable oases of silence suddenly come into being. The maddening din that rages next to the bar and in the corridors dies away, respectfully, at the frontier of those privileged tables where people can talk without being overheard by those at the neighboring ones. Perhaps that's why nobody ever sits at them. When I arrived, the fringe of silence was there, aloof, out of harmony with the hustle and bustle of the all-night restaurant. In Buenos Aires, many people don't wake up from their long siestas till midnight and then go out to trawl for life. Part of that fauna was coming awake at the Tabac.

Nobody signaled to me when I came in. I studied the faces, not knowing which way to turn. All of a sudden, I felt the touch of a finger on my shoulder. The individuals who had phoned me were behind me. There were three of them: two of them must have been over seventy. The third one, a bald man with high cheekbones and a hairline mustache, was a carbon copy of Juan Duarte, Evita's brother, who had fallen out of favor with Perón in 1953 and, out of desperation or guilt, had put a bullet through his head. It seemed to me that the past in person, arbitrary, implacable, was coming to get me.

"I am Colonel Tulio Ricardo Corominas," one of them said. He was ramrod stiff, tense, ill at ease perhaps. He didn't even put out his hand, and I didn't either. "We had best sit down."

I entered the acoustic fringe. To my relief, I noticed that my depression was lifting all by itself. I began once again to look upon reality as a vast present where everything, in the end, was possible. The tallest of the three army officers sat down next to me and said, in a hoarse, brusque voice:

"I wasn't in the group that carried the corpse off. My name is Jorge Rojas Silveyra, the one who returned it."

I recognized him. In 1971, the military government had given him full powers to negotiate with Perón in Madrid. He came back to Buenos Aires empty-handed, but he gave Perón two poisoned gifts: Evita's body, which he didn't know what to do with, and fifty thousand dollars in back salary as president, which burned his hands.

The bald man clicked his heels with a martial air.

"My name is Maggi, like the soup," he said. "On one of my identification papers I was once Carlo Maggi."

"I came because there was a story," I reminded them. "Tell it to me and I'll be off."

"We read that novel of yours about Perón," Corominas explained. "It's not true that the body of that person was in Bonn."

"What person?" I asked cagily. I wanted to find out what name he called her by.

"Her," he answered. "Eva." He raised his hands to his imposing, drooping double chin, and immediately corrected himself: "Eva Perón."

"As you said, it's a novel," I explained. "In novels, what is true is also false. Authors rebuild at night the same myths they've destroyed in the morning."

"Those are just words," Corominas said emphatically. "They don't convince me. The only thing that means anything are facts, and a novel, after all, is a fact. But the corpse of that person was never in Bonn. Moori Koenig didn't bury it. He couldn't even find out where it was."

"Perhaps he had a copy and thought it was the real body," I ventured. "Articles have appeared in print that mention copies scattered all over the world."

"There were no copies," Corominas said. "There was only one body. Captain Galarza buried it in Milan, and it was there from that time on, until I recovered it."

For two hours, he recounted with the thoroughness of an anatomist the misfortunes of the Deceased in her wanderings: the Colonel's failed attempt to hide her at the Waterworks, the night of the storm at the Rialto movie theater, Arancibia's crime in the attic in Saavedra, and what he called the "sacrileges" of Moori Koenig, which he learned of, he said, "only through rumors and anonymous accusations." He also spoke of the dogged, ubiquitous offerings of flowers and candles. Then he showed me a sheaf of documents.

"Look," he said. "Here's the paper Perón signed when he received the body. Here you have the customs invoice I was given when we shipped the Deceased to Italy. This is the title deed for the grave. Have a look at it."

He handed me a document, yellow with age, dog-eared, useless.

"This title deed is no longer valid," I said, pointing to the expiration date.

"It doesn't matter. It's proof that the grave was mine."

He put the paper away and repeated: "It was mine."

I ordered another coffee. I felt that my muscles had been crystallized or flattened by the weight of those memories that were not mine. All the others were smoking a lot, but I was breathing a different air: that of the street with no movement or light, or that of the river, close by.

"Do you believe it was hers, Corominas?" I said. "In one way or another, it was always everyone's."

"It's no one's now," he said. "It's finally where it should always have been."

I remembered the place: the far end of a crypt in Recoleta cemetery, beneath three plates of steel four inches thick, behind steel bars, bulletproof doors, marble lions.

"It's not always going to be there," I said. "It has all eternity to decide what it wants. Perhaps it's turned into a nymph that's spinning its cocoon. Perhaps it will come back someday and it will be millions."

I went back home, and until day dawned, I went on pondering what to do. I didn't want to repeat the story they'd told me. I wasn't one of their number.

That's how I spent three years: waiting, brooding. I would see her in my dreams: Santa Evita, with a halo of light behind her chignon and a sword in her hands. I began to see her films, to listen to recordings of her speeches, to ask questions everywhere: who she had been and how and why. "She was a saint, period," the actress who had taken her in when she came to Buenos Aires told me one day. "You can take my word for it, since I knew her from the beginning. She was not only an Argentine saint. She was also perfect." I accumulated floods of file cards and stories so as to be able to fill in all the unexplained blank spaces of what, later on, was going to be my novel. But I left them where they were, leaving the story, because I am fond of unexplained blank spaces.

There was a moment when I told myself: If I don't write it, I'm going to suffocate. If I don't try to know her by writing her, I'm never going to know myself. In the solitude of Highland Park, I sat down and wrote these words: "On coming out of a faint that lasted for more than three days, Evita was certain at last that she was going to die." It was an impassive autumn afternoon; good weather was singing out of tune; life wasn't stopping to look at me.

Since then, I have rowed with words, carrying Santa Evita in my boat, from one shore of the blind world to the other. I don't know where in the story I am. In the middle, I believe. I've been here in the middle for a long time. Now I must write again.

Acknowledgments

My thanks:
- To Rodolfo Walsh, who set me on the path to Bonn and initiated me into the cult of "Santa Evita."
- To Helvio Botana, who allowed me to copy his archives and revealed to me almost everything I know today about the Colonel.
- To Julio Alcaraz, for his story of Evita's withdrawal as a candidate for the vice-presidency.
- To Olga and Alberto Rudni, to whom I owe the character and the story of Emilio Kaufman at Fantasio. Both of them are well aware of who Irene is.
- To Isidoro Gilbert, who recorded everything that Alberto had forgotten to recount.
- To Mario Pugliese Cariño, for his memories of Evita's first journey away from home.
- To Jorge Rojas Silveyra, who, one morning in 1989, told me the end of this novel. For his long conversations concerning the return of the corpse, for his loan to me of invaluable documents, and for his aid in the search for witnesses.
- To Héctor Eduardo Cabanillas and to the noncommissioned officer who pretended to be Carlo Maggi, for their stories.
- To Colonel Moori Koenig's widow and to his daughter Silvia, who, one evening in 1991, recounted to me the misfortunes of their lives.
- To Sergio Berenstein, who interviewed the person who is called Margot Heredia de Arancibia in these pages. To those who were

once projectionists and ushers at the Rialto movie theater, as well as to the heirs of the former owner.

• To my son Ezequiel, who taught me, as no one else could have, how to do research in military archives and back files of newspapers and magazines. To my daughter Sol Ana, who helped me set up theaters with dolls she named Santa Evita and Santa Evitita.

• To Paula, Tomy, Gonzalo, Javier, and Blas, my sons, for their love, during these longs months of absence.

• To María Rosa, who searched through the daily papers of 1951 and 1952 for the feats undertaken and the records attained in an effort to restore Evita's health.

• To José Halperín and to Víctor Penchaszadeh, who patiently corrected the innumerable medical references in the text and facilitated my research in the archives of the Otamendi and Miroli clinic.

• To Noé Jitrik, Tununa Mercado, Margo Persín, and, in particular, to Juan Forn, who read the manuscript more than once and rescued it from obscurities and lapses that I had failed to notice.

• To Erna von der Walde, for her lessons in German via computer. All the sentences in that language—except for two trivial ones—are taken from Rainer Maria Rilke's requiem "Für eine Freundin."

• To María Negroni, to whom I owe a line from "Venecia."

• To Juan Gelman, who gave me permission to include a number of lines from his poems, above all from "Preguntas."

• To Mercedes Casanovas, for her aid and her patience.

• And, above all, to Susana, to whom this novel owes every word, every revelation, every felicity.